SHADOW HOUND

BLOOD & SHADOWS BOOK 6

BOOKS BY ALIANNE DONNELLY

BLOOD AND SHADOWS
Blood Moons
Blood Trails
Blood Debts
Blood Hunt
Shadow Hawk
Shadow Hound

THE REBEL COURT
Catch Me
Dearest Love
Sweetest Kiss

DAWN OF RAGNAROK
The Royal Wizard
Dragonblood
Prince of Deceit

THE BEAST
Bastien
The Beast

OTHER TITLES
Wolfen
Virtual
Function: LIVE

ALIANNE DONNELLY

SHADOW HOUND

BLOOD & SHADOWS BOOK 6

For the ones who are too badass to fit the standard mold.
We ride at dawn.

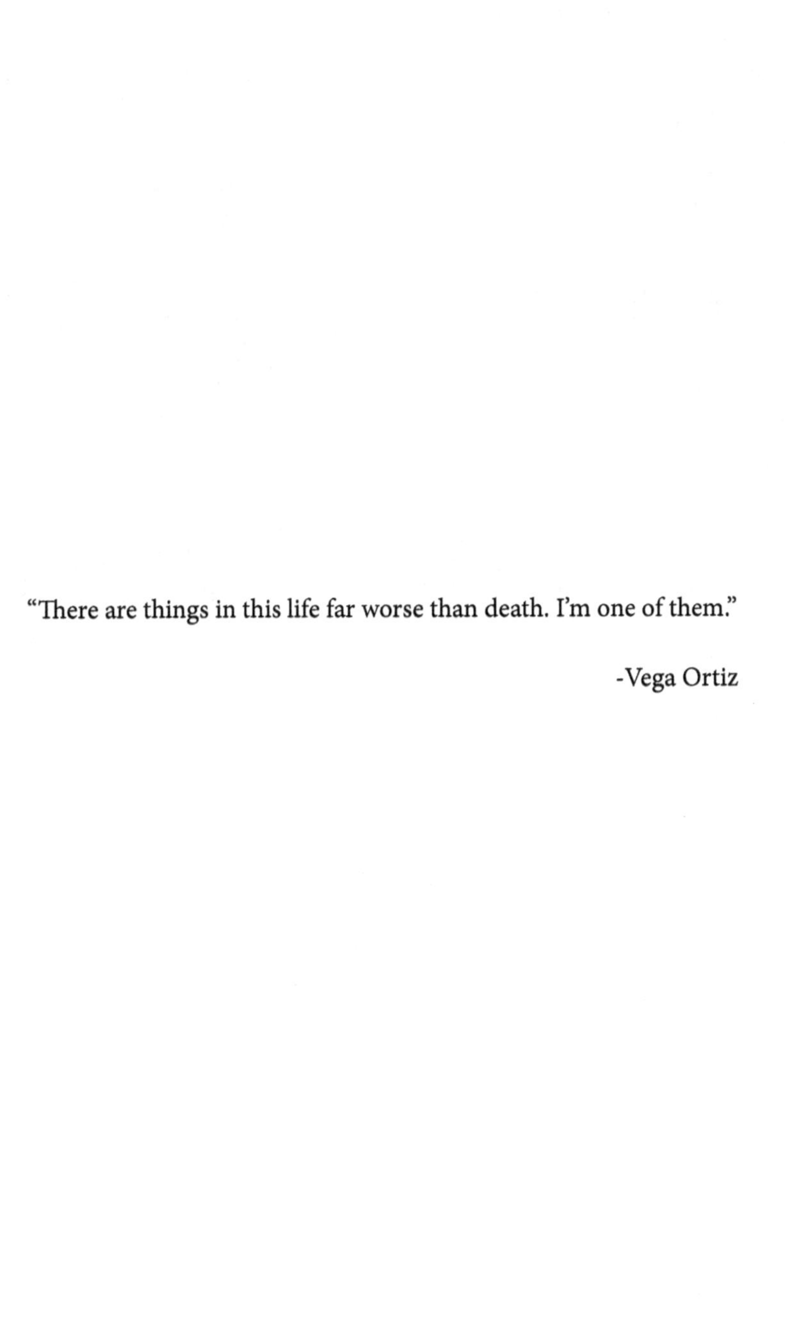

"There are things in this life far worse than death. I'm one of them."

-Vega Ortiz

May 6, 3038 – Blue Lake Village, Anamtaigh

There were lines a soldier wasn't supposed to cross.

Vega Ortiz had been watching the Shadows under Talon's command jump rope with those lines for months. But this...

No other choice.

Not one she could live with, anyway.

As if that made a difference.

Her knees quivered as she walked back out into the night, breathing through her nose to keep down the bile churning in her stomach.

It was so quiet.

The others clocked her exit, and Wight spoke into her com. *"What's the status?"*

Better me than them.

But was it? Dead was dead.

So fucking quiet.

Vega measured her footsteps around the corner and heaved in relative privacy beneath an awning. She had to get the shakes under control. If she showed remorse, any sort of weakness, they'd eat her alive. Fuck, she needed a hit. Two of them. Fifty of them. Just keep them coming until the sound of that last sigh stopped vibrating her eardrums to near-bursting. Anything to erase the sight of that pulse beat going still.

But no.

This was on her.

Vega rolled her shoulders beneath the impossible weight and used it to ground herself until her breathing evened out. She let it settle over her features, turning her face into a death mask, leeching all emotion from her voice as she replied to Wight, "Abort mission."

"The fuck?"

Sorrenson peeked around the corner from the back of the house and threw his hands up in question.

Higgins stepped out from behind the civilian transport in the driveway, frowning at her. "What's going on?" he whispered.

Aleric would be somewhere near the hedges—he liked to lurk.

She was surrounded. They'd expected her to run.

"The asset is non-viable."

She could feel Sorrenson tense and suppressed a shiver.

Higgins jerked back, and his face went hard as he quietly entered the house. A couple of minutes later, his hushed voice came through the coms. *"Confirmed. Asset non-viable."*

Her stomach heaved again, but she swallowed it back and marched out from the darkness toward the hover waiting above the park green at the end of the block. Higgins slammed the front door shut as he exited the house and fell into step on her right, tension radiating from him in furious, pulsing waves.

On her left, Sorrenson still hadn't said a word, but his jaw twitched in a rapid beat.

Aleric brought up the rear. With all their footsteps naturally aligning into one uniform rhythm, the sound of his knife slapping against his palm made her eye twitch.

No response from the others.

Vega didn't notice while she grappled with the invisible weight, trying to somehow settle it on her soul in a way that wouldn't crush the last, tattered bits of it into oblivion.

And then she heard the scream.

She didn't look back to see the lights turning on all over the house—all over the street. She didn't pause when the wailing cries of a grieving mother filled the air. She didn't hesitate to board the hover as concerned neighbors began to spill into the night.

She found her seat so easily and sat there perfectly calm and composed as the hover rose into the sky and returned to the Roost with no one below the wiser.

The others were pissed. No one was talking to her or even looking at her.

Fuck them.

Vega pulled a knife to sharpen. Keep her hands busy—that was the ticket. Keep her thoughts on other things.

The first stroke of the honing stick along the blade sounded out a sigh. The sigh. The final exhale of life as it ebbed out of the body of a thirteen-year-old girl.

The hover touched down in the saddle.

Vega was first out of her seat before the engines stopped whirring. She was on the ramp before its edge had touched the landing pad. She marched into the vault with her eyes forward and her hands loose at her sides.

Someone must have reported ahead of their arrival. The chest-pounding music had been turned off, and the women were gone, but the air was still thick with the musk of sex, alcohol, and vomit. The main vault chamber was filled with sour-faced soldiers who glared at her like it was her fault. Every time she met one of those gazes head-on, a tiny bit of weight lifted. But it left behind a dark void where something should have been. Honor, maybe? Or compassion.

Vega's life had always been a shitshow. But how the fuck had it managed to come to *this*?

A blow to the back of her head sent her face-first to the ground.

She must have blacked out for a second. When she came to, her cheek was pressed into the vault floor, and she was pinned with her hands at her lower back and a heavy weight between her shoulder blades. Her ears rang too much to make out the voices around her, but she was acutely aware of the many Shadows looming over her.

Vega had no leverage, and only a vague sense of self-preservation fluttering through her mind, trying to tell her she was in danger.

Someone was yanking on her braid. Someone else's hands were groping along the back of her waistband, tugging up her shirt. A Shadow fell over her vision as someone hummed garbled words in her ear on a blast of hot, moist breath.

"…take away our entertainment, guess what you become, bitch."

Vega flexed against the body that pinned her down, finding no leverage, no angle to exploit, and no opening for escape. This wasn't a typical mob falling over her. These were *Shadows*. Trained from youth to kill before they got killed. Pitted against each other and taught to exploit each other's weaknesses—so they would know that none of them was better than the others.

And now all that violence was about to be unleashed.

On her.

Vega couldn't tell which of the animals was currently on top of her, but she felt him shift his weight to undo his pants. He had to let go of her hands to pull down hers.

A fatal mistake.

Vega still had her knives strapped all over her body. And she only needed one.

Muscle memory brought her palm to the handle of a knife. She yanked it out and blindly stabbed at the body on top of hers. Her position and the angle of her limbs limited her range of motion, but she did strike true. Somewhere.

The Shadow shouted and reared away, but before she could take advantage of the opening, he was back, his big hand on the side of her face, shoving her down into submission.

And then he was gone.

The pressure eased as his weight tipped off her and collapsed sideways, blank eyes staring at her. She could see the others backing away through the smoking hole in the middle of Aleric's head.

Silence.

And then *he* spoke. "We may be Hounds, but we will *not* turn on each other like dogs."

The proclamation was met with an uproar of protests as Vega attempted to raise herself off the floor.

Someone stepped forward, reaching for her, and promptly dropped.

No arguments. No mercy.

This time, the silence lasted.

Vega held still, fighting through the dizziness, trying to think her way out of this death trap, but part of her didn't want to. No more bodies on top of her, but that impossible, invisible weight was still there, pinning her chest to the floor. It weakened her limbs too much to escape the pull of the grave they were about to shove her into, probably in pieces.

"Disobeying a direct order from your commanding officer is a corporal offense. Get her up."

Two soldiers split off from the crowd. Each took hold of one of her arms, dragging her up from the floor. They didn't take her far. A few feet, maybe. Then they deposited her face-first onto a gurney. Mechanized shackles locked around her ankles and wrists. Flexible straps whipped across her lower back and shoulders, tightening until she could barely breathe.

She recognized the rhythm of Talon's footsteps as he approached the gurney and tossed her braid aside to bare the back of her neck. The barrel of something cold and metallic kissed her spine, and she squeezed her eyes shut. No way was her last sight in this universe going to be some brainwashed, sadistic asshole's crotch.

Only she had no more pleasant sights to call up. Her memories were a cesspool of shit and horror, swirling in a haze of misery. She desperately sought her mother's face, but time and countless EMC treatments had eroded her image to a blur of caramel skin and long, black hair curled into big, glossy waves around her face and shoulders. Vega remembered the dress she'd used to wear and the smell of her perfume, but that was it.

She had nothing.

She was no one.

No, that wasn't quite true. She was something—a murderer.

The trigger compressed, and Vega felt the impact of the payload stab through the back of her neck. For one terrifying moment, she lost all feeling from the neck down but remained fully alive and conscious. Her heart raced, but her lungs wouldn't expand to accept air.

And then electric fire seared down her spine. It scorched her nerve endings, made muscles all over her body contract and twist, contorted her fingers and toes while the rest of her was immobilized. It went on for so long that Vega's eyes started to feel like they were cooking out of her skull. Her teeth cracking in the unbreakable vise of her locked jaw barely registered.

When it was over, Vega could breathe again and wished to fuck she didn't. She got a five-second reprieve before the electric current struck her again, trying to arch and break her back.

She screamed, tasting metal on her tongue as tears overflowed without her say-so.

Another pause.

Another jolt.

By the time the force released her, Vega's mind was shredded beyond any ability to reason or comprehend. Her entire body was one massive muscle spasm, with only her restraints keeping her prone. Her chest hurt with every breath she forced in and out of her lungs. Her dry eyes burned, even as the tears kept coming.

She blinked, and there was Talon, with his blond hair and bloodshot eyes, without a hint of ire on his face. "Your little stunt cost me two good men today," he said.

The fuck did he expect her to do? Apologize? Far as Vega was concerned, two out of sixty-five was a piss-poor score. *Let me up, motherfucker. I'll take you all out before I let you lay a finger on a fucking child.*

She couldn't tell whether her fury translated to her face when it was so completely numb. Whether he read her silence as resignation or mutiny, Talon sighed. "The punishment is regulation. Not giving you to *them*—that's mercy. I own you, pretty bird. And you will not disobey me again." He stared her down to make sure she got the message. Then he pushed to his feet, and she was once again eye-level with his crotch. "Your job is to follow orders. If you forget, the leash will remind you. Let's make sure the lesson sticks."

And for the next five days, all Vega knew was pain.

2

October 20, 3039 – Station, Persephone 5

Tripping balls on Bliss was so much better at a Mile High. The music had color. Ethereal butterflies fluttered all around, trailing sparkling lights. Laughter prickled Vega's tongue like champagne, and she felt love envelop her in a cloud of warm mist that showered her skin in millions of tiny fairy kisses.

The air swayed her hips into the rhythm of a new song. She liked it. A lot. It matched the whoosh of blood coursing through her veins. Vega raised her arms, and her breath caught at the gorgeous rainbows she traced in their wake. She brought them down, then up again, then held them out and twirled around and around, laughing as the butterflies in her chest took flight, bursting out of her in an explosion of magical confetti.

She knocked into something. A tall glass spun off a table, struck the floor, and turned into glittering diamonds.

"Heeyyyy, waaatch it…"

Vega glanced up at the speaker. A troll who'd been slowed down until she could barely make out his words. She smiled. It wasn't his fault he was so ugly.

He pushed to his feet. "Whaat diid youuuuu saaaayyy?"

Had she said something? Vega reached out to touch his cheek in consolation, but he knocked it away. Angry sparks struck out from the impact.

Oh, there was another glass. Vega picked it up, shushing the troll's little goblin as she held the glass up to the strobing lights. Where were the diamonds? *Meh*, this one was boring. She dropped it and turned away. Dancing was better.

But the troll grabbed her arm and spun her around as he pulled back his fist.

Sooooo sloooow.

Vega punched him in the nose.

He squealed. Or someone did. And then there were five more trolls, climbing over and around their tables toward her. They looked ridiculous with their stumpy fingers, big, flat noses, and green mouths snarling around tusks.

Vega laughed, and the sound echoed, then split into a separate version of her. They laughed harder together than on their own, and the ugly trolls' eyes shrank and started to glow red. She danced her other self away from the first troll who grabbed for her. The twirl turned the butterflies into a tornado. She didn't see the next hit coming until it was almost too late.

Vega ducked under the swinging log of an arm, ended up behind the troll, and watched him punch another troll. But there was a third one, and he had smoke billowing from his flippy ears. He pointed a banana at her, and when he squeezed it, an invisible demon hit her in the chest.

She flew back and collided with a wall with arms. They caught her up and held her there with her feet dangling off the floor and her head drooping back against the shelf. This was not a good position. The ceiling spun too fast, and her stomach roiled with angry, angry rats.

Vega brought her head up and forward. The trolls were buggy-eyed, backing away from her and the wall. The goblin didn't like that. It yapped, flinging its hair and pointing sharp fingers, but none of the trolls moved.

The wall set her down and gave her room to turn around. She blinked at the surface of a suit. Why was a wall wearing a suit? Tracing the collar up, she found a neck and then a head carved out of stone. Marble eyes glared at her. "You got it out of your system now?"

Not good. She didn't want to leave yet, and the wall could make her. That was its job. She thought. Maybe not. It looked familiar, but it was hard to tell with the stone cracking when it moved to speak.

Better safe than sorry. She had one more shot of Bliss waiting for her at the bar. Couldn't let it go to waste. Smoothing a hank of hair behind her ear, she pulled back her shoulders and said, "Yyyep."

The wall let her go.

Vega whirled and flew at the trolls with a banshee wail that made them scatter.

The wall caught her back up again, and she laughed as it swung her to drape over the shelf. She bounced up and down to five steps off before her stomach let out the rats.

Quinn VanWarren stopped and closed his eyes for a second to gather his patience, then kept going. At least she wasn't squirming anymore. Probably passed out cold. A pair of bouncers ran up after the fighting was long over, shouting at him to get out. Where the hell did they think he was heading?

The strobing lights gave him a headache and made everything look the same. He got turned around twice before he found the exit and breathed a sigh of relief as the soundproof door closed behind him. The hallway was blessedly quiet and illuminated by soft, steady lighting. He stopped at the coat check and adjusted Vega in his arms. Sleeping like a baby doused in perfume. A side effect of Bliss, but not usually this strong. Quinn pressed each of Vega's fingers to the pad, but none of them worked. She hadn't left anything there.

His personal transport was waiting out front. The black finish, polished to a mirror shine, had attracted some attention, but when the looky-loos saw who was coming for it, they prudently removed themselves to gawk from a safer distance.

He tried not to hold it against them. Even in this new age of DNA manipulation and extreme body modification, it was rare to see someone of his height and build walking around town. But, no matter how often he reminded himself of it, it never did anything to ease the old, bitter resentment. Nobody liked being the freak in the ointment. He didn't snarl and bark at them only because it tended to make things worse.

The door opened automatically, and the vehicle raised higher off the ground in deference to his height. Handy feature. One of many. Quinn laid Vega on the back seat, checking her pulse to make sure she still had one, then shucked out of his vomit-covered jacket before getting in after her. Vega didn't stir once.

"Good evening, sir," the AI navigation greeted through the speakers. "Did you enjoy the Mile High?"

"Predictably, no."

"I'm sorry to hear that. Shall I set course to a different establishment? I have a number of recommendations. Or would you like to return home?"

"Hospital."

"Right away, sir." The transport pulled away from the curb, and an emergency blue light blinked on the dashboard. It allowed the vehicle to circumvent traffic rules by rising above the street to take the fastest, most direct route to a preapproved location. "The closest hospital is Boma Centrale. I have notified them of our ETA."

The temperature rose inside the cabin, and Quinn opened the top three buttons on his shirt in deference. The heat was probably good for Vega, but he was sweltering.

They arrived at the hospital in ten minutes and pulled over in the parking space assigned to them. Quinn pulled Vega out and carried her through into the emergency room. An android nurse was already prepped with a glass tablet displaying Quinn's personal information ready for his approval. He canceled it—he wasn't the patient. The next screen that popped up had only one question: HOW WILL YOU BE PAYING TODAY? Quinn passed the back of his hand over the screen to scan his chip. His identity checked out, and a confirmation message wished him a good day.

"How can I assist you?" the android asked.

"My friend needs a detox."

"I see. My sensors indicate a possible overdose. I have called for a medical consult. ETA: two minutes and fifteen seconds. Please stand by."

The doctor arrived with a gurney and didn't waste time. "What do we know?"

Quinn laid Vega on the gurney and stepped back so the doc could scan her. "She threw up and passed out at a club. Bliss. Possibly other stuff."

The scanner started flashing red all over the place. "Woof. Must have been one hell of a party. All right, let's get her on some fluids."

The gurney followed the doc as he turned to lead the way down the hall. He didn't ask any questions. As long as they got paid, all doctors cared about was fixing the problem and sending the patient on their way. "I need her detoxed, not stabilized."

"Are you sure?" the doc asked dryly. "It'll ruin a hell of an expensive high."

Quinn frowned. "How expensive?"

"At this point, her blood is about point fifteen percent Bliss."

"Isn't that deadly?"

The man shrugged a careless shoulder. "Yes, no, maybe." Such a caring soul. "I've seen it kill at a fifth of these levels. I've also seen a guy dosed up twice this much walk in, get his broken arm fixed, and head straight out to another den. Individual tolerance levels vary."

Quinn breathed down his frustration. Of all the stupid shit he'd seen people do in his life, drugs were the stupidest. He'd thought Vega was smarter than this. "Just get her detoxed. We don't have time for a hangover."

The doc nodded. "In the tank she goes." But he stopped before a door to do something medical with the scanner. "What the…?"

"What?"

The doc didn't answer, so Quinn came around to his side to see what he was staring at. The screen showed an enlarged scan of Vega's cervical spine and a crazy, alien-looking device attached to it with a lot of thin tentacles.

What the fuck was that?

The doc stiffened as he realized Quinn was standing beside him. He slowly looked up, his face turning ashy. Quinn saw the shudder go through him before the man swallowed hard and masked his fear. But he fumbled the device and almost dropped it when he reached for the scanloc to open the door.

Quinn caught it, and the doc flinched away. The hell was his problem? "How much to get that thing removed from her spine?"

The doc looked seconds away from pissing his pants. "Listen, I don't want any trouble."

"And I'm all out of trouble to hand out," he said in as reasonable a voice as he could muster while holding the device out to the shivering little man in a lab coat. "I'm asking you about the cost of a medical procedure."

The terrified doctor shrank a few inches more as he snatched his device back, slipped into the room, and pulled the gurney in after him, putting a lot of space between himself and Quinn. "Y-you're here for a detox. That's what we're going to do."

A chorus of androids swarmed around the gurney, relieving Vega of her clothes. "The clothing articles are dangerously saturated," one of them informed him. "We will remove any salvageable personal items and incinerate the rest in the biohazard furnace."

As it talked, the others carried Vega to a sophisticated medical tank that looked like a fancy one-person submarine turned inside out and filled with a thick fluid. They submerged her into it carefully, not so much for her sake, but so they wouldn't spill the liquid. Quinn had spent a day or two in one himself—for different reasons. The artificially engineered amniotic fluid used in them was one of the most expensive substances in existence because it literally saved lives.

"Your deluxe medical plan includes a complimentary replacement of any destroyed items," the android continued.

Quinn ignored it and turned to the doctor. "So you're just going to leave that thing in her neck?"

The doctor swallowed hard and squeezed his eyes shut, nodding in a twitchy tick. "Yes. Yes, that's exactly what we're going to do." He turned his back on Quinn to fiddle with the controls.

"The hell kind of a doctor are you?"

Okay, maybe he'd said that a little louder than he intended. Still, there was no reason for the doctor to hunch over like he expected Quinn to beat him over the head. "Please, I have a family."

"What are you talking about?" Quinn knew he could be intimidating, but this level of overreaction bordered on insulting.

"Boma Centrale has a strict non-involvement policy with the Shadows. We don't touch your tech. We don't want any trouble."

Wait… "You think I'm a—"

"The saturation levels will require a six-hour detox to clear everything out of her system and balance her hormone production. She will be placed under sedation for the procedure and for twenty-four hours afterward. I am prescribing a time-released nutrition booster and putting an auto-discharge on her chart. She'll be ready to go when the bots remove her from the tank. Keep her warm and make sure she hydrates when she wakes up."

Rattling instructions off at the speed of light, the doctor edged around Quinn and fled from the room, leaving him speechless.

"New articles of clothing will be provided for the patient prior to discharge," the bot said. "For your comfort, we have a waiting room down the hall with—"

"I'm not leaving."

"As you wish. Please use the console at your convenience to request anything you need."

The bots filed out the door, leaving him alone with Vega in an artificial detox womb, sound asleep and oblivious to the world. The glass had frosted over to obscure everything but her face as soon as they'd placed her into it.

She looked so different now than in the club. In sleep, her features relaxed not into peace but the careful blank mask she'd worn when he'd first met her a few months ago.

"You believe that guy? Two people in the room, and he pegged *me* as the Shadow."

Little had he known…

Vega reached for the gun under her pillow before she'd fully awakened.

It wasn't there.

She kept her eyes shut, pretending to sleep while she took stock of the situation. The bed wasn't hers. The pillow was too soft, the covers too silky. The lights didn't flicker and buzz like the ones in her cheap apartment, and there was a distinct lack of any smells whatsoever.

Someone else was in the room with her. Vega heard them shift around in a seat—which she didn't have. "I know you're awake."

She knew that voice. But there was no possible way…

Vega gave up the pretense and sat up, turning toward the stranger who was more familiar than he should have been.

"I'd say good morning, but we're in flux."

She blinked at him, then got out of bed to pull back the thick drapes beside him. Sure enough, there was a pill-shaped window, sealed from both sides against subspace forces. "This ranks on a whole new level of suicidal."

"More like desperate." He cleared his throat. "Would you mind putting some clothes on?"

Vega raised an eyebrow at Quinn. "Weren't you the one who took them off me?"

He dipped his head, more to avert his gaze than nod, but conceded, "Fair point. I thought you'd be more comfortable sleeping without them." He sat so still, as if he thought he'd take up less space if he didn't move around. It didn't work.

"Finally got that new heart, did you?"

He grinned and, damn, it was a good look on him. "Better than."

The last time they'd met, Quinn VanWarren had already been taller and wider than any soldier in Talon's messed-up gang of miscreants. His unique genetic glitch had essentially gifted him with superhuman strength, but it had come at the price of a failing heart. Stuck on the backwoods planet of Anamtaigh, cornered and cut off by the Shadows, he'd suffered the defect for years, limited in ways that would have driven her crazy.

But all his former weakness was now gone. As big as he'd been a few months ago, he'd expanded at least three more sizes. His shoulders stretched the seams of his dress shirt, and his arms bulged in the sleeves when he set aside the digital reading device to give her his full attention. He kept his gaze firmly above her lack of a neckline.

"I assume you have questions," he said.

"Just one. How would you like to die?"

Quinn's gaze made a sweep down her body and back up. The answer he tried so hard to hide was written all over him: *With my head between your legs.* She might have obliged him if he had the balls to say it out loud. It had been years since Vega had had good, hard-driving, satisfying sex—not counting drugged-out escapades, which didn't qualify as "good" or "satisfying" in any sense of the word. And, despite all common sense, there was something about Quinn that made her want to arch and purr.

It was his hands, she decided. They were huge—and capable. Yes, he could haul around mechanical equipment that usually took five normal people to budge, but she'd also seen him tinker with children's toys without crushing a single one.

Vega's gaze trailed down to his lap as she shifted her weight to one leg, cocking her hip. *Say it,* she silently willed him, her body priming for a hard, punishing ride. She could make his eyes roll back in his head. One word, and she'd climb into his lap and help him break that flimsy chair he sat in. Her body hadn't felt this good, this *ready*, in a long time. And the way he was looking at her… Quinn VanWarren had never and would never flinch from her. He would take anything she dished out and give it right back to her, and, holy fucking shit, did that sound good right now.

He was staring at her thighs. More specifically, a pale scar from the knife wound Talon had gifted her last year for not giving him the fawning praise he'd expected from his minions. Vega rested her fingers over it, hiding the mark and drawing Quinn's attention elsewhere.

Say it…

Quinn flushed and shifted in his seat to prop an ankle on his knee. "I have a proposition for you." That didn't sound like it was heading where she wanted it. And yep, there went his gaze, turning uncompromising as it met hers. He'd mentally shelved any possibility of something physical between them to keep things *professional*.

Vega almost sighed. "And the suicidal keeps on coming." She left the window to explore the spacious, expensive-looking room, giving him a view of her back. Not that she was trying to torture him or anything. After all, he'd probably already seen every inch of her when he'd undressed her. But if he wanted to ignore this, she could, too.

"I think you'll find some interest in what I have to say."

"Do you? Why's that?"

Aha! Clothes.

Not her clothes.

"I'm not dead yet." She could hear the shrug in his voice.

Vega sorted through the pile of garments, hoping her stuff was buried underneath. There was only one outfit, consisting of serviceable underwear, a nondescript black T-shirt, and pants. The socks were short and white, and instead of her good boots, someone had issued her neon green, lace-up running shoes. A matching jacket completed the outfit.

Standard issue hospital fare. Vega had worn her fair share of it in the past.

She would be chucking it out of an airlock straight toward the nearest burning star.

There were two doors to the room. One opened onto a sitting area with couches and an entertainment center. The other was the bathroom. She grabbed the outfit and closed herself in there to take care of business and wash off the neutral smell of a hospital with one of the many soaps and perfumes lining the shower.

Six minutes later, Vega emerged to Quinn looking up from his reading device as if he'd forgotten she was there. She went through the bedroom straight to the sitting area. This place looked like a hotel suite rather than a shuttle unit. It even had a refreshments console with a long list of food and drink options.

"How are you feeling?" Quinn asked behind her.

"Better than I should." Which meant he must have spent a fortune on a total detox. "Second question: who'd you kill to get all this money?"

Quinn winced. "It's a long story. It's actually what I want to discuss with you."

Vega made her selection through the console and, ten seconds later, retrieved a fresh-made hot breakfast of scrambled eggs, bacon, and toast with a steaming mug of coffee. She took it to the dining table, sat down, and waited.

It took her raising an eyebrow in question for Quinn to understand that he should do something, like start talking.

"Oh." He scratched the back of his head, then got his breakfast and brought it to the table. He walked with all the confidence of his formidable size but sat gingerly in deference to furniture that might not have been made to support his weight.

His eyes had acquired faint crow's feet at the outer edges since they'd last talked. And there was a bleakness to him he hadn't had when he'd been dying of a severe heart condition and fighting his way through a battleground of trained soldiers to save her life. *Now we're even*, he'd told her that day. But they weren't. Not even close.

"In your own time," she told him sweetly because sitting in awkward silence, staring at each other, and not eating scrumptious food was getting old.

"Why aren't you mad?"

"About what?"

"Being kidnapped."

Vega forked a fluffy chunk of eggs into her mouth and almost melted. Best thing she'd had in her mouth in months. "Is that what I am?"

"I suppose, with your background as a Sh—"

"Don't say it." Fancy as this suite was, it probably had security monitoring every corner. And Shadows didn't rank very high in humanity's esteem at the moment. It was a wonder so many of them were still alive, herself included.

He compensated and continued, "—shit-kicking badass, you could get yourself free the second we land. Which is why I'm glad you have nowhere to run for another"—he checked his device—"twenty-nine and a half hours. We have time to talk."

Vega took a bite out of a crispy strip of bacon. Holy shit, when was the last time she'd had bacon? Thank the galaxy for her Shadow training. Without it, she'd never have been able to mask her reaction. It was almost worth losing the high she'd built up over the last two weeks.

Seeing she wouldn't respond verbally, Quinn took a bite of his toast, chewed and swallowed, then blurted out, "I want to hire you. As a bodyguard and an investigator."

Vega stopped chewing for a full second. "I'm waiting for the punchline."

He took a deep breath and shook himself off a little, squaring up as if for a battle. "Okay, here goes. My family is rich. Not Laura-rich, but enough that none of my siblings, cousins, or their offspring have to even think about working."

"Father, Derek Kitsuto, famous director, married into mother, Holly VanWarren's family fortune. Actress by trade, she inherited the bulk of her money from her parents, Amundsen and Beatrice VanWarren, the inventors of the motion-responsive 3D holoflick. You have two brothers, four half-sisters, and nineteen first cousins, all celebrities in some way, shape, or form. Most of it undeserved."

The type of fame the VanWarrens enjoyed and got paid for was referred to as being a dashie. With the possible exception of Derek Kitsuto, none of them had done anything to earn their place in the galactic spotlight, but the notoriety of their name alone brought them money from advertising contracts and ensured instant success for any business venture they did endeavor at least in the short term. Which was why anyone marrying into the family automatically adopted their last name. They made their quick fortune using cash-grab rip-off deals with the VanWarren brand slapped all over them and then let the businesses run themselves to the ground while they sipped expensive drinks on their private islands all across the galaxy.

"How do you…? Never mind."

"Your parents disinherited you at sixteen when your genetic differences started to manifest and kicked you out of the house. Your father divorced your mother soon after. You spent two years on the street, then signed up for a work-study program at the public library, which sent you to Anamtaigh, where you ultimately got stuck. None of which explains how you're rich again."

"Honestly? Not a clue. Last time I saw any of my family was eighteen years ago when they slammed the door in my face. Fast forward to earlier this year, I wake up after heart surgery on Torrey, to a lawyer sitting in my room, telling me my grandparents are dead and I'm the sole beneficiary of their entire estate."

Vega whistled.

"And that's when all the shit hit the fan."

"I'll bet." Her meal finished, Vega sat back to sip her coffee while he spilled the poison with an obvious distaste.

"There was no explanation in their will, so, naturally, the entire family contested it and got nowhere. The document is ironclad. I was summoned to Ela to take over management of the estate because no one else is allowed to touch it, not even the estate manager—seriously."

Ela was the second planet in the Karos System and an orbital neighbor to Mai, where Laura McNally recently made her new home. Curious proximity. Vega would bet it wasn't accidental. With two other planets in the habitable belt, the Karos system was considered something of a universal miracle. It attracted the rich, the famous, and the unscrupulous, keeping everyday rabble out with astronomic property prices and travel costs. Tourism was highly discouraged, but once in a while, a film crew got special dispensation to access restricted regions for movie projects, which only added to the system's popularity.

"So I dig into the books and find out that my grandparents had financed most of my family's projects and ventures. The actual operations they left to the respective brain trusts, but they retained controlling interests in all of them. Every single one could be shut down or sold off in an instant, and the family wouldn't be able to do a damned thing about it."

"And now you're in charge of it all."

Quinn nodded. "The boy they kicked out into the cold to fend for himself has all of them by the proverbial balls."

"They try to take you out yet?" she snarked.

Rich people were a stratum of society she'd never wanted to deal with. Her experience with them was limited to what she'd seen represented in movies and holoflicks, and that was already more than enough for her. Vapid, petty, shallow, and vindictive, the people who controlled humanity's wealth could barely be considered human themselves.

Which, naturally, meant that a good number of them had been included in the class whose interests the Shadows unknowingly protected. Luckily, any missions involving one of them required a level of finesse not included in Hound training, so the pleasure of their completion always went to a Hawk.

"Twice," Quinn said with a bitter twist to his mouth, and Vega felt an uncomfortable chill race up her spine and into her hairline, making her scalp itch.

She set down the coffee cup to give him her full attention.

The moment he said it, Quinn felt the temperature in the room plummet. Vega's veiled humor iced over, and she became the Shadow she was—one of the boogeymen lurking behind the scenes, watching, and waiting for the perfect time to strike.

Even three and a half years ago, the Shadow armies had been nothing but a rumor. People had whispered about them and threatened their children with them, but no one had believed they were real.

Until they'd decided to step out into the light and struck out with such malice, it had crippled society on too many worlds to count. The three-year war had been declared finished by most public media, but anyone with eyes, ears, and two brain cells to rub together knew better. The Shadows might have been scattered, but they were far from finished.

And no one knew that better than Quinn.

"First time, they put a bomb in my new transport. I didn't know how to work the controls yet and managed to trigger it from a distance."

He paused there to gauge Vega's reaction.

She showed none.

She didn't even blink, staring at him blank-faced, and he couldn't tell if she would shrug it all off and go back to drinking her coffee or take an escape pod straight to his family's mansion and burn it to the ground, along with everyone in it.

Slightly concerning.

"At first, I figured it was someone with a grudge against the family. I would have made a prominent target as the newcomer without the dedicated security the rest of them have. Plus, my name had been on the news a bit. The long-lost heir to the VanWarren fortune." He waved it aside. "But then a cousin invited me to dinner."

"Poison?"

"I spent the night in the ER with the worst case of indigestion. Doctor said it was supposed to have caused cardiac arrest. Apparently, Cousin Elspeth remembered my bad heart from when we were kids. She didn't know that I got a new one of the artificial variety and some additional modifications to my DNA." Said modifications were the only reason the poison hadn't caused permanent damage.

Vega blinked. "Your new heart is artificial?"

"The latest invention to come out of the laboratories of Dr. Hailey Chase-Calen."

The younger Chase sister worked closely with the Special Unit on Torrey. Hailey and her older sister, Amelia, were legends among Quinn's telepath friends for reasons no one wanted to discuss with him. All he knew was that the things they'd invented and engineered had changed the way the SU approached medicine for chem-re-sistants—people like Quinn, whose DNA didn't stabilize with the government-mandated chem-treatments.

Hailey had taken over the research after Amelia had gone into hid-ing. Her methods were unorthodox, to say the least. But although her bedside manner bordered on sociopathic, she was still the most capa-ble doctor Quinn had ever had. And, given the miracle she'd worked on him, he was willing to overlook a few minor character flaws. "It's made with my DNA. But it works more like an engine than a pump. It doesn't beat, it whirrs." To make sure his body didn't reject it, Dr. Chase-Calen had also administered some top secret and probably illegal serum to ramp up and calibrate Quinn's healing. "Not, strictly speaking, approved for public consumption, but the all-benevolent Special Unit pulled some strings for me."

In the absence of his own family, Quinn had been adopted into the organization made up of telepaths and "other freaks," as their acting director, Emma Wayland, referred to them. Sweet lady. Bit scrambled in the brains department. He and everyone who'd made it out from under the Shadows on Anamtaigh owed her a great debt, which Laura, as their self-appointed matriarch, had decided to repay on their behalf.

Vega pushed back from the table and came to his side, bending over to put her ear to his chest.

Quinn froze as the hum of his new heart raised in pitch, the equivalent of an elevated heart rate. His body heated, and his face flushed. Just because the heart worked didn't mean it was perfect. He was still getting used to the fluctuations in blood flow. And Vega's cheek pressing against his chest wasn't helping.

The overwhelming flowery scent of Bliss had been detoxed out of her, but a trace of it still lingered beneath the citrusy perfume of whatever soap she'd washed with, and Quinn had an overwhelming urge to put his nose to her smooth, warm brown skin to look for the truth of *her*.

He knew her scent in ways that made him feel more animal than human. He'd dreamed of it more times than he cared to count. He'd smelled it in those last moments before the surgical anesthesia kicked in and thought for sure he'd never wake up again. And, when he had, it had been from a chemical coma and twisted dreams of her legs tangling with his, her mouth at his ear, and the scalpel-sharp edge of her blade at his neck.

"Interesting." Vega returned to her seat, ignoring his physical reaction. "Continue."

"Like I said, the heart's not approved." Neither was the regenerative serum, which Dr. Chase-Calen had warned him not to brag about too much. "So, I had to pay off the ER doctor to keep it quiet." The price of erasing all records of his visit had been a small fortune and a round-trip ticket to Mai. "Which means I can't bring attempted murder charges against Cousin Elspeth."

"Hmm."

Now came the tricky part. "I have reason to believe the Shadows are involved somehow."

Pause for a reaction.

None came.

Quinn kept going. "The doctor analyzed the substance used on me and found no record of it in any database. He had to feed it into a simulator just to figure out its structure and intended function. So, I went home and did some more digging. Because of the whole controlling interest thing, I have access to the family's financial records. I found a pattern of recurring payments going back several years. There are many different source accounts, negligible amounts per transaction, and a seemingly random schedule. But it works out that the same total sum leaves the family coffers every month to untraceable recipients. And I'm talking down to a thousandth of a credit."

"I'm not surprised."

"And that brings me to my point. I want the Shadows out. You're the only one I know who has a chance in hell against them."

"Try again."

"The SU said no," he admitted. They were stretched too thin as it was, and after the victory they'd pulled off on Anamtaigh, they'd decided it would be prudent to lay low for a while.

"What about the others? Rowe would have stepped in."

"Rowe's been wiped," he reminded her. The former Shadow had been captured by Talon shortly after Vega had led the attack on Quinn's makeshift family. Rowe had had his entire past and identity ripped away, replaced by a mindless code of Shadow conduct. He'd retained enough of himself to turn on Talon and help the prisoners escape but not enough to remember the love of his life. "I don't trust him."

"But you trust *me*." The statement dripped with sarcasm. "You do remember what I did to you, don't you?"

"I remember you led the attack on the inn and then stabbed one of your own men to set Rusty loose." The teenage girl he considered his little sister had come out of that fight with little more than a bruise. She was one of the lucky ones. "I remember you shot me and then restarted my heart. And I remember you took three of us prisoner but then released Miguel and me from the ledge and sent him off in a transport with five terrified kids." Quinn remembered her hiding him from the other Shadows, saving his life a second time after that, and the battle she'd waged to protect Laura and the SU telepaths. "I haven't forgotten any of it. And I meant what I said that day. As far as I'm concerned, we're even."

He could tell she didn't like that. But instead of arguing, she said, "Catton and Zigmann jumped ship, too, didn't they?"

After the dust had settled and before all the blood had dried on Anamtaigh, only a handful of Shadows had remained standing—the ones Emma's telepaths had chosen to spare. Two of those had ultimately decided to leave with the Special Unit, but only Brent Catton had stayed with them. "Zigmann's disappeared. But I did ask Catton. He wished me good luck and hung up on me."

"Yep."

What kind of response was that? "Here's the thing. If I go in there by myself, I'll get myself dead before I can find out where the money leads. And I don't want to hurt the family, either. As shitty as most of them are, they do have kids who didn't do anything wrong. I know I can bring at least half of the adults around to my side, but if I do that, and the payments stop—"

"The Shadows will retaliate against all of you."

Quinn breathed out the air holding up his spine. Vega had just confirmed his worst fears in a straight-forward statement of fact.

She took a sip of her coffee. "I'm assuming you have a plan?"

Sort of. But to get Vega to help him, he had to make it worth her while. "I heard you're still looking for Talon."

If possible, her face hardened even more.

The leader of Anamtaigh's Shadows had escaped the battle to save his own skin and left his men to die. He might have disappeared into thin air, but no one who knew him expected Talon to lay low for long. It wasn't in his nature to accept defeat. He would seek out other Shadows to start rebuilding his forces again. The Special Unit, Talon's surviving Shadows, and even Laura all agreed this could not be allowed to happen. But, of all of them, Vega was the most invested in hunting him down, and the evil-looking betentacled device on her spine was the most likely reason why.

Given the state in which he'd found her on Persephone 5, "I take it you don't have any actionable leads as to his whereabouts."

Vega's cup rattled slightly when she set it down on its saucer. "No."

"Well, I don't know much about Shadows, but I would assume finding one to question would probably be helpful in your quest."

"Probably."

"And my current situation just so happens to give you the safest and most direct path to a Shadow—through me and my family. So, here's the deal: you help me get the Shadows off my family's back, and I'll help you find Talon."

She looked duly unimpressed. "How?"

Wasn't it obvious? "With money. Tracking people requires information, travel, gear, bribes—everything you need will come at a significant cost. And I find myself burdened with a great deal of money at the moment, which I'm eager to put to good use." He brought up a banking screen on his device and pressed his thumb to the corner for identification to unlock it. The screen refreshed to an authorization page. Quinn put the device on the table and pushed it across to Vega.

"What's this?"

"Thumbprint in the lower left, then scan your ID chip across the screen, and you'll have full access to my estate bank account."

Vega raised an eyebrow at him. "The bank account which controls all your family's resources?"

"That's the one."

"What if I decide to drain it and run?"

Quinn shrugged. "I know how to live without money. And it'd be one way to get rid of the Shadows." And ruin his family in the process. A small part of him almost wished Vega would do it, give them a taste of what they'd put Quinn through when they'd shunned him at sixteen for being too different to fit into their public lives.

But he knew she wouldn't. He was betting his entire fortune and the lives of every last family member on the belief that, despite her hard exterior, her dark past with the Shadows, and all her arguments to the contrary, Vega Ortiz did, in fact, have a heart.

4

"How long have you been rehearsing that speech?"

"A while. How'd I do?"

Vega shrugged to cover for the shudder. Thanks to the detox, her mind was perfectly clear of any drug-induced haze, and it was reeling at his offer. Near-unlimited funds and one more chance to finish what she'd started.

Vega prided herself on her self-control, but at the moment, she had a hard time holding on to her stoic expression. Talon was a nightmare that kept her from sleeping longer than two hours at a time. He still had the trigger to her leash. As long as he was out there, Vega continued to live with the constant threat of pain and torment shadowing her every step. She *needed* to take him out, not only for the greater good but for her own sanity.

And here was Quinn, offering her the means to hunt him down—at the cost of more time. Under normal circumstances, a month was enough to turn a minor irritation into a lethal threat. These were not normal circumstances, and Talon was much worse than an irritation. He'd already had several months' head start. Months which Vega had spent in constant anticipation of a debilitating electric shock, followed by death at any moment. Truth be told, she'd been ready to call it quits in a way most permanent.

But this offer changed everything.

"We're headed to Ela?" That's what the shuttle's flight tracker said.

"Yes, to the family resort on Crescent Island. They're holding a reunion in my honor. Everyone will be there for roughly three Earth-standard weeks. It's our best chance to find the Shadow link."

"We won't." If the Shadows were involved—and Vega wasn't convinced—the payment plans would have been established at the height of their power before the war. And if the payments had kept up through the three-year conflict, then the VanWarren family was dealing with a well-funded, trained, and coordinated unit of professional assassins. They'd be more likely to find a unicorn.

"We will," he countered. "*Someone* gave Cousin Elspeth the poison she used on me and the necessary instructions to pull it off. Believe me, that bulb is not bright enough to have come up with it on her own."

Cousin Elspeth had overlooked a critical detail about his biology, implicated herself with her presence, and used a substance that not only failed to kill Quinn but also remained in his system long enough to be extracted and studied. Three mistakes a true Shadow never would have made.

Unless their plan had been to take out Quinn and Elspeth at the same time. "You think they made direct contact."

"It's the only possible explanation."

Vega rolled her eyes. "Yeah, sure. We'll pretend that's what it is."

"What else could it be?"

"The Shadows aren't the only criminals in the universe capable of building bombs and synthesizing poisons." Quinn had no evidence the Shadows were involved. In his mind, that meant it had to be them. Far more likely, his family decided to try to eliminate him before he messed up their lives too much. The payments could be going to the Shadows—they did like to tap the super-rich for resources—but it could also be a VanWarren relative or employee skimming off the top. All this could be a wild goose chase for Vega and more time for Talon to mobilize.

"Are you saying no?"

Now we're even.

Vega closed her eyes and breathed to a count of ten. Quinn had presented this madness as an opportunity, a choice, but it wasn't. It was the universe forcing her nose into the dirt to make up for everything she'd done and allowed to be done as a Shadow. Getting free of them, stopping them and herself, wasn't enough. The scales had to be brought to balance, even if it cost her everything. And if she didn't choose to do it herself, the choice would be made for her. Finn

Rowe had taught her that.

She opened her eyes. Quinn looked almost disappointed.

But he was holding his breath.

"Obviously, I can't walk in there as a bodyguard."

Quinn exhaled, and his shoulders relaxed. "Obviously. I'm not an idiot."

"I will need unrestricted access."

He indicated the tablet and the authorization screen, still waiting for her mark.

"No, I mean everywhere. I can't have any doors closed in my face."

Quinn nodded. "I already thought of that. We're going to introduce you as my girlfriend."

Adorable. "A girlfriend who has full access to your *estate* bank account? You honestly think someone will believe it?"

He frowned. "What do you suggest?"

"There's only one way this can possibly work. You're not gonna like it."

~

Eight hours later, Vega had an entire dossier on their fictitious relationship spanning the last eighteen months and change, with minute details he was supposed to memorize by the time the shuttle touched down on Ela. Meanwhile, Quinn's head spun from the fact that she'd pulled it all out of thin air on the spot as if repeating it from memory.

But every single detail fit. Vega knew the date he'd first arrived on Anamtaigh. She knew he'd been staying in Hadran City when the Shadows had attacked three and a half years ago. She even knew that he'd spent a week in a hospital there last year, thanks to a good Samaritan gifting him a ride and emergency treatment until the hospital's goodwill had run out.

That was the scariest part.

Vega knew *everything* about his life on Anamtaigh, and the way she inserted herself into his past after the fact was so seamless it was majorly fucking with his brain. It was like reading an alternate universe version of his life where, somehow, he'd ended up married to Vega Ortiz, and Quinn was half convinced it had really happened.

"Where did we meet again?"

"Coffee shop off of Grand," he rattled off on pure reflex now.

"When did we get married?"

"December fifteenth of last year," he answered. The one detail he couldn't get wrong no matter what. But then he thought, fuck it. If they were making up an entire fake life together, he'd get his say, too. "It was snowing. The farmhouse roof had a hole in it the size of a transport, and you were freezing, but you kept saying that snowfall made the perfect backdrop."

Vega raised an eyebrow and tapped on the device.

"We couldn't find a proper wedding dress," Quinn continued, warming to the fantasy. "So, the local museum curator dug out a relic from the late twenty-eight hundreds. Floor-length white satin with light blue lace."

"Did it fit?"

He ignored the sarcasm. "Just about. You had to cut off the sleeves, and the waist needed to be cinched in the back, but you were right. With the snowfall, you walked through beams of sunlight like an angel descending from the heavens."

Vega snorted. "Make sure you say it exactly like that to your family." Marking down the added details, she swiped through the pages. "How did we get off-world?"

This was the tricky part. They had to stick close enough to the truth not to slip up but keep it vague enough to prevent people from making connections they shouldn't be making.

Quinn couldn't remember the story she'd made up, so he changed the subject. "How do you take your coffee?"

"What?"

"Coffee. Black? Milk? Sugar? What's your favorite thing to eat? Which side of the bed do you prefer to sleep on?"

Vega swiped across the screen a few more times, drumming her bare heel on the floor. "We should stick to the basics."

"I am. The big things might come up once. The details of everyday life, though… If I don't know how my own wife likes her eggs cooked in the morning, no one's going to buy this charade."

She didn't answer, and Quinn got the inexplicable sense that he'd somehow managed to catch her off guard—and not in a good way.

"We're supposed to have been living in each other's pockets for the last year and a half. Give me something. Make it up if you want to."

"I'm ambidextrous," she finally said.

"Great. Which hand decides how you take your coffee?"

"Hounds don't make decisions." Her restless heel settled in an ominous thump. "They have decisions made for them."

"Are you se—"

"If we're going to Ela for three weeks, I'm going to need some gear."

Study time was officially over. "You have the funds. Order whatever you want." He'd already put in a few requests for delivery to the Ela shuttleport before they'd left Persephone 5.

Handy thing, money. You could get anything, anywhere, in any way you wanted, as long as you were willing to pay the premium. Meanwhile, billions of people displaced by the war were starving out in the cold, their bodies breaking down from the fallout, and instead of dispatching aid, officials poured public resources into reelection campaigns and propaganda machines.

Vega took the invitation and relocated herself from the couch to the entertainment unit that doubled as a com. It couldn't send or receive messages until they emerged from subspace, but it still had cached access to everything in the galaxy. Vega could put in her orders, and they'd be relayed to the vendors as soon as the com lines opened.

"What about Hawks?"

"What about them?"

"You said Hounds don't make decisions. But Finn was a Hawk, right? What's the difference?"

She was silent for a moment as she brought up multiple vendor screens to find what she needed. No hesitation there; she probably had a standard issue supply list memorized down to the item's make and model numbers.

Quinn was about to pick up his digital book, figuring Vega would ignore whatever question she didn't want to answer. But then she spoke again, and he was almost sorry he'd ever asked.

"Imagine a soldier trained in every method of combat known to man, with unquestioning allegiance to the chain of command and no fear of torture, death, or whatever hell might be waiting for them after. That's a Hound. Now imagine that soldier with the ability to mimic personalities and mannerisms and blend in anywhere at any time. That's a Hawk. A Hound will rain down death and destruction upon you and everyone you've ever known. A Hawk will become your best friend, and you'll never suspect them. Not even as you watch them bury the blade in your heart."

There'd been a time, years ago, when Vega had wanted nothing more than to become a Hawk. She'd almost made it, too. In between combat training, test sessions, and live missions, she'd spent months going on maybe three hours of sleep a night to accommodate extra lessons. They'd taught her the psychology of charm, emotional manipulation, and the intricacies of body language. She'd learned the best techniques for infiltrating a social environment and how to quickly map a building and find the vulnerabilities in its security measures.

They'd forged a hammer into a scalpel and then sent her back into the toolshed as unworthy. Because, despite her immaculate service record, her pre-Shadow past made Vega a liability.

"It goes without saying that, when it comes to your family, you trust no one."

"Not going to be an issue," Quinn retorted.

"You don't go off property without me."

"Obviously."

"And try to resist getting seduced by any spouses at the gathering."

Silence.

Then, "Are you trying to be funny or just cruel?"

Surprised by the odd note in his voice, Vega turned to face him. "Neither."

He didn't look convinced.

"Do I need to draw it for you in crayon? You just got handed total control over your family's financial lives. Your blood relatives already hate you enough to want you dead. What do you think their spouses will do when they realize their cash cows are about to be put out to pasture? Without the family's money, their separation agreements will be useless. People who get comfortable get desperate to maintain their comfort—by any means necessary. Taking you out is only one of the available options."

Quinn squeezed his eyes shut and rubbed the bridge of his nose. "I need to get some sleep."

What he needed was to escape the reality of what he'd been signed up for. "Go ahead. Plenty of time." *Rest while you can.*

"What about you?"

"I still have work to do."

Back when they'd first settled in Karsengale, Talon had been eager to learn all there was to know about its residents. Who better to carry out the task of research than the one with an eidetic memory? Vega had spent weeks reading up on William and Laura Belden and the charity cases under their care. Quinn's famous last name had made him a prime target for exploitation—until they'd confirmed that he'd been disinherited, and Talon decided to focus all his attention on the soon-to-be-widowed Laura Belden instead.

As much as Vega had memorized about the VanWarrens, there were still too many relatives she needed to research before she stepped foot into their territory. Knowledge equaled leverage. And a soldier could always use some of that.

"Vega-speak for 'Don't wait up, honey.' Or is it, 'Don't hold your breath'?"

Before she'd fully processed what he was saying, Quinn was already through the door, and it closed between them.

Frowning, Vega turned back to the com. Apparently, two years off the Shadow grid wasn't enough time to overcome close to two decades of muscle memory. With each search she brought up, Vega had to consciously stop herself from looking for familiar Shadow contacts.

It was bad enough that Quinn had scanned her default ID chip to get her on the shuttle. She'd augmented it as much as possible, but it wouldn't keep the Shadows from finding her if they went looking. Vega just had to hope they weren't looking.

With secrecy no longer being an issue, a Shadow going AWOL wasn't as much of a concern as it had been back when John Wayland had made off with their most prized asset. And, unlike Hawks, Hounds were plentiful enough to be expendable.

Vega's shuttle had gone down during her last mission on Anamtaigh, killing forty-two of her unit on impact. When the remaining twelve had failed to report back within the scheduled timeframe afterward, no one had come looking. They'd been left stranded and likely presumed KIA. By now, Vega would be less than a forgotten memory.

That suited her fine. The Shadows had their hands too full with their battle out in the galaxy to bother coming after someone like her.

As long as she stayed low and didn't give them a reason.

But the second she decided to interfere in whatever they had going on with the VanWarrens, Vega would become a person of interest again, and Shadows weren't the forgiving types. She would have to play a cautious game to keep half a step ahead of them.

At least until she'd found and dispatched Talon. After that, she had three other ID chips, and with access to Quinn's resources, she'd have the means to disappear forever.

Maybe then the nightmares would finally stop.

Two hours after emerging from subspace in the Karos system, Quinn stood before the com screen, palms sweating and throat dry. They were on final approach to Ela, and the captain had activated communications with the planet's surface. Quinn had managed to track down an official on the dayside who was willing to do what they needed—for a proper bribe, of course—but the son of a bitch had insisted on following procedure to the letter "for the sake of appearances."

Behind him, Vega emerged from the bedroom and came to stand by his side. Quinn steeled himself before he turned to her, and his breath hitched. She'd somehow managed to find an onboard clothing directory and bought a white, strappy dress. The fabric was obviously expensive, sheer enough to allow the outline of her nipples to peek through, and it clung to her body from chest to hip, where the narrow, ankle-length skirt slit open on either side.

The only thing it lacked was a bit of pale blue lace, and Quinn knew she'd chosen it with all the snark in her soul. It didn't change how beautiful she looked in it, with her naturally tan skin and long black hair left unrestrained in glossy, voluminous waves. Barefoot and free of any weapons, she looked almost innocent, except for the sharp humor in her dark hazel eyes.

The official cleared his throat and straightened in his seat. "Looks like we're ready to begin. Place your thumbs where indicated."

The screen showed two red squares and a miniature simulation of a paper document in between. Quinn and Vega pressed their thumbs into their respective squares to confirm their identities. The squares turned green, and an image of their prints and digital signatures floated up and over to the appropriate places in the document.

"Do you have rings?" the official asked.

Vega brought forth a set of golden hoop earrings. "Closest thing I could find."

"Then let's get started. I, Olanre Wabasu, Clerk Official of the Karos system, do hereby witness the marriage of…" He checked his console. "Quinn Gerhart VanWarren and Vega Analisa Ortiz. Do you, Quinn, accept Vega into your keeping, free of malice and coercion?"

"I do," he rasped.

"And do you, Vega, accept Quinn into your keeping, free of malice and coercion?"

"I do," she said.

"The exchange of rings symbolizes the bond of your covenant to one another."

The earrings were the wrong size for both of them, too large for Vega and too small for Quinn, but they put them on each other's fingers because the clerk wouldn't finalize the ceremony otherwise.

"And now, by the power vested in me by the Interplanetary Council of Governance, I declare this marriage legal and binding. The license will be backdated to December fifteenth of last year, as per your request, and your respective identification chips will be updated upon entry scan at the Ela shuttleport. *Felicidades*, and good health to the baby."

The call terminated, leaving Quinn and Vega still holding hands.

"The baby?"

Quinn flushed. "I told him you were pregnant so he wouldn't ask questions about the backdate."

"Smart."

"Should we, uh…kiss or something?"

Vega didn't twitch a smile, but her eyes laughed at him. "If you feel it's necessary."

The official was gone. The ceremony was finished. No one except backwater world romantics kissed at weddings anymore, but Quinn had always considered it an essential part of the ritual. The exchange of breath, and with it, life, to seal a pledge was a lot more personal than a few words and a digital stamp on their profiles.

But how personal was this marriage supposed to be?

Quinn leaned down and pressed a chaste kiss to Vega's lips. He only meant to satisfy his own need for at least a pretense of something between them. After all, if they were going to play at husband and wife for the next three weeks, they'd have to show some affection between them, so they might as well start getting used to it.

But then she kissed him back, and he felt the puff of her breath hitch the slightest bit. Quinn pulled her closer, and she let him. He increased the pressure of his kiss, and her lips parted for him. It shocked him how much he wanted to take her up on the invitation, to steal a forbidden taste of her while the option was still on the table.

Vega was not the kind of woman he'd ever pictured himself marrying, but, at the moment, hovering between kissing and not kissing, he had absolutely no regrets. They fit together so naturally, with his hand resting on the curve of her hip and her leg sliding along the outside of his. Vega was tall enough that he didn't have to contort himself into grotesque angles to claim her lips and, goddamn, those lips tasted addictive. He could easily see himself doing this for the next few days—the next few decades.

And that right there answered his question.

How personal would their fake marriage be?

Very.

Easing back from the kiss, they put a scant two inches of space between them. "You're careful with your strength," Vega said, hovering on tiptoe in the circle of his arms, and Quinn released his tight grip on the fabric of her dress.

"I'm not a monster."

"I know," she returned. "And I know that, when it comes to family, your first instinct will be to hold back. So you should know that I won't. You're not a monster. But you'll have one watching your back."

6

Day 0 – Emerald Belt Province, Ela

Ela was roughly half the size of Earth and had a rotational axis perfectly perpendicular to its circular revolution, which kept its global environments in one season all year long. As the second closest planet to its star within the habitable belt, the season was perpetual summer. Ela had a twenty-three-hour day and two hundred eleven days in a year, but no one cared except the shuttleport's AI systems responsible for scheduling arrivals and departures. For everyone else, it was day when the sun was out, and night when it went down.

Vega learned this as their shuttle touched down, and the AI system greeted them with current weather conditions but no date or time. Looking out the window provided no clues, either. The sun was slightly off its zenith, which could have been morning or afternoon.

Their cabin doors automatically opened when it was time to disembark. She didn't see any other passengers, which with this level of luxury, was likely deliberate. They stepped onto a conveyor belt and stood like idiots all the way to the concierge desk.

Vega donned the persona of a loving wife and linked arms with Quinn.

"Hello, and welcome to Ela!" The concierge was a beautiful dark-skinned woman with big, almond eyes and a genuinely friendly smile. "Please scan your ID chips here."

Quinn went first, then Vega.

"Mr. and Mrs. VanWarren, I do hope your flight was comfortable?"

"It was," Quinn replied.

"Excellent! That's what we like to hear. I see your luggage is already on its way, and your packages are waiting for you by your transport."

"Were there any issues with my orders?" Quinn asked.

"No sir, everything passed through customs about an hour ago."

Vega lightly touched the counter to get the other woman's attention. "We have a transport waiting?"

"Yes, ma'am. The VanWarren family was notified of your arrival and sent an automated personal transport vehicle to meet you."

Likely with an extra welcome package tucked away where the shuttleport's security scans wouldn't detect it.

Before Quinn started glowering and scared the poor woman to death, Vega cocked her hip and pouted. "Aw, that's disappointing."

"Ma'am?"

"Well, I mean, it's a nice gesture and all, I guess, but I was hoping for something more sporty. I mean look at this place. It's paradise! I want to *see* it."

"What did you have in mind?" Quinn asked.

Vega pretended to think about it, then faked a gasp and clutched Quinn's arm. "How about a HOVR?" HOVR was not an acronym. It was a not-so-clever but effective brand name for a transport vehicle that could fly. They were programmed to follow the same roadways and traffic rules as regular transports, but the higher elevation limit allowed them to get above buildings or tree canopies. Expensive, inefficient, and lacking any comfort features, they were marketed as "a one-of-a-kind offroad transport for the true sportsman."

In truth, the manufacturer simply recycled an outdated chassis model, stuffed it with the cheapest materials available, and reprogrammed the same operating system used in standard transports to adjust the lev height limitations. Ten times cheaper to make, but with a price tag three times the average, it made the company fortunes on top of fortunes.

Quinn tensed a little at her touch, but he graced the concierge with a smile. "What the wife wants, the wife gets."

The woman didn't miss a beat. "Of course, Mr. VanWarren. We do have a HOVR available for rent. Let me send it through the wash to get it ready for you. It'll be waiting in place of the VanWarren transport by the time you get to the first-class departure bay. Is there anything else I can help you with today?"

"Yes," Vega said at once. "Where can we get some food?" The meal service on the shuttle had been excellent, but she could do with something less gourmet and more burger-and-fries.

"Your HOVR will include light refreshments for your trip. If you're in the mood for something more substantial, I can call ahead to the shuttleport's Treetop restaurant in the first-class terminal or provide recommendations along your travel route to Crescent Island."

Vega wrinkled her nose at Quinn. Anything the woman recommended would likely be the same brand of high-end fare. Hard pass. "Where do you like to go?" she asked the woman. "Not any fancy white tablecloth place. I'm talking hole-in-the-wall joint only the locals know about."

The woman looked delighted by the question. She leaned over her counter to say in a conspiratorial stage whisper, "I know just the place."

There were no more conveyor belts to get them to the HOVR. The concierge did offer them a levpad, but Vega politely refused. She'd been too stationary for too long.

As promised, the vehicle was waiting for them, along with one suitcase and six boxes of various sizes. The attendant greeted them as warmly as the concierge had. "Would you like to get any personal items out of your luggage before I load it for you?"

"I think we can handle the loading ourselves."

The attendant nodded a weird bow. "As you wish. For your convenience and comfort, the guest suite is available through that door if you need it." He returned to his station, far enough to give them privacy while remaining within sight and earshot.

Nothing about his body language said he was watching them, but Vega was still creeped out. "Is it me, or does all this service feel a bit over the top?"

Quinn shrugged. "You get used to it." He tossed his suitcase into the storage compartment, turning it on its side to take up less space. Then he took the smallest box off the top of the stack and handed it to Vega. "This is for you."

"What is it?" Whatever it was, it had some weight to it.

"Something Catton said would keep you from killing me. Seemed a bit counterintuitive, but I figured you're a woman. You probably appreciate shiny things."

Vega glared.

"You, uh, might want to wait to open it until we get going."

The HOVR was already pre-programmed with their route, including a stop at the Monkey's Tail Shake Shack in Jaqar, a village north of the shuttleport. Their ETA to reach the Van Warren compound was marked as "dinner time." Whatever that meant. The HOVR raised up and took off on its own—no manual operation needed.

"Well?" Quinn prompted. "Aren't you going to open it?"

Vega peeled off the seal sticker and opened the box, mentally preparing herself for whatever joke Catton had decided to play on her. But when she pulled out the soft layer of insulating material, the contents were not what she'd expected to see. "Catton did this?"

"Sort of. We didn't have time to go back to your place for your stuff, and I figured there were probably things you had there that you would need. I called Catton, and he said these were the kind you preferred."

Vega pulled out a light silver throwing knife, sharpened on both edges of the blade, and polished to a shine. She could tell it was brand new and made of a special alloy that hardened with use. She'd had a full set of six back in the day. Down to four by the time she'd joined Talon. At the end of the fight last July, she'd had two left, and both had stayed behind on Persephone 5 when Quinn had whisked her off-world.

The silence stretched so long that Quinn began to worry she really would kill him. "They, uh, come with sheaths." He knew she liked knives—they'd been her signature weapon of choice back when she'd still been working for Talon.

Watching her handle the one in her hands, Quinn realized her liking was more akin to obsession. The shining blade totally transfixed Vega. If she was breathing at all, he couldn't tell.

Vega blinked at him. "Thank you."

Quinn unclenched with relief. "You're welcome."

She dug through the box to take out all six knives, their sheaths, and the honing block. Each blade went through a full inspection before she tucked it into a sheath. There was a belt and an assortment of straps for maximum versatility. Vega strapped one knife to each ankle underneath her pants. Two knives each got threaded onto what he assumed were thigh straps, which she tucked underneath the seat.

They were coming up on the restaurant which, as its name suggested, looked like a weathered shack held together with cordage and a prayer.

The HOVR descended onto a parking spot and idled down.

There was no seating area, only a counter and a greasy-looking cook behind it. "Two for lunch?" he said without preamble or any discernible change in his facial expression.

"Can we see a menu?" Quinn asked.

The cook pointed sideways.

Next to the counter window, a wooden board on the wall had a pre-printed DAILY SPECIALS label, underneath which someone had written *Breakfast*, *Lunch*, and *Dinner* by hand.

After considering her options, Vega turned to him and said, "Lunch sounds good."

She was enjoying this far too much. "Make it two," he conceded with a long-suffering sigh.

The cook grunted and disappeared into the shack.

Vega turned around to lift her face to the sun. "I can see why rich people come here."

Tropical trees filled with songbirds surrounded them. The day was warm but not stifling, even with the humidity, and it smelled like Quinn imagined paradise would smell: rich, wet earth, flowers, and a hint of salt from the sea.

Then their lunch arrived.

Quinn cast a dubious glance at the wooden bowls stacked with cut-up sections of purple crustacean and a pile of something white and mushy.

"Forty credits," the cook said.

"For *this*?"

"Tourist surcharge."

Before Quinn could argue, Vega extended her hand, scanned her chip against the payment portal, and paid for their meal. "Got anything to drink?"

The cook disappeared again and returned with two glasses of something ice cold and bright pink. "Twenty credits."

Vega scanned her chip again. "Thanks!"

"Enjoy," the cook said, still wearing the same sour expression.

Vega took her meal and hopped up onto the HOVR's hood. She sat cross-legged, with her bowl in her lap and her glass beside her. Quinn didn't want to risk the vehicle, so rather than sit, he ducked inside to raise it high enough for the hood to serve as a counter for him. Then, he joined Vega outside.

"Well, cheers," he said, clinking his glass against hers. To his surprise, the pink stuff was delicious and had a slight, alcoholic kick, like spiked fruit punch. He downed half his glass in two swallows.

Vega, meanwhile, had already dug into her meal, breaking open a crustacean segment to pull out its bright blue meat. She used it to scoop some mush into her mouth in the same bite. Quinn watched her reaction. If she spat it out, he would be having a talk with the cook.

Instead, she breathed in deeply and said, "Oh, my God."

Quinn, still dubious, followed her example and took a bite of his own. "Holy shit."

He had no idea what he was eating, but it was the perfect blend of sweet and savory, the salty crustacean meat firm enough to chew but not rubbery, and the mush, which had to be made of some local vegetable, providing a soft, sweet counterbalance. The drink, whatever it was, highlighted every note of the simple meal. Quinn couldn't get enough.

He finished his plate before Vega was halfway done and returned his dishes to the counter, asking for two more portions. That seemed to put the cook in a slightly better mood. The two new bowls he brought out each had a flower next to the mush. The price didn't go down, but Quinn didn't care. He would happily pay it three times a day to keep eating.

"I think this is the best thing I have ever eaten," Vega said around a mouthful.

Quinn grunted in agreement. "I'm gonna ask what it is."

"Don't!"

"What—why?"

Vega's gaze shifted to something behind him, then back to him. "Just trust me."

Quinn swallowed a big chunk before he'd chewed it all the way. He looked down at his half-eaten third plate and didn't take the next bite. "Vega, what's behind me?"

Again, she did that shifty glance and shrugged. "Paradise."

He turned around slowly but didn't see anything strange.

At first.

Then, "Why's that tree bark moving?"

As if to demonstrate, a huge, colorful bird swooped down from overhead straight at the tree. The bark broke apart into hundreds of skittering creatures, and the bird came away with one in its talons. A hard-shelled, brown centipede the size of Vega's forearm, with about a dozen lashing tentacles spewing from its mouth as it scream-hissed and writhed in the bird's clutches, spraying a stream of white liquid from its other end.

Quinn shuddered and turned to Vega, determined to wipe the sight from his memory forever. His stomach felt like the centipede chunks he'd eaten were reconstituting back to life.

"So…yeah," Vega said.

He returned the rest of his meal to the counter unfinished.

The navigation still estimated their arrival at "dinner time." The sun hadn't made much progress toward the west during their meal from hell, and Crescent Island was fairly remote. Quinn figured they still had a lot of miles and several hours to go. He let the nav take them away from the shack and back over the road but eased it down to solid ground a few miles away at a rest stop with a gorgeous view of the jewel-green sea.

When the engine shut off, Vega gave him one of her signature deadpan looks. "Are you going to throw up?"

He glared at her in response. Most people who found themselves on the receiving end of his glares usually cowered and made a quick retreat. Vega just chuckled. For some reason, it improved his sour mood a great deal.

"We're playing house," he explained, getting out of the HOVR. "We probably shouldn't greet the family with shipping boxes for luggage."

He took all the remaining boxes out of the back and set them down in a row on the roadside. "Dig in," he invited.

Vega shrugged and opened the largest box, pulling out a suitcase. It wasn't empty. The set came complete with an umbrella, beach towel, tote bag, and various travel sundries, like earplugs, eye masks, an emergency kit, and the like.

The next box held clothes, which got him a raised eyebrow.

Quinn shrugged, unrepentant. "I estimated your size and got nano-fiber where possible." The garments were the most expensive on the market because they adjusted to the wearer's size and shape for a perfect fit. There were two categories of nanofiber: formalwear and survival gear. Quinn had gotten some of both. Plus regular clothes, because not every occasion called for a two-thousand credit outfit.

As he'd guessed she would, Vega sorted through the pile and packed all formalwear into the suitcase. She selected a pair of gauzy, tan, wide-leg pants in deference to the heat and a clingy, dark green top.

Quinn swiveled on his heels to give her his back when she started undressing then and there. The woman had not an ounce of bash-fulness in her body.

"Very husbandly," she mocked. "You can turn around now."

He did. The clothes fit her fine, but what should have been a ca-sual outfit looked like a uniform on Vega. She had the physique of a soldier, with toned arms, six-pack abs, and modest breasts, but that wasn't unique nowadays. Plenty of women exercised or enhanced their bodies to achieve her kind of athleticism. It was the way Vega carried herself. She was all efficiency and economy of movement, with no superfluous sway.

Quinn had seen her fight, and she'd made it look as seamless as a dance. But he had a feeling if he asked her to dance, she'd make it look like a fight.

Box three had shoes. He'd asked the AI shopping app to select ones to match the outfits while maintaining reasonable comfort. It had primarily chosen flats, with a couple of pairs of heels, neither taller than three inches.

Vega ignored them all in deference to the military boots he'd added to the order as a joke. He rolled his eyes but didn't comment when she put them on and flexed the heels and toes to test the range of motion. They appeared to meet with her approval, and she chucked the rest of the shoes into the suitcase.

The next box—toiletries and makeup—got immediately upended into the suitcase.

Moving on to the last one, she pulled out the electronics one after the other. Quinn had figured she would need gear but hadn't known what kind, so he'd settled on the best available e-pad and a com cuff for each of them. The cuff was a flexible bracelet that generated a holographic screen when making video calls. It also came with an earpiece for conversational privacy.

Vega tossed him a cuff and put on her own, then tucked the earpiece into her ear. With her knives strapped to her ankles, she was now as geared up as she could get without making it too obvious. She pushed to her feet, rolled her shoulders, and appeared to settle into her skin as if she hadn't been complete until then.

Quinn couldn't look away.

Her former rigidity was gone. She looked like a whole new woman, and though she would probably never be wholly feminine, Vega's innate, subtle grace gave her an air of danger and mystery, like a sleek panther stalking out of the jungle.

An insane thought popped into his head. What would it be like to walk up to the deadly predator and pet her until she purred like a house cat? To make her writhe in his arms and dig those nails into him, to feel her shudder with pleasure, see it on her face, hear it in her—

She smiled at him, and Quinn forgot to breathe. "Ready, husband?"

Her voice went straight to his balls, and Quinn turned away and quelled all thoughts of Vega Ortiz before they elicited a noticeable physical reaction. His feet felt disconnected from the rest of him as he shuffled them around to the other side of the HOVR, needing a physical barrier to keep him from doing something stupid and quite possibly suicidal.

Nope. He was far from ready.

He was in big, big trouble.

7

Dinner Time

Crescent Island had no bridges to the mainland. It was only accessible by vehicles that either flew or floated. The HOVR had no issues crossing the water, and from their vantage point, Vega had a stunning view of the bay, the island, and the crystal-clear waters all around.

The island itself was, true to its name, shaped like a crescent moon, no doubt the rim of an ancient volcano. It was outlined by a thick forest of tropical trees for privacy, but the interior had been cleared to make room for a posh compound the size of an amusement park. Vega counted three sprawling structures, none of them taller than three stories. In the triangle they created, the grounds were manicured and subdivided into different sections for various entertainments, including a crescent-shaped pool.

The HOVR made a loop around the perimeter, then touched down outside a tall gate. Quinn had to scan his ID chip against the console for the gate to admit them, and then the HOVR hugged the winding roadway toward the compound. All automated security measures set to enforce protocol on any arriving vehicle, no matter the type.

Efficient.

But easily hacked.

Vega made a mental note of it for future reference.

"Have you been here before?"

Quinn shook his head. "First time for me. Think anyone will give us a tour?"

"I prefer to do my own recon." That way, she could snoop in places tour guides conveniently omitted.

When the HOVR stopped in front of what would be the northern-most building and idled down, Quinn puffed out a dramatic, bracing breath. "Here we go."

A uniformed attendant with a ridiculous tiny hat on his head came running out of the building to greet them when Vega emerged. "Welcome to Crescent Island, Mr. VanWarren."

Vega got unpleasant goosebumps when he snapped his heels and saluted Quinn, ignoring her completely. She shook herself off and rounded the HOVR to retrieve her suitcase.

The attendant beat her to it. "Allow me, miss."

"Mrs.," Quinn corrected. "This is my wife, Mrs. Vega VanWarren."

The attendant blanched and then flushed bright red. "A thousand apologies, Mrs. VanWarren! We weren't aware you would be joining us."

His panic freaked her out. "Relax, kid. I like to make an entrance."

He ducked his head and started to tug on the luggage. Quinn had had no trouble loading it, but the kid couldn't budge the suitcase an inch out of the storage space.

"Here," Quinn offered, taking pity on him. "I'll handle the bags. You just tell us where to go."

"Yes, sir! Thank you, sir."

"What's your name?" Vega asked him.

"I'm Gareth, ma'am, at your service."

"Fantastic. Here's something you can do for me. Stop calling me ma'am. I'm Vega. This is Quinn."

Gareth's eyes went buggy. "I'm sorry, Mrs. VanWarren, but we're strictly forbidden to address any of the family members by their first names."

"Even the kids?"

"Yes, ma'am."

Wow. She looked at Quinn, since this was his turf now, but he only shrugged, holding the two suitcases like shopping bags.

Vega schooled her face into a neutral smile. She did not like this place. At all. "Which way are we going?"

Gareth pulled a metallic pentagonal disc from his pocket. He looked to Quinn, who was burdened with their luggage, then motioned for

Vega's hand and stuck the disc to the back of it. "This has a map of the entire island and is connected to the service staff. Tap it once to bring up the map." He demonstrated by tapping Vega's hand as gently as he could. A holographic miniature of the island appeared above it. Gareth manipulated it with his fingers, pinching them together to shrink the image, spreading them to zoom in on a particular section. "You can say what you're looking for, and the navigation will trace the path for you."

Meaning it also functioned as a personal locator and whoever was at the security controls would always know her whereabouts. Yeah, this baby would be staying in the room for the mission's duration.

Gareth tapped her again to make the map disappear. "Tap twice to reach the service center. All requests are routed to the proper departments, and we respond within five minutes, regardless of the time of day."

He let go of her and ran off, returning seconds later with a small levpad and another disc. "A trailer for your luggage, Mr. VanWarren." He let Quinn set the bags on top, then attached the disc to Quinn's hand the same way he'd done with Vega. "You can also ride it if you wish. It's synced up with your map, so it will go wherever you tell it to." Gareth beckoned Vega closer. "Ma'am, if I may?"

Vega gave him her hand again. Gareth tapped it to bring up the map so they both could see it and expanded it to explain, "We are right here. The garages. All the guests are staying at the main house, here. Your suite will be on the second floor, Master Suite West. Your personal attendant will meet you at the front door and take over your luggage from there. Your belongings will be unpacked for you during the *formal* dinner."

Curious emphasis. Almost like the kid didn't think she was dressed appropriately for the occasion. But she admired his diplomacy in getting the message across.

"Is everyone already here?" Quinn asked.

"Yes, sir. They've been waiting for you." A diplomatic way of saying they were late.

"Thank you, Gareth."

"My pleasure, sir. I hope you have a wonderful stay."

The main house was visible down the long gravel path but was a fair distance off. Still, Vega welcomed the opportunity to stretch her legs and walk off the uneasiness of meeting their first VanWarren staff member.

"You want me to carry you across the threshold?"

The sarcasm was unnecessary, but it brought up a good question. "How much can you lift?"

Quinn shrugged. "Don't know. Never bothered to measure."

Walking beside her, he cast a big enough shadow to hide Vega completely from the setting sun. It picked out the gold in his light brown hair in a way that would have seemed almost angelic on anyone else. But Quinn was too hard for anything so delicate.

At close to seven feet in height and thick with muscle, his body was intimidating enough already. His face didn't do him any favors, either. Quinn was far from the modern definition of male beauty, which leaned more toward smooth and androgynous. But his features fit him, and he wore them with a confidence that must have been hard-won. A prominent brow ridge shadowed his dark amber-colored eyes. A wide nose bisected his sharp cheekbones. His mouth was the only soft thing about his face, and it was surrounded by thick stubble that entirely covered his hard, square jaw and reappeared within hours after he shaved.

Vega had seen how people looked at him and moved out of his way. Did it ever bother him? The thought didn't sit well with her. She knew what it was to stand out, to be seen as dangerous, even when she wasn't trying to be. But she had earned that fear. Quinn hadn't.

"How much do you weigh?"

He grinned, and suddenly, his formidable features became something altogether different and inviting. "Isn't that supposed to be a rude thing to ask?"

Vega shrugged. "Wouldn't know."

"More than I look, but less than you're thinking. Higher bone density."

"Makes sense."

"Tell me something about you."

"I'm five-eleven and a hundred and eighty-two pounds." Most of it muscle.

He chuckled. "No, I mean something personal."

More personal than her body measurements? "Like what?"

"I don't know. Anything. Tell me how you ended up…where you ended up."

And just like that, Vega ran out of words.

Good thing the main house wasn't too much farther. She picked up her pace a little, Quinn matched her, and they reached the front door in three minutes flat, by her count. As Gareth had promised, another attendant was waiting for them, a dour-faced older woman dressed in a matching uniform but without the hat.

"This way, please," she said without preamble, leading them through the massive, gilded entry hall to an elevator tucked away in a concealed nook. It was large enough to fit the levpad and three normal-sized people, but with Quinn and Vega in there, the attendant's expression turned to thinly veiled disgust. She pushed the button and said, "I will meet you upstairs," as the elevator door closed.

"Bitch," Vega growled.

When the door opened again, the attendant stood in the hall in the same pose, not a hair out of place. She must have run like hell up those stairs. "Your suite is at the end of this hallway. Please follow me."

Vega didn't realize her fists were clenched until Quinn's hand enveloped one of them. "Stop glowering," he murmured in her ear. "She's just doing her job."

The attendant opened the double doors to their suite and stepped back to let them enter.

It was like the shuttle suite, only bigger and fancier. The anteroom alone was as big as her shitty little apartment on Persephone 5. Beyond that, there was a bedroom with a massive four-poster bed, a fireplace, and a walk-in closet the size of a normal person's living room. The bathroom had a huge tub and a separate shower set against a glass wall Vega hoped would frost over for privacy.

"When you're ready," the attendant said stiffly, "Your maps will guide you to the grand hall where everyone is already gathered. The family prefers to dine in formal wear. We can offer you a choice of appropriate clothing, should you need it." She gave Vega a nasty once-over when she said it, then transferred her judgmental gaze over to Quinn. "And we retain a tailor and seamstress on staff for alterations. Shall I place an order for you?"

"That won't be necessary," Quinn said before Vega could tell the woman where to shove her opinions.

"Very good. The staff is at your service day and night."

It wasn't until she'd closed the doors that Vega noticed the woman had never crossed the threshold.

Quinn changed in the bathroom while Vega took over the closet. When he came out to check on her, she was waiting by the door, sheathed in a form-fitting strapless crimson gown. He turned his stutter-step sideways toward the closet on the pretext of putting his travel clothes away before he dropped them. All their belongings were neatly set out—with the notable exception of her knives. Since he hadn't heard anyone else come in, it must have been Vega's handiwork, and she'd probably hidden the knives somewhere safe but still accessible.

How the hell did she keep doing things so fast? He'd only been in the bathroom fifteen minutes, max.

Quinn took a couple of deep breaths to compose himself before coming out again. "You look stunning." The dress clung to her like a second skin, lovingly displaying her sleek figure and accentuating her modest cleavage. She'd put on minimal makeup, and arranged her hair to drape down her back with a few strategic strands left loose to frame her face. Everything about her beckoned, *Come closer—if you dare.* A siren poised to lure men to their inevitable demise.

"Likewise," she returned with an approving once-over that made heat rise up his neck. "Nanofibers?"

Quinn adjusted his shirt collar, still not used to the cut. "Only thing that'll fit me."

"Stop tugging." She pulled his hand away to readjust his tie. "And wipe that look off your face."

He frowned. "What look?"

"Your signature fee-fi-fo-fum glower."

"We can't all be blessed with your natural good looks."

Her fingers paused on the knot of his tie. "Looks don't count for much these days. But they can be as useful as any other weapon if you learn how to wield them."

Of course. The standards for beauty might change over time, but its privileges remained universal. Except when Vega talked about wielding them, she didn't mean getting lonely slobs to buy her shots at a club.

Quinn's gaze went straight to Vega's left cheek. When they'd first met months ago, it had been marred by a smooth inverted C cut that Talon had given her to remind her of her place in his hierarchy. He couldn't decide what was worse. The fact that the man had been unhinged enough to cut up his best soldier in a temper tantrum or that he'd retained enough sanity to allow her to treat the wound before it scarred.

Beauty could be wielded both ways.

"This isn't working. It looks like a leash." With a quick tug and yank, she pulled the tie off him, slipped a couple of fingers beneath the edge of his collar, and popped open the top two buttons. "There. Much better. You realize this is going to be a logistical nightmare."

He'd thought about that, too. He had no idea how many of his family members wanted him dead. Surely not all of them, but enough to make him nervous about dining with them, much less staying under the same roof for any length of time. If anyone made a third attempt on his life, he and Vega would be outnumbered in unfamiliar territory, and their getaway vehicle was way back there in the garage, where anyone could tamper with it at any time.

Vega knows what she's doing. It was why he'd asked her to do this in the first place. But even so, "I keep thinking about the poison," he admitted. A physical attack, he knew they could handle, no problem. But poison was something different. Vega couldn't protect him from something she never saw coming, and Quinn was not about to let her be the one to take the first bite.

"They won't try the same thing twice. You survived once. They'll expect you to be prepared for something like it again. Smell everything before you take a bite or a sip."

"What will that do?"

"It'll make them think you have a way of detecting unsafe substances."

Clever. But not enough to put his mind at ease. "Maybe we should skip it tonight."

"We can't," Vega said. "They threw this shindig for a reason. It's a test to size you up. You accepted the invite. Your only option now is to see it through. If you show weakness, they'll eat you alive."

"How can you be sure—of anything?"

She shrugged, smoothing her hands down his shoulders and arms. "Soldiers, rich people—no difference. In the end, they're all just predators with an established pecking order. And I know how to get to the top."

The last thing she did was to take off his guidance disc and toss it onto the side table next to hers. Quinn didn't ask. "Tell me you're armed." If they were heading into a den of wild animals, she would need her claws.

Vega grasped the slit of her long skirt and pulled it across her lap to reveal a black sheath strapped to the inside of her opposite thigh.

Quinn gulped.

"Shall we?" She tucked her arm through his, and off they went.

The mansion was immense, but Vega navigated its hallways and staircases as if she'd memorized the blueprint—which she probably had. Once they made it to the ground floor, all they had to do was follow the sound of voices to a grand hall filled with people.

All conversation stopped when they entered, and every gaze turned their way. He'd only met a small handful of his relatives after returning to the family fold. For the vast majority, this was their first look at the new heir, and their expressions ran the gamut from shocked to horrified and everything in between.

Quinn almost backed right out again, but Vega tightened her hold on his arm. "Smile and say hello," she said between clenched teeth.

"Hi," he said. "Sorry we're late."

"Quinn!" His brother pushed his way forward and held out his hand in welcome. "We were starting to get worried."

Quinn grasped the offered hand, pretending not to notice the size difference. They had a similar coloring, but his younger sibling had been blessed with far better looks and a reasonable height several inches shorter than Quinn. "Holden, allow me to present my wife,

Vega. Vega, this is my younger brother, Holden VanWarren."

She had to let go of him to shake Holden's hand, and Quinn gritted his teeth against a protest. "It's nice to meet you, Holden."

"I didn't know Quinn was married. Welcome to the family."

Holden was considerably less venomous than the rest of Quinn's family. He'd been about five when everything had happened, so he didn't remember much of the drama from those times. When Quinn had reappeared, Holden had been the only one who'd seemed genuinely happy to have regained his long-lost brother.

Seeing it was safe, a few others came forward to introduce themselves as well. They tried and failed not to stare, but Quinn didn't hold it against them. That they were willing to shake his hand at all was progress, whether or not they flinched at the contact. It wasn't his ugly mug and fee-fi-fo-fum glower that made his relatives so afraid, but rather what it represented. Everyone in this room knew all about his secret. The underlying strength that could crush those carefully offered hands into bloody mulch if he happened to sneeze.

That's what they feared.

Times like these, he really missed the easy camaraderie of the group Laura Belden had forged on Anamtaigh. No one in Laura's care had ever treated him as anything other than a big brother or uncle. He'd had children hanging off his arms and legs at least twice a day, and no one had ever run from the room when he'd raised his voice. In fact, the kids had begged him to roar more than once, giggling madly when he'd made the cups and plates rattle in their cabinets.

He missed every single one of them. Those who now resided in Laura's new compound, those who'd returned to the lives they'd had before the war, and those who had become a cherished memory.

When the line of introductions started to taper off, Quinn leaned toward Holden, who'd stayed by his side. "Where's Mother?"

"She, uh, she's not here."

Quinn stiffened and felt Vega's hand on his arm as if she'd sensed it, but she never interrupted her conversation with Cousin Maurice.

"Her health's been pretty bad," Holden explained, lying with the truth. "She decided to stay home with baby Ash."

"Right." Holden had told him their mother had remarried for the fourth time shortly before the war. At the dynamic age of three, Ashley VanWarren was officially his mother's first and last daughter. Along with the four on his father's side, it made baby Ash the fifth half-sister Quinn would never meet. But both Quinn and Holden knew that neither her health nor her daughter was why Holly VanWarren chose not to attend the reunion. Or why Quinn had yet to meet her face-to-face.

A delicate chime turned everyone in the direction of an open doorway, and the congregation filed into the formal dining room like a well-behaved pack of trained dogs. Quinn took Vega's hand, keeping a careful hold on his temper so he wouldn't crush her bones.

She leaned into him. "Look at me."

He did.

"Now smile," she said, demonstrating with a smile of her own. It was as genuine as anything he might have seen on other women, but though it reached her eyes, it didn't soften them. She was pissed, and somehow, that made him feel better.

Quinn leaned down, intending to thank her for being there, but ended up brushing a kiss across her cheek. It was enough. He did smile, then, savoring the veiled surprise in her expression, before he led her through to their seats at the table.

An eidetic memory sure came in handy when meeting an entire army of people with the uniform last name of VanWarren. Vega did some preliminary character analyses during the introductions, but the biggest info dump came during dinner.

While Quinn struggled to keep a neutral face with those around him, Vega did her best to introduce herself to as many strangers as she could talk to at the long, formal table. Most of them were civil enough to her, with the notable exception of cousin Elspeth VanWarren, who went out of her way to ignore Vega and Quinn as much as socially allowed.

She was a woman who'd aged before her time. By Vega's estimate, Elspeth was around forty years old, but her face already showed signs of cosmetic updates, not all of them successful. Her full lips, painted a deep red, pulled down at the corners in an expression of perpetual disgust. Her eyebrows were artificial and a tad too high for her face, and her nose showed a slight ridge where the augmentation had gone awry. Her failed assassination attempt had marked her in posture and attitude. She had given up and sunk into bitter defeat.

Vega judged her a waste of space.

"So, how did you and Quinn meet?"

Vega gave Cousin Geraldine a smile. "On a world far, far away," she said, delivering the story she and Quinn had concocted on the shuttle.

Geraldine was one of the younger cousins, still innocent and somewhat naïve. Harmless, as far as Quinn's safety was concerned, but a potential ally if they ever needed one, so Vega made an effort to put on a kind face.

"My shuttle got rerouted to Anamtaigh because of technical issues and I got stranded there."

She touched Quinn's arm to pull him out of a tense exchange with Uncle Trent. Amundsen and Beatrice's oldest son must have expected to inherit the estate. But despite being clearly unhappy about Quinn usurping him, Trent was a dog with more bark than bite. He would make his complaints loud and clear, but he didn't strike Vega as the type to do anything as dramatic as murder. More like he had an army of lawyers on retainer ready to fight the battle for him.

In fact, despite some expressions of distaste, most of the VanWarrens gathered at the table showed a remarkable lack of concern about Quinn's presence. They had to already have a plan in place to keep him out of their hair.

"Quinn found me in a coffee shop, bawling my eyes out." Vega continued her tale of woe while mentally sorting through possible scenarios for the next three weeks.

Best case, Quinn would hit a wall of restrictions and objections when it came to the family's money. Worst case, they'd try to keep him from leaving the island alive.

"They didn't even have proper cups anymore. I was drinking out of a chipped soup bowl."

The first two attempts on his life had been amateur—public and sloppy. Rushed by someone desperate to stop something before it started. It appeared their strategy had evolved since then. In a place as remote as this, an accident would be easy to orchestrate. A body would be easy to hide. And the authorities would happily look the other way for a proper bribe.

Three weeks was a long time to plan and execute the perfect murder. Especially with multiple accomplices working together.

Geraldine looked horrified. "Was it really that bad?"

"Oh, yes!"

"Anamtaigh is a ruin," Quinn offered, covering Vega's hand with his. "Outside the shuttleport, it's mostly burned-out buildings and a whole lot of nothing. Hadran City is about the only place that still has some infrastructure, and only because the transport agency needs it to keep the shuttleport functional."

Geraldine gasped. "Holy shitballs."

"I couldn't even find a place to stay for the night, can you believe it? I was going to go back to the shuttleport to sleep at the terminal." Vega leaned into Quinn in a silent prompt.

He smoothly picked up the story. "So I walk in to get my morning coffee, see this gorgeous creature crying in the corner, and what am I gonna do? Leave her there?"

Vega gave him her best doe eyes with a hint of tears for full effect. "He was so gallant. A perfect gentleman."

Geraldine put both hands over her heart. "Aww! Tell me about the wedding!"

Quinn shrugged humbly. "Well, it wasn't anything fancy…"

Vega let him tell that part of the story while she resumed her recon.

Her impression of the family gradually evolved from cold-blooded murderers into something more sinister. The VanWarrens were decent actors. They were cautious around Quinn but went out of their way to be cordial to both him and Vega.

It was a good strategy. Emotional manipulation was much cleaner than murder. Quinn had already shown his cards by agreeing to meet with them at all. His need to be welcomed back into the family was so obvious it hurt.

"…we found an official in Avencore…"

Quinn's older brother was named Matthew, and he'd been seated as far away from them as he could get. He was handsome in a cold, heartless way. Married to Kendry, who was about as affectionate as a porcupine. The two of them acted as if no one else was at the table, keeping to themselves unless someone had the audacity to address them directly.

"…think it was daisies, right darling?"

Vega smiled and nodded. They'd agreed that whatever details one of them needed to fill in on the fly, the other would confirm, maintaining a united front. "They were the only flowers growing in town."

Geraldine made a face. "Ugh, at that point, I would have bought something artificial."

"We didn't care," Quinn said.

As his family began to relax, Quinn became more open and animated. He soaked in the smiles they cast his way and missed the sharp looks they shot back and forth among themselves.

They'd picked up on the same thing Vega had. Quinn was a push-over at heart. He would give them anything for a smile and a kind word. "It wasn't about the wedding," Vega added. "We just wanted to be married. I mean, the wedding's one day in a lifetime. It's what comes after that's the important part."

Quinn gave her another of his sweet smiles and leaned down to peck a quick kiss on her lips. "Agreed." Then he resumed telling the story, and Vega transferred her attention to the end of the table she could see while her head was still resting against Quinn's shoulder.

Uncle Ulrich was a jovial old drunk with a handlebar mustache and a rounded belly the size of a beach ball. His husband Jackson was pleasant enough and seemed to genuinely care for him—a rare quality among the VanWarrens. Vega couldn't see either of them trying to take out Quinn. They appeared too content with their lives and not interested in causing waves.

Aunt Ylva was instantly identifiable as Elspeth's mother. Both had similar features and the same unattractive expressions. But there was a sharpness to Ylva that Elspeth lacked. Vega would guess Ylva had been the mastermind behind the poisoning—her disappointment over her daughter's failure to see it through was palpable.

"It's like a fairy tale," Geraldine said with a sigh. "And you two look so in love! I hope one day I find someone who looks at me the way you look at Vega."

"Yes," Cousin Emmett retorted. "We should all be so lucky."

His sarcasm caused Quinn to tense against her, bringing Vega's attention back to their little section of the long table.

Seated on Geraldine's right, opposite her and Quinn, Emmett was now on his third tumbler of whiskey since sitting down and, unlike Uncle Ulrich, he was a bitter, unpleasant drunk.

Vega wasn't the only one who noticed.

"Maybe we should get you some coffee," Geraldine suggested, subtly shifting her chair away from him.

Emmett belched in her face. "Who are you again?"

Geraldine blinked at him. "W-what?"

"Who. Are. You?" Emmett repeated, swigging the last swallow of his drink. "Don't remember ever seeing your face before today. So maybe what we should do is shut the fuck up while the adults are talking."

Geraldine's face paled to nearly gray, but two hot spots of color burned in her cheeks. "For your information, I'm a musician. I released an album just a few months ago…"

"I do not care," Emmett proclaimed, then jerked his chin at Vega, dismissing Geraldine before she could finish asking what he'd accomplished in his miserable life so far. "So tell us, how much did Cousin Quinn pay you to agree to this?"

Vega met his drunken gaze head-on, momentarily forgetting her happy wife mask. "Excuse me?"

Geraldine tensed, shifting in her seat. She looked one sharp gesture away from making a run for it. Hard to say if it was because of Vega or Emmett.

Quinn, apparently, decided it was Vega's fault and knocked his knee against her under the table.

She didn't care.

Neither did Emmett. "I think we can all agree that you fit my cousin about as well as a golden bow on a pig. There is no way he could land someone like you unless he paid for the privilege. And whores of your caliber don't come cheap. Believe me, I know."

His little speech was met with dead silence from the entire table.

Emmett held up his empty glass for an attendant to refill with more whiskey.

Vega breathed down a sudden murderous rage. He was less than five feet away. At this range, she couldn't miss if she tried, and her fingers itched to bury her steak knife between his eyes. She wanted to see it embedded in the middle of Emmett's forehead, and it was all she could do to keep still.

Then, from the far end of the table, opposite Matthew, a new voice spoke up. "Yes, well, we all know you're a revolting waste of flesh, Emmett. That's never been a secret."

Vega picked out the speaker, a man roughly her age whom she hadn't met yet. Dark hair, tan skin, even features, a long, thin nose, and a mocking smirk. But his dark eyes were a tad too cold, too calculating.

The cut didn't miss its mark. Emmett went stiff but compensated by downing another two fingers of whiskey. "I still don't hear you denying it," he said to Vega.

"I have nothing to prove to you."

"Don't you?"

Quinn pushed to stand, but Vega dug her fingers into his arm to keep him seated. Emmett was after one thing: getting Quinn to explode with his superhuman strength and turning everyone here against him. The moment that happened, it wouldn't matter how much he fought to ingratiate himself back among them. He'd never be anything other than a monster holding them all hostage, and they would hate and fear him for as long as he lived. Vega was not about to let Emmett have that satisfaction.

"I can tell you're trying your hardest to insult me," she told Emmett. "You should know it won't work."

"Is that so?" He leered at her.

She graced him with an ice-cold smile. "In order for me to be insulted, I would first have to give a damn about what you think of me."

"Well said." Her as yet unidentified defender pushed to his feet and raised his champagne flute in a toast. "To Vega and Quinn. Long may their happiness last."

One by one, the VanWarrens raised their glasses and echoed the sentiment.

Vega swept her gaze around the table and took careful note of everyone's less-than-congenial facial expression.

Quinn had hired her to keep him safe. By her definition, that directive extended to all aspects of his life. If any VanWarren dared to break his heart again, she was prepared to collect theirs.

~

The family made a palpable effort to somehow salvage the occasion after that. They chatted a little too loudly and smiled a little too much through four more courses before the meal was finished, and the congregation broke up into their respective cliques for after-dinner activities.

Quinn didn't have the stomach to stay any longer, so he excused himself and Vega both, blaming exhaustion after a long trip. No one protested. So, still holding Vega's hand, he pulled her out into the hallway, where he immediately lost his bearings.

"This way," Vega said, guiding him back to the entry hall where they'd first arrived. It was long past sunset, but the entire building and the garden outside were lit up bright enough to fool a body into thinking it was day.

Once they were back in their suite, Quinn let go of Vega, picked up one of the decorative pillows on the anteroom couch, and hurled it at the wall. Paint cracked outward from the point of impact in an impressive spiderweb pattern, and pillow seams popped where the stitching was weak, exploding the stuffing in a shower of white fibers.

"Feel better?" Holding one of her new knives, Vega looked unimpressed with his outburst. She pulled the honing block out of a nightstand drawer and toed off her heels, aligning them by the wall with military precision. She made herself comfortable on an overstuffed armchair, tucking one foot under her ass. Her supple leg stretched out in front of her through the gown's slit as she applied the block to the blade over and over again.

Any one of the people downstairs, people who were supposed to be his loving, accepting kin, would have either attacked him or run from the room screaming to see him in a temper. But Vega… "You're not afraid of me in the least, are you?"

She flipped the blade and resumed honing its other edge in the same rhythmic motion. It looked almost meditative. "Are you afraid of me?" she countered.

"Honestly? A little."

The corner of her mouth twitched in an almost smile that got firmly straightened back into a no-nonsense line. "You let Emmett get to you. He's not worth it."

"He could be the guy." They'd decided to talk in code until Vega could confirm no surveillance devices were hidden in the room. He figured if his family were so intent on getting him out of their hair, they would dig out whatever dirt they could use against him, which meant Quinn and Vega would get no privacy for the duration of the reunion.

"Did you notice how many whiskies he had during dinner?"

Quinn shrugged. "Three? Four?" What did it matter?

"Nine. He's too busy drowning his woes to do anything practical about them."

She'd put on such a friendly, non-threatening façade downstairs that, for a while, Quinn had forgotten Vega was more of a threat to the family than they could ever be to her or Quinn. The way she took everything in stride, calmly observing everyone without being influenced by them, was amazing. Not one single VanWarren seemed to rate high enough in her esteem to cause the slightest change to her mood. He envied that.

And he was profoundly grateful to have her there with him. "Thank you," he said.

"For what?"

"For being here. Being you." He wouldn't have lasted an hour down there without her.

She looked at him then, acknowledging his words with a solemn nod. "You should get some sleep."

"What about you?"

"Soon as the party breaks up, I think I'll go for a walk."

Part of him wanted to caution her and offer to go with her. Then he woke the hell up. Vega could take care of herself. Plus, she probably wouldn't react well to having her expertise questioned.

So, rather than make an ass of himself, he went to take a long shower to wash off the disgust lingering on his skin. By the time he came back out, the grounds outside were dark, and Vega was gone.

As tired as he was, Quinn waited up for her. Strange bed, strange surroundings—not exactly the recipe for a good night's sleep. Instead, he took out his glass tablet and pulled up the book he'd started reading on the shuttle. It was an anthology of classical myths with a modern twist. A way to keep the nearly-forgotten history of millennia past fresh and exciting—if grossly inaccurate.

His favorite so far was the story of Aria, the daughter of a heartless king who fed young men and women to a demon in exchange for more power. Aria helped the brave hero, Theo, defeat the demon, but she ended up betrayed and abandoned when Theo tired of her affections.

Moral of the story: Handsome heroes were assholes.

Vega didn't say a word when she returned, just slipped into the bathroom to wash up and came out wearing one of his T-shirts. One thing he'd forgotten to add to her wardrobe order: sleepwear. Although, he couldn't say he felt bad about it.

"How'd it go?"

"Good." She took a pillow from the bed and headed for the anteroom.

"What are you doing?"

"Going to sleep."

Quinn set the tablet aside and followed her out there. She'd put the pillow on one end of the couch and was settling in for the night. "Are you kidding?"

She didn't deign to respond, so Quinn pulled the pillow out from under her head and scooped her up with one arm around her waist. "Hey!"

"You're not sleeping on the damned couch. We're married."

She could have done any number of things to make him let her go, and he half expected her to send him face-planting into the nearest wall, but she stayed still until he dropped her on the bed. Then she bounced right up and slipped around him, heading back out. "I sleep alone."

Quinn caught her up again and deposited her back on the bed. "Get over it."

When she opened her mouth to argue or, more likely, threaten him with bodily harm, he cut her off with, "Privacy." Or rather, their current lack thereof. They were likely being watched. A staff member could come in without knocking on the pretext of performing some service they never asked for. If they found Vega out on the couch while Quinn slept in the massive bed all on his own, they'd never be able to explain it.

Vega glared at him but didn't respond. Instead, she yanked the covers out from under her and tucked herself in. "You better not snore."

"No promises," he said, rounding the bed to get in on his side. The mattress was wide enough to fit three additional people between them. They could toss and turn and never come into contact unless one of them went looking for it.

Quinn turned off the lights and lay on his side, facing away from Vega, as she was facing away from him.

It was going to be a long night.

9

The Office of Shadow Affairs was an actual, unmarked office building inconspicuously tucked away in the city's financial district. The ground floor had a lobby lined with a handful of touch screens to vet visitors and direct them to the correct department—or back out if said visitor didn't have the proper clearance.

The upper floors were reserved for the "top copper," as they called themselves—people whose job it was to read through piles of paper reports and make decisions on where to allocate resources in the continued efforts against the telepath threat.

In an age of infinite digital interconnection, paper was impossible to trace. Boxes of it got delivered daily. Clerks performed bureaucratic triage, discarding petty requests, escalating serious ones, and sending the most dire straight to the desk of Commander Armitage Lee Hughes.

Hughes liked to think of himself as the *secret* secret weapon hiding in the stacks. He'd started his career as one of the first Hounds in his then-newly-established outpost of Blue 4. He'd distinguished himself with exemplary service and unquestioning loyalty.

And then he'd made the mistake of not dying.

As a "reward" for such an auspicious achievement, the powers that be had put him in charge of the financial heart of Shadow operations. He spent his days reading himself blind while his ass went flat and his belly grew round from sitting at a desk from morning 'til night.

But on occasion, something requiring direct action would cross his desk and break up the monotony of his inertia. He got to organize a tactical strike that no one else knew about because, since their Commander in Chief, Senator Matthew Griffith, had been rendered deaf, blind, and dumb, his authority had fragmented down to the highest-ranking COs in each sector.

On this world, where the only thing resembling an outpost was the OSA, that was Hughes.

Any other time, Hughes would take immense pride in doling out efficient, decisive solutions to pesky problems throughout the sector. But the most recent one seemed to be sticking and leaving a bad taste in his mouth.

Today, he found said problem lounging in the armchair facing his desk. He glared at his secretary, who shrugged.

Hughes slammed the door behind him when he entered, causing his visitor to shove to his feet at attention that would have earned him fifty push-ups and ten laps around the building back in the day. "What are you doing here again, Mr. Bigellow?"

The Hound had slinked into Hughes' office weeks ago, "reporting for duty" in civilian clothes, looking like a common street thug. Since then, he'd had his head tattoos removed, his hair cut, and his beard shaved. But even dressed in the proper uniform, cleaned up, and as presentable as someone like him could get, there was still something distinctly unsavory about him. Which was why Hughes had buried him deep in the residential part of the building reserved for off-duty Shadows and forgot the man existed.

Yet it seemed Latham Bigellow was determined to remain a thorn in Hughes' side.

"Sir! I was hoping for a minute of your time, sir!"

Hughes rolled his eyes. "At ease."

Instead of stepping his feet apart, Bigellow parked his ass back in the armchair before Hughes had taken his seat.

"Are your quarters not to your liking?"

Bigellow's cheek twitched. "I thought I'd be sent out into the field when the medics cleared me for active duty. It's been almost a month, and I haven't received any gear or assignments."

"Gear is reserved for Shadows on assignment. You don't have an assignment. Therefore, you don't need any gear."

Bigellow's state of mind was questionable at best, and the last thing any of them needed was a loose cannon running amok out there. Hughes judged him in dire need of a treatment, but as the nature of their duties here was so benign, they didn't have the necessary equipment to administer it—they'd never needed it before.

He had already requested a treatment unit and a trained medic to be brought in just for Bigellow—a massive expense he'd have to offset on the budgets now—but their ETA wasn't for another two weeks. Bigellow could cool his heels in storage until then.

"I don't understand, sir. I was cleared for duty."

"Your physical condition notwithstanding, I'm not convinced that you're an asset we can use at this point in time."

Bigellow's face flushed. He put forth a visible effort to calm himself—which shouldn't have been necessary if his conditioning was still effective. Whatever he'd endured had had a profound and disturbing effect on him. Hughes' former CO would have taken one look at him and retired him immediately. Back in those days, there'd still been plenty of soldiers to go around. Now, every Shadow was a precious resource. Even one as damaged as Latham Bigellow.

"I noticed the roster for this unit consists of all Hounds," Bigellow remarked.

"That's what the roster says." Sometimes, it served Hughes' purposes to keep his most valuable assets off the books, so to speak.

Among the Shadows, Hounds were a dime a dozen. Not to say they were disposable. Hughes himself was a Hound, and he took pride in his rank and the camaraderie he'd developed within it.

"Since the war started, we lost contact with most of our Hawks out in the field," he explained for Bigellow's benefit, and it was true. For the most part.

Though neither designation outranked the other, Hounds and Hawks operated in different ways. Hounds trained and worked together, much like any other army. Hawks were more like spies who were dispatched for solitary assignments requiring surgical precision rather than a show of brute force. They were masters at blending in, becoming part of their environment, and carrying out their mission in such a way that no one ever suspected their involvement.

The standard ratio for a typical Shadow unit used to be four hundred and eighty Hounds to twenty Hawks. In Hughes' mostly bureaucratic unit of two hundred and seven Shadows, only one was a Hawk, and it was still more than many other units had.

At the moment, his Hawk was on assignment and, therefore, off the roster.

"What if I could get you a Hawk?"

Hughes responded to the offer with the exact level of credulity it deserved. "Get out."

"If I can get you a Hawk," Bigellow pressed, "that means I'm an asset you can use, right?"

Hughes sighed.

Bigellow leaned back in his seat and grinned. "I guarantee I can get you a Hawk."

"You mean, poach one from another unit."

"I mean *return* one who's gone AWOL from a unit that got obliterated."

Despite himself, Hughes waved him on to continue.

"Look up the name Vega Ortiz."

Hughes took a few seconds, debating with himself the wisdom of humoring the unstable Hound. In the end, he figured he had nothing to lose. And there wasn't a Shadow unit anywhere whose CO couldn't use an extra Hawk. He pulled up the Shadow databases and searched the name Bigellow had given him. "Are you done wasting my time? It says here Vega Ortiz was a Hound." She was also listed as KIA, not AWOL.

"She was fully trained as a Hawk. Passed all the tests. Her CO flunked her back to Hound at the end on a technicality."

"What was the technicality?"

"A history of substance abuse. He didn't feel he could trust her on her own for extended solo missions. But I happen to know he was a misogynistic dirtbag, and Vega is capable enough that she's still alive out there, all on her own."

"And how would you know this?"

Bigellow shrugged. "We crossed paths recently."

Hughes tried and failed to read the subtext in Bigellow's face. It didn't make any sense. He decided to pull up the full roster from Ortiz's unit. The CO's name was familiar enough that Hughes could well believe Bigellow's story. It was linked to a number of disastrous mistakes and decisions that had cost the Shadows a number of outposts and the entire outcome of the war.

The name John Wayland glowed an angry red—a deserter who'd been instrumental in obliterating the unit, as Bigellow had said. There was a standing Kill-On-Sight order against him across all Shadow units with an active connection to the database.

Hughes also found Bigellow's name there, which further corroborated his knowledge of Ortiz and her qualifications. His service record, however, included several red flags he found worrisome. Compared to Ortiz's, it painted a much more dubious picture. Hughes couldn't imagine any crossing of paths between the two of them ever ending well.

But if, by some miracle, Bigellow had the means to deliver her back into the Shadows' fold, it would, in fact, make him an asset Hughes could use. For the time being. "You're saying you can deliver Vega Ortiz back to us."

"Without question."

"How?"

Bigellow rubbed the side of his neck. "Let's just say I know what makes her tick."

The way he said it almost made Hughes send him to the brig to get his head on straight. But a Shadow of Ortiz's caliber, one who had been passed up for a Hawk pin, was worth a risk or two.

"Understand, your only value to me right now is your ability to walk Vega Ortiz through that door alive and in one piece."

"Oh, I can do a lot more than that."

"Not without my direct order."

Bigellow's smug grin withered, and the angry flush returned. He definitely needed to get his head treated before going out there. But time, as always, was of the essence.

"Bring me Ortiz, and maybe we can talk."

Bigellow pushed to his feet and gave Hughes a mock salute. "Yes, sir!"

"I'll send instructions to the quartermaster to get you whatever you need. And, Bigellow? I'd think twice before darkening this office again without her. Dismissed."

As soon as Bigellow left, Hughes forgot he existed. He scrolled through Ortiz's record again, memorizing her history from early childhood to the day she'd dropped off their map about two years ago. She was a remarkable specimen, distinguished by an exemplary record, flawless missions, and unflappable courage.

Why hadn't she reported back? What must she have endured to keep her isolated and without the support of her unit for the last two years?

Whatever it was, the lost Hound had been scavenging trash out there in the cold for long enough.

It was time to bring her home and give her wings.

~

What are you doing here again, Mr. Bigellow?

Gear is reserved for Shadows on assignment. You don't have an assignment.

Talon was fuming.

Bureaucrat fucking piece of shit talking down to him?

He veered off the main hallway and charged the wall, throwing his whole weight behind a punch that split his knuckles bloody. He couldn't get Hughes' pudgy face out of his head. The condescending tone—the *disrespect*!

His bulging eyes and fishy lips hovered in the bloodied smear on the wall. Talon hauled off and punched it five more times in rapid succession until his knuckles went numb, and the pain in his carpals radiated up his arm into his shoulder.

And still Hughes' face mocked him, dripping Talon's blood down the wall from the corner of his sneering mouth.

Talon slammed his flat palm over it and screamed in rage until he ran out of breath.

Negotiating for breadcrumbs. That's what he'd been reduced to. *Him!*

If Hughes knew the shit Talon had done on Anamtaigh, the fucker would be quaking in his shiny dress shoes and falling to his knees to beg forgiveness.

Not without my direct order.

Talon had opened Shadow throats for so much less.

"New guy, right?"

An animalistic growl built up in his chest, hackles rising and back curving as he turned his head toward the intrusive voice.

"Latham, something?" the Hound clarified, looking him up and down like something the cat had chucked up into his shoe.

Talon bared his teeth, fists clenching tight again, itching to beat his unremarkable face into the same bloody pulp he'd just left on the wall. "The fuck are you looking at?" he snarled.

The Hound, in full uniform, neat as a pin, crossed his arms and shook his head. "You won't last long here."

A tiny, still rational part of Talon's brain told him to stand down. The Hound wasn't worth his time, and he couldn't afford to piss off the wrong people. He didn't have the same pull here as he'd had on Anamtaigh. This glorified office building was still a certified Shadow outpost, with a commanding officer on site to call the shots, and it wasn't Talon. Hughes would send him straight into the chair if he stepped too far out of line.

Too bad the rational part of him was so faint that the rush of his blood drowned it out completely.

Talon's vision went red, and he charged.

The Hound moved at the last possible second, but he moved lightning fast. He sidestepped Talon's flying fist, twisted his arm behind his back, and slammed him face-first into the wall, pinning him in place with a forearm across his nape. "What did you say?"

Talon roared, shoving his free hand into the wall to push himself off, but he had fuckall for leverage. Pinned like a bug.

The Hound drove his knee into Talon's side. "Say it again. Didn't quite catch it the first time." Talon's shoulder stretched just short of dislocation as the Hound applied more pressure, crushing his ear against the wall as he leaned close. "I don't know what shithole you crawled out of, and I don't care. *No one here does.* You look at one of us crooked again, and we'll save the medics the bother of frying you back into your place."

Talon reached back in a desperate, sloppy claw.

A second knee to his side subdued him. "Acknowledge, soldier!"

Talon's roar turned into a pathetic whimper.

A hand on his face shoved him harder into the wall. "*Acknowledge!*"

"Understood!" he barked.

The Hound shoved himself away, releasing Talon. He wished to fuck that he still had his sidearm or even a brace of knives. But they'd disarmed him as soon as he'd checked himself in.

Gear is reserved for Shadows on assignment.

The Hound looked down his nose at Talon, his mouth twisting in distaste. He hadn't even creased his uniform.

Meanwhile, Talon's hand was split open, he was sweaty and disheveled, his ear was already swelling up, and if the throbbing pain in his side was any indication, he'd be pissing blood tonight. His men on Anamtaigh would have taken one look at him in such a state and recognized that heads were about to roll. Literally.

This son of a bitch had no notion of what Talon could do.

Could have done.

Not anymore, the annoying, rational voice reminded him. He was back to where he'd begun. At the bottom of the chain of command, where every prick with an attitude could wipe their boots on his face.

I'm not convinced that you're an asset we can use, Hughes had said.

And Talon couldn't show them the error of their ways.

"You're a fucking Shadow," the Hound spat. "Act like it."

Talon was breathing too hard and shaking too much to form the proper verbal response. Humiliated twice over, he jerked his chin down to acknowledge.

The Hound turned his fucking back on him and walked away like Talon was nothing.

Because, in this outpost, he was.

Shaking the dripping blood off his knuckles, Talon stomped back into the main hallway and took himself to the quartermaster.

He'd been there three times since he'd arrived, and each time the Hound on duty had turned him away. Without the CO's clearance, the only gear he could requisition was a replacement uniform.

The woman behind the desk rolled her eyes when she saw him enter. "Sure, yeah. I have five minutes to waste on you."

"I have an assignment. Commander Hughes sent in the order."

She looked skeptical but turned to her screen to search her records. "Congratulations," she deadpanned. "You're cleared for standard gear and weaponry. Go down the corridor and to your left. Everything you need will be set out for you."

"I'll need a wrist unit."

She snorted. "Don't we all?"

"Check with Hughes. He'll confirm." The fucker had better. Hawk or not, Talon was going out there solo. He would need a weapon that wouldn't attract attention.

The woman sighed and swiped across her screen a few times. She typed something in, then swiped again and waited.

The silence was punctuated by the wet drum of Talon's blood dripping onto the floor. He gave exactly zero shits. If she wanted to make him wait, she could deal with the mess.

Two minutes later, the screen flashed, and she read the response. "Looks like you get your wrist unit."

Talon tried not to gloat. It was hard, but he was a Shadow, after all. He could act like one and keep his glee in check.

The woman glared at him. "What are you still standing there for? Down the corridor and to your left."

"Yes, ma'am," he gritted out, pivoting on his heel to march away.

Fuck her.

Fuck the Hound, fuck Hughes—fuck all of them.

All he had to do was get Vega and walk her into Hughes' office. Once they got *her* measure and realized Talon had brought her in on his own, they'd have to give him his due. It would be proof positive of what Talon was made of.

Then maybe they'd finally show him some fucking respect.

He'd always know Vega would be good for something one day.

10

Day 1 – Ela

Quinn was awakened from sound sleep by strange, muffled noises. He tried to ignore them at first. Probably just the kids playing outside his door.

But then he remembered where he was. There were no kids outside of his door. And the noises didn't sound happy.

He opened his bleary eyes facing the window. Day was starting to break outside, illuminating a forest of strange, tropical trees.

The noises quieted for a moment, and he almost closed his eyes again, but then a louder yip behind him startled him wide awake, and he turned around.

"Vega?"

She was facing away from him, curled in so tight she barely took up any room on the giant bed. Only her hair showed from underneath the covers, but he could see her shivering and twitching. And the noises she made—had it been anyone else, Quinn would have thought they were crying out in pain. But this was Vega.

"Hey, you okay?"

A hard twitch, and then she froze, and Quinn held his breath.

Then she cried out again, and he couldn't take it anymore.

He crossed the ridiculous expanse of the mattress and reached for her. "Vega, wake up."

Until his dying breath, Quinn would never be quite sure of the sequence of events that followed. It happened faster than his brain could process. He put his hand on her shoulder, blinked his eyes, and then he was on his back with Vega on top of him, nightmare-hazed eyes unseeing, and one of her knives pressing into his throat.

Quinn shoved her off and put a hand on the cut to stop the bleeding. By the time she landed softly farther down the mattress, the shallow wound had already closed.

The impact seemed to jar Vega fully awake. She sat up in a daze, looking around until she spotted Quinn, and recognition took hold.

"What the hell was that?" he demanded, louder than he should.

Whatever tumult of emotions she might have displayed in her confusion got shut down instantly. "I told you I sleep alone."

And that made it all so much worse. "Talk to me."

"No." She reclaimed her knife and rolled away over the foot of the bed, heading for the bathroom.

Quinn followed. "That's it? Just *no*?"

"That about sums it up. Shower on, cold." At her command, the shower woke to life, lighting up from the inside as the glass wall frosted over. Water started dripping from overhead in a simulation of rain filling the entire large pen.

Unabashed, Vega shrugged out of his T-shirt and her panties and stepped right in underneath a waterfall so cold Quinn could feel its chill from four feet away. He didn't turn his back this time. He traced the icy rivulets as they raised goosebumps over the enticing swell of her ass and the long, supple lines of her limbs. But he didn't miss the rigid set of her spine and the slight, defensive curve of her tense shoulders. The way she tilted her face up to the cold rain, then pulled aside her hair and dropped her chin to her chest to catch the water on the back of her neck.

He didn't think the word 'defeat' existed in Vega Ortiz's dictionary. But, standing beneath that chilling waterfall, she became its embodiment. Defeat and misery.

And all he wanted to do was pluck her out from the cold and tuck her back into the soft, warm bed.

She stayed there for several minutes, and Quinn didn't say a word, too stunned to come up with anything that might break her out of it. Indignation didn't seem to register with her. Sympathy would probably get him maimed.

He didn't imagine her tenure with the Shadows to have been pleasant, but with each tiny glimpse Quinn managed to steal past her armor of cold indifference, he realized Vega carried more darkness and hurt than he ever could have guessed.

First, the device on her spine, then the nightmares. And now her Bliss binge on Persephone 5 made a lot more sense. What the hell had Talon and the Shadows done to her to turn her into this? It went beyond being a loner. Vega seemed almost incapable of showing any kind of emotion unless it was part of an act.

When Vega shut off the shower and stepped out, Quinn was still there, glaring at her.

"At least make yourself useful and hand me a towel." She was pointing at the ones folded on a shelf.

He gave her one from the warming rack instead. "I'm going to make you tell me eventually."

Vega ignored him, drying off in adroit sweeps of the towel over her skin, nowhere near slow enough for the towel's warmth to transfer to her. Then she wrapped her hair in it and stepped around him, heading for the closet as if he didn't exist.

Her anger, he could have handled. Tears, he could have soothed. But she just shut him out, leaving Quinn helpless to do anything at all. But, stubborn idiot that he was, he tailed her and kept on trying. "Does this happen a lot?"

Vega had already put on fresh panties and a bra and was sorting through her clothes for the rest of an outfit. She didn't answer him.

"We're going to be sharing a bed for the foreseeable future. I don't get to know if you're liable to kill me in the middle of the night because you happen to have a nightmare?"

"Don't touch me, and you'll be fine."

If possible, her words pissed him off even more. "That's not good enough." Not for him, and definitely not for her.

"That's all you're getting." She'd put on a pair of skin-tight pants, a sports bra, and a sleeveless top that only reached a couple of inches below her breasts, leaving her midsection exposed. "I'm going for a run."

When she would have brushed past him, he put out his arm to stop her. "Vega—"

"They're *my* nightmares," she snapped. "I earned them. Back off."

It wasn't the anger in her voice that got to him. It was the despair in her eyes and the icy shower's lingering chill still radiating off her. She never raised her voice or a hand, physically as loose as a person could get, but Quinn recognized a ticking time bomb when he saw one. Vega was ready to blow in a big way.

For her sake more than anything, he dropped his arm and let her leave.

~

The humidity slammed into Vega as soon as she stepped foot outside. It stuck her loose top to her clammy skin. The air was thick with scents of burgeoning life.

It was suffocating.

And not a drop of Bliss anywhere to be found.

Which left her only one alternative: run until her muscles gave out.

She picked a direction and took off hard and fast as if she could leave all her bad dreams in the dust. But they stuck to her heels, dragging along in her wake and slowing her down.

This morning, she'd been incapacitated, at the mercy of Talon and his trigger. She'd heard him laughing as he'd activated it over and over again, just to watch her writhe. And then she'd somehow broken out of the paralysis, and there'd been a knife in her hand, and she'd held it to Talon's throat, savoring the final moment before his shit stain of a soul fled his body.

Only it hadn't been Talon, but Quinn.

Quinn, with his big heart and eyes filled with fear.

Quinn, whom she'd almost convinced that she wasn't dangerous—at least to him.

Quinn. Her *husband*, who kissed like the whole universe depended on him getting it right, and whose sexy thoughts she clocked by his bashful blushes.

He would have been too good for her long before she'd ever crossed paths with a Shadow, but Vega still kept wanting to pretend that if she played the part well enough, she could somehow mold herself into a decent human being. Maybe not enough to deserve Quinn, but at least enough to stand beside him for a little while.

Except she couldn't. Whatever goodness she'd once had was long gone.

And this morning proved she would never get it back. She knew it; even Quinn had to know it by now. But rather than turn her out and tell her never to shadow his doorstep again, he wanted to play therapist.

He should have kicked her in the head instead. It would have hurt a lot less.

Fucking pity.

Vega shook her head hard and pushed herself to run faster until the forest trail spat her out on a beach on the outer curve of the island with black sand and crystal clear, green-hued water. She had no idea what order of beasties swam in those waters. It wasn't fenced off, so Vega figured it should be safe. The dainty waves lapping in and out beckoned with the promise of a bracing respite from the growing heat.

But her nightmares were still too close, and now they had a new flavor of guilt, thanks to Quinn's near-beheading with a throwing knife. She was tense all over with the anticipation of a full-body muscle cramp, and she couldn't get Quinn's horrified look out of her head.

Vega had seen him angry while in her custody; she'd seen hate in his eyes and a strong desire to end her; she'd seen him defeated and accepting of death.

But not once during everything she'd put him through had Vega seen him scared of her—until this morning. It had only lasted a second, but it was now permanently burned into Vega's memory. Another nightmare to add to her collection.

She could never get rid of them. Not even with a steady diet of Bliss. All she could do was exhaust her body and hope her brain got too tired to dwell on it. So she turned south and took off along the beach.

Vega ran all the way to the sharp tip of the island, where she had a view of its inner curve. There, she stopped for a break. The island's lee side was almost completely encircled by the landmass, leaving an opening only a mile wide. The water was as calm as an inland lake, and the beach was studded with umbrellas and cushioned seats. It was eerily pristine, like an abandoned resort that hadn't given in to nature yet.

Then she noticed a figure jogging along the beach in her direction. Definitely male but too small to be Quinn.

She could have run back the other way to avoid him, but he spotted her and waved. It'd be rude to run away now. Vega ripped and clawed and shoved her dark thoughts to the back of her mind and pulled herself into the persona of Quinn's happy wife to meet the intruder halfway.

She recognized him immediately: her gallant defender from dinner last night. "Good morning," he called ahead. He was a few inches taller than her, with a lean, muscled build. His coloring was similar to hers, but his features were of a different ethnic background.

"Good morning," she echoed.

He stopped at a polite distance, breathing hard, but he wasn't sweaty, and his heartbeat pumped out a steady rhythm in the side of his neck. He'd run a decent distance to get to her but hadn't strained himself at all. "We didn't get a chance to meet properly last night. I'm Zach."

Vega shook his offered hand. "It's nice to meet you, Zach. Which branch of the family tree do you hail from?" He looked nothing like the aunts and uncles she'd already met. Someone's spouse, maybe?

"The poor one," he said with a self-deprecating smile. "I'm the branch they wish they could prune out. The illegitimate son of an illegitimate son."

"Ah, I see."

"Yeah, I think I got invited by mistake. But, hey, free vacation. And, besides, there are so many VanWarrens, most of them don't even know who everyone is."

So she was learning. As prolific as the VanWarrens were, calling the family tight-knit would be a wild stretch.

Emmett's jab at Geraldine last night had been aimed with the expertise of endless practice. Vega had witnessed more than a few snubs like it throughout the night, but no one else seemed to take them as hard as Geraldine did.

The young musician seemed to be unknown in more ways than

one. On top of not having any close connections at the reunion, her public resume only went back about a year. And, while her production contract appeared to be legit, and her music, from what Vega could tell, was good, her following was tiny. Almost as if she'd been living under a rock her entire life and never once tried to capitalize on the infamy of her family name. Even her stage name was unique: Whisper on the Wind.

Very un-VanWarren-like.

And an instant red flag.

"Do you think that's a good thing or a bad thing?" Vega asked.

"You're getting the spotlight treatment. You tell me."

Vega found herself smiling. "Fair. Well, I don't want to keep you."

He shrugged. "I don't mind the company. Keeps me honest. Unless you want to be alone."

She wanted to say yes. But he was presenting her with an opportunity to get more personal information on the family. Regardless of her own shit, she was on mission. The smallest detail could mean the difference between heading off an attack on Quinn and watching him go up in flames.

Her nightmares could wait until she went back to sleep.

"Can we circle the entire island this way?"

"Let's find out." He turned back the way he'd come but let her set the pace, falling into a steady rhythm beside her. "I don't get to run on a beach very often. It's nice."

"It is," Vega agreed. "So tell me about the family. What did I get myself into?"

"Oof, I don't think I'm qualified to answer that. But, I mean, you saw the dinner show last night. Hell, you were part of it."

"Yeah, what's Emmett's problem?" *And what's your problem with him?* It hadn't escaped Vega how strongly Zach had reacted to Emmett's attack. It had the whiff of a personal vendetta.

"Emmett is… Emmett." The short sentence contained a lot of bitterness.

Vega gave him a curious eyebrow lift for encouragement, though it didn't look like he needed much. Once he started talking, the poison bled out all on its own.

"He tried to start a shipping and distribution business and got a few of us involved in the scheme. I was just starting to make contacts within the family, wanted to prove myself, I guess. So I did the dumbest thing ever and invested almost every credit I had to my name. It was going to be my ticket to a better life. 'Cuz there was no way a VanWarren enterprise could possibly fail, right? And even if it did, my *family* wouldn't let me go broke." He shook his head. "I was such an idiot back then."

"I think I see where this is heading."

"It fell to total shit as soon as the war hit."

"So you all went broke?" She made a mental note to look into it more later. If Zach was telling the truth, there would be exploitable grudges within the VanWarren family that Vega could leverage in the future.

"I did. The rest of them not even close. Emmett least of all."

"Let me guess. He invested *your* money so he wouldn't have to risk his own."

Zach clicked his tongue and winked at her for confirmation. "But *he* was the first one to go to the old guard for a bail-out. That's what we called Pop-pop Amundsen and Oma Beatrice: the old guard. Way I heard it, he pissed them off so much they didn't talk to him again for months. And he pretty much ruined it for the rest us. I sure as hell wasn't gonna risk going to them for help after him."

"Oh, to have been a fly on the wall during that meeting."

"Wait, it gets better. 'Cuz it turned out, Emmett used the war as an excuse to tank the business on purpose and cash out a fortune for himself—before he ever went to the old guard. When they found out, they were so pissed, they took the money from his inheritance and used it to repay the investors, with interest."

"As one does."

"Yeah, Emmett wasn't exactly jumping for joy over it. And he decided it had to have been my fault. Like I talked them into it, or something, because I needed it the most. He's been trash-talking me to the family ever since."

"And you still came to the reunion? What's wrong with you?"

Zach shrugged. "Bastard bastards make convenient scapegoats. But there are still connections here I could use. You just never know, you know? Someday, something might actually break my way for a change. But not if I crawl back under a rock and let them forget me."

"So you're using them."

"Give it a few days," he retorted dryly. "You'll see—everyone uses everyone in this family. And Emmett's an expert at exploiting the system."

"What do you mean?"

A massive chunk of driftwood barred their way. They jumped over it in tandem.

Zach made a face. "This isn't a topic suitable for ladies."

"Then pretend I'm an expensive whore," she said.

"Emmett shouldn't have said that." His tone carried the right amount of offense and something else, a sharp note she couldn't identify.

Vega shrugged. "Still don't care. Spill it."

The beach ended in a rocky barrier, but a wooden pier marked out a straight line from the black sand to the tip of the island. They hopped up onto it and kept going, their feet drumming out a steady rhythm.

"Think of a sin," Zach said carefully, "and he's probably guilty of it."

Vega turned to him with a dramatic gasp. "Even…*murder*?"

Zach snorted, amused, but his tone dropped low with disgust when he said, "With his sordid sexual appetites? I wouldn't be surprised."

"How—*why*—do you know all this?"

He shrugged. "Being ripped off so royally by my own blood taught me it's always in my best interest to dig until I find what I need to know. Emmett is an embarrassment to the VanWarren name. They've spent a lot of money cleaning up his messes over the years. And they like to complain about it when he's not around, but aside from staying out of his business ventures, no one cares enough to put a stop to it."

"Good to know."

"What about you? Any sordid skeletons in your closet?"

"Just the usual," she lied. "I work, I party, I enjoy life to the fullest extent of my limited bank account."

He chuckled. "I'm guessing it's not so limited anymore. Will you be partying it all away the first chance you get?"

"Haven't decided yet." But she'd be lying if she said she wouldn't go for a shot or ten of Bliss if someone offered it. The detox might have cleared her physical cravings, but her mind remembered the sweet, sweet embrace of happy oblivion. The things she'd seen, the things she'd done—it was easier to set them aside than face up to them. Easier to fade away and disappear. Bliss could do that for her, give her some peace for a while.

But not yet.

Not while Quinn still needed her to watch his back.

The pier ended at the crescent tip, forcing them to a halt. "Well, for what it's worth, I'm always a good source of bad ideas," Zach offered. "But seriously, there are so few normal people on this island, I think it's safer if we stick together. If you ever need to talk, I'm here."

"Ditto." Wouldn't hurt to have another set of eyes and ears around here. Zach seemed happy to be able to have a laid-back conversation. He was practically doing the hard work for her and going out of his way to establish a personal connection.

He tipped his head toward the beach. "Shall we head back?"

"I think I'll stay here for a bit. Enjoy the view." There was a fine line between establishing a friendship and leading someone on. But more importantly, she wasn't ready to face Quinn and his probing questions yet.

"It is a hell of a view," Zach acknowledged. "Thanks for the run!"

Vega watched him jog back to the beach and disappear through the trees. Only when he was out of sight did she let her happy face relax back to neutral.

She now had two suspects to keep an eye on. The mysteriously unknown Cousin Geraldine and the unlikely Cousin Emmett.

Brunch was served buffet style out in the curve of the crescent pool. This time, the children were in attendance and had the run of the place. Quinn could tell their antics annoyed the adults, some of whom were still nursing a hangover from last night, but he liked having them there. They broke up the tension with guileless fun and honesty.

Like the little girl with her hair dyed a dark blue, who ran up to the fruit table next to Quinn. She gaped at him as she reached for a strawberry. When he delivered a deep-voiced "Boo," she gasped and giggled. "You're funny," she declared before returning to her cousins.

When his plate was full, Quinn turned away from the spread to go to his seat and found his path blocked by an elderly attendant. "Allow me, sir."

Quinn immediately stood aside. "Of course. Knock yourself out."

"Your plate, sir. I shall carry it to your table for you."

Quinn scowled. "I can carry my own damned plate. How about you take an empty one instead and fill it for yourself? You look like you haven't had a proper meal in a decade."

The attendant didn't even blink, bowing to Quinn before he walked away as if he endured such abuse on a regular basis.

And Quinn felt like shit.

He did his best not to talk to anyone else after that. Clearly, despite his morning meditation, he was still raw from Vega's outburst and unfit for polite company.

His table started out empty, but encroachers descended soon after he sat down, forcing him to put his digital book away. Uncle Trent's wife, Ivy, was the first, sporting a shapeless dress and a wide-brimmed hat. Their introduction yesterday had been brief but not unpleasant.

She was a remarkably self-possessed woman for being married to a windbag like Trent. Unlike some of the others, Ivy had chosen to age naturally. It made her a little more human in Quinn's eyes. Her face might not have been perfect, but her wrinkles mapped out a happy, content life and a genuine inner kindness that marked her as an outsider within the VanWarren clan.

"I was wondering how the children would react to you," she said.

"And did I pass the test?"

Ivy smiled. "Children are the truest judges of character, don't you think? For example, none of them would ever approach my Trent unless summoned. Oh, he's not a bad sort. He's just not child-friendly, and they can sense it."

"They're not exactly lining up to see me, either."

"They will," Ivy predicted. Quinn got a distinct motherly vibe from her. Curious, since Trent and Ivy didn't have any children of their own. "Uma is their scout, and she walked away laughing. As soon as she reports back to the rest of them, you'll never get a moment's peace."

"Somehow, I can't see their parents letting them near me for too long." They'd swoop in to rescue their little angels from his monstrous clutches as soon as they looked up from their Chablis long enough to notice them in his proximity.

Ivy laughed. "Dear, there are so few parents here. They sired their children but they don't raise them. Don't you remember how it was for you?"

His already dark mood got a little darker. "I blocked out most of my childhood." He'd had to—otherwise, the total abandonment that had ended it so abruptly would have stopped his bad heart before he'd had a chance to live.

"I'd like to say I'm surprised, but after what your mother did…" She took a sip of her champagne. "Do you know why Amundsen and Beatrice left their estate to you instead of the rest of us?"

"Do you?" Quinn had been under the impression it had been kept secret from all of them.

"Not officially," she said. "But I've seen things and heard things over the years. Dear, they didn't know your mother planned to cast you out."

"Really? Not even after I called them from a public com and begged them to take me in? They didn't, in case you were wondering." His grandmother had only kept the connection open long enough for him to sob out what'd happened. She'd told him how sorry she was, but she and her husband couldn't get involved beyond transferring two thousand credits to his ID as a parting gift. She'd never even said goodbye.

"Yes, well, by then, acknowledgment of any kind would have meant public drama. And if there is one thing at which the VanWarren old guard excelled, it was quelling public drama unless they were its masters. But you should know the family was never the same after you left."

"After I was kicked out."

Ivy ducked her head in what might have been humble agreement. "Holly would get into vicious fights with her parents and even Derek. I can't be sure, of course, but I do think it was why he ultimately divorced her. He went no-contact with all of us, cut himself off from the family accounts, and even your brothers."

If it was true, it would explain Matthew's animosity. Unlike Holden, Matthew would have been old enough to blame Quinn for their father abandoning them. Although Ivy was right about one thing. Quinn didn't remember either of his parents showing much interest in any of their children beyond the bare minimum required to keep up appearances.

"And as for your grandparents," Ivy continued, "I think they went to their final rest still weighed with guilt over it."

"If you're expecting sympathy, you're wasting your time."

"No, dear, I'm well aware we don't deserve any. In the end, we all share in Holly's guilt, because none of us did a thing about it all these years. Not even me. And I think that was ultimately why Amundsen and Beatrice willed you the estate. To assuage their own guilt and remind us of ours."

"I would have preferred if they'd taken it to the grave with them."

"Nonsense! This family has needed someone like you for a long, long time. You still know how to look up and see the world instead of your own reflection. Think of all the good you can do with the money."

"If I survive this reunion," he retorted darkly.

Ivy rolled her eyes and gently slapped his shoulder as she stood up to make her exit. Her parting words were spiced with a healthy dose of dry humor. "You know how I can tell you're a true VanWarren? You inherited their flare for drama."

Her guileless retort immediately crossed Ivy VanWarren off Quinn's list of potential murder suspects.

If nothing else, the compound had a stellar kitchen staff. Dinner last night had been delicious. Brunch today was a revelation—although he stayed far away from the familiar-looking chilled crustaceans in the center of the buffet.

He was starting to enjoy himself when his brothers joined the table. Matthew was accompanied by his wife, Kendry. Holden, the bachelor, had two beer bottles. He set one in front of Quinn before taking his seat. "Sleep well?"

"For the most part." Quinn ignored the bottle, which was already opened. Vega would kill him if he got himself poisoned again while she wasn't there to stop him.

"A bunch of us are going for a boat ride later. You want to join us?"

Quinn wanted to trust Holden—he wanted there to be one person whose motives he didn't have to question. But as genuine as his younger brother appeared, Quinn still didn't know enough about him as a man to fully let down his guard. "Who else is in the bunch?"

Holden shrugged, "Matthew, me, Emmett—"

"Pass."

"Emmett didn't say anything we weren't all thinking last night," Matthew said. "And can you blame us?"

"I can, and I do." Did Quinn go around asking Matthew what inbred rich bitch cesspool of hobgoblins had spawned his shrew of a wife? No. Did he ask Kendry where she kept her pitchfork when she was done pegging Matthew with it? Also no. There were some things you didn't say out loud, unless you wanted to get your face pummeled.

"So that's a no to the boat ride, then?" Holden pressed.

"That's a no to the boat ride."

Kendry sniffed.

Quinn raised an eyebrow at her. "Something to say?"

There was a sharp frailty to his sister-in-law that was uncomfortable to look at. She seemed to exist in a perpetual state of agitation as if the smallest thing would send her careening into destructive and self-destructive hysterics. "Yes," she said tightly, and though he couldn't see her skeletal hands under the table, Quinn would bet the entire estate that her fingers were curling into claws. "Grow up."

Quinn couldn't help it—he burst out laughing. Everyone within hearing distance turned to stare at him as if he'd grown a second head, and the baffled, bug-eyed look on Kendry's dried-out face made it so much harder to rein back in.

"What did I miss?"

The voice behind him went straight to Quinn's gut, choking off his mirth, but he held onto his grin when he stood up to greet Vega as a proper husband should. "There you are."

Her social persona was firmly in place, along with an open smile. She'd chosen a simple sun dress for the brunch, with a knee-length skirt to conceal her knives. In deference to the grass, she was barefoot, her sandals swinging from their long straps looped around her hand.

She didn't hesitate when he held out his arm for her. She came to him and raised up on tiptoe for his kiss, keeping up the pretense of a happily married wife. "Hey, you," she purred.

"Hey, you," Quinn echoed. He didn't release her. Mentally, he knew it was all an act and that whatever had happened this morning would come back again to bite him on the ass. But right now, the way Vega smiled, the way she relaxed into him, the way her fingers absently traced patterns over his shoulders made it all seem like a bad dream. He knew better, but he didn't want to.

Quinn wanted this version of Vega to be real. It was a version whose worst memory was getting stranded on a foreign world for a few days. This Vega didn't have shadows haunting her eyes and didn't wear a stiff mask that kept her from smiling too much, just in case.

And the fact that this version *was* a mask fully hammered home how dangerous a trained Shadow could be. She made Quinn want to be the one who made her feel this safe without it.

The attendant who'd followed her to the table set her plate between Kendry and Matthew since the seats on either side of Quinn were taken, and neither of his brothers had so much as stood up at Vega's arrival, much less thought to move so she could sit next to him. Quinn reclaimed his seat and pulled Vega down to perch on his lap—because he could. Because while all eyes were on them, she couldn't shut him away from the demons that haunted her. And he was too selfish not to take full advantage.

It felt too good to be holding her, even if it was an act. The relief he felt to be able to offer her at least this much comfort was real enough.

"Sorry I'm late to the party," Vega said, making herself comfortable. "My morning run stretched a little longer than I anticipated. Matthew, would you be a dear and pass me my plate?"

The look on Matthew's face said he'd rather stick the fork in his eye, but he did move himself to comply. Kendry probably would have hurled the plate at Vega's head.

"You run?" Holden asked, one golden eyebrow rising toward his perfect dark-blond hairline.

Vega picked a morsel from her selection to pop into her mouth. "I do."

She didn't seem to mind Quinn's arm around her. No issues with physical touch and affection—while she was awake and in character. Quinn decided to milk it for all it was worth. He brushed his thumb along her side while she ate and nuzzled her shoulder when she leaned back against him in between bites. The chill of their wake-up call was completely gone now. Her skin was sun-warmed, and her body was free of all tension.

If he didn't know better, he'd think she enjoyed being in his arms.

"I did a circuit around the island today. It's so beautiful. I get why you all live here."

"Please, we don't *live* here," Kendry said as if the mere idea offended her. "Ela is as backward as its people. But I suppose it is a nice break from all the attention on Jericho."

Vega picked up a crustacean and broke it apart with her hands. "That's right. Quinn mentioned you have a… What was it, babe? A daily fashion show?"

He'd told her no such thing.

"An advice column," Kendry corrected, her eye twitching.

Matthew took a swig of his beer.

It was Holden who stepped in to smooth his sister-in-law's ruffled feathers. "It's pretty popular, too. Right, Kendry? Don't you have something like five million followers?"

Kendry preened. "Eight and a half as of last week."

Vega was still chewing when she asked, "What kind of advice?"

"The kind that helps people."

"Hmm." All conversation paused for an awkward moment while Vega scooped out the last bits of meat from her crustacean with her fingers and sucked them clean. "God, I love these things." She picked up the second one and twisted in Quinn's lap to offer it to him, hazel eyes dancing with teasing humor. "Want a bite?"

Quinn's stomach roiled. "Thanks, I'm full."

Kendry got a nasty smirk watching her. "Do you know what that is you're eating?"

"I do! I ran into one of the cooks. He said it's a local delicacy."

"Yes," Kendry confirmed, clearly enjoying herself. "It's an oversized insect native to Ela."

"Kendry, come on," Holden tried.

His sister-in-law kept going. "They're the jungle's garbage disposal system. They break down rotting carcasses—by eating them. I understand it's their mating season now."

Vega paused for effect, then shrugged and dug into her second helping.

Quinn was learning to appreciate her compartmentalization skills. She liked the bugs. It didn't bother her what they were or where they came from. There was a kind of nobility in her acceptance that was sorely lacking in much of his snobbish family. For no other reason than to distinguish himself from them and aspire to be more like Vega, Quinn decided he would give those things another taste.

Later. When the memory of them swarming by the hundreds up a massive tree trunk no longer made his skin crawl.

Denied the spectacle of disgust she'd been fishing for, Kendry's face went bright red.

Finally, Matthew decided to step in before she detonated. "We were just telling Quinn about the ride we're taking on Emmett's boat later."

"He turned us down," Holden said.

"Emmett will be there," Quinn supplied.

"Oh."

Kendry rolled her eyes. "He's still sulking over last night. Men are so emotional, aren't they? But you didn't take offense over Emmett's comments, and that's what matters, isn't it? Can't you persuade your husband to be the…bigger man? For the family's sake."

Quinn could have happily snapped the harpy's neck.

Vega twisted in his lap to look at him, all innocence and concern, but her eyes were Shadow-sharp. "Well, if he doesn't want to go…"

"I really don't," Quinn gritted out.

She tilted her head a little. "What *do* you want to do?"

"We have a schedule of activities all planned out," Kendry informed them.

Ignoring her, Vega prompted, "Quinn?"

He wanted to find a secluded spot and spend the day reading with Vega tucked against him, sharpening her knives. Just one day to relax and not think about his family, Vega's nightmares, or the Shadows lurking nearby.

"Mrs. VanWarren."

Quinn flinched. The attendants were so quiet they kept sneaking up on him when he wasn't looking.

"Yes?" Kendry snapped.

"Apologies," the attendant said with a bow. "Mrs. *Vega* VanWarren."

Vega smiled at the man. "That's me."

He smiled back. "We received notification of packages being held for you at the post depot in Port Cain. They require authorization for pickup. One of our drivers is standing by to fetch them for you. We only need your ID scan."

"Well, I know what I'm doing today. You want to go with me to check out Port Cain?"

Quinn would swim there if it got him away from Kendry. "Sure, why not?"

Vega graced him with a sunny smile. "Larkin, could you please ask the garage attendant to prepare our HOVR? We'll be leaving within the hour."

"Right away, ma'am."

Holden frowned. "How do you know his name?"

She shrugged. "I asked." As simple as the concept was, Quinn could tell by the look his brothers and sister-in-law exchanged that it was totally foreign to all three of them. He made a mental note to ask the name of every uniformed attendant who crossed his path.

Kendry traced the rim of her champagne glass, producing an even tone. "I see you're not shy about spending our money."

Enough. Time to put the hateful shrew in her place. "It's *my* money," Quinn said, making a show of brushing Vega's long hair aside to kiss her neck. "And, just so we're all perfectly clear, I already named Vega as my sole beneficiary."

"*WHAT?!*" Kendry screeched as Matthew choked on his beer, and Holden paled.

12

"That was smart," Vega said as the HOVR raised off the ground and set course for Port Cain.

"Thanks."

"I was being sarcastic."

"I wasn't. I thought it was a brilliant idea. Now, if they want to get their money back, they can't just kill me. They'll have to get rid of you first."

"Or torture you until you sign the estate back over to them."

He winced. "I didn't think of that."

"At least you had the good sense not to strand yourself alone on a boat with any of them."

"Well, yeah. I'm not a total idiot."

Vega sighed.

Quinn's announcement, whether true or not, had made their situation a lot more complicated. Last night, the VanWarren family had been in a stable holding pattern, willing to give the beast a chance and themselves an opportunity to come to a non-violent resolution. Now, even the least concerned relatives would be frothing at the mouth to secure their own standing. The uncertainty might force them to take desperate measures sooner rather than later. And, with so many of them under one roof, Vega would have a hell of a time predicting where the attack came from.

"What are we picking up in Port Cain?"

"A few friends."

The ride only took ten minutes. They touched down in the harbor parking lot and left the HOVR in the care of another VanWarren family attendant named Jackie.

Port Cain was a metropolis by Ela's standards. From the air, the five-street province sprawled over about seven square miles along the coast. The marina took up at least half of that, with a main thoroughfare stretching alongside, lined with posh shops, restaurants, and other establishments. Vega's com cuff had voiceless navigation, making the bracelet vibrate in various patterns to indicate where she had to turn.

At the first intersection, Quinn took her hand in his, exerting enough pressure to get her attention. "Do you want to do some sightseeing while we're here?"

Vega forced a little more leisure into her driving march. No telling who might be watching and reporting back to the family. "I did see ads for guided wilderness tours in the marina."

Quinn made a face, and she laughed. He was definitely not the intrepid explorer type.

"Maybe we can just take a walk down the peninsula," she offered.

"That, I can do."

As it was everywhere else, the post depot was fully automated to eliminate human error. The counter only had an ID scanner and a touch screen.

Vega scanned her chip. The screen listed four packages with their points of origin and asked for confirmation. When she tapped the button to add her digital signature, the screen went blank, and a conveyor belt activated over the counter, bringing her packages from a different, inaccessible part of the facility. Vega took two, Quinn the other two, and off they went.

"I was expecting something bigger," Quinn said as they strolled down the paved path toward a seating area.

"Didn't anyone teach you size doesn't matter?"

"Yeah," he muttered, "that one's a lie."

Quinn's self-esteem issues raised her hackles in a bad way. She stopped him in the middle of the path, took one of his big hands, and pressed her palm to his. Her narrow fingers were on the longer side yet still utterly dwarfed by Quinn's. "See this?"

"The grotesque difference in proportions? Yeah."

"Grotesque difference, maybe, but not because of proportions. That hand"—she nudged against his palm—"can rock a baby to sleep. This one"—she turned her hand palm up in his—"has spilled more blood than I care to acknowledge." Vega twined her fingers with his and squeezed as tight as she could. "Size *doesn't* matter. Actions do. The way people look at you is a reflection on them, not you."

Quinn's jaw went tight enough to twitch, but he did move himself to nod. Vega doubted her little speech made a difference to his frame of mind but, unsure of what else to do, she let it drop.

At high noon, most of the town's visitors were holed up in temperature-controlled restaurants. The peninsula had no tree cover to obscure its water views, which also meant no respite from the heat of the sun. They had it all to themselves.

Vega sat on the farthest bench and tore open the first box.

"At least introduce me to your friends."

She took out a small black device and held it in the middle of her palm. It had a flat bottom and a slightly rounded top. It looked like a pointless piece of neomodern chachki with no markings or discernible seams. Vega presented it to Quinn. "Meet Monty."

Quinn took it from her and gingerly held it up to the light. The device was tiny in his grasp. "What's it stand for?"

"It's not an acronym. The model is called Monterey 45-G15. I call it Monty for short."

"Is it gonna explode?"

She grinned and took it back. "No. It's a privacy net. You twist it like so, and when the blue light blinks, it means it's blocking any surveillance devices from spying within a set perimeter. Won't work on true Shadow gear, but it's highly effective against pretty much anything else." The light only blinked once. Anything more than that would draw too much attention. She left it activated and set it down on the bench between them.

The second box was no bigger than the first. "Duo," she introduced, pulling out a square about half the size of Monty and a flat disc about a quarter-inch in diameter. "The sensor goes above the door. The relay sticks to your skin. When the door opens, the relay heats up to let you know your perimeter's been breached." She planned to slap the sensor over their suite door the second they got back. As nice as most of the family attendants were, Vega didn't trust any of them, or the VanWarrens themselves, to keep their noses out of her and Quinn's business.

Slipping the devices into her dress pocket, she motioned for the boxes in Quinn's lap.

"Where did you get all this stuff?"

"Lox-N-Moore," she said. "Your run-of-the-mill personal security gadget marketplace. I put in an order from the shuttle."

Vega would love to get her hands on some proper Shadow gear. They still had caches scattered on every inhabited world, with gear and rations for Hawks who ran into trouble while on assignment. Finding one would be easy—she'd memorized all the locations during her Shadow training. Getting in, not so much. They were bio-locked to Hawks. Even if Vega hadn't yet been flagged in the system as AWOL or KIA, her former rank of Hound would set off alarms and paint a target on her back.

She opened the third box and pulled out a baggie full of crystal coins. "Minions. Programmable spybots. They network together and sync up with any personal com. You tell them what to look for and listen for, scatter them in strategic locations, and they do the dirty work for you." They had built-in algorithms to compile everything matching user-set criteria into one daily report. But there was also a hidden feature that would alert the user immediately in certain cases.

Quinn whistled. "Won't Monty mess them up?"

"Out here, it would. That's why you only use these indoors. Monty detects walls to frame its boundaries. It'll only work inside our room. Any place outside of it—hallway, closet, bathroom—will be unaffected."

He held up the largest box. "And this?"

Vega checked a grin. "Open it."

The look he gave her said he expected it to blow up in his face, but he did open the box long enough to look inside. And then he slammed it shut again.

Vega laughed. "You should see your face right now."

"What the hell, woman?"

"You have very nosy relatives. If we came back empty-handed, they'd ask too many questions."

"So instead, we'll go back with a box full of sex toys?"

"And edible lingerie—for both of us." Plus some discreet canisters of substances that could induce mild drowsiness, uncontrollable itching, severe nausea, or a slew of other symptoms, up to and including death, depending on the dosage. But he didn't need to know that.

Quinn went beet red, and she knew he was trying not to picture all the things they could do with that box. There were so many options. And Quinn's reaction all but confirmed he would enjoy exploring all of them.

Vega would love nothing better, even if the thought stabbed anxiety through her belly. Sex for her wasn't the same as it was for someone like Quinn. She'd never done the long foreplay and drowsy cuddles thing. The lovers she'd taken in the past had had one purpose and one only: to fuck the darkness out of her and wear her out enough to sleep through a night without dreams.

It had worked, too. For the most part.

But it wouldn't do for Quinn. He was a romantic who fantasized about the kind of wedding dress his bride would wear, for fuck's sake. A hard ride and a kiss goodbye would never be enough for someone like him. Quinn would want the long foreplay and the afterglow cuddles.

And, for the first time in her life, Vega wasn't opposed to the idea. She could take her time with him, let him explore every inch of her before she put him on his back and drove him beyond the threshold of his self-control. She wanted him out of his mind for her until he fucked her with everything he had. Nothing less would do. Nothing less would convince Quinn that she could take whatever he dished out. Vega liked her pleasure spiced with a little pain.

"Considering our audience, I'm pretty sure this will lead to more questions, not less."

It was a hard crash landing back to reality. This wasn't a honeymoon, and Vega wasn't a doe-eyed young bride. All of it was just an act for his family's benefit. No matter how easy it was to pretend otherwise while they were on public display, in private, she still had a job to do.

There was a reason why Quinn had picked her to be his bodyguard.

"Speaking of questions, you asked me one yesterday about how I ended up with the Shadows. You deserve an answer."

Quinn instantly put down the box and turned to sit sideways so he could face her.

The weight of his focus made her want to be anywhere but there. She picked up Monty to keep her hands busy. It didn't make the words any easier to say. "I was a junkie. I was…bored, I guess. Stupid for sure. Tried Bliss at a party one time, and that was it. My senior year of high school became a blur of hallucinations and hard, *hard* crashes afterward. One day, I woke up, didn't know where I was or how I got there. No money, no drugs, and no way home.

"I, uh, bartered for a ride to the closest city. Payment in advance. He got rough, I fought back… Next thing I know, he's dead, and I'm sitting in a café across from two tough guys in nondescript clothes telling me they can make it all go away. All I had to do was trust them."

"Shadows."

Vega nodded. "Turned out, my ride was their trainee, and I was his test. He got himself killed by a strung-out teenage girl. They couldn't forget him fast enough."

"And the strung-out teenage girl took his place."

"I was shaking so hard they had to help me scan my chip to sign on. They promised to take care of everything—which they did. When we got to the outpost, they showed me my obituary in my hometown's community news. It said I was attacked and killed eighty-seven miles away when I'd never gone farther than the town limits before. They manufactured a body double so my mom would have something to bury. Made sure to bruise it up so much she wouldn't want to look too closely. I actually thought it was for the best."

"Is your mom still alive?"

Vega shook her head. "I ended up back there for an assignment a few years later. Looked her up, but she was gone."

"That's… Shit, I'm sorry."

Anger bloomed like a thunderstorm in her chest. "Goddammit, I just told you I ended my childhood as a drug addict who killed someone. Stop pitying me."

He had the nerve to look offended. "It's called sympathy. Compassion. Look it up."

"It's called pretending I'm something I'm not so you can rationalize what I did."

Quinn rolled his eyes. "Right, I forgot. Big bad Vega, the Shadow Hound. Terrified teenager turned into a brainwashed soldier with a gizmo in her neck that will zap her whenever she steps out of line."

"That 'gizmo' didn't get put in until six months after I joined up with Talon. You want to know all the things I did for the Shadows before the war? Want to know what I did for Talon, all on my own, before he put the leash on me?"

"No," he snapped. "I want to know what you did to make him put the leash on you."

Son of a bitch. He wasn't going to let it go.

"Fine. May, 3038. Talon just brought down the last official shipping hover to ever make it to Karsengale. Crates upon crates of bioengineered meals. Not war rations. Real food. And a hell of a lot of booze. Talon decided to get shitfaced and have himself a party. He gave me a direct order to fetch the entertainment. He heard there was a special kind of telepath outside the region. A true mindfucker, he called her. Was supposed to be able to induce orgasms in people with a thought, and he wanted to test how she'd perform under pressure. She was thirteen years old."

Quinn didn't look away, but he went pale. "What did you do?"

The bitter curl of her lip couldn't even be called a smirk. "I killed her."

Quinn shoved to his feet and turned away from her. He took all of two steps before he rounded on her. "You're a real piece of work, you know that? Think you can manipulate me like the others back there—well, it's not gonna work. I can hear the things you're not saying."

"Then you're hearing what you want to hear."

Quinn wasn't about to let her turn this around on him. "You forget, I lived in Karsengale for years. I know all about Talon and what he's capable of."

Mad was too mild a term to describe him. Like all Shadows, Talon had had his mind wiped multiple times using a brutal method of electromagnetic shocks coupled with a chemical cocktail injected straight into the brain to reorganize neural pathways.

It was a horrifying glimpse into the impermeable Shadow secrecy that had only recently come to light. To make their soldiers wholly compliant with their directive, the Shadows administered these EMC treatments not just once but regularly and as often as necessary, to ensure no one ever asked questions or refused an order.

But something must have gone wrong with Talon or had been wrong from the beginning. The sheer sadistic psychopathy with which he'd taken over the Karsengale region had made even his own men live in fear of him.

"I knew the girl you're talking about, too. Her name was Sandy Eléa Wottkins. And I know she died in her sleep."

"Yeah, because of *me*."

"In defiance of a direct order—from *Talon*. Because the alternative would have been unthinkable."

Vega went toe to toe with him. "Are you listening to yourself? You're seriously trying to justify the murder of a *child*?"

He didn't give her an inch. "Walk me through it, Vega. What really happened that night? Because you were sent to fetch this girl alive. And instead, *she* ended up dying peacefully and painlessly in her bed. And *you* got a torture device embedded in your spine. I'm filling in the blanks here, and I'm thinking Talon didn't send you out there alone."

He waited for her to deny it. She didn't.

"There were more of you, weren't there? Backups in case one of you got cold feet." Hell, knowing Talon, the whole mission might have been a test to see who would obey without question and who needed to be culled from the herd.

No response.

"And you weren't going to just let them take Sandy because, let's face it, *you're not a fucking monster.*"

Vega's face turned an angry red, but she still didn't say a word.

"Which would have left you with an impossible choice. One against an army—sorry, but even you're not that good. So fighting back—out of the question. Running, with or without Sandy… Talon had the whole region locked down and under constant surveillance. Even if you'd managed to take out the backups, he'd have been on you before you reached the next town over. And he wouldn't have stopped at punishing you. He'd have taken it out on Sandy, her family, and everyone else you happened to pass by along the way."

It was what he'd done with everyone who'd decided to stand up to him in the early days. It was how he'd taken control of the region in the first place. No mercy. Comply, or have your entire community wiped off the face of the world.

"So how do you keep a thirteen-year-old from suffering unimaginable torture when you know the second you let her out of your sight, someone else will swoop in to snatch her?"

Vega was so rigid she was quivering. But she still didn't offer one word in argument.

He spelled the answer out for her slowly, enunciating each word with sharp precision. "You use your limited means and short window of opportunity to do the only thing you can do to make one hundred percent sure no one will *ever* get the chance to hurt that innocent little girl."

Had she done anything else, left any quarter, Talon would never have stopped hunting either of them. He would have caught them and retaliated in ways that would have made both of them wish for death over and over again for as long as it amused Talon to hear them scream.

"You gave her mercy and took the punishment upon yourself."

Put in the same impossible situation, Quinn didn't know if he would have had the strength to do it. But he'd seen what Talon and his men did to their human playthings. More than once, he'd helped pick up the pieces of their broken bodies. And, though he mourned for the girl and the life she might have had, Quinn knew in his whirring heart that sparing Sandy the same fate had been the kindest thing Vega could have done.

"Does believing so make it easier for you to cope with—"

"I'm gonna stop you right there because this whole self-flagellation bullshit is already getting old. Whatever you did in the past—I don't care. But, since you seem to need to hear it, I'll say this once. *I—forgive—you.* For all of it. Even if you don't want to forgive yourself. Because, sometimes, all your options suck, and all you can do is choose the one that sucks the least. And that's what you do—every single time. Even when you know you'll end up hurting for it."

She started to speak again and again, he cut her off.

"I don't care! As far as I'm concerned, your past was over the day you decided to put your life on the line for me and mine. You chose to fight alongside us, and you bled your way out. That makes us square. Clean slate. End of story. Or, you know, new beginning. Whatever. You know what I mean."

They faced off for a moment, fraught with pent-up aggression. But, once again, Vega proved his point when she blinked and stepped back. The space she opened between them pulled an exhale out of his lungs, and some of his tension eased. No more fighting, no more arguments. They'd both said their piece.

"Believe what you want," she said without looking at him. "We should get back before someone misses us enough to come looking."

She twisted Monty to turn it off, pocketed the device, and picked up the box full of sex toys.

Quinn gathered the empty ones to drop into a waste disposal chute in town and fell into step with her, heading up the peninsula.

They didn't talk the whole way back to Crescent Island. In fact, they didn't speak at all the entire rest of the day. By chance or by design, the family split them up for different activities, and they didn't see each other again until it was time to call it a night.

Ensconced in their suite, Vega installed the bigger half of Duo over their door, turned on Monty, and got ready for bed. Quinn half expected her to head out to the couch again, but she didn't.

When she tucked herself in on her side, Quinn turned the light down low so he could keep reading without disturbing her. He was too wired to sleep.

He was just starting to get into the story of an undertaker falling in love with the flower shop girl when Vega spoke up. "What are you reading?"

"A collection of short stories with questionable endings."

"Will you read one to me?"

"Why?"

She shrugged against her pillow. "I like the sound of your voice."

Taken aback, Quinn stared at her for a moment, waiting for the punchline.

But all she said was, "Please?"

So Quinn turned the digital pages back to the beginning and started over for her.

14

Day 2

Vega's skin prickled with goosebumps at the same time as her still-half-sleeping mind registered a deep voice murmuring her name. She startled awake to find Quinn standing over her, his big hand hovering a couple of inches above her bare arm.

He pulled back and cleared his throat. "I, uh, didn't want to wake you, but the stupid schedule thing keeps going off. We're being summoned to a picnic lunch on the beach. Dress *semi-casual*, whatever the hell that means."

Vega released her grip on the knife she kept beneath her pillow before she sat up and rubbed her face. "What time is it?"

"Somewhere between breakfast and lunch. Closer to lunch, I'd say."

"Ugh, right. Ela time."

Quinn cocked his head at her. "You okay?"

"Yeah, why?"

"You slept really late, that's all." He gave her a slow, crooked smile. "You also have pillow creases on your cheek."

Vega rubbed her face. It felt too warm to the touch. "I do crash sometimes, you know." On the rare occasion when her body decided to drop her into a near-coma for her own good.

"Any nightmares?"

"Not that I recall. Why are you looking at me like that?"

Quinn opened his mouth to say something, then seemed to change his mind. "No reason. Bathroom's all yours. Meet you down there?"

"We should probably try to keep our entrances and exits synchronized." Vega tossed back the covers and climbed out of bed, stretching her arms up as far as she could. "Just give me a few minutes to wash up."

To which Quinn responded with a baby-voiced, "Big stretch," and put his hands on her waist, lifting her up like she weighed nothing. "See if you can reach the ceiling."

When she brought her hands down and mutely stared at him instead, Quinn flushed, that adorable smile fading in a hurry.

He set her back down and stepped away. "Ah, sorry. Force of habit. The kids in Karsengale used to love it when I picked them up like that."

Vega blinked her brain back online. "Uh, no, that's fine. I just wasn't…expecting… I'll go wash up."

"Yep, I'll wait out here."

Out of habit, she didn't close the bathroom door all the way. She also didn't get in the shower for a good thirty seconds while her mind replayed what just happened at triple speed. When Vega finally got moving, it took her all of three minutes to finish her morning routine and head to the closet for clothes. And all the while, Quinn's handprints warmed her sides as if he was still touching her.

It was an awkward, quiet walk down to the beach.

When they got there, the picnic was well underway. Not on the sand but around formal tables, with two attendants at each one. They served portions of select dishes from heated food tray carts and wine out of chilled glass carafes.

The VanWarrens liked to eat in style, no matter the setting.

"Quinn! Vega!" Cousin Geraldine hopped up from her chair, flipping it over in her enthusiasm. She waved at them, smiling big and bright in welcome, while her table attendant righted her chair. "Over here! I saved you a seat."

Damn. Vega had meant to do some more research on Geraldine last night, but the Minions had been higher in priority. She'd left at least one in every room she'd entered while playing the part of Quinn's wife. She might have looked up the singer this morning, except she'd slept half the day away.

Vega put on an appropriate smile and looped her arm through Quinn's to pull him toward Geraldine's table. "Here we go."

They exchanged big hugs before taking their seats. Vega noted a fourth place setting that already had a half-finished glass of wine but clean plates and no occupant.

"Have I mentioned how glad I am you're here?" Geraldine said. "Ever since Emmett decided to be a jackass at dinner, whenever I try to talk to someone, they look at me like I'm a bug." She mimicked a sour expression and pitched her voice for comedic value. "*Who are you again?*"

Quinn winced. "That bad?"

"Worse. Kendry organized a music festival for tonight. I was supposed to be headlining solo. Now she's making all the musicians do it together. I know their songs. But do they know any of mine? Nope! *Augh!* This is going to be a disaster."

"Can't you just play your tracks?" Vega suggested. "Maybe if it's loud enough, it'll drown out their mistakes."

Geraldine squeaked a little unhappy noise. "I can. I hate it, but I can. I just… This was going to be my chance to show them what I can do, you know? If they saw me perform, they would know that I'm not a hack. Now all they'll see is the family holding my hand up there."

"Speaking of performing, how come you haven't done any concerts yet?" Quinn asked around an attendant filling his plate with a mountain of food.

"My producer refuses to let me do one until I sell two hundred million copies of my album. He says that's a *reasonable benchmark* for an unknown artist."

Vega sampled a strange looking berry off her plate. "Sounds like he wants you to grow your audience."

"Yep."

"So what's the problem?"

Geraldine glared at her. "I'm working on it, okay? I have a coach, a therapist, and a publicist who are all telling me I have to get out there and connect with people if I want my music to sell. Show them my approachable, human side, or whatever."

"You know they're right," Quinn said before sipping his wine. As Vega had instructed, he sniffed it first. She still watched him closely to ensure he had no adverse reactions.

Geraldine downed her wine and lifted her glass at the attendant for a refill. "Yeah, Zach said the same thing. *And* he gave me a lecture about not using my name on the album. So we can skip right over that part of the debate."

"Out of curiosity," Vega said, "why aren't you using your name on the album?"

"Because dashies never last. I want to get famous because of what I can do, not who I am. I want people to hear my music without the 'VanWarren trash' chorus repeating in the background." She drank down half of her refreshed wine. "I want people to be singing my songs fifty years from now. And not ironically. Can't do that as a VanWarren. Most of us are an expensive joke."

Right as she said it, Aunt Ylva walked past their table on her way back toward the main house. She stopped in her tracks to give Geraldine a look full of hatred from beneath her wide-brimmed sun hat. "And you wonder why none of us bother remembering your name."

"Go stick a cactus up your ass, *Auntie*."

"Okay!" Quinn pried the wine glass out of Geraldine's hand and gave it to the attendant. "I think that's enough happy juice for you. Don't forget, you have a show tonight."

Ylva scoffed. "If we let her."

Geraldine attempted to stand but with Quinn's hand on her shoulder, she wasn't budging an inch.

Ylva smiled. "You'll learn your place. Or we'll teach you. The hard way."

Quinn had to cover Geraldine's mouth to muffle her shrieking tirade. Poor girl was shaking with the force of her rage.

Vega decided she didn't like that so, when Ylva stuck her nose in the air and whirled away to make her dramatic exit, she knocked her fork off the table. "Oops!" She leaned over to pick it up, sticking her foot out into Ylva's path, deciding at the last second to only bruise the older woman's shin, not fracture it.

Ylva squawked and went down face-first into the sand. Her big hat sailed into the air like a white flag of defeat.

The table attendants sprang into action immediately. One rushed to Ylva's side to assist her back to her feet. The other chased after the stupid hat, which was so aerodynamic the breeze sent it out to sea before the poor woman could catch it. She ended up wading thigh-deep into the water to retrieve the thing.

"I am so sorry!" Vega gushed. "I can't believe I did that. Are you okay?"

Ylva spat out gobs of black sand. A layer of it was crusted over her face, and when she huffed, it came out of her nose like smoke. "Y-you stupid, gold-digging mongrel bitch!"

Vega gave her a vicious little grin. "Woof."

Ylva shook off the attendant and took one step toward Vega, her fingers curling into claws.

"Careful," Vega warned, "I bite."

It was enough to make Ylva hesitate for a beat. Enough for her to realize she wasn't dealing with another hothead like Geraldine. She looked at Quinn and Geraldine, both of whom had gone suspiciously quiet, then made a show of brushing sand off her skirts. "This isn't over," she said before flouncing off in a huff.

Vega straightened in her seat and forked a piece of fruit into her mouth. Around the bite, she said to Geraldine, "You do understand you'll still need to put yourself in the spotlight to get your music out there. And it'll be ten times harder without using your VanWarren notoriety."

Geraldine and Quinn both stared at her, shocked into silence.

Then Geraldine snorted and burst into laughter so loud that even the handful of VanWarrens who weren't already staring in their direction turned to look.

When Quinn shook his head at her, valiantly fighting a smile, Vega shrugged and kept eating.

Not like she hadn't warned him well ahead of time.

The afternoon transitioned smoothly from lunch at the beach to the newly erected concert venue on the back lawn. A large stage had been set up facing the house so those who didn't want to sit outside after the sun went down could comfortably enjoy the show from one of the rooms facing that direction.

It turned out that the family boasted several musicians aside from Geraldine.

Cousin Andras played bass guitar in a small indie band. The teenage twins Jek and Juni were drummers who'd brought their drum sets to the reunion. Aunt Amanda was a classical cello player, and her daughter, Cousin Maya, played electric violin.

As they went over their respective repertoires, the scheduled playlist was updated every five minutes on the night's program.

Not that anyone else cared.

The family had split up into cliques. The elders were ensconced in the parlor, lounging on cushioned couches, enjoying a selection of expensive liquor and finger foods, and trash-talking their latest target.

The rest of the adults were scattered across the lawn, circled around flameless firepits that kept the insects at bay. They nursed fruity cocktails and laughed loudly at the latest inappropriate joke. The few who weren't drinking appeared to have deep conversations going on that involved covert looks being shot Vega's way.

Quinn knew she was aware of those looks, but you wouldn't know it to look at her. She was busy talking to Aunt Amanda and Cousin Maya about how different it was to be part of a classical orchestra versus a neomodern one.

As for Quinn, after he'd made it clear to Uncle Trent earlier that he would not be discussing the Aunt Ylva incident or "talking to his wife" about it, no one else broached the subject to him again.

None of them came to talk to him at all. Which was perfectly fine with Quinn. He was happy to just hang around Vega and listen in on her conversation with the two musicians while watching the kids run around with their light-up toys.

But the lower the sun set, the more he felt everyone's attention arrow toward him and Vega. He could feel them judging him, and he couldn't keep the glower off his face whenever he happened to meet someone's sneering gaze. Their dislike of him stung his nose with a near-palpable scent. He imagined it smelled like burned rubber.

How tragic that, on an island filled with his blood relations, he counted potential friends on one hand. And those were questionable at best.

Maybe it was a fool's errand to try to make them like him. Despite knowing how much they all wanted him out of their hair, Quinn had still come here thinking he could prove them wrong—prove himself worthy. He still believed he could, given enough time.

But was it worth it? Beyond their obvious hatred of him, these people didn't seem to like each other, either. Cousins glared at their aunts and uncles, parents ignored their children, siblings fought against siblings…

There was a great aunt somewhere in the house who was so old she couldn't walk ten steps without assistance. And all Quinn knew about her was that she hated absolutely everyone.

Coming here had been a necessary evil. Staying long-term and continuing to fight the uphill battle into their good graces would be a choice. Quinn hated to admit it but if it hadn't been for Vega, he would have taken care of business yesterday and washed his hands of the whole family. Left them to the Shadows and moved on with his life.

But then he thought of the kids growing up under their constant threat, and he couldn't bring himself to walk away. No child should go through what his chosen family had gone through in Karsengale. No matter how messed up their elders were.

"I thought it was brilliant," Aunt Amanda said beside him. She'd extricated herself from the feminine triad to talk to him.

"Sorry, I wasn't listening. What was brilliant?"

Amanda grinned, her eyes crinkling slightly at the outer edges. "The way Vega handled Ylva. I was at the next table over, and let me tell you, I will treasure the sight of Ylva eating dirt for the rest of my life." Her irises didn't quite match. One was darker than the other. But both twinkled with mischief as she said it.

"I knew there was a reason I liked you."

Amanda chuckled. "Excellent. That'll make talking to you about funding my music program a lot easier."

Quinn's heart sank. Of course. Of course, the only reason a VanWarren would voluntarily strike up a conversation with him was money.

Something of his inner thoughts must have shown on his face because Amanda immediately backpedaled. "Oh, shit, that didn't come out right. I'm sorry. I was kidding. Well, half kidding. I mean, I do have a music program I wanted to talk to you about, but not right now. I—"

"It's fine."

"No, it's not. I swear, I'm not like the others. I just don't always think before I speak. Can we start over?"

Up on the stage, Andras plucked a string on his guitar for sound check.

"I think you're needed up there. We can talk another time."

"Oh, but I…"

Quinn walked away in search of a drink to wash the bad taste from his mouth.

"Will you be gracing us with a song, too, Cousin?"

Quinn had no idea who'd tossed the question at him. Every man around that particular firepit looked identical in the dusk.

"We can find you a bow tie and a unicycle if you want. Maybe some cymbals?"

Before he could formulate a response, the group did for him, cackling at his expense. He didn't know if it was their slightly pointed canines or the flickering light of the flameless firepit, but Quinn got a distinctly demonic vibe from them.

He moved on in a hurry.

At the bar, he ladled himself a cup full of spiked punch.

Vega took it out of his hand. "They'll be shitting their guts out by tomorrow morning," she murmured around the rim, then took a big gulp.

Quinn stared at her. "What?"

"The giggle boys," she clarified, tilting her head the slightest bit toward the demons still laughing at their own joke. "They'll get theirs."

"What did you do?"

She fluttered her eyelashes at him. "I don't know what you mean."

"Vega."

"Quinn?"

He had no follow-up, and she knew it. But she still waited, gazing up at him oh-so-innocently as she returned his drink. He curled his hand around hers on the glass. "Try not to kill anyone, wife."

She raised up on tiptoe, and Quinn leaned in so she wouldn't have to stretch too far. "No promises, husband," she whispered at his ear but when her lips brushed his cheek, it felt like one.

The musicians struck a chord, and all eyes turned toward the stage. They cheered not out of excitement but exasperation.

"Finally! They took their damn time," someone complained.

"Better be worth the wait," someone else muttered.

"Can't wait to see how the chit butchers Andras' set."

Quinn honestly didn't know why they'd bothered to show up to this, other than Kendry making it mandatory and there being no other live entertainment available on the island.

Geraldine took a seat at the keyboard they'd set up front and center. A spotlight found her immediately, and she squinted against its glare, even as she smiled at her audience. "VanWarren clan, make some noise!"

Vega whistled and shouted in support, which got a bit of applause from the others but not much.

"We'll work on that," Geraldine said to herself, but she happened to be angled toward her mic, and her voice amplified to fill the night. Quinn could see her cheeks heating with embarrassment from a distance and winced in sympathy.

But then she counted off, and the music began, and no one cared anymore. The song was one of Andras' compositions and clearly a popular one, given how the atmosphere changed with the first few notes. People even got up to dance, and a small crowd formed at the base of the stage, bobbing and swaying to the rhythm.

Quinn wasn't much of a dancer, but he did love music, and Geraldine had a sweet, lilting voice. Coupled with the classical string accompaniment, it added depth and character to what would otherwise be a hard-driving, cold beat.

By the time the first song ended, the crowd had warmed up to them considerably.

Three more songs followed: one from Maya's collection, a classical song with a new age twist, and one from Geraldine's new album. After that, Geraldine paused so the musicians could drink some water and set up for the next set. Quinn was about to go over to congratulate Geraldine on what was shaping up to be a huge success for her, but someone else beat him to it. Quinn recognized the guy from dinner their first night. Vega's valiant defender.

Tonight, he seemed to be totally enamored with Geraldine, talking at her with animated hand gestures and making her laugh with delight. She nodded to something he said, and then he stepped away to let her get back to it, but his eyes never left the stage.

"He knows they're related, right?" Quinn said in an aside to Vega, assuming she was seeing the same thing.

"Zach? I would assume so. Although I doubt it matters all that much in his case."

"How do you mean?"

"I'll tell you later."

Geraldine was back in her place, and Andras was plucking strings on his guitar to tune it while she fiddled with the settings on her keyboard. "This next song is very special to me," she said, adjusting her mic. "I was waiting for the right time to debut it, and I think tonight is perfect. We have some new faces among us, someone who has been lost to the family for a long time. Quinn, I know it hasn't been easy for you, and I'm so sorry that none of us could be there to stand up with you and Vega at your wedding. I know it's probably too little too late, but I'd still like to dedicate this next song to you both. Maybe you can have your first dance again, among family this time." She smiled at him and Vega with so much warmth Quinn's throat went a little tight. "Let's clear a little room on the dance floor. Ladies and gentlemen, for the first time among us, please give a warm welcome to Mr. and Mrs. Quinn VanWarren!"

The crowd parted, clapping for the sake of appearance, but it was clear most of them were humoring Geraldine to keep things polite.

It left Quinn no choice but to go along with it and put on a show.

Might as well make it a good one.

He bowed at the waist and offered Vega his hand. "Shall we?"

Vega didn't hesitate, playing her part to perfection with a gentle smile and happy tears glistening in her eyes. "Do let's."

He led her out onto the lawn and took his place in the half-circle of space the family had opened for them. "I hope you're quick on your feet. Wouldn't want you to lose any toes."

"You just keep time, and I'll follow along," she quipped back.

Geraldine struck up a soft, slow melody, and Quinn moved. His first steps were wooden and awkward. Every time he took one, he thought he'd step on Vega. But she flowed with him, effortlessly following his lead as if they'd practiced it.

"It was a sweet gesture," she said before moving away into a spin.

Quinn pulled her back into his arms. "Yeah. I just wish she'd told us beforehand. Also, that we weren't the only ones dancing."

"Oh, I don't mind. The best time to study your enemy is when they're too busy watching your every move."

"That doesn't even make sense."

Vega grinned, giving the impression that he'd said something romantic. "Doesn't it?" She pulled in closer to him. "Look over my shoulder."

He did. "What am I looking for?"

"Do you see Ylva talking to Trent?"

Sure enough, there they were at the edge of the crowd. Ylva looked heated, gesturing angrily at Quinn and Vega. Then Trent cut her off with a short burst of words spoken through tight lips.

Quinn spun Vega again and danced them into a turn, losing sight of Ylva and Trent for a few seconds. When they came back around, Emmett had taken Ylva's place, a glass of liquor in his hand as he spoke to Trent, who was now rubbing his forehead. Ylva had stomped off back into the house.

"What was that about?"

"If I had to guess, I'd say Ylva is trying to recruit other family members into her scheme to get rid of you," Vega said. "Doesn't look like it worked with Trent."

"Guess we can cross him off our list of suspects."

"You're adorable." That didn't sound like a compliment.

He changed the subject. "What do you think of Zach and Geraldine?" They would make a cute couple if it weren't for the shared DNA. They were both equally untouched by the general bitterness of the VanWarren horde.

"Haven't decided yet."

"You're not jealous, are you?"

Vega blinked at him. "Of what?"

The song ended, and the crowd cheered—for Geraldine more than Quinn and Vega. They swarmed back, closing the open space, and the concert atmosphere ramped up with another hard-driving song from Andras' collection. Between half-hearted congratulations tossed their way and a few shoving pats on the back, the relative privacy of their dance disappeared.

Quinn had to lean over and speak directly into Vega's ear to make himself heard. "Thank you for the dance." It was on the tip of his tongue to ask for another, but Vega squeezed his shoulder to stop him.

"I'm going after Ylva," she said. "Stay close to the stage, and don't eat or drink anything until I get back."

Then she slipped out of his arms and disappeared, blending into the shadows like a ghost.

Like hell.

Quinn pushed through the dancers toward the main house, fully aware that he was about to make a royal ass of himself. He didn't care. Ylva was dangerous, and she'd already threatened Vega once.

At the very least, he wanted to be there to see the woman get her ass handed to her.

The elder VanWarrens were still lounging along the couches, unbothered by the concert outside. Quinn spied a quick flash of movement through the door and went after it, coming out to the hallway in time to see Vega silently mount the last three stairs in one leap and disappear out of sight again.

He was nowhere near as silent. If he raced up there the way she had, the whole damn house would probably shake. Better to pace himself and not attract attention. Head down, watching the carpet runner beneath his feet, he picked his steps to make as little noise as possible. He almost ran into someone on the second-floor landing.

Someone standing with her feet perfectly aligned at the edge of the top step.

Uh oh.

Quinn was already wincing when he dragged his gaze up to meet Vega's glare. "Missed you?" he offered with a shrug.

She rolled her eyes at him, then signaled for silence before tapping the inside of her left elbow where she'd attached the smaller part of Duo. By the time Quinn caught on that the device had alerted her to their suite door being opened, she was already at it, hand on the ornate handle to keep it from opening wider as she pressed her ear to the gap.

Quinn came up behind her, but if any sounds were coming from their suite, he couldn't hear them. Vega was all business, tense and loose in a way that seemed physically impossible. He gave her plenty of room to move, but even with three feet of space between them, he felt her as if she was pressed against him. He smelled the spicy scent of the shampoo she preferred and wished he could bury his nose in the generous fall of her hair.

Then she cocked her head, and his brain belatedly processed the sound of feminine rage inside their suite. Whatever Ylva was up to didn't sound like it was going well.

But then there was a gasp, and Vega pushed through the door with, "Hey, Autie!"

Quinn bit back a curse and followed to find Ylva by their bed with one of Vega's knives in her hand.

"What the hell is this?"

"Well, it looks like a gross invasion of privacy to me," Vega said, her tone unbothered.

"How dare you bring a weapon into our home!"

Vega shifted forward one step.

And Ylva screamed, shielding her face with one arm while slashing the knife through the air between them. *"Help! Help! She's trying to kill me!"*

In three seconds flat, Vega relieved Ylva of the knife and pinned her to the wall by her throat, cutting off the screams. "That'll be enough of that."

Ylva clawed at Vega's hand. She could still breathe, but her voice was no more than a croak when she cast a desperate look at Quinn and pleaded, "Help…"

With the music blaring and most of the compound residents outside to enjoy it, no one would have heard her screams. Still, just to make a point, Quinn turned toward the door and softly clicked it shut, taking a casual lean against it for good measure. The look of sheer terror on Ylva's face might have elicited sympathy at one time. But that was before she'd had her incompetent daughter put poison in Quinn's food.

Vega traced Ylva's jaw with the tip of her knife. "Tell me, Auntie, do you enjoy having a pulse? Feels good, doesn't it? The thump of your heart in your chest. The rush of blood in your veins. The stretch of your ribs when you take a nice, big breath of fresh air…"

Ylva whimpered, her hands falling down at her sides. She was shaking in Vega's grip.

"Personally, I love it. And so does my husband."

Ylva gasped and didn't breathe out, her eyes going wide.

"Isn't that right, husband?"

Quinn grunted in response. What did she expect him to say?

A shuddering exhale from Ylva prompted another quick squeak of a breath.

"You had one shot and missed. You don't get another," Vega told her. Soft and gentle. But each word she spoke was a threat. "Do you understand what I'm telling you?"

Tears streaked down Ylva's face as she jerked her head up and down.

"So you'll be gone by morning. Yes?"

Another jerky nod.

"Good. That's very good. I'm going to let you go now, and you'll go back to your rooms and start packing. And you won't tell anyone about our little chat, will you?"

Ylva twitched her head sideways with a sob.

"No, you won't. Because you have a number of soft spots I could aim for. Your widowed sister-in-law, for example. Or one of her three beautiful little children. Or that sweet, curvy neighbor, who I hear comes over for *tea* at your place every single day when your husband is out. And, Auntie, please believe me when I say… *I never miss.*"

Even Quinn was starting to get uncomfortable now.

Vega stared Ylva down for a full thirty seconds. "It's good to have a pulse, isn't it?"

By the time she slowly released the woman, Ylva looked shell-shocked.

Quinn pushed away from the door, but not fast enough to avoid Ylva barreling past him.

"Don't forget to smile," Vega called after her, and Ylva froze by the door, wiping her face with shaking hands and squaring her shoulders before she walked out.

"You think she'll really leave by morning?"

No response.

Quinn turned back to find Vega staring at their bed. "Vega?"

"Pillows are wet," she murmured.

"What?"

"No, Ylva won't leave. Not until she sees us alive at breakfast."

Quinn's heart sank to his heels, leaving a cold, heavy void in the middle of his chest. "What did she do?"

"Stupid, amateur bitch." Vega turned to him, face hard, eyes burning, but her grip on the knife remained loose, and she kept her voice even when she said, "I'm going to need you to make a choice. It will have consequences."

The pillows were wet.

And a professional assassin was asking him to make a choice.

Quinn couldn't think. Vega wouldn't need more than a nod or a gesture. If he indicated his permission in any way, she wouldn't question it for a second. She would do whatever it took to eliminate the threat—one that, it appeared, would not be going away on its own. And she wouldn't lose a minute of sleep over it.

But Quinn would.

"I can't… I want her gone. Not dead."

Vega nodded. She yanked the blanket off the foot of the bed and threw it over the pillows before she picked them up and dumped the whole bundle into the shower. A couple of minutes later, she'd doused it all in some expensive liquor from the sitting room bar and lit it on fire with one of the scented candles. The security system doused it almost immediately, using the built-in air conditioning vents to suck out the toxic fumes, and both of their estate discs wailed with an alert to let them know that security was on their way up.

"Tell them we got a little carried away with the candles," Vega said, tossing the half-empty bottle onto the bed and handing him the candle. "Have them strip the bed completely and replace everything, even the mattress. The water will have diluted whatever Ylva dumped on the pillows, so they'll be safe for the staff to handle. The shower will clean itself of any leftover residue—but wait for the cycle to finish before you get into it."

She stashed her knife back into its usual spot in her nightstand drawer, then headed out the door.

"Where are you going?"

"To make sure Ylva doesn't miss her flight."

He didn't ask any more questions as a small army of attendants rushed in following her exit.

The bed was replaced, and the entire suite was cleaned and restored to order within the hour.

And Quinn knew with absolute certainty that Ylva would not be joining them at breakfast the next morning.

16

The inn swarmed with panicked civilians as her Shadow team swept through. Vega tuned out the noise, listening for status updates.

She was inside.

That wasn't right; she was supposed to be out on the street to head off anyone who ran.

The quaint interior she'd seen on the inn's business page was a scene from hell. Flickering lights threw everything into shadow. Figures clashed and ran in flashes of terrified faces and echoing wails—but they were only ghosts.

The carpet depressed into thick wetness beneath her bare feet, and Vega sank ankle-deep into blood. She looked down at herself and saw nothing—she herself no more than a spirit. But she felt her nakedness as a disconcerting absence of her uniform and her arsenal of weapons.

Vega shuddered.

Thud.

Talon's voice crackled through her com piece. "Whatever it takes, understand?"

Thud.

Yes. She had a mission. Bring back the Belden bi—

"Bring me back the big one."

Thud.

What was that noise?

Thud.

"Whatever it takes..."

The light pouring in from the front door only reached halfway up the stairs.

Thud.

Civilians, Shadows—all the ghosts shrank away into silence as a heavy foot dropped onto a stair above the light.

Thud.

The other emerged out of the darkness to the next stair below.

Thud.

Thud.

Thud…

Step by step, Quinn descended the stairs, and step by step, Vega sank a little deeper into the blood. He was so tall, but his face was ashen. Sweat sheened his skin, and his mouth was pressed into a tight, angry line. But his eyes… Sunken deep beneath the shadow of his brows, they stared at her with pure hatred.

Vega wanted to run.

"I own you," Talon whispered in her ear, and a shiver of a spasm raced down her spine.

Vega clenched her teeth against the pain she knew she would feel if she disobeyed.

But this was Quinn.

Thud.

He stepped down off the last stair, towering over her, his breath sawing in and out in such ragged pants Vega felt her chest constrict. She clenched her hands into fists, and her fingers curled around the handle of a knife.

"Disobeying a direct order from your commanding officer is a corporal offense."

The device on her spine activated, sending Vega into a tense, full-body shudder, but without any pain. She reversed her grip on the knife.

"Bring him to me!"

Quinn heard the voice, too. His lips pulled back in a vicious snarl.

Another painless zap twitched through her, and her knife arm came up of its own volition. No! She stopped the blade's descent. Talon might own her, but he didn't control her.

But the blade demanded blood and would not go down without it.

Vega fought it with everything she had, even when a stronger zap arched her back and locked her knees.

She couldn't lower the blade.

So she turned it on herself.

As soon as the painless charge released her, the blade took over, forcing its way down toward her chest.

Quinn's massive hand wrapped around her wrist, stopping her. The blade screamed, but it was powerless against Quinn's massive strength. He pried it from her grip so easily, and Vega was relieved.

Until he turned it on himself. With a merciless flex of his arm, he buried the blade in his chest and yanked it down, then reached in and pulled out his heart.

He proffered the still-beating organ to her without a flinch as blood poured from the gaping wound in his torso.

More of it dripped from his lips as he growled, "Now we're even."

Talon screamed his rage through the static of her com, and the device on her spine delivered another bone-wrenching charge.

This time, she felt it…

~

Day 3

Vega yelped as she bolted upright in bed, hunching over to somehow shield the rest of her body from the thing in the back of her neck. The memory of pain shuddered through her limbs as her fingers and toes zinged with the unpleasant sensation of an oncoming storm of cramps.

She breathed through it, breathed herself back under control. Just a nightmare.

Recalling where she was and with whom, Vega glanced over to Quinn's side of the bed. He wouldn't like the repeat performance. One time was bad enough. When he learned her nightmares came almost nightly, he—

He was gone.

The covers went flying as she surged to her feet. "*Quinn!*"

Something dropped in the bathroom, and then he was there, all the way naked and all the way wet, with foamy suds dripping down his forehead. "What? What happened?"

For a few seconds, her brain misfired, and she couldn't answer.

Vega didn't have a poetic bone in her body, but Quinn was a god-damn work of art. And there was so very *much* of him. It didn't take more than a glance for her eidetic memory to map out a scene, and he was giving her a lifetime's worth of memories in under two minutes. A reckless thought occurred to her. If she licked him from head to toe, there was enough moisture clinging to his skin to quench her thirst and then some.

Vega closed her dry mouth and sat down hard on the edge of the bed.

Quinn reached over sideways to snatch a towel and wiped the suds off his face before they got into his eyes. Vega became transfixed by the play of his muscles as he wrapped the cloth around his waist and came to her, big hands reaching out in what she understood on some level to be concern, but her brain still fell like a halfway-cooked egg, and it anticipated an entirely different scenario. And *son of a bitch*, she froze halfway between kicking him away and tumbling him onto the mattress beneath her.

Then she saw his face and the sharp focus in his eyes quickly put a damper on both. He folded those big hands over her shoulders, brushing her long hair back. She heard the snap of a static spark, but Quinn showed no reaction to its bite. "You okay?"

Vega squeezed her eyes shut and dug the heels of her palms into the sockets. *Get a fucking grip!*

"Hey, stop that." Quinn pulled her hands away. "Look at me. What do you need?"

No pity. No censure. She had raised an alarm, and he was in action mode. Except it wasn't her brand of, *Tell me whom to shoot.* His had been honed by three years of living in a house full of refugees where people had no choice but to take care of each other or die.

Did he see her as one of those invalids now?

"I need Talon to stop breathing," she growled.

He nodded like he was making a mental To-Do list. "What do you need that I can get you?"

Right now? He could ditch the towel and let her take him for a ride. That would go a long way toward dispelling the tingling numbness in her fingers. Her hands needed something to do, and Quinn looked like a veritable playground of sensory stimulation.

"Vega." He said her name a little softer, a little lower. Like a secret. "It's okay. He's not here. I am. Tell me what you need." He was still holding her hands, his thumbs brushing back and forth across the inside of her wrists, sending her pulse into overdrive.

Could he feel it?

She licked her dry lips, swallowed nothing, and dragged air back into her lungs. *Get it together.* "I'm okay." *Good. Words are good. Now pull your hands free.*

They didn't move. The hypnotic back-and-forth across her skin was slowly restoring feeling back into her fingertips. Even in the heat of another stifling Ela day, Vega's nightmare had left her chilled to the bone. Quinn radiated heat and vitality. She didn't want to lose it.

Pathetic.

One more breath, then she gripped his wrists for a second in reassurance before pulling away. "Where's your com?"

He retrieved it from his nightstand and handed it over without question, his towel-covered crotch directly in her line of sight.

It took her another second to get her head on straight. She activated the device and put in the same settings she'd programmed into hers last night. "I have about half of the main building covered by minions. They're already doing their thing, but it'll take a day or two to map any patterns. For now, I set up SOS locators on our coms. If I'm not with you, say my name three times, and it'll return a location. Works both ways." Pointedly ignoring the loosening fold of his towel, Vega took Quinn by the wrist and secured the com cuff around it. "This is weatherproof. Meaning, you don't take it off, even in the shower. Got it?"

Quinn subjected her to a piercing scrutiny that made Vega want to hide. He stared into her eyes as if he could see inside her mind and pick up on all the things she wasn't saying. She braced herself for another interrogation about her nightmares but, after a moment, Quinn simply nodded. He glanced down at the cuff, then gently twisted his wrist in her hold.

Flushing, Vega released him.

Quinn brought the cuff up, staring her down as he murmured

her name into the device. A second later, the inside of his forearm illuminated with a holographic map and a glowing red dot indicating the location of her com in their suite.

Vega raised her left hand to show him the blinking red light on the com she wore at all times as a matter of course. "You see where I am, I know you're looking for me." She swiped her thumb across the device, and a matching map appeared on her forearm to show Quinn's location.

He was still looking at her as if expecting something more. When she didn't say anything else, he shook out his com arm to deactivate the device, a quicksilver frown flashing across his features. "My brothers want to meet today to discuss the estate."

"Okay."

"It may take a while."

The scar of his heart transplant created a thin, pale line down the center of his chest from the hollow at the base of his neck to his solar plexus. Most of it was obscured by chest hair he hadn't had back on Anamtaigh and practically invisible from a distance, but she could see the endpoints clear as day at close range.

A clean scar, fully healed. No gaping hole. No blood pouring down his torso.

"Vega?"

She blinked. "Hmm?"

Quinn's mouth compressed into a thin line. "Stand up."

When she did, he took her by the elbow and pulled her forward.

Vega hesitated. "What are you doing?"

"Humor me for thirty seconds, okay?"

She took the one step needed to put her toe-to-toe with him, and then, to her utter shock, he did something she could never have anticipated.

Moving slowly and with the utmost care, he folded her against him, his thick arms circling around her tight enough to immobilize but not hurt. His right hand curled into her hip, his left covered the back of her head and pressed her cheek against his chest. Then he hunched over her smaller frame and rested his chin against her crown.

"Erm…"

"Shut up. Thirty seconds. Time it if you have to."

The awkwardness could not be put into words. Vega concentrated on her breathing as his body heat soaked into her skin and made her flush. With her ear to his chest, she heard the whirr of his heart like an efficient little generator tucked inside his rib cage.

After ten seconds—she counted—Vega rolled her shoulders to loosen the stiffness in her spine and relax against him.

After ten more, she tentatively put her arms around him. He didn't make a sound, but she felt him stiffen the slightest bit, and the whirr in his chest raised in pitch.

At thirty seconds, he tilted her head back and his mouth pressed against her forehead in a brief kiss, for all the world as if she was some precious, delicate thing. And for a brain-scrambling instant, Vega almost felt like it.

Then he set her loose and drew back, taking all that delicious heat with him as his gaze searched hers. "You gonna freak out on me?"

Vega slowly shook her head.

"Good," Quinn said, flashing a hint of his strong teeth in a quick-silver grin. "That's called progress."

He returned to his shower, leaving Vega at a loss.

This was not how she'd expected to start her day.

17

Quinn was smiling when he left the suite. The day had barely started, but he felt like he'd already accomplished the impossible, and he wanted to whistle as he strolled down the hallway toward the main staircase.

Progress.

Some guys bragged about the notches on their bedposts. A thousand of them wouldn't compare to the triumph of holding Vega Ortiz in his arms for a full thirty seconds and walking away without a scratch on him. Better, he'd left her flushed and discombobulated. Someone give him a fucking medal.

As far as places of business went, the ground floor office was pretty cozy, with a big window to let in soft light and a wall-to-wall bookcase filled with books that had never been opened. On the other side, a liquor cabinet with glass doors and interior lights showcased bottles of highly expensive vintage booze. And in the middle of the room stood a massive desk with two armchairs for guests and a thronelike seat for the man of the house.

Guess that would be me.

His brothers were already waiting for him. Holden, dressed in casual pants and a button-down shirt, had parked his ass on one corner of the desk. Matthew, wrapped up in a tight black suit and tie, was leaning against the bookcase, swirling a glass of liquor, deep in thought.

"Morning," Quinn said in greeting.

Matthew straightened away from the books.

Holden stood up and offered him a smile. "Morning. Hope we didn't pull you away from anything important."

As a matter of fact...

"Heard you had a bit of fun in your suite last night," Matthew said, downing the contents of his glass in one swallow. "And did you hear Aunt Ylva left? Apparently, she refuses to stay under the same roof with you and your wife. Wonder what that's about."

Quinn shrugged. "If you're expecting me to apologize for Vega, I already told Trent what happened at brunch was on Ylva. My wife has nothing to apologize for."

"I guess it's too much to ask for some people to show a little class."

Quinn grinned. "So we agree it's a good thing Ylva's gone."

Holden coughed to cover up a laugh as Matthew's eye twitched.

"Good. Then we can get down to business. I hear there's a full schedule of activities all planned out. I'd hate for us to miss them."

Matthew took the invitation to go straight for the throat. "What are your plans for the family estate?"

Quinn raised an eyebrow in silent question.

"I mean, aside from breaking all the prescribed rules of inheritance and handing it over to your *wife*."

The eyebrow he'd raised went right back down as something dark and ugly roiled inside him. Quinn felt it bubble up and had to swallow against an insane desire to growl at the man who dared to call himself his brother.

Holden quickly stepped between them, raising his hands. "Okay, we're not here to fight. This is a family matter, and we are all mature adults here. We're going to sit and have a rational talk and *not* say anything stupid." The last part he directed straight at Matthew.

Matthew snorted and dropped into one of the armchairs facing away from them.

Holden gave Quinn a look of silent entreaty.

For his little brother's sake, Quinn rolled his eyes and rounded the desk to take the ridiculous-looking throne chair.

But that was as far as his benevolence stretched. Matthew clearly had no desire to put up even a pretense of goodwill behind closed doors, and if that was how he wanted to play this, Quinn had no problem getting on the same page.

"Before we begin, I want to make something clear to both of you. I have no family here. We may share blood but, let's face it, it's not blood ties keeping the VanWarrens together. The only thing most of you have ever cared about is the money."

"We're not—"

Quinn held up his hand to stop whatever bullshit platitudes Holden was about to deliver. "Spare me. I don't care what lies you've been fed," he said to his little brother, "and I don't care what you let yourself believe all these years," he said to Matthew. "Far as I'm concerned, it's all water under the bridge. We're going to be starting over. From scratch. You're all strangers to me, and you have no idea of the man I grew into. So if the choice ever comes down to Vega or *family*, understand that she *is* family, and that makes her a very easy choice for me."

Matthew's mouth twitched in a grimace of a smirk, his eyes hard and ruthless. "The record shall so reflect."

"Quinn," Holden tried, yet again putting himself into the middle. "You may not see us as family anymore—can't say I blame you—but none of us want to be your enemy."

Of course not. Why would they risk their cushy lives by openly antagonizing him?

"All of us got caught off guard by this. We're just trying to figure out where to go from here."

"Can't imagine what that feels like."

"I wouldn't get too comfortable on your high horse if I were you," Matthew remarked, studying his empty glass as if he could conjure more alcohol into it with the power of his thirst.

Call him paranoid, but that sounded an awful lot like a threat. Come to think of it, Matthew's entire demeanor didn't match up with someone who had any concerns about his life getting turned upside down. Food for thought.

Later.

For now, Quinn activated the glass desk to bring up the family estate financials. Files upon digital files exploded across the surface, organizing themselves into as neat a grid as could be contained on one piece of furniture. It was organized chaos. Quinn had done a great deal of reading since he'd been granted access to this mess. He'd learned quite a bit about the most affluent members of the VanWarren clan but as far as the family name stretched, it would take a year or more to get properly acquainted with all of their portfolios.

Quinn had focused on what should have been the old guard's immediate heirs: children and grandchildren. They were the ones who'd benefitted the most from the estate's resources. They'd received the greatest percentage of financial support from Amundsen and Beatrice, and many of them had continued to exploit his grandparents' goodwill directly or through underhanded means right up until the old guard had put in their notice to life.

"You want to know my plans for the estate?" He was going to clean house in a big way. "Get comfortable. This is going to take a while…"

Quinn knew he had their full attention when the first order of business he brought up wasn't their mother. As the source of all his hardships, they naturally expected him to retaliate against her the hardest. And yes, Holly VanWarren had been the first one Quinn had looked into when he'd begun to dig through the family financials.

But, as it turned out, Holly's parents had already done the dirty work for him. His mother's accounts were no longer connected to the family estate. She did not have a trust fund or inheritance account in her name. The only document in the archives with her name on it was a lengthy non-disclosure agreement containing several provisions for her biological offspring.

On the outside, she was still a VanWarren and benefited from the collective notoriety of the family's publicity. But behind the scenes, Holly VanWarren's financial life was totally cut off from the rest of the family. Whatever money she had, she'd made all on her own through business ventures or divorce settlements.

It was unclear whether his brothers were aware of this.

Truth be told, Quinn was relieved.

Despite everything, Holly VanWarren was still the woman who'd given him life, fucked up as it was. If she hadn't kicked him out, he never would have met Laura and the others. He never would have become the man he was today. Quinn couldn't change his parentage, but he could choose to be better.

And if pretending indifference and ignoring his mother's existence caused her and the others to wonder and stress for the rest of their lives, waiting for the other shoe to drop… Good.

Over the next several hours, Quinn outlined what he'd learned about his family's businesses and what he intended to do about it. Not surprisingly, both of his brothers had a great deal to say about their own ventures, but neither put up too much of a fight over the ones that didn't concern them.

Until Quinn casually mentioned that he had hired a team of forensic accountants to calculate what his grandparents' shares of said businesses amounted to today. And that he would be withdrawing that exact amount from them to donate to charities of his choice.

The ensuing argument took their meeting well past lunchtime.

Attendants interrupted twice to bring refreshments and clear away empty plates and platters. Kendry poked her head in once and quickly retreated when all three brothers glared her out of the room. Quinn figured Vega would show up to check on him at some point, but she never did.

It wasn't until he stood up to stretch out his sore back that he found the little minion disc lying flat on a bookshelf above his brothers' line of sight. Almost like she'd placed it there for him to find.

From what she'd explained, the little gadgets were so sensitive they didn't need to face whatever they were spying on. They used echolocation to paint the picture with enough precision to reconstruct a scene down to individual hair follicles. Vega would know not just what Quinn and his brothers had discussed, she'd be able to see who'd sat where and analyze the subtlest changes in their body language and facial expressions.

He was curious about how much of the discussion she'd listened to and what she thought of his strategy for dispersing his family's riches. He hadn't even gotten to the part where he planned to set up work-study funds for each VanWarren child under the age of twenty. Anyone who wanted to walk their own path and make their mark on the world would have the means to do so. But they'd have to give up their claim on the VanWarren estate first—until they became self-sufficient, contributing members of society.

"I hope you realize you just issued a declaration of war," Matthew said. He'd calmed down from the temper he'd displayed when talking about the failing merchandise line his wife had set up for her advice show earlier to something akin to numbness. But his tone was all steel and intent. "We will fight you with everything we have by any means necessary."

Holden didn't speak up anymore. Sometime in the last hour or so, his demeanor had changed as he'd realized the full extent of Quinn's plans and how adamant he was about them. Quinn's charming, open-hearted younger brother had stopped trying to advocate on behalf of the family. He'd stopped pretending to be Quinn's ally as he realized how badly they'd all misread him.

Yes, Quinn wanted his family's acceptance. And before last night, he would have gone to great lengths to attain it.

Yesterday, he'd danced to Geraldine's song and chatted with Maya, Andras, and even Amanda as if they were all friends. He'd had Holden in his corner, smoothing the way with some of the more difficult relatives, and Ivy sending kids his way to show him their toys. If any one of them had asked, he would have given the whole estate over to them without batting an eye.

But after Ylva's attempt on his life—and Vega's—everything was different. Quinn still had their best interests at heart, but he was done bending over backward for their approval.

Matthew was right. Quinn had no desire to maintain the status quo.

Now that Holden had accepted it as well, he looked like he wanted to be anywhere but there. He slumped in his seat, his head bent to hide the angry flush Matthew's words had brought up. And he didn't look at Quinn again.

Quinn had expected this to happen, but for some stupid reason, he'd still hoped his brother would prove him wrong. "What do you know about war, Matthew? Hmm? You think calling up an army of lawyers to fight the battle for you is war? Throwing a fit over losing some money? Throwing a punch? Go ahead. Take your best shot."

Matthew's jaw twitched, and he practically vibrated where he stood, but as pissed as he was, he wasn't stupid pissed—yet. He knew he'd be no physical match for Quinn.

"War, *real* war, is watching your entire life and everything you hold dear blow up in fire and blood—the literal kind. War cuts through your bullshit like nothing else. It strips you down to the soul and forces you to live with whatever's left. So you go ahead and call up your armies. Give it everything you have and then some. Because I know what I'm working with. I know how many hits I can take before I go down, and I guarantee it's a lot more than you and the rest of the clan can deliver."

"You were there, weren't you?" Holden asked softly, breaking the tense stand-off. "When the Shadows showed up."

Matthew didn't back down from his aggressive stance, but something flickered in his gaze. Some brief awareness that maybe the brother they'd forgotten had been through some shit they'd only ever seen on the news before. The change was subtle, nowhere near enough to make him warm up the slightest bit, but it brought his chin down as he waited for Quinn to answer.

"I never left." Vega wasn't the only one who still nursed nightmares.

Matthew's flush drained so quickly that it left him ashen.

All of a sudden, Quinn felt a hundred years old and tired. So very tired. "Let's call it a day. You have troops to muster, and I'm all talked out." He walked out on them with no idea where to go next. The last thing he wanted was to get dragged into whatever "family fun" Kendry had going on. He wanted to go for a walk, but, in his current glowering mood, he might end up scaring the genteel rich people in residence.

Maybe he—

A heavy, muted thud dropped in the parlor a few doors down, followed by a string of curses. Quinn went to investigate and found Geraldine's biggest fan glaring at a big five-seater couch.

"Did you just kick the couch?" Quinn asked.

"I'm trying to *move* the couch," the guy said. "Sent one of the attendants for a couple of levpads half an hour ago and he's still not back."

"So you thought you'd give it a go by yourself?"

The guy raised a dark eyebrow. He definitely didn't have the typical VanWarren look—or attitude, for that matter. "You see anyone else around?"

"Okay, here's a better question. *Why* are you trying to move a couch that's five times bigger than you?"

"Because," came the tight answer, "I got drafted into prep duty for the parlor games tomorrow night. Kendry wants this room set up with all the furniture around the walls to keep the middle clear. And then she sent all the attendants to work on the *other* rooms and left me holding the couch." When Quinn gave him a blank look at such a glaring lack of common sense, he shrugged. "Distant poor relation. Trying to make a good impression."

That Quinn could understand.

He rolled up his sleeves. "Where is it supposed to go?"

"Buddy, it's gonna take an army to move this thing. I barely lifted one corner by my…"

Quinn grasped the bottom edge and tipped the monstrous piece of furniture onto its backrest. It was soft enough to slide around without damaging the floors.

"Okay, how'd you do that?"

"Easily," Quinn said. "Where do you want it?"

The guy pointed in the direction opposite to the garden-side glass wall.

Quinn slid the couch into place, tipped it back over, and pushed it flat against the wall. Piece of cake. "Don't think we've been formally introduced. I'm Quinn," he said, offering his hand.

His distant, poor relation stared at him, then at the couch, then back at Quinn. "I know. Everyone's talking about you and your wife." He matched his smaller hand to Quinn's. "I'm Zach. Wanna help me with the rest of this stuff?"

Eh, why the hell not? He took hold of one side of the large, solid marble table as Zach took the other. It would have been easier for Quinn to pick it up on his own, but he liked to make people feel included. "I wanted to thank you for what you did the other night."

Zach frowned, grunting as they started moving. "What did I do?"

Quinn tilted his wrists to take more of the table's weight without being too obvious about it. "You stood up for my wife." Man, he liked saying that. *My wife.* He didn't even have to fake a smile. It came to him naturally, just for thinking about her. "I appreciate it. And so does Vega."

"Oh." He snorted. "Consider that my pleasure. Worth it to put Emmett back in his place."

They set down the table flush with the couch. "Just saying. You wanted to make a good impression on your rich relatives—that was your winning move right there."

Zach grinned at him as he shook out his hands. "I'll take it. Thanks, man. I like Vega. Not in a creepy way," he quickly amended. "She seems like good people, you know? The kind of gal a guy doesn't get to rescue a lot."

You have no idea.

Zach shrugged, looking sheepish. "Call me a sucker for damsels in distress."

"We have that in common." Zach was all right in Quinn's book. "So. Parlor games?"

"Yeah, I don't know either. Thinking I'll probably have myself a bad case of the stomach flu."

The last thing they needed to move was some kind of freaky art piece that looked like someone had taken a sledgehammer to a mirror ball and froze it in the moment of explosion—in the middle of a cyclone. Shards of sharp, polished metal pointed outward in a chaotic twist around a central rod. It had been set on a marble pedestal in the most inconvenient place, just so the light coming through the glass wall could reflect off the many surfaces and cast rays of light over the floor and ceiling. The effect was pretty. But there were safer ways to create it than this.

Zach seemed to be thinking the same thing. "Rich people, am I right?"

Quinn grunted in agreement. "It doesn't look like it's bolted to the pedestal."

Zach bent at the waist and carefully snaked his arm beneath the shards to test the base. "Definitely not. We need to move them one at a time. Want me to take the hellpiece? It looks lighter."

Lighter, maybe, but one wrong move, and Zach could end up shredded. "Safer if we work together. I think I can grab it near the top. I'll take the weight and make sure it doesn't come down on anyone. You take the bottom and guide it somewhere safe."

"Got it."

Easier said than done. There was only one spot where Quinn was able to fit his arm in between the blades, and it was a tight fit. He carefully grabbed hold of the central rod and lifted the whole thing off the pedestal. The weight wasn't an issue for Quinn. The angle proved problematic for both of them.

Zach was bent double to keep it steady, twisted at the shoulder to keep his head and neck safe from its sharp edges. Every careful step tilted the contraption. Quinn winced each time he felt metal bite into his arm. By the time they set it down in the far corner behind the couch, his arm was braceleted in blood all around his elbow.

Zach noticed. "Shit, why didn't you say anything!"

"Don't worry about it," Quinn said, turning his back on the man as he hastily wiped his arm on his dark pants. "Just a scratch or two. No big deal." Because the wounds had already closed. He rolled down his sleeves for good measure.

"You want me to get a medic?"

"Nah, I can take care of this. Let's get the pedestal out of the way, and then you can handle the rest on your own."

As they had done with the marble table, Quinn carried the bulk of the weight and let Zach steer the course.

"You sure you're okay?" Zach asked as they set it down. "That looked like a substantial amount of blood."

Quinn waved the concern away. "Must have been a trick of the light." He held up his arm, the white shirt sleeve unmarked. "See? Not even a drop."

Zach frowned. "Lucky."

He needed to exit the situation fast. "You got this now? I think I might have pulled something in my shoulder. I'm gonna go check out the spa and see if the family has a masseuse on staff."

"Uh, yeah, absolutely." Zach held out his hand again. "Thanks for your help."

Quinn shook it quickly. "Don't mention it." Then he was headed out the door.

"Hey, Quinn?"

He stopped at the threshold. "Yeah?"

"Ask for Tomas. He's got magic hands. And get someone to clean your scratch, too. That thing looks like it has rabies."

"Thanks for the tip."

18

The VanWarren family didn't like children. Looking over the schedule Kendry had organized, Vega noted that every single activity, except for a meal or two, segregated the minors to a different area of the island with attendants for supervision.

Today, the men were out on their boat again, the kids were soaking up the sun at Crescent Beach, and the women had themselves a spa day.

The third building in the compound was nothing less than a luxurious retreat for the body and mind. Any form of relaxation or exercise a rich person could think of was made available under its roof. Or on it—half of the roof was dedicated to a yoga Zen garden, and the other had massage tables discretely obscured by billowing tents.

The women had chosen to start their day at the salon and had yet to remove themselves elsewhere. Vega had never been one to put too much effort into her appearance. Though she had learned about hair and makeup as part of her Hawk training, it had been nothing like the subtle art form she'd seen the professionals use here.

By noon, all of the women had completed a relatively quiet and conversation-free course of cosmetic rejuvenation treatments, and Vega had had enough of the clusterfuck happening on Quinn's end of the audio feed in her ear. She turned it off and tuned in to the present moment.

After they'd hosed off the mud, Kendry announced lunchtime, and they all gathered in a lounge that opened out onto the lawn. A gorgeous spread had been laid out with an array of sumptuous offerings, some of which Vega couldn't even identify.

"You might like to try this," Kendry said, offering her a bowl filled with a lumpy gray goop. "I know how you enjoy exotic dishes."

Vega returned her saccharine smile, then dipped her finger into the bowl and scooped up a sample. The texture was smoother than it looked, more creamy than gritty, and the taste was somewhere between fruity and meaty. A strange combination, but it worked for her. "My compliments to the chef." She took one of the salad bowls and ladled herself a hearty portion of the stuff, then topped it with chopped fruits and toasted flatbread wedges.

Kendry's smile froze as she set the serving bowl down. "What are you trying to prove?"

Vega shrugged. "I could ask you the same."

Her sister-in-law had no response. She pivoted on her heels and walked away.

The rest of the women were much more inclusive. If the subtle art of female interrogation could be called inclusion. They drew Vega into conversations, shared some of their stories, asked about hers, and in general, used their highbred charm to delicately pry information out of her.

"Tell us, what's it like to be married to Quinn?"

"Where do you plan to live? The galaxy is literally your oyster."

"Have you traveled much?"

"How does it feel to go from destitute to untold riches?"

"Does Quinn have any interest in a career in entertainment?"

And on and on and on.

Each time, Vega expertly delivered a response that felt satisfactory without revealing a single thing and then changed the subject back to them.

If there was one thing these women loved to do, it was talk about themselves. And, without meaning to, they told Vega far more than they realized. Within a couple of hours, she had learned enough to be satisfied that none of them harbored any homicidal impulses where Quinn was concerned.

The younger VanWarren women were all too oblivious about finances to be concerned about what Quinn might plan to do with them. They were either happy homemakers who filled their days with trivial pursuits or secure enough in their own careers not to be concerned about Quinn's return throwing off their public image.

The older ones were a different breed. Most of them remembered the days of Quinn's banishment. Their attitudes ranged between quiet shame and glaring resentment. Few bothered to acknowledge Vega's presence at all, aside from some covert glances at her that were quickly followed by pointed looks at Elspeth. Aunt Ylva's hasty exit had not gone unnoticed. And, seeing as she'd departed on her own, her daughter was left to weather the fallout.

She seemed confused as to why the rest of the family was giving her the cold shoulder.

And then there was Amundsen's half-sister, Ingrid.

The fearsome centenarian had a mean gaze and wasn't shy about voicing her opinions. While the women around Vega talked about the woes of their favorite stores now having such long shipping times, Aunt Ingrid piped up with a loud, "Bah! Everything goes to shit when there's war. People just going about their lives can't get one simple thing done when it counts. And it's all because of those goddamn antichem morons. All they had to do was keep their mouths shut and their freak children locked up in the basement. That's what proper people used to do back in my day. We were less selfish back then. Cared more about our neighbors. Not like now. All you younger people care about is yourselves and your *natural rights*. And now look! The whole damn galaxy's gone to hell." She huffed and shook her head. "Should have just kept their mouths shut."

Her younger relatives subtly distanced themselves from the old bitch while she spoke, but no one said a word in reprimand. They only flushed and looked away, maybe tried to laugh it off with an awkward chuckle. Several of them cast Vega wary glances to see how she would react, having married one of those, "freak children."

People in their advanced years were often some of the most dangerous. Frail bodies didn't mean frail minds. The opposite—having been respectfully shuffled out of positions of authority, they tended to radicalize deep-seated beliefs into fanaticism. And, with nothing left to lose, they were not only free to act but also protected by their age. Someone like Ingrid would have easily been dismissed as an old curmudgeon. But behind the scenes, she fit the profile of the Shadows' ideal collaborator.

Vega made a mental note to spend some quality time with Auntie Ingrid one of these days. See what kind of cocktail her medics had prescribed and which compounds needed a little adjusting. It was a complicated balancing act to keep someone of Ingrid's age in good working order. One could never be too careful.

Someone must have alerted the attendants because three of them came to escort Aunt Ingrid back to her rooms for an afternoon nap. As soon as they left, the atmosphere lightened considerably. Out of sight, out of mind.

And no one said a word about any of it.

Then, in the middle of a heated discussion about the latest trends in impractical footwear, Vega picked up on a disturbance out in the hallway. Heavy footsteps, the sound of a familiar deep voice speaking in low tones to a spa attendant, and a melodic reply. She couldn't see Quinn from her position, but it didn't take a genius to figure out something was wrong.

Kendry clapped her hands. "Ladies, our hair stylists are ready. If you'd like to follow me."

Vega flinched at the responding chorus of energetic squeals, and as she did, a subtle zap of electricity bit the back of her neck.

Talon.

She froze, her heart rate ratcheting up to a wild gallop as her face went cold and sweat broke out all over her scalp. Holding her breath, she waited, fingers curling into the edge of her seat.

Nothing happened.

Vega took advantage of the inward exodus to step outside onto the lawn and scan the tree line for movement. She didn't expect to see anything. That kind of terrain could hide anyone. It wasn't even difficult. And Talon didn't need line of sight to activate the leash. All he needed was to be within a one-mile radius in any direction, including up. He could be anywhere on the island or above it.

"Vega? Are you joining us?" Kendry's voice sounded brittle and on edge.

Vega cracked her knuckles one by one, then dug her nails into the fabric of her fluffy robe. The anticipation of a shock was almost worse than the shock itself. She waited for it and braced herself for the searing pain that would leave her writhing and incapacitated for an hour after.

"Did you hear me?"

It didn't come.

What the fuck was going on?

Vega released her death grip on the robe and took a couple of breaths to get back into her wifey persona before she turned to face her sister-in-law. "You know, it's so gorgeous outside. I think I'll skip the hair appointment and go up to the roof instead." She needed a high-ground position to properly sweep the area. And, if Talon was around to kill her from a distance, she wanted to be somewhere beautiful, away from her viper in-laws.

Kendry's eye twitched. "But we have stylists waiting. And yoga time isn't until later."

"I'm sure I won't be missed at either," Vega said with a finality that dared Kendry to argue. "Enjoy the makeover."

Brushing past the seething Kendry, Vega took the ornate stairs two at a time up to the roof. She couldn't get her heart rate under control. The need to go on the offensive was so strong that her body tensed to act, but what could she do? Throw on a pair of fatigues, smear camo paint on her face, and go stalking a Shadow through the trees? Leave Quinn exposed and unprotected?

And that was assuming Talon was on his own.

Vega emerged on the roof and raised her face to the sun, breathing hard. She couldn't go on the offensive. She couldn't defend against a threat she couldn't see. And neither she nor Quinn could just take off without drawing too much attention to themselves and possibly bringing a storm of violence down on their heads.

Vega was not geared up to handle a full-on tactical assault on the compound.

If Talon was in range, and he wanted her dead, she would be. If the Shadows had gotten past the island's security, their targets' death warrants were already signed, and there was nothing Vega could do to stop it.

But if Talon was already in range, why hadn't he killed her yet?

The shock she'd felt earlier had been a flea bite compared to what she knew it could do to her. Come to think of it, she'd felt the same thing that morning, only she'd assumed it had been part of her nightmare. It didn't feel like Talon's MO. He wasn't exactly a subtle kind of guy.

Could it be a glitch? If the device was damaged or degraded, it was possible for it to malfunction.

Or maybe it was all a figment of her imagination. Maybe her mind couldn't process a life without the constant threat of pain and violence hanging over her head, and it was filling in the blanks to make the world make sense in the only way she understood.

Maybe she was the one malfunctioning.

And not a drop of Bliss to be found.

Fuck!

She needed something familiar and tangible to ground herself back into reality.

She needed—

Quinn.

The diaphanous white curtains of a tent blew apart in a gentle breeze to reveal the towering shape of her fake husband, naked, except for another towel wrapped around his waist, staring off into the distance with a pensive look on his face. The afternoon sun gilded his hair in gold, and the flowing white curtains somehow softened the harsh lines of his body.

Vega had no right to admire his body or think about those big hands stroking her all over. It definitely wasn't her place to keep imagining what it'd feel like to have the full force of his untapped power between her legs.

But that little zap had completely short-circuited her ironclad self-control. She was about to spiral, and she didn't have the luxury of a Mile High to change course. Her adrenalin was through the roof; her heart was racing, and her brain was beyond rational thought. Right now, she could only handle action. Hard, violent, muscle-burning, heart-throbbing action. And there was no one around for her to beat to a bloody pulp.

Deep in thought, Quinn didn't notice her presence as he sat on the edge of a massage table and stretched out on it face-down. She heard the flimsy contraption creak from twenty feet away.

An attendant dressed all in white came up behind Vega. "Pardon me, ma'am."

Vega reacted on instinct, catching his sleeve to stop him as he passed by. "What's your name?" she asked, putting all of her effort behind a bland smile while her thigh muscles twitched to *fucking move.*

"I'm Tomas," he answered politely.

"Tomas, I wonder if you could maybe let me take this one?" She gave him her sweetest, girliest wink, willing her fingers to release their death grip on his shirt.

He blinked at her fluffy spa robe, then glanced over at Quinn's prone form and bit back a grin as he handed over the tray of oils and candles he'd brought. "Of course, Mrs. VanWarren. I'll make sure you're not disturbed."

"Thank you, Tomas. Your discretion is appreciated."

He dipped one of those infuriating bows. "I'll be on standby downstairs if you or Mr. VanWarren need anything."

Once he was gone, Vega carried the tray over to Quinn's tent and placed it on the waiting side table, trembling.

Breathe.

Breathe…

"That was quick," Quinn said without raising his head. "I'm ready when you are."

With a shaky hand, Vega picked up a bottle of warmed oil and brought it to her nose. She inhaled the smoky, evergreen scent deep into her lungs and exhaled to a count of five.

Breathe, she told herself when her body forgot to take the next breath.

Her skin felt too tight over her bones. Her knees wobbled as she turned and took the two steps toward Quinn's massage table.

Breathe…

Control. She had to get control of herself. She had to give him a choice.

And if he chose to say no, she had to be able to walk away.

He'd loosened his towel to drape across his ass, leaving the rest of him exposed.

Breathe, she reminded herself again, even as her body demanded,

Touch. Feel. Taste.

Vega poured a little drop of the oil into her hands and rubbed them together. She could do this.

Quinn twitched a little when she applied her thumbs to the juncture of his neck and shoulders.

She could do this. Be normal. Just enough to work the edge off until she could think again. And if he said no…

Leaning over him, she murmured in his ear, "Good afternoon, Mr. VanWarren."

19

Quinn was ready to zone out, maybe doze off a bit while Tomas worked on his back, but at the sound of Vega's voice, his eyes snapped open, and he arched up off the table. "Vega?"

She pushed him back down. "Relax," she said, digging her thumbs into his spine.

Quinn bit back a pleasured groan. "Didn't realize massage therapy was in your repertoire of skills."

"I am a woman of many hidden talents. Would you like me to show you?"

She couldn't mean that the way it sounded. No way. She was messing with him.

Too bad he couldn't make his body agree. Her sultry voice raised goosebumps over his skin. The steady, expert pressure of her hands totally disarmed him. And when she leaned down to nip at his shoulder, he shot harder than a flag pole.

"Tell me where it hurts," she whispered, her lips grazing his neck.

What was this, some kind of joke? He tried to raise himself up again, and again she pushed him down. "What are you doing?"

"I'm taking care of my husband."

So it was an act. Part of the persona she put on for his family's benefit. "Who all is watching?" The words came out as bitter as they felt. Quinn was used to people staring at him wherever he went, but this was a new low. He didn't care if it messed up their act. He was not about to—

Her lips brushed across his nape. "The only people up here are you and me."

Quinn's brain went quiet.

Vega's knuckles ran down either side of his spine all the way to the edge of his towel, pushing it a couple of inches lower. There, she spread her hands over the small of his back and pushed them up toward his shoulders. "You're so tense." Her hands disappeared, and then warm oil dripped along his spine.

Either it had something extra mixed into it, or Quinn was so touch-starved it didn't need to. Everywhere the oil made contact with his skin, his nerve endings zinged with sensation. And when Vega once again applied her hands to his muscles, Quinn's eyes rolled back in his head. "Fuck, that feels good."

And, for a moment, that was all he let himself think about. The feel of her hands on him, the firm, expert pressure rubbing away all the lingering tension from his meeting earlier. The steady, near-hypnotic rhythm of her deep breaths.

For a few moments, he didn't question what game she was playing. He didn't want to know. Vega was touching him—of her own voli-tion—and Quinn didn't want to waste a single second of it wondering why. He let himself sink into the massage table, willing his cock to stand down, not wanting to jeopardize this…whatever it was. He matched his breaths to hers and concentrated on nothing but her hands on his back.

He knew he'd made the right call when she hummed her approval.

Leaning harder into him, she dug the heels of her hands into the space between his shoulder blades, kneading until the last of his ten-sion melted away. Then, as she had done before, the steady pressure of her knuckles traced his spine down to his waist.

She spread her hands out at the small of his back, but instead of rub-bing up to his shoulders, her finger slipped down his sides to his front.

Shocked right out of the Zen he'd almost gotten going, from half-mast to full-on, raging hardon again in an instant, Quinn twisted sideways, almost tipping over the narrow table. Thank God for Vega's lightning reflexes and the oil making his skin slippery enough for her to pull her far hand free, or he might have broken her arm in the process. He caught both of her wrists, searching her face for a hint of what the fuck she wanted from him.

He had to be reading too much into it. The touch could have been completely innocent and…

The fire in her eyes said otherwise.

Quinn watched her gaze drop to his mouth. Her tongue slipped out to moisten her lips, daring him to chase it down and coax it out of hiding. Her pupils were blown, her pulse fluttering wildly in her neck, but her breathing remained even and controlled if a little fast.

Raw, almost desperate need in the tense lines of her body, but she held still in his grasp, watching him right back. Waiting for him to decide the next step.

One word from him, and she'd back off.

And he'd never get this close to her again.

But if he gave in, if they crossed that line…

Vega must have read his leanings in his expression because she tilted her head at him, and he could have sworn something like relief flashed across her expression even as a small smile teased at the corner of her lips. She twisted her hand in his hold in a request for release.

It did something to him, that tiny tell, the tentative movement so very different than her usual, confident self. He didn't know what was going on with her, but he knew she'd come to him. She wanted—needed—*him*.

Still, he needed her to be sure. "Don't start something if you don't mean it." His tongue felt thick in his mouth, stumbling over the words.

Instead of pulling away, she leaned closer, twisting her hands again. When he released her, Vega took his hand and brought it to the overlap of her white robe. The belt holding the garment closed came loose, and she put his palm flat against the inside of her thigh. His fingers curled into her supple flesh and moved reflexively to follow her lead to the top, where he couldn't possibly miss how wet she was. She braced her free hand at his shoulder and leaned so close her nose brushed against his. "Tell me if I mean it."

A few months ago, it would have stopped his failing heart dead. Quinn's head dropped back onto the table as a dizzy spell assailed him while his new heart caught up with the demands Vega was putting on it.

But he never let go.

He played with her slick folds and watched her eyes grow heavy-lidded, watched that feral edge dull a little. Everything about this felt unreal. Maybe it was. Maybe he'd never woken up from surgery, and this was all just another fevered dream inside his comatose mind.

Vega lifted her knee onto the edge of the table, spreading herself wide to give him better access, and Quinn lost it. He flexed his arm and lifted her off the ground. "Get up here."

The table protested as she straddled his lap and shucked her robe. Quinn had never seen anything so beautiful as when she put her hands on her breasts and aligned her soft, wet heat with the length of his dick.

He tried to sit up to taste her, but the table emitted an ominous creak beneath them, and something cracked. He laid back and stilled. Clearly, this thing wasn't made for someone of his considerable weight, much less the added stress of any vigorous activities.

Vega chuckled. "Guess I have you at my mercy now," she purred, bucking her hips to deliver a long, wet stroke.

"*Mercy.*" Denied a taste, he contented himself with petting her gorgeous body on top of his as she rocked back and forth. Quinn wanted inside her so badly it hurt, but he needed to give her time. Even if it killed him. Watching her take her pleasure from him might put an end to this before it even began.

He pushed the backs of his calves against the edge of the massage table and forced himself to breathe as he slid his hands up beneath hers to lay claim to her breasts.

She arched into his touch and bore down harder on his cock, not in the least bit shy about showing him where she liked to be touched and how. Quinn's mouth went dry with a desperate thirst for those dusky nipples.

Vega bucked her hips over him, stroking a bead of pre-cum from him, and he barely stopped himself from surging up to her. "*Vega.*"

Not enough.

Not enough contact.

Not enough *her.*

He needed to feel her everywhere. In an imitation of the massage she'd delivered earlier, Quinn swept his hands up and down over her torso, over her hips and thighs, savoring the way her lithe muscles stretched and flexed beneath his touch.

Vega was quiet in her passion. She moved without hesitation, but tension kept her body rigid, her breaths so even he could set a clock by them. They were out in the open. It made sense that she would want to keep herself under tight control. But the primitive part of him wanted to make her lose it. Quinn wanted her moaning his name and screaming her pleasure to the heavens as she sank her nails into him. He wanted to be the one to make the restrained assassin let loose and go wild.

Nothing less was good enough.

He clamped his hands around her hips, pulled her down harder on top of him. He couldn't move without breaking the damned table beneath them, but he could move *her*. She breathed in a little harder, just short of a gasp and leaned over him, changing the angle between them.

Quinn took immediate advantage and captured her mouth. She was all sun-warmed silk and honey, and he couldn't get enough. Her hips stilled as he plunged his tongue into her mouth. Quinn tangled his fingers in her hair to keep her with him and guided her back into motion with an arm around her ass.

She bucked her hips faster, and he felt her body go taut, felt her quiver through a climax, and tasted her quiet moan.

Not good enough.

Pleasure rocked through Vega, enough to dull the edge of her need but not truly satisfy. But it allowed her spine to melt a little, for her body to lean into Quinn until her nipples pressed into his chest. And once she got that close, his arms clamped around her, keeping her there.

Keeping her contained.

Vega sighed against Quinn's mouth with equal measures of pleasure and relief.

He hadn't said no.

He was strong enough to handle her, to keep her from shattering herself to pieces.

At least for a little while.

It was enough for her to regain control of herself, for the clawing tension to release enough to let her think her way to the next breath, the next step.

It had to be enough.

Because as her mind cleared, Vega began to realize what she'd done.

She was legally married to Quinn, and they were stuck together in an extremely intimate setting for at least another month. Whatever boundaries Vega might have had, wanted, or needed to maintain were already blurred.

And she had just complicated the ever-living fuck out of an already tricky situation, crossed a line she never should have crossed.

Vega pulled back to gauge his reaction, bracing herself for censure, rejection, and more questions she didn't know how to answer.

Quinn's heavy-lidded gaze tracked her retreat, and he raised his head to nip at her lower lip. "Ready for the main course?" His hips curled up, rubbing the head of his erection against her hypersensitized clit, and Vega gasped.

It was the most selfish thing she'd ever done, and she knew she'd hate herself for it later, but right now, Quinn was still in this, still hard and needing, and Vega was desperate enough to want to take what he offered. All of it—all of him.

The thought of it made her pussy squeeze hard for the thick rod sliding so smoothly against her. "Are you?" she returned, curling her hips against him. His fingers dug into her hip and instantly released, as if he was afraid to hurt her.

No way.

She raised herself up and reached between them. He was bigger than any other man she'd ever been with. Curling her fingers around his girth, she stroked him down to the base and back up to the head, squeezing hard enough to make his jaw twitch and his hips buck up. Another careful flex of his fingers.

The table wasn't wide enough for her to shift her legs apart any more than they already were, so she arched her back, pressing her chest into his as she fed him into her pussy inch by slow inch. He trembled beneath her, but held still and let her set the pace. Vega sank herself onto him, embracing the light burn and the glorious feeling of fullness. It was almost too much—and she suddenly knew that for the rest of her life, she'd never be satisfied with anything less.

The thought was too disturbing to contemplate, so she shoved it aside and concentrated on the moment, with Quinn panting at her ear, and her bones buzzing with sensation. She took him as deep as her body would allow, then slowly pushed herself up, letting him slide almost all the way out before she ground back down on him.

Quinn groaned and, lightheaded, Vega reminded herself to breathe again.

Up and down a little faster.

She savored the burn as her body adjusted to him, clamping down on him as she picked up the pace, keeping low so that every move rubbed her nipples against his chest.

Quinn's hands roamed over her back in long strokes that were as soothing as they were stimulating. When he gripped her ass, her pussy clenched on him in reflex, and he puffed an explosive breath against her neck, releasing his hold immediately.

Panting, Vega pulled back and gripped his chin to make him look at her. His pleasure-hazed gaze wasn't all the way focused, and he strained up to kiss her again. She nipped at his tongue hard enough to get his attention. "Don't you fucking dare hold back."

He blinked, and fire blazed in his eyes. The table groaned and tilted as he braced his feet on the edge to gain leverage. Then his thick fingers curled into her ass again to hold her in place and he bucked up hard enough to make her squeak. He watched her for a second, and Vega met his gaze in a head-on challenge.

He did it again and again, and it was everything she'd never known sex could be. Vega braced her hands at his shoulders and let him take over, let him fuck her so hard the table beneath them rattled. She couldn't hold his gaze anymore, couldn't hold her head up at all, so she let it drop next to his, licking at his neck as the driving force of him inside her left no corner for retreat.

She'd thrown down the gauntlet, and he'd picked it up.

She'd told him not to hold back, and now he wasn't letting her do it either.

Her body coiled so tight she thought she might explode. She couldn't breathe fast enough to keep up or hold on hard enough to maintain her balance. Noises built up in her chest, and she couldn't hold them back.

So she sank her teeth into his shoulder to muffle them instead.

Quinn shouted something incomprehensible and clamped his arms around her again, one across her lower back, one at her shoulders, his big hand on the back of her head, pressing down as if demanding that she stay, bite harder.

So she did.

She felt his answering growl like the rumble of an earthquake beneath her, and he fucked her hard, hard, *hard*, until her body simply… shattered.

Vega bucked and quivered as the intense pleasure turned her muscles into mush and plunged her mind into a blissful blankness. She was vaguely aware of Quinn gripping her tight enough to bruise, fucking her hard enough to make her sore after. She felt and heard him take his pleasure inside her, and a crazy thought briefly crossed her sex-addled mind: *Mine.*

It was gone in an instant, leaving nothing behind but a low hum of satisfaction buzzing up and down her spine in the wake of his roaming hands.

The tension was gone. Her mind floated in a pleasant, dreamy haze. Her body melted on top of his, limp from head to toe. She didn't have to remind herself to breathe anymore. The rise and fall of Quinn's chest set the rhythm for her, rocking her through the aftershocks. His hands rubbed her hip to soothe away the ache of a blooming bruise and brushed through her hair, massaging her neck.

For a while, neither of them moved or spoke, content to relax until the burning heat of their bodies began to cool.

And then her leash sparked again.

"Ow!" Quinn pulled his hand away, breaking a few strands of hair in his haste. "The hell was that?"

Vega pulled back, wide-eyed, her body rigid.

His gaze met hers, and his body tensed beneath her as he frowned. "Vega?"

He'd felt it.

It wasn't in her head; she hadn't imagined it. It was real.

Instant panic twisted her insides. "I have to go."

"What? What are you talking about? What's going on?"

Vega pushed off of him, wincing as he slid free of her body. She ignored the trickle of moisture between her legs as she hopped off the table and grabbed for her robe. "There's something I have to do."

"Just hold on a fucking minute!"

He reached for her, but she moved out of the way, tying off the belt to hold the garment closed. She didn't bother with her slippers. "Stay in our suite, and don't wait up."

Quinn was already up and reaching for his clothes, even as he tried to go after her. "Goddammit—*Vega*…"

She ran down the stairs as if the shadows closing in around her had claws—because they did. And she needed to do something before they sank those claws into her neck.

Crescent Island security was a fucking joke. The automated measures forced any vehicles that didn't have proper authorization to return to the mainland, but it had no rules for individual people. Like, say, a Shadow who didn't like to be turned away at the door and decided to jump out of said vehicle before it left the island.

The fact that Talon was now without proper conveyance was a minor nuisance. The VanWarren compound didn't even have a dedicated security team. There were only two guys with coms that connected to a central station he wasn't even sure was manned. He could literally walk into their three-story garage and avail himself of any transport that struck his fancy.

When the time came to escort Vega out of there, that was exactly what he planned to do.

But first, he had some business to take care of.

From the cover of his tree canopy perch, he watched as Vega exited the far building. She was too worked up to keep the stiffness from her marching stride and the sharpness from her gaze. Poor little bird had grown too comfortable without a proper chain of command. She'd let down her guard so quickly after their last tango.

Activating the wrist unit, Talon winked, and the lens in his left eye captured Vega's image as she reached the main residence and looked over her shoulder. Then she disappeared indoors and out of sight.

Tilting his head, he twisted the dials on the wrist unit to bring up a hologram of the image and enlarge it to actual size. The likeness was so detailed, he could almost smell her skin and feel the brush of her long hair over his wrist. He recognized that sharp stare, the cold calculation no doubt churning in her mind.

But there was something else underneath her Shadow mask that he hadn't seen in her in a long time. Her gaze was sharp but haunted. Her face was set but pensive. The elegant line of her throat was tense enough to make him want to crack his neck.

His little Vega was scared. It suited her so well.

Talon smiled and settled back against the tree trunk.

For the life of him, he couldn't wrap his mind around the depths she'd sunk to.

One general search.

One single search was all he'd needed to find her ID scan leaving Persephone 5 as Vega Ortiz and arriving on Ela as Vega VanWarren.

By what twisted mind-fuck of an illogical skip had she decided to go from that point A to that point B?

Was it the money? Money, at least, would make sense. It sure as shit couldn't be for love, and Talon sincerely doubted attraction had anything to do with it. Vega was as cold as they got—in every sense. She didn't catch feelings, and she sure as shit didn't indulge in sexual escapades. Any vulnerability was too great a risk in their line of work.

It definitely had to be the money.

And it was beneath her.

The very idea offended Talon to the marrow of his bones. Shadows were supposed to be above such bullshit. And Vega was supposed to have been one of their best. Impulsive and sometimes too defiant for her own good, sure. But that was nothing a treatment or two couldn't cure. When it came to skill, Vega still put every Hound he knew to shame.

She belonged with them. She belonged to the Shadows, not this overbred herd of chattel, prancing around in their fancy clothes like piglets decked out in ribbons. And he would make sure she never forgot it again.

No one left the Shadows—except in a body bag.

But there was no need to rush. After all, how often did a Shadow get an opportunity to let loose and enjoy himself these days? Especially with a pudgy bureaucrat CO breathing down his neck.

Well, Hughes wasn't there. Talon was on his own, with no one to tell him what to do. He could indulge himself a little.

He traced the elegant line of Vega's eyebrow, the hologram brightening into colorless hotspots everywhere he touched.

For everything she'd cost him, his little bird would pay.

With a rapid series of taps, he activated the com and sent Vega's image to Hughes with a message: TARGET LOCATED. Then he waited for a response.

The fatass paper pusher had fallen so far from his Hound training Talon didn't even consider him a soldier anymore. But, like it or not, Hughes was the only one with the authority to get Talon what he wanted.

The response was terse and to the point: PERMISSION TO PROCEED.

Talon's jaw twitched, and heat gathered in his chest, ready to explode.

Permission to proceed? Like he was a fucking dog waiting to be let off the leash. Son of a bitch had another think coming.

He flexed his hands and breathed down his welling rage. This had to be managed with level-headed logic. Level-headedness wasn't usually his strong point, but that didn't mean he wasn't capable of it.

A few more controlled breaths cleared the red haze from his vision and calmed the shaking in his hands.

Then Talon tapped out his answer. MISSION PARAMETER MODIFICATION: HAWK PIN IN EXCHANGE FOR TARGET.

Because of the distance and the relays involved, the coded transmission delivery had a delay of several minutes. Still, it took almost twenty for his wrist unit to vibrate with a new message.

NEGATIVE. PROCEED AS ORDERED.

Talon slammed his cuffed wrist against the tree trunk with everything he had. And then he slammed it a few more times. Conscious of his position, he swallowed back his roar, but just barely. He was shaking too hard to offer a response, so he didn't bother.

The high and mighty fuck thought this was a negotiation?

Let's see how that works out for him.

Breathing hard, Talon wiped the sweat off his burning face and blinked the compound back into focus. Had Vega slipped back out already? He hadn't seen her.

Regardless, she'd be stalking through the trees in no time. But she wouldn't find him, not with a heat shield disguising his thermal signature. She would hunt herself to exhaustion, chasing her own tail. She would convince herself that her target was in range and when she failed to locate him, she'd convince herself she'd imagined the whole thing.

And then he would strike.

Talon didn't forgive and forget. Vega had made a fucking fool of him and cost him command of the entire unit he'd spent years building up. He might never get command again the traditional way, but a Hawk pin on his shoulder would go a long way toward mollifying his temper.

If Hughes wanted Vega alive, he would have to pay the price for her delivery.

And if he refused, Talon would take great pleasure in ripping Vega apart from the inside out.

With that satisfying thought in mind, he leaned back his head and closed his eyes as the creatures around him settled their feathers and scales and resumed their song.

Then he reached up and ever so lightly ran his finger down the trigger in the side of his neck one more time.

Operative M was unique among the Shadows—a true chameleon. M's earliest memories were of gray walls and a nondescript, monotone voice reading from the Shadow field guide at the pivotal age of three.

Drafted Shadows always had their memories incinerated at the earliest opportunity. But the complexities of the human mind made it a messy, imperfect process that often left a Shadow haunted by dreams and visions they couldn't explain.

M had no such issues. M hadn't been *drafted* so much as *adopted*. From a hospital delivery room without the mother's consent.

It had been classified as an experiment to craft someone who, at their core, was no one. And the best way to do that was to start with a blank slate. Why waste resources on continuous memory wipes when you could simply circumvent them altogether?

As a result of this early intervention, M's entire life was nothing but Shadows. Schooling, training, and field missions. Not always in that order.

No other Shadow existed quite like M. Not even other Hawks. Where others might put on a mask to blend in with the crowd, if one knew what to look for, they could always see it slip. A glance here, a gesture there, a turn of phrase slightly out of character, or a chuckle that didn't sound quite right. Because it was all just a mask—the role, the training, even the treatments—and, underneath it, the truth of a person always fought toward the surface.

That was why the average usefulness and, therefore, life expectancy of a fully trained Hawk was limited. Masks always deteriorated. Their weight eventually became too heavy to bear across the damaged infrastructure of a traumatized brain. The Hawk's mind became too fractured to keep it on any longer.

M didn't wear masks. M assumed a soul. Becoming someone else was a simple matter of sliding a puzzle piece into its designated slot—and there was always an empty slot to accommodate it. And when the new personality settled into place, it was everything to M until the mission was complete. Manufactured memories became real. Personal preferences ingrained themselves into M's skin, eardrums, and taste buds. A lifetime of hobbies and passions altered physical movement, gestures, and mannerisms. Even M's face and voice adjusted in subtle ways, from winks to smiles to accents.

When the mission was complete, M wiped the slate clean once more and walked away nothing but a Shadow in the night.

In fact, there had been only two times in the past when a particularly sticky personality had refused to let go, necessitating a treatment, but even then, M had only needed a light zap to remind those pesky brain cells who was boss.

WHO ARE YOU? *"No one."*

WHERE DO YOU RESIDE? *"Nowhere."*

WHAT DO YOU DO? *"What needs to be done."*

It was a game. But, like all games, once a routine of rounds established itself, it became boring. The fun only lasted while the threat of discovery, such as it was, was still fresh and acute. Once the targets became complacent and wholly accepting of M's presence, the game quickly lost its appeal.

Long cons were the worst. And the VanWarren assignment was the longest M had ever had. But it would be over soon.

M reviewed the latest report one more time, making sure there were no errors or omissions. It was imperative for Command to receive full details on the situation as it developed. Anything new and unexpected needed to be communicated immediately.

Satisfied, M reached for the Send button.

An incoming transmission stopped M's finger mid-action.

M stared at the blinking red light, head tilted with curiosity and a small thrill for the unknown.

Hawk communications were usually one-directional to minimize the risk of discovery. Unless the mission parameters unexpectedly changed.

Unexpected was a good thing. Unexpected broke up the monotony of an established game.

M accepted the transmission.

The screen flashed twice in what, to the untrained eye, might look like a glitch. Then it cleared, and new data streamed rapidly across the surface. Speed reading had been one of the first lessons M had received—it was vital in the field, as briefs were only delivered once. If M missed a single word, it could jeopardize the entire assignment.

Hmm. Another CO was tapping in on the mission. The update didn't come with a name, meaning whoever it was had not been briefed on the details and would not receive updates until the requested task was completed. But M's CO appeared to have deemed the request an acceptable addition to their original plans.

The text trailed off the screen, and then two images popped up side by side for three seconds flat. Two faces, each with specific orders for processing. Two new mission parameters, delivered in a flash, and then everything was gone again. When the screen reverted to its original state, M sent off the most recent mission report and turned toward the window. The scenery disappeared behind a mental image of the two faces of a new twist.

The first was a stranger. Not a pleasing face to look at. Something about the eyes. Like staring down a tweaked-out animal. M had a feeling that, despite the order to locate and monitor only, this particular assignment would eventually turn into a hunt-and-kill. It was unlikely to present much of a challenge.

The second—now there was a surprise. Not only because of the familiarity of features but because M recognized the sharp focus in that piercing gaze. Given this new turn of events, M wondered what Command would make of the report they were about to receive.

When a small smile threatened to bloom, M allowed the brief indulgence, the thrill of anticipation.

At last, a worthy adversary.

The game had just turned very, very interesting.

22

Day 4

Stay in our suite and don't wait up.

Quinn was going to kill her.

He had no idea what time it was, but the night had come and gone while he'd paced around the suite. *Don't wait up.* Yeah, right. His arm kept twitching to use the SOS locator on his com and go fetch her, wherever the hell she'd run off to. He stopped himself by picturing her sitting on the edge of the bed as she'd demonstrated how it worked. If he tried to find her, the blinking light on her com might give away her position. If he went after her, he'd be a walking target and a potential liability.

Vega was out there on her own, with nothing but her knives for protection, and there wasn't a goddamn thing Quinn could do to help. He kept reminding himself that she was a fully trained Shadow, and then he remembered the look on her face right before she'd left him.

She'd been terrified. And Quinn had just frozen there in shock to realize there was something the woman feared.

And now she was out there all on her own while he was stuck in here with an endless loop of horrible scenarios playing out in his mind. It was the worst kind of hell.

The estate disc chimed with a notification of the day's planned activities.

It was now late enough for the family to be awake.

Quinn swore, spearing his hands into his hair and tugging hard.

The door opened.

He was across the suite in five ground-eating strides, snatching

Vega to him before she'd closed the door behind her. His heart was whirring like mad, making his arms twitch, straining not to crush her outright as he lifted her off her feet.

She sighed, a sound of resignation more than anything else. She didn't relax so much as collapse against him. Like she was too tired to keep her spine straight anymore. Like she had given up.

A quiet panic twisted Quinn's gut as he set her back on her feet so he could check her over. She looked exhausted but unharmed. Except for that wounded animal weariness in her eyes.

"I'm okay," she said before he could ask.

"Not good enough," he growled, dragging her with him to the bathroom and snatching Monty off the side table along the way.

Something had happened yesterday—before she'd ever come up to the roof. Something had spooked her badly enough to throw caution to the wind and let down her guard. And it had cost her something vital.

"You're going to explain."

He half expected her to bolt when he let go of her arm, but she stayed put while he drew her a bath. Hot. None of that icy shower shit. And he added scented bubbles for good measure, to poke the predator back to her usual surly charm.

By the time he turned to face her, a soft haze of steam had filled the room and Vega was fully naked already stepping around him into the half-filled bath. No arguments, no glares.

But sure, yeah, she was totally fine.

Quinn sat on the ground and drummed his foot against the tub, waiting for her to speak before her weary silence ate away the last remnants of his sanity.

"We can't stay here," she said. There, but not there. He was looking right at her, and she was miles away from him. A ghost.

His drumming foot stilled. "You say *we*, but somehow I'm hearing *I*."

"*I* can't stay. But *I'm* not leaving *you* here without protection. That better?"

Not remotely. "You skipped a few steps. Back up and tell me what's going on. What happened up there on the roof?" When she'd slid off his post-coital dick straight into fight-or-flight without so much as a wink for transition.

"I don't know," she said, and he fucking felt how much it tore at her to admit it.

"That thing in your neck went off," he prompted, hands going numb with dread. The torture device Talon had put on her and used to electrocute her from a distance—the one the doctor on Persephone 5 had refused to even consider removing.

"I thought I was imagining it."

"But I felt it too."

The tub was full. The flow of water stopped, plunging the bathroom into dead silence. Vega hugged her knees to her chest, and Quinn wanted to kill something for her. Preferably that son of a bitch Talon. Quinn would love to rip off his limbs one by one and watch him bleed out.

"Talon is the only one who has the trigger."

"So you figured he found you and went out there looking for him. But you didn't find him, did you?"

Vega shook her head, then rested her cheek on her up-drawn knee to look at him. "I'm still alive. If he's here, he's fucking with me because he wants something."

"*If* he's here?"

She squeezed her eyes shut.

"Hey." He shifted over to put his arm around her. She didn't pull away, but she wouldn't look at him. Quinn couldn't take much more of this. "Talk to me." He needed to understand so he could figure out what the fuck to do about it. There had to be something. There always was if you had enough money, and Quinn was drowning in it.

"There's a chance it's not him. It went off three more times while I was out there, but it didn't feel like it usually does." Debilitating pain that dropped her on the spot and left her body in muscle-ripping spasms for an hour afterward. Quinn had seen it first-hand. Still had nightmares about it sometimes. "There's a chance the device could be misfiring."

He took a second to absorb that. "Okay, so we get it removed." Simple enough.

Vega shook her head. "Can't. Not without killing me, anyway. At least that's what your new telepath friends told me. The way it's attached, it will destroy my spinal cord if anyone tries to remove it while it's active. And deactivating it will fry my nervous system beyond repair. Something about a biofeedback loop."

There was no absorbing that. "What are you saying?"

Vega shrugged. "I was deluding myself. I thought all I had to do was get rid of Talon, and everything would be fine—piece of cake. But it's not enough. Even if he dies, that thing won't go anywhere. It's a death sentence, no matter what. And I'm so fucking tired of… I'm just so tired, Quinn."

Quinn pulled her in tighter as if he could hide her from the reaper.

"No one leaves the Shadows," she whispered, haunted and so small. "Except in a body bag." The finality of it closed a cold fist of fear around his artificial heart.

No. Fuck that. They'd waded through way too much shit to give up now. "You did leave. And so did Rowe and the others. You're free of the Shadow for good. You beat the odds how many times now? You'll beat them again." He wouldn't accept anything else. "You're Vega-fucking-Ortiz. Don't go soft on me now."

Out in the bedroom, the estate disc chimed again with a summons to brunch.

It barely registered with Quinn, but Vega sat up, pulling away from him. He watched her build her mental armor back up until it straightened her spine and blanked her face, but her eyes were still shadowed with defeat. "We can't pick up and leave out of the blue. We'll need to come up with a proper reason and say our goodbyes."

"And then what?"

"Then I guess we'll take a trip to visit with your friend Laura."

Quinn hadn't spoken to Laura since he'd left the hospital after his heart surgery; hadn't wanted her to know about the shit show that was his family and their attempts on his life. But the Special Unit had been keeping him up to date. Laura's new facility on Mai was now fully operational and receiving a steady influx of new residents in need of refuge from all over the galaxy, courtesy of Emma Wayland spreading the word throughout the SU network. With what had to be a good number of telepaths *and* Finnegan Rowe in residence, Laura's new home was probably the safest place in the whole galaxy.

A convenient place to ditch a guy.

"You're going to disappear again, aren't you?"

"If Talon is after me, he'll follow. I'll lead him far away from you. You don't want to be there for what happens next."

Quinn wanted to start breaking shit. And keep breaking more until there was nothing left. Somehow, he managed to unclench his jaw enough to grind out, "And if he's not?"

"Then you *really* don't want to be there for what happens next."

Something shuttered in Quinn's expression. Vega had seen the look before, usually moments before she burned a hole through a prisoner's head. She hated being the one to put that look on Quinn's face. He deserved better.

Too bad all she had was the truth.

When he pulled away, when he stood up and turned his back to her as if he couldn't stand the sight of her anymore, Vega's bath water turned cold. With a sigh, she washed off the night in quick, efficient sweeps, and drained the tub.

The annoying chime out in the bedroom was getting louder. They were going to be late for brunch. As much as Vega longed to be left alone, she and Quinn couldn't miss another family event. Not after the way Vega had brushed off Kendry yesterday. And they needed to start laying the grounds for their departure.

Vega had some ideas. She could tell them she'd received some bad news from her family. As worked up as she was, it wouldn't be hard to play the part of a distraught damsel. And, of course, as her husband, it would be logical for Quinn to want to be there for her.

Then, after dinner, they could announce that the situation had gone from bad to worse and they simply couldn't stay any longer. Deepest regrets, blah, blah, blah. She'd have to book multiple shuttle flights out from Ela to make them harder to track. Maybe go the long way around before they touched down on Mai.

All that mattered was making sure Quinn was safe.

"For what it's worth, I don't think your family is in direct contact with the Shadows." They were all too comfortable and oblivious. Including the vitriolic Great Aunt Ingrid, and the homicidal Aunt Ylva.

Meeting a Shadow face to face tended to leave an impression.

It was by design. Before they'd made their existence known far and wide, the Shadows' most powerful currency had been fear. They'd operated in secret, leaving enough evidence of their involvement to make powerful people dread and ordinary people wonder at the possibility that everything they'd ever heard might be true.

They'd become almost mythical. Urban legends to scare children into behaving. But that was the thing—childhood fears tended to stick. People could reason themselves out of irrational fears of the dark; they could rationalize away strange noises in the night and shake off the hair-raising feeling of being watched every now and then.

But when the thing they'd been taught to fear made itself known, when it became *real*, when it insinuated itself into their life… There was no shaking that.

If one of the VanWarrens was truly communicating with a Shadow, there would be signs. And Vega hadn't seen a single one in any of them.

She stepped out of the tub. "The attempts on your life were too sloppy to be Shadow work. They would have been traceable and left too many loose ends." She took a towel off the rack to dry herself. "That said, we already know your family isn't above trying again." Which was another good reason to put some distance between Quinn and the rest of his family. "And as far as the payments go, the fact that they're so small and scattered means they were never meant to be found. Whoever set them up didn't intend for anyone to be directly involved. As long as it stays that way, the VanWarrens should be fine."

Quinn stood frozen, barely breathing, tense from head to toe. She reached out to touch his arm, and he flinched.

He might as well have struck her.

Vega pulled back and stepped away.

Quinn caught her hand to stop her before she got out of reach. He still wouldn't look at her, or even turn in her direction. She waited for him to say something, to pull her into his arms again like he'd done before. She wouldn't have resisted.

The chime shrilled again, so loud it echoed through the silent bathroom.

"Thank you," Quinn rasped and let her go.

Vega nodded. She ought to say something. Something meaningful. Something to chase away that bleak look on his face, but she'd never been much good with words.

Turning away felt wrong. Walking out of the bathroom felt worse. Vega was a trained soldier; the prospect of death, even an ugly, painful one, had always been part of her life. She would adjust and deal with it.

But Quinn…

Leaving him behind the way she knew she'd have to do for his own good made something in her want to howl and rage.

Because he would mourn her.

No one was ever supposed to mourn her.

23

Brunch was once again served poolside. Vega and Quinn arrived late but, despite the heavy silence between them, once they emerged into the gathering, Quinn put on the appropriate expression and held a united front with her.

They excused their tardiness with the story Vega had concocted before they'd left the suite. "I got a message from my father's hospice care this morning. He's not doing very well."

The news was met with sympathetic murmurs and polite questions about his condition.

"Fallout," Quinn said. "He got hit with it pretty bad. We thought the hospice had him stabilized, but these days…"

Geraldine launched herself at Vega, hugging her tight around the neck and Vega had to let go of Quinn's hand to return the embrace. "I'm so sorry. Is there anything we can do to help?"

There was so much sincerity in her voice, Vega swallowed hard. "It's just the way it is. The war took a lot from all of us." *Some more than others*, she thought, glancing over at Quinn. He looked away rather than meet her gaze. "I hope you'll understand why we can't stay for the rest of the reunion."

Geraldine's eyes went wide. "You're leaving?"

"As soon as we can book a shuttle flight," Quinn supplied.

"We still have business to discuss," Matthew injected. In deference to Vega, he kept his voice low and even, but he clearly had no sympathy for anyone's personal problems.

Quinn didn't take that well at all. He straightened from his slouch to his full height, looking down his nose at Matthew. "Business will have to wait. I'm not leaving my wife to bury her father alone."

I'm not leaving my wife.

Matthew seemed to recover enough sense to let the matter drop. He dipped a curt nod and made himself scarce.

"Do you really think it'll come to that?" Geraldine asked.

"They said it's only a matter of time now. They're keeping him comfortable, but he doesn't have long." Vega brushed away a tear and sniffled a little for effect.

Quinn made a small sound and pulled her into his side, tucking her head under his chin. It was all for his family's benefit but Vega still took comfort from the gesture. Far more than she deserved.

"Please know that we're here for you," Geraldine said, then walked away.

Vega tracked the girl's retreat to the buffet table where Zach was piling his plate with food. A quiet conversation made Zach look over at them with a frown, but Geraldine slapped his shoulder as if to say, *Don't stare!*

The two of them were definitely on friendly terms. Not VanWarren friendly, either. Normal person friendly. It was almost sweet.

"You want something to eat?" Quinn asked gruffly.

"Don't have much of an appetite right now."

His fingers curled around her nape. "How's your neck?"

She frowned. "Quiet." She hadn't felt a sting since before dawn. It only intensified her anxiety over when the next one might strike. Being on display like this wasn't helping, either. She was holding on to her persona, but just barely. If the device did go off on her in this crowd, Vega didn't know if she'd be able to hide it. She wanted to retreat into the darkest closet available and stay there until she could get a grip.

Hell of a mindset for a Shadow.

One day. A few mild zaps, one amazing fuck, and a single night without sleep was all it had taken for Vega to completely lose her shit.

She was embarrassed at herself.

The news of her and Quinn's upcoming departure spread through the gathering in seconds. They hadn't even reached their seats yet when Holden approached with a caution one might show a wild animal. "Hey, I just heard. I'm really sorry about your father, Vega."

"Thank you."

"I know this is too little too late, but if you give us a contact for his care provider, we can have our family physicians take over. Maybe we can get him somewhere nice, give him a little peace."

Before she could respond, Quinn said, "Thanks, but I already took care of all that."

Holden smiled, and it looked truly genuine. "Of course you did. That's good." He turned to Vega. "You'll let me know if there's anything I can do, won't you?"

She nodded.

"Good. Quinn, you think I can borrow you for a minute?"

He looked at Vega, and she caught a flash of concern in his gaze warring with his valiant effort to feign indifference.

"Go on," she said. "I'll be fine."

But she wasn't.

The minute Quinn let her go, Vega felt a stab of panic. It made about as much sense as everything else in her life recently. She swallowed it down and breathed in the tropical breeze. The sun was muted through a haze of white cloud cover today. It was a lovely, mild day, but Vega only saw a battlefield filled with too many potential casualties. No defenses and no sight of the enemy she could almost feel breathing down her neck.

Quinn got folded into a group of his male relatives, and all she could think was that there was too much distance between them, too many bodies in the way. If there was an attack, she'd have no hope in hell of reaching him in time.

The VanWarrens milled about in their fancy clothes, drank their expensive drinks, and smiled their fake smiles, filling her vision with too many moving targets, and Vega couldn't breathe. The air itself felt like a cage around her, trapping her in place when her entire body quivered with the need to move.

Without conscious thought, she did. Her feet had walked her a good twenty yards down from her original position before her mind caught up to what she was doing. Keeping Quinn in her line of sight. Palming a thin, curved knife off the buffet table, even though she had four of her own blades strapped to her legs beneath her skirt.

"Don't you look pensive this morning."

Vega blinked.

"What's the matter?" Emmett asked, eyeing her up and down as he smothered a belch. "Too much of a good time? Or not enough?" He reeked of alcohol, and, true to form, his left hand was curled around a crystal tumbler of hard liquor.

She didn't bother hiding her disgust or making any pretense of civility. "What do you want?"

Over his shoulder, she met eyes with Zach, who frowned at her. *You okay?* he mouthed.

Vega gave him a quick nod.

"Baby, I'm a greedy son of a bitch," Emmett said. "I want a lot of things. But right now, I just want to give you something I think you want very much."

"What could you possibly know about what I want?"

He grinned. "A lot more than you think. See, I did some digging about Quinn's pert little piece of ass. I know all about your fake ID, and how you like to party. And right now, you look like you could use a bit of *fun.*"

Vega swallowed hard. She had multiple fake ID chips and used them at random for different things to dilute her footprint.

But she'd only used one repeatedly—on Persephone 5. It was a burner persona she'd been planning to erase once she'd emerged from her Bliss binge. Except the binge had turned into a marathon, and the next thing she remembered was waking up in Quinn's shuttle cabin.

"I'm good, thanks."

She was far from good. The mere idea of a possible hit was giving her chills. More than ever before, Vega craved the feeling of all her worries fading away until there was nothing but light and music, and the delicious euphoria of a chemical high.

Her mouth parched for it. Her knees went weak for it.

Emmett noticed. The smirk he gave her was a lot sharper than it had any right to be, given his state of inebriation. "Oh, I think you'll reconsider. Wonder how much Quinn knows about your secret double life."

"What—do—you—want?" she growled. Quinn might already know about her addiction, since he'd been the one to pluck her out of her most recent relapse, but he didn't know everything it made her do.

Vega herself didn't, but she'd come to her senses in enough strange places with enough strange people to hazard a guess.

Emmett's shoulders hitched up to his ears. "Maybe I just wanna do a good deed for once." By feeding her mind-altering drugs? "Maybe I want a taste of Quinn's life. The sweeter parts, anyway." His gaze raked down her body and back up, but only as far as her breasts. "What do you care, as long as you get yours?"

Vega would be gone in a matter of days. She didn't give half a shit about what any of these people thought of her.

But Quinn would. He'd care a whole hell of a lot if Emmett started spreading unsavory rumors about her among the clan after Quinn had gone to such lengths to convince them all that he and Vega were genuinely in love. After he'd given her full access to their money.

And it would get so much worse if she then disappeared out of the blue, never to be heard from again.

How long before someone discretely took a chunk out of those accounts and blame it on her?

And once the general VanWarren opinion turned against her, how long before Emmett, or even Matthew suggested that Vega had been playing Quinn from the start—or worse, that he might have had a hand in her disappearance?

They already eyed him sideways for how he looked, and what his body could do. It wouldn't be that much of a mental leap for them to go from thinking of him as a freak to a full-on criminal. And, the way they'd stirred shit up in the last couple of days, Vega was willing to bet there were several VanWarrens who wouldn't need an ounce of persuading before they dug out their pitchforks and led the charge.

It's what she would have done. It would be the easiest way to take out both targets and restore the status quo they'd enjoyed before Quinn had reappeared to wreak havoc in their miserable, complacent lives.

Vega glanced over to where Quinn stood deep in conversation with his relatives.

Family was everything to Quinn—the one he'd forged on Anamtaigh, and the one he'd been born into. Regardless of what he ultimately decided to do about the money, he'd been given a chance to rebuild the relationships his mother had broken all those years ago, and he was well on his way to making genuine connections with a few of them already. A handful of awkward starts notwithstanding, there were VanWarrens here willing to meet him halfway.

Fuck if she'd let a wasted piece of shit like Emmett take that away from him.

The emotional haze lifted, clearing her mind, and she instantly pulled back her shoulders. In the midst of her mentally checking out of her entire existence, Vega had almost forgotten why she was here in the first place. She had a mission: keep Quinn safe, by any means necessary. That's what she'd signed up for, and that's what she would do until she couldn't anymore.

Leash or not, she was still a Hound, and she would damn well bite. *Hard.*

Vega turned her gaze back to Emmett and let him see a tiny hint of the Shadow lurking beneath her painted lips and her pretty summer dress.

When she smiled, he gulped.

But he followed her like a dog when she sashayed her way from the gathering toward the cool, shadowed entry of the main house.

24

Holden, Quinn decided, was a decent kind of guy. A little young and rash, but smart enough to know it. His short, awkward apology for the way he'd acted during their meeting had gone a long way to softening Quinn toward his little brother. "Forget about it," he said, offering his hand. "We all say shit we don't mean when the stakes are high."

And sometimes there's so damn much to say, the words don't come at all.

Quinn kept reminding himself that Vega was a Shadow as if it would somehow ease the invisible clutch he'd felt around his throat since she'd told him her plans in their suite.

She was everything he should fear, hate, and want to flee from. It wasn't as if she'd ever bothered to hide it, either. In fact, she'd gone out of her way trying to make him fear and hate her. Really, it was his own goddamn fault for being so stubborn.

What was it she'd told him? *A Hawk will become your best friend, and you'll never suspect them, not even as you watch them bury the blade in your heart.*

Vega might not have been a Hawk, but she was a true artist with those knives of hers. Until this morning, he'd had no idea his artificial heart could hurt as much as it did. And, stupid son of a bitch that he was, Quinn was just happy she still held on to the hilt.

Twist it hard, wife. Just don't let go.

But she would. It was the only thing she knew how to do: walk away and face the storm alone. And Quinn had no logical reason to give her for staying.

Cousin Andras was droning on about the humanitarian services he'd setup under his band name. Clearly, word had spread about Quinn's experience with the war as well as his plans for the estate. All of a sudden, everyone was eager to explain why their ventures deserved to stay fully funded. The group of four had already grown into ten, and Quinn was starting to get a headache.

He tried to pay attention, but it all sounded like inconsequential bullshit compared to the one conversation he really wanted to have.

When Uncle Trent pushed his way close and opened his mouth, Quinn had had enough. He held up his hand in front of Trent's face. "No. Your vintage cell phone factory is done. I already sent the papers to start shutting down operations."

Trent gaped at him.

"I'm liquidating the assets and transferring them to Aunt Ivy's book business."

Ivy, it seemed, had a dreamer's heart and couldn't resist bringing fantasies to the worlds at large. Most of her portfolio of published authors was woefully underperforming but, in this particular instance, Quinn didn't see failure. Only a deep desire to inject a little beauty and magic back into the human race. He hadn't told her yet, but he planned to put a condition on the investment. She had to set up a printing press on every world where a VanWarren maintained a residence and convert at least thirty percent of her portfolio into print editions.

Books should have pages that yellowed with time.

Mumbling under his breath, Trent turned right around and walked away.

Now that he had everyone's attention, Quinn studied the faces around him, then pointed to one after the other. "No, no, no, yes, no, yes, maybe, no, definitely not, and I'm willing to discuss—later."

Half of the group dispersed.

The other half shocked him by sticking around. Holden was keeping as straight a face as he could manage, but his eyes watered with the effort not to laugh. There were a few lighthearted chuckles, a few claps on the back, and then the conversation magically shifted to other things. Everyone was curious about the parlor games Kendry had planned for that evening. Apparently, it was a beloved tradition in the VanWarren family, and something they looked forward to.

Kendry being in charge of organizing them every single year made the shock all the deeper. Who would have thought Quinn's shrew of a sister-in-law had a whimsical side?

Second cousin Jacen was the first to share his favorite experience with them, and it set off a chain reaction that had Quinn scratching his head. Everything they recounted sounded like…fun. The kind of fun his refugee family would have had on Anamtaigh. Board games that incorporated wild dares, impromptu theatrical performances, scavenger hunts, and stunts people sometimes took a bit too far.

The sense of camaraderie he felt from them around the topic made Quinn want to be part of it. Was he finally starting to see the human side of the VanWarrens?

The group shifted as people wandered off, and others came over. Quinn listened more than he talked, but he was fine with that.

Then Geraldine and Zach pulled Quinn's attention away from the others.

"How are you holding up?" That was the thing about Geraldine. She was all about the people. She would have fit right in on Anamtaigh. Maybe he could introduce her to Laura, arrange for a concert on Mai.

"Fine."

When she smiled, it was with her whole heart shining in her eyes. "Good. That's good." Quinn hoped she never lost that spark. It was sorely needed. "So hey, have you seen where Vega went off to? Zach and I wanted to take her out…"

Quinn didn't hear the rest. He was on his feet, scanning the crowd for her dark hair and blue-green dress. *She wouldn't just leave*, he told himself. Vega was still on the job he'd hired her to do. At the very least, she would want to deliver him somewhere safe before she disappeared out of his life forever.

But where the fuck was she?

"…figured she could use a little distraction, you know?" Zach was saying. Something about an excursion to some club on the mainland.

Cousin Andras paused beside them on his way to the buffet table. "You're looking for Vega?"

"Yeah," Geraldine said, "you know where she is?"

"I think I saw her go off with Emmett earlier."

Quinn's gut tightened.

"Why?" Zach snorted. "They don't even like each other."

Cousin Andras shrugged. "Beats the hell out of me. Emmett's been acting weird as shit the last few days."

"*Our* Emmett?" someone else snarked. "No, I don't believe it."

"It's true," Geraldine chimed in. "You know my attendant Kora overheard him getting pissy with the house manager. She sent the wrong attendant to run an errand for him and the poor kid told someone else what he was picking up." She leaned in to stage whisper, "It was a whole bottle of Bliss—*whoa!*"

Quinn shoved his way out of the group so hard it sent a couple of them stumbling back. Then he was running, his com raised to his mouth. "Vega, Vega, Vega."

~

Most of the rooms were already covered by Vega's minions, which limited her options where Emmett was concerned. She didn't want any record of what she was about to do. With Emmett trailing her footsteps so close she could hear his ragged breath at her back, Vega led the way to a small nook of a room that only had a weird half-couch-looking seat by the window and a shelf of books to one side.

Vega imagined some long ago VanWarren had built it out as a private sanctuary of peace and quiet and then never returned again. As small and antiquated as it was, no one ever used it. The VanWarrens liked their environments to be grander, more stimulating. But they had left the room untouched, perhaps in honor of its original owner.

As soon as Vega closed the door, Emmett grabbed her and shoved her back against it. "I knew you were a whore," he whispered. "I knew it the second I saw you in that dress the first night."

His hands were clammy on her skin. She broke his hold easily and shoved him back. A flash of alarm briefly cleared the drunken haze from his eyes, then anger returned, spiced with disgust. He was gearing up for an attack, but she cut him off before he could move. "I'll take my payment in advance."

Taken aback again, Emmett lagged a second catching up to what she was saying. With a leer that triggered her gag reflex, he went to the bookshelf and pulled on one of the books closest to the door.

A hidden compartment clicked open two shelves below. He pulled out a couple of glasses and a mini bottle of champagne. Handing her a glass, he opened the bottle and split the contents between them. It was barely enough for two swallows once the foam settled. Tossing the empty bottle aside, Emmett reached into his jacket pocket and pulled out a small vial of shimmering pink liquid.

Vega stopped breathing. It was Bliss—and not the cheap knockoff stuff, either. She could tell by the iridescence that he'd paid a premium for the pure, uncut version. The high didn't last as long, but it was so much more intense. Pure happiness. Pure *Bliss*.

Emmett noticed her intense stare.

He was too close, the toe of his shoe sliding between her feet. They were roughly the same height, but Emmett had a weight advantage, and Vega was distracted. Having momentarily lost her bearings, she retreated a step and her back met the wall. She blinked up at Emmett's face in time to see the triumph in his eyes as he brought the vial to his mouth and bit down on the stopper to pull it out.

The scent hit her straight in the nose and her head reeled back. Sweet flowers, warmth and sunshine concentrated in a liquid that looked like it shouldn't exist. A magical potion to take all her troubles away.

Vega's breath came faster as she watched him tip the vial over his glass, then hers, depositing three drops into each. Enough to knock a normal person on their ass for hours. Enough to give Vega a light, nerve-tingling buzz and help her relax for a little while.

Emmett clinked his glass against hers. "Here's to a delightful new partnership."

His toast brought Vega down to her senses as she speared him with a sharp stare. *Partnership*. Because, as with all attempts at blackmail, it wouldn't stop at one payment or even twenty. Emmett was stupid enough to think he could keep her on the hook for as long as it entertained him.

She brought the glass up to her lips and drank. Butterflies took flight in her belly almost immediately. Her muscles loosened; her spine relaxed against the wall's support. Emmett weaved in and out of focus as her pupils pulsed with her heartbeat.

He fell forward, catching himself on his hands on either side of her. Already drunk, the dose of Bliss sent him over the edge. With a lusty groan, Emmett put one hand on her throat and squeezed, angling his face to lick at her mouth as his other hand groped her skirt up her thigh. A couple of inches higher, and he'd feel the knives.

Vega caught his roving hand by the wrist to stop him.

It was the kind of instinctive, feminine retreat he expected, and he used his hold on her throat to choke her harder as he slammed her back against the wall. "Easy or rough," he purred. "Your choice."

The bite of pain, the pressure on her throat, awakened Vega's fight response. "Took the words right out of my mouth," she said around a feral little smile. She was seconds away from ripping his eye out of his skull, hand raised to strike, when the blinking red light on her com cuff caught her attention.

Quinn.

At the last second, Vega changed tactics, grabbing him by the ear instead. With a hard yank, she distracted him enough to give her room to breathe. A jab at the inside of his arm broke his hold on her throat and gained her the few inches she needed to bring her knee up between his legs—*hard.*

He went down on his knees with a howl of pain, clutching at his crotch and cursing her to hell and back. The pitiful state she'd brought him to within seconds disgusted Vega more than anything he'd done so far. He was the worst kind of waste—the kind that shouldn't be breathing the same air as her.

Bliss coursed through her veins, and she felt invincible. Untouchable.

She could end it. She could put Emmett out of everyone's misery, and no one would ever have to know. All she had to do was snap his neck and stash his body in some closet until dark, then row his ass out to sea and dump it over the side. No blood. No evidence left behind.

Vega was reaching for him, ready to follow through, when she heard the heavy thud of rapidly approaching footsteps.

Sanity returned, and she pulled back.

One second.

Two seconds.

She reached again.

Three seconds.

No, she couldn't kill him.

Not without a good reason.

And then he gave her one.

Emmett looked up at her and she saw no semblance of rationality in his snarling gaze. Only pain, and hate, and violence. The same Bliss-fueled feeling of invincibility that coursed through her had him in his clutches, too, except he didn't have enough experience to control it. Vega braced for an explosion of fury, ready to strike and put him down for good.

Three things happened then, all at the same time.

Emmett grunted and surged to his feet.

The door opened with enough force to rip it off its hinges.

And Vega met Emmett's face with one blow, angling her fist to lay him out flat and break her own hand.

But Quinn didn't seem to register that the threat had passed. He looked murderous, intent on Emmett's prone form.

Vega would have happily let him go to town, but she picked up on new voices outside in the hall. In a bid for damage control, she whimpered his name and threw herself into his path, slamming into his middle and wrapping her arms around him. She didn't have to fake the pained moan as her broken hand clutched at his back.

Quinn stopped in his tracks.

Gasps and curses filled the small room as other VanWarrens poured in to witness the scene, and she knew what they saw. She knew what she had to do.

"Thank God you're here!"

Quinn flinched so hard it brought his arms up around her. He picked her up and removed her to the far side of the room, hunching over her to shield her from Emmett, who hadn't made a sound since he'd hit the floor.

Vega turned her face to make her voice carry before she launched into the most important performance she'd ever give. "I was so scared.

He said he wanted to apologize for the other night and start over, but I think he put something in my drink, and then he was all over me, and I was so scared…"

The rumble in his chest was a balm to her nerves. But she sensed the others retreat as if Quinn was a bomb ready to go off. Which, to be fair, he was. Vega felt the tension coiled inside him. Given half a chance, the smallest excuse, he would set her aside and rip Emmett apart—literally. She squeezed him tighter and gave a little shiver.

"He's out cold," Zach said somewhere behind Quinn. "Someone get the medic."

"It's true." Geraldine sounded shaken. "Oh my God, he really did it. This is Bliss."

They needed to leave—all of them. Their voices were winding Quinn tight as a string. Vega wasn't sure she could keep him still much longer. "I don't feel so good," she murmured.

In seconds flat, Quinn had her out of there and two doors down in a room that echoed in a weird way. He sat her on a couch and knelt before her. His big hands cupped her face as he looked into her eyes. Her pupils were dancing wildly, causing light to flare and dim all around her. Quinn had a halo one second, and in the next, he grew demonic horns as his face transformed into something wild and feral and utterly beautiful. His eyes glowed with the golden light of twin full moons, and she wanted to howl at the sky with him.

Then his thumbs brushed across her cheeks and brows, and he frowned as his mouth moved. "…Vega, can you hear me? Are you okay?"

She blinked hard, curled her fingers into her palms and flinched at the pain. Oh, right. She'd broken something.

Quinn reacted as if she was about to pass out. "*Where the fuck is the medic!*" he roared sideways.

She blinked again, and he was gone, and a stranger was sitting before her, fiddling with a limp, black mesh glove. "…just a fracture. You were lucky you didn't shatter your wrist. But don't worry, we'll have you fixed up in no time."

He gently took hold of something that looked like it was attached to her but didn't feel like it, until he did something and pain shot all the way up her arm and into her brain. The glove slid onto her rapidly swelling appendage, loose mesh settling into place from her knuckles to a good several inches up her forearm. The soft material caused thousands of needles to prick her skin from underneath—and that was before the mesh thickened and solidified into a hard brace.

"This will keep your wrist stable while you heal. It'll adjust in size as the swelling goes down, and is perfectly safe around water. Although you may want to be careful with it for a few days. The padding is minimal. If you bump yourself, it'll hurt. I put a time-released pain patch on the inside of your wrist. It should keep you comfortable for the next twenty-four hours."

Vega nodded.

The medic disappeared and she rocked on a fluffy cloud, floating down a lazy river of sunshine. Voices around her rose and fell. Many of them. She picked up on a few words here and there, piecing together what was happening.

Quinn was livid. He wanted Emmett booted off the estate.

Several voices agreed, but a few others argued back. Emmett might be an ass, but he was still family, and he belonged there. She picked up on the unspoken, *She doesn't,* and it sounded like Quinn did, too.

While the bickering continued, Vega became aware of bodies bracketing her on the couch. She glanced to each side. Geraldine and Zach. They looked bored, watching the drama. Neither of them said anything for a while until Geraldine murmured, "Shame the rest of the stash got spilled."

Vega snorted and giggled. "It was the good stuff, too."

Zach grinned, but then he shook his head. "Still can't believe Emmett would pull something like that."

"With Quinn's wife," Geraldine added. "You gotta figure he's either high or suicidal."

"Or both," Zach agreed.

Vega sighed, content with the fruits of her labors. It didn't matter if Emmett stayed or went. Didn't matter what he tried to tell the others. They'd seen the evidence of his transgression and heard *her* version of it first. It was the word of a drunken reprobate with a sordid history and demonstrated animosity toward Vega against her broken hand

and Quinn's murderous fury. Emmett stood no chance in hell.

"I think it's fading," she said to no one in particular. It was true. The lights weren't pulsing as much anymore, and voices were starting to regain their sharp precision. Her body would float for a little while yet, but her mind was pretty much clear.

"Here," Zach said, offering her a glass. "Lemon water. It'll help with the cotton mouth."

"Spoken like someone who knows."

"Maybe."

His sheepish shrug made Geraldine laugh.

So very normal. So comfortable with each other and, surprisingly, with her. She might have liked being friends with them.

"We *are* friends," Geraldine assured her.

Oh, okay. Apparently, Vega had said that out loud.

"Technically, we're family," Zach corrected. "But I won't hold that against either of you."

Vega inclined her head. "Much obliged." She took a tentative sip of water, then gulped down the rest in two swallows.

When she came up for air, she almost jumped out of her skin to find Quinn crouching before her again, looking worried. "How are you feeling?"

"Mmm…" She rolled her shoulders and smiled, her lower lip catching beneath her teeth for a second. "*Good.*"

Zach coughed and made a quick exit, Geraldine right on his heels.

Quinn grinned, scooping her up against his chest. "Come on, let's get you to bed."

"Will you be joining us for parlor games this evening?" Kendry's voice snipped out, but it sounded like she was making an effort to be polite and considerate. Almost like she would accept if they declined without arguing, for once.

"No," Quinn said at the same time as Vega chirped, "Of course!"

Quinn missed a step but kept going, tossing over his shoulder, "We'll think about it."

"But we'll be there," Vega assured her with an exaggerated wink.

Back in their suite, Quinn closed and locked the door, then set her on the bed. "Now, you wanna tell me what really happened?"

Vega sighed. "Emmett tracked down my clubbing history on Persephone 5. He was trying to blackmail me."

"Did not know who he was fucking with," Quinn said, grinning. Almost like he was proud of her for beating the shit out of his blood kin.

Vega's spine straightened a little at the praise. But then her head swam and she listed sideways. Drugs on top of injury, on top of no sleep, were not a good combination. She didn't resist as Quinn slipped his big, deft fingers up along her thighs to remove her knife straps. Before she could ask him to, he set them down on the nightstand where she could reach them.

"You would have killed him," she observed as he rearranged her to lie down properly beneath the covers. Cradling her injured arm against her chest, she turned on her side.

"I still might," Quinn groused, and then the mattress compressed as he stretched out on the bed at her back.

"Why? I didn't." As murderous as Vega had felt, even riding a Bliss high, rational thought had won out in the end.

One of the softer pillows appeared in front of her. "Exactly," he said, as if that made perfect sense. Quinn arranged her arm on the pillow, and she sighed. That was so much more comfortable. "Get some rest. I'll wake you when it's time for the games."

She nodded, already halfway under, but a frown tugged on her brows as she felt the bed decompress. "You not gonna leave, are you?"

A pause, and then Quinn's big arm settled over her waist. "Try and make me."

25

Birdsongs pulled Vega out of a bottomless black pit. Loud, chirpy birdsongs that kept getting louder.

Something big rumbled behind her, and a heavy weight lifted from her waist. The pleasant heat retreated, and the chirping stopped.

Vega wanted to sink back into the glorious abyss of sleep, but then there was a hand on her arm bigger than felt natural, and then soft lips pressed to her bare shoulder as stubble scratched along her skin.

She pried her eyes open, blinking her vision back into focus, and groaned.

"Way I see it," Quinn's voice rumbled at her back, "we can either drag ourselves out of bed, put on *casual attire*, and go downstairs for the parlor games…" His fingers trailed down her arm to her elbow in a butterfly-soft caress. "Or not."

Another of those shoulder-twitching zaps cracked the back of her neck, and she was wide awake, waiting for the electrical inferno to fry her spine and brain.

Quinn must have felt it, too. He wrapped himself around her and held on so tight, and her jaw was clenched too hard to warn him. If that thing went off full force, it would kill her. And if he was touching her, he would die right along with her.

In the endless seconds of silence, as they both waited for the other shoe to drop, Vega started wondering if maybe that was why he did it. Not because he wanted to die but because he didn't want her to die alone. That big, mighty heart of his, artificial though it was, wanted her to have in death what the Shadows had taken from her in life—someone to hold onto when everything fell to shit.

And it fucking hurt.

So much worse than anything Talon had ever done to her.

After a full minute passed and the torture didn't come, Vega made herself relax in Quinn's hold, hoping it would loosen him up a little. One of them needed to keep a level head. He unclenched enough to let her take a deep breath but didn't let go.

"If we stay," she said to distract him—and herself, "Emmett wins." They'd already left themselves wide open to his machinations by hiding away for so long. He would have had ample opportunity to plead his case and, as optimistic as she'd been during her happy high, she wasn't a complete idiot. With so many VanWarrens still keeping a cold distance from Quinn, it wasn't out of the realm of possibility for Emmett to convince someone to his side of things. Even if it was only one person, Vega and Quinn needed to be there, right in front of them, playing their parts to remind them that *she* was the victim.

"Does it matter?" Quinn countered, absently trailing his thumb over her bare shoulder.

"Yes." Of course it mattered.

And he made that clear when the soothing motion paused for a breath, and his big body tensed again, turning to rock behind her.

"I have no problem walking away from all this."

For her? "You would regret it for the rest of your life."

Quinn snorted. "I told you I know how to live without money."

"You wouldn't walk away from your family." Not while there were still VanWarrens who didn't openly hate him. Quinn would go to hell and back for them.

Vega turned over, careful of her fractured hand. She could have crushed Emmett's jaw and never shown a mark, but that wouldn't have helped her case. People didn't stand behind strength—they feared it. But they would flock together with a righteous fury to play hero for the underdog. As long as it didn't require too much effort.

"Here's the thing. If you leave, you're back to square one. No money, no family. No one of consequence. But once they get their hands on the accounts, your family will rock a lot of boats trying to get their shares."

Understanding cleared the grouchy scowl off his face. For the moment, no one seemed to know about the monthly payments except Quinn. And Quinn knew better than to touch any of them. But once the family started changing things and the payments stopped, they might end up in a shitstorm of pain. The Shadows had no mercy for ignorance.

"Right now, you're in the perfect position to live a long, happy life. As long as the status quo holds, the Shadows won't have any reason to look your way—so don't give them one. Put a little distance between yourself and the VanWarrens you don't like. But keep control of the estate. Keep the payments going, and your family will be safe." The Shadows wouldn't jeopardize their cash cow unless said cow became more trouble than it was worth. "And, with your SU connections, you're protected from both sides."

"Until they find out my family is funding their enemy and costing them lives."

"The telepaths can take care of themselves," she said ruthlessly. "Your family's ignorance will protect them from the SU, and you will have the means to mitigate any damage on your end. Offset the payments with humanitarian aid. Fund the SU's projects. Set up another refuge house like Laura did."

"And carry the guilt for the rest of my life."

"What's the alternative?"

"What we agreed to! We find the Shadows together—"

"And, what? I go in with my six shiny knives to take them all out? Hoping I don't drop dead all on my own before I clear the door?"

Quinn's face set into lines so harsh she wanted to kiss each one to make it relax. His anguish made her chest ache, knowing there was nothing she could do to make it better. There was no fixing this.

"The plan was to protect you, make sure your family was safe, and find Talon. This is how we do it." It was the only way.

The alert chirped again.

When she moved to retreat, Quinn caught her hand against his face, forcing her gaze back to his. She waited for him to say something, but he didn't.

The chirping rose to a deafening pitch, and he growled. "I'm going to smash that thing to dust."

A few minutes later, they walked into the designated parlor hand in hand and dressed in what Vega assumed would pass for 'casual attire' in the VanWarren world. She'd opted for loose-fitting pants, a stretchy tank top, and a cozy hoodie in similar shades of off-white. Her favorite running shoes and a knife strapped to each ankle completed the outfit.

She glanced over at Quinn in his black T-shirt and slacks and decided this should be what he wore half the time. The other half, he should be naked. His body radiated warmth. Thanks to her injury and mellow Bliss crash, Vega was struggling to retain any body heat whatsoever. She wanted to rub herself all over him to soak up his.

The gathering was smaller than usual. No children, very few elders. Quinn cursed under his breath.

Following the direction of his cold stare, she spotted Emmett lurking in the far corner. His face was a bit bruised but other than that, he looked the same as he always did, complete with a drink in his hand and a surly disposition. He kept his head down and wouldn't make eye contact, which suited Vega just fine.

She raised her broken hand a little to keep it visible. The mesh brace didn't do anything to hide the bruised, swollen mess underneath, and Vega had deliberately chosen light-colored clothing to make it stand out.

Scanning the faces around them, she smiled at Zach and Geraldine and returned Holden's nod of greeting. Matthew looked as jovial as ever, but his expression softened the slightest bit with what might have been familial shame or regret when his gaze touched on her injured arm. He flushed and turned away. Definitely shame.

The parlor had been rearranged, with all furniture shoved toward the walls. There were tables laid out with finger foods and drinks against one wall, and all the doors were opened onto the dusk outside.

Kendry clapped her hands to get everyone's attention. Vega had never seen her like this before. She wore pants with *pockets* and an oversized, worn shirt with the sleeves rolled up and the hem knotted at her waist. Her hair was up in a ponytail, and her face was so bright and open Vega half thought the woman had a twin.

"Who's ready to play?" she asked, her voice naturally amplified by the cavernous room.

The family cheered, drawing closer to their mistress of ceremonies, so eager for whatever was about to come. Having never played anything other than war games before, Vega didn't know what to expect. But it was kind of nice to see them all so uninhibited in their excitement.

"This year, the honor of choosing our first game goes to our newest family member, Vega."

Vega tried and failed to spot any malice in her sister-in-law's pronouncement. There was an approving hum, and Kendry beckoned her forward.

Quinn was no help. When she looked up at him for guidance on how to proceed here, he shrugged, then leaned down to murmur, "You wanted to play."

Vega pasted on a smile and stepped forward.

"As is tradition," Kendry explained, "All of our games tonight have been planned out to the last detail. There are some that will take minutes and some that might take all night. The next game will be chosen by the winner of the previous one." She brought out a glass bowl filled with little paper squares. "Pick one, open it, and read it out loud for the rest of us."

Easy enough. Vega reached in with her good hand and rooted around to give the rest of them a little thrill before she picked one of the squares and pulled it out. The paper was so thick that whatever was written on it didn't bleed through the fold. It was also sealed shut.

Vega took her time, struggling to unfold it, then cleared her throat and read the word written on the inside: "The first game of the night is called… Savages."

A few woops rose up, but mostly, the VanWarrens didn't seem to know this game any more than she did.

Kendry took the paper from her, then explained to everyone, "I guess our first game of the night will be *the* game of the night." She smiled wide, raising her glass tablet as she read the game's description for the rest of them. "The challenge is simple: Spend one night beneath the open skies, find the treasure in your camp, and bring it to the judge once the sun has cleared the trees. You may choose to work alone or in pairs. Each team will be dropped off at a different location on Midnight Island to make camp and look for their treasure. This game can have as many winners as there are teams. Once you find your treasure, you can choose to keep it or trade it in for another prize of equal value."

Great. Another night out in the elements. She was almost looking forward to it.

"Now, here are the rules," Kendry continued. "Stealing another team's treasure is not allowed. Players who sabotage another team will be disqualified. The distance from each camp to the judge will be the same—but the tools you get may just make or break your chances for success."

An excited hum moved through the crowd. Vega could tell this was something foreign and exotic to them. Every single VanWarren present was chomping at the bit to get going.

All of them, except Quinn, who looked like he'd rather shoot himself in the foot than spend a night outdoors.

"When I give the signal, the game will begin. In the western solar, you will find an assortment of packs filled with a variety of tools and gadgets to help you through the night. Not all packs are created equal. Some will include the barest necessities. Others will have tools to help you retrieve your treasure. There might be comfort items or useless things that only add more weight for you to carry.

"Your first and perhaps the most important task of the night is to choose a pack—*without* knowing what the contents are. You will then make your way to the front lawn, where HOVRs are waiting to take you to one of the designated camps on Midnight Island. Make sure you have your pack with you when you exit the transport. Once all passengers are out, the HOVRs will automatically return to the compound."

Simple enough. Ela's mild climate kept the nights at a comfortable temperature, so no one would need to worry about freezing. It also didn't have much in the way of natural predators, so safety wouldn't be a concern. Vega didn't know where Midnight Island was, but if it was anything like Crescent Island, this would be a vacation with the added fun of a treasure hunt.

Kendry lowered the tablet. "Is everyone clear on what we're doing?"

The family sounded off their approvals.

"Excellent. The game starts…*Now!*"

Someone screamed, and then they all ran. Most of them bottlenecked at the door, and Vega prudently shifted out of their way. But she noted that a few people went in the other direction, outside onto the lawn, where there was less traffic.

"If you're not feeling up to it," Kendry said, "you're welcome to sit this one out. I didn't anticipate anyone having a serious injury when I set up the games."

Quinn had shoved his way across to them and as the parlor emptied, he said, "We're bowing out. Right?"

She almost laughed, knowing he was more eager to stay in for his sake than hers. Biting back a grin, Vega said, "I never back down from a challenge."

"Then you might want to hurry before all the good packs are taken," Kendry advised and followed the rest of the family to the western solar.

By the time they reached the solar, there were two packs left, and everyone was already on their way out. Quinn shook his head as he picked them up. Of all the ridiculous things…

"I still don't like this," he said.

"One night out in the open won't kill you," Vega said, holding out her good hand for one of the packs.

He scowled and herded her ahead of him. "You sure about that?"

Vega grabbed a fluffy throw pillow on her way out the side door to cross the lawn. "I may be one hand short of a full deck, but I'm still the baddest bitch here. Something tries to hurt my man, it'll have to go through me first."

Quinn tripped over the threshold. "Your man?" The words made his heart whirr like mad until a fine sheen of sweat covered him from neck to toe.

But before he could savor them too much, Vega schooled her features and shrugged. "Figure of speech."

Right. No big deal. Just like that blush, she was trying to hide. If it weren't for her busted hand, he'd haul her into the nearest closet and make her say it again. And again. Until she actually believed it.

Anything to give her second thoughts about leaving him in the dust.

Three HOVRs rose off the ground as Quinn and Vega rounded the corner onto the gravel path. Quinn led Vega to the nearest one left and helped her into it before climbing in after her. As the vehicle rose up into the sky, a folded piece of paper fell off the front dash moments before the interior lights turned off and the roof cleared into a shell of polished glass, giving them an all-around view of the brilliant night sky.

Vega sighed and leaned her head back. "Would you look at that?"

The sun had set a few minutes before their take-off, but the night was far from dark. A tail of galactic gasses trailed overhead in star-studded hues of violet and pink. Diaphanous veils of strange clouds floated on gentle air currents, flickering and pulsing with soundless flares of green bioluminescence. Quinn spotted a flock of flying things, their spines and wings lit up one moment, then disappearing into darkness the next.

The dance of colors all around them was breathtaking, and he almost regretted that he hadn't bothered to look up at the night sky a single time since their arrival. If Vega hadn't insisted on coming out tonight, he might never have known such beauty existed.

Too soon, the HOVR descended low over the water, and a dark landmass grew and stretched in front of them. Quinn braced himself as treetops scraped along the HOVR's bottom, and then they descended into a clearing barely large enough to accommodate the vehicle.

The HOVR doors opened, but the engine didn't idle down. Kendry hadn't been kidding about them getting stranded here. "Did you see where the other HOVRs landed?"

"A few," Vega said, retrieving the fallen paper thing. "Our extraction point is about three miles back toward the south. I saw the light beacon on the beach we passed over."

That made one of them.

"Are you going to get out?"

"I'm thinking."

Vega chuckled and slipped out on her side, giving him no choice but to follow or leave her out there on her own with a pillow and a broken hand.

Quinn cursed whatever genetic defect had fooled otherwise sensible people into thinking the great outdoors were anything but miserable. There was a reason why humanity had spent millennia perfecting indoor living.

He tossed their bags to the ground and then climbed out of the vehicle. As soon as he'd cleared the door, it closed, and the HOVR rose up into the sky and disappeared. Mild panic caused sweat to break out along his spine, and he checked his com to make sure it still worked.

Just in case.

The device worked perfectly. It turned out they weren't too far from Crescent Island, and the mainland wasn't too far beyond that. As long as he could call out, a rescue should be able to reach them within the hour. Barring massive bleeding, Quinn could survive an hour out in the woods. Piece of cake.

Behind him, Vega was sitting on the pillow, pulling stuff out of one of the packs.

"Did we get anything good?"

In answer, she set a round metal canister on a flat patch of the ground, twisted the top, and pulled it up. The core inside lit up and in seconds, the clearing around them got downright hot. Flameless fire. Next, she pulled out a light sleeping bag, and it dawned on Quinn that if they wanted to sleep tonight, they'd have to do it on the ground.

"Well, we have food and water," Vega said, lining up three small containers and a good-sized bottle close to the flame. More of the finger foods he'd seen in the parlor, neatly packed for their convenience. "And emergency beacons," she added, tugging on a little device clipped to the outside of each pack.

The last thing she did was unfold the piece of paper someone had left in their HOVR for them. It was a printed map of the island, with an X marking the extraction point to the south and a circle around their current location. Both of their coms had built-in navigation, but how many of the others would have had such gadgets on them when the game began? For their sake, Quinn hoped at least one person on each team knew how to read a map. He didn't.

Vega turned the map over, read a few lines of text printed on the back, then set it aside without interest and reached for the other bag.

This one was about as useful as earplugs in the rain. There was a small night light, a fluffy toy, and a set of three heavy black balls. Quinn recognized them as parts of a stupid art piece he'd seen in the spa lobby.

"I don't like this game," he complained, taking a seat on the ground beside Vega.

She chuckled. "It's good for you to get out of your comfort zone."

"I don't have a comfort zone."

Well, that wasn't quite true. He'd been pretty damn comfortable a few hours ago in their suite. The nap he'd taken with Vega hadn't been nearly long enough to make up for the sleepless night before, but it had been the most restful sleep he'd had in weeks.

"When I was in basic training, they would take us out into the middle of nowhere with nothing but a compass and a multi-tool, and we'd have two days to find our way back to camp. The first ten would get a half-day rest period. The rest of whoever made it back was taken right out again to a different location for the next round."

"Okay, what the actual fuck? Were they *trying* to kill you all?"

Vega shrugged. "You don't get good by being comfortable. And they didn't want good. They wanted the best." Her voice softened a little as she lowered her gaze from the sky above to the flameless fire before her. "The worst part wasn't how many died, but how many fought to live."

She became lost in whatever nightmarish memories still haunted her, and Quinn had no idea how to get her back without her thinking he was pitying her again. He wasn't. The thought of everything the Shadows had put her through just to breathe another day twisted his gut with rage. She was sitting right there within arm's reach, but somehow they still had a tighter hold on her than Quinn ever would.

In a few days, Vega would be gone, and he might never see her again.

He knew it was for him. Quinn had given her a mission to keep him safe, and she was prepared to do that at any cost, including her own life.

It was unacceptable.

And there was nothing he could do to stop her from walking out the door.

He sat there in silence for a while, listening to the woods around them. "Do you think those centipede things are nocturnal?"

Vega looked at him, and her blank expression cracked beneath a small, wicked smile. "Why? Do you want me to catch you one?"

Quinn almost managed to hold back a shudder. "Maybe we should look for the treasure instead." It might help take his mind off their inevitable goodbye. He reached for the map. The writing on the back had to be a clue to finding—

"Or we could have sex."

The map crinkled in the crush of his fist. His artificial heart ramped up its whirr so much he heard it humming in his chest. Quinn didn't trust himself to move as a fever took over his body, blanking his mind.

There was no mockery on her face, no humor in her eyes. She watched him without blinking, and he knew that whatever he said or did next would change everything. He felt it in the sudden stillness in the air around them, the steady warmth blazing from the flameless fire.

Vega gave a small, careless shrug. "It might change your mind about the benefits of sleeping outdoors."

In an instant, he shot so hard it hurt as he recalled their little interlude on the rooftop massage table. The light playing over her skin, the feel of her hands on him, the arch of her back as she took him inside her.

All the things he'd wanted to do to her but couldn't.

She'd just presented him with an open invitation to do them all.

Don't you fucking dare hold back.

"You're hurt," he said lamely.

A flash of amusement. "Then I guess you'll have to peel my clothes off for me."

Quinn stared at the map in his hand. The markings bled together into a cloud of nothing. The writing became a meaningless squiggle of ink on the page.

She's going to leave.

Was that why?

Did he care?

Yes. Vega might be able to disengage from the intimacy for the sake of pleasure, but Quinn didn't work that way. He'd been through enough shit to know that when a good thing came your way, you held onto it with everything you had.

He didn't know when exactly Vega had become one of those good things, but he found himself reaching for her more often than not.

He thought about her—*worried* about her—when she wasn't there.

If she walked off into the woods right now and never came back, Quinn might still have a chance to let her go and move on with his life.

If he let himself have one more taste of her, tomorrow morning would be a different story.

He was still and quiet for so long, Vega frowned. "Your choice," she said, as if either way made no difference to her.

And suddenly, Quinn wanted to pull her beneath him and break down every last shield she'd spent a lifetime building up. He didn't want to peel her clothes off; he wanted to strip her down to her soul and make her shine so bright it banished all remnants of the Shadows.

Whatever she saw in his face made her throat work on a nervous swallow. But she met him halfway to take his kiss, and Quinn didn't hold back. He breathed her in, savoring the earthy, feminine scent of her skin, lightly spiced with a flowery perfume of Bliss. He couldn't taste it on her tongue, but somehow it still kicked him in the gut as she brought her arms around his neck and leaned in close.

With a smooth sweep of his arm, he transferred her onto his lap, and she straddled him, finding the ridge of his hardon. Quinn's hands shook as he reached over to spread the sleeping bag on the ground without breaking their kiss. It was too sweet, and he was too hungry to leave the smallest morsel untasted.

Vega pressed down on him, clawing at his shirt, and he hazily remembered her injured hand. He swept his palms up her sides, scrunching her hoodie up to her chest. She pulled away long enough for him to get the garment off her and send it sailing away into the night, but he suffocated until he found her mouth again and breath returned.

She was shivering, her hands on him chilled despite the heat of their artificial fire. Quinn pulled her tighter into him, then carefully shifted sideways, depositing her on the sleeping bag beneath him. He raised himself up enough to look into her face, a question on the tip of his tongue and an answer she would never ask for. Words locked up in his chest as he watched her gaze soften and her kiss-reddened lips tease into a smile that set his heart humming.

Then something changed.

He registered the tension in her body too late; she'd already surged up, throwing her entire meager weight against his to roll them over.

A flash of light, a hiss in his ear, and then she moved, raising up astride him, a knife in her hand. It left her grip so quickly Quinn didn't have time to flinch before it disappeared in the darkness off to his right.

Vega swore, shoving to her feet, her second knife already gripped in her fractured hand. "Stay here," she snapped, then disappeared into the woods.

Quinn had no idea what the fuck just happened.

But as he sat up, fingers curling into the sleeping bag, waiting for Vega to reappear, his mind caught up to the sight of her running for the woods.

And the black burn of a plasma blast across the back of her exposed left shoulder.

26

The snap of a branch.

That was it. One tiny mistake and Vega's lifetime of military training were all that had prevented the plasma blast from burning a hole through Quinn's chest.

One mistake. *One mistake.*

It kept repeating in her head as she hurtled through the darkness, blindly following the sound of running footsteps.

One mistake…

Hers.

She'd let down her guard. She'd assumed she'd chosen the game at random and that they'd be safe in terrain as unfamiliar to her as it was to everyone else.

Vega had become too emotionally compromised to do her job. She'd let herself forget this *was* still a job.

A larger branch snapped in front of her.

Vega veered a few degrees to the left. Running water somewhere ahead. It would help camouflage the enemy's movements. He was heading right for it.

Even without the benefit of sight, Vega knew things about him. His stride and the weight of his footsteps said he was male. Estimating height and weight was tricky, without factoring in unknown variables like gravity and the surrounding environment, but she knew she'd be able to take him if push came to shove—which it would.

He was a civilian with black market contacts and a lot of money. He couldn't have gotten his hands on a gun with a kill setting otherwise. The general public's access to such weapons was pretty much nonexistent. It would have taken a fortune and significant determination to even find a trader, much less convince one to sell him a piece.

Vega picked up more speed, ducking low branches, squinting in the darkness to pick out shadows of protrusions that might trip her. She was usually light on her feet, but the texture of the ground was spongy, absorbing some of the impact of her footfalls and the bounce-back that propelled her forward.

She was still catching up to her prey. The amateur who had aimed at the widest possible part of his target because he hadn't felt confident enough in his marksmanship to aim for the head.

One mistake.

If Vega hadn't moved as fast as she had, Quinn would be dead now.

Her shoulder burned. Her hand throbbed. She ignored both and pushed forward. The target was less than ten yards ahead. She could almost make out his shape as he passed through pools of starlight where the canopy thinned.

Definitely heading for the water.

A choked grunt, and then the footsteps stopped.

Vega slipped to a halt, holding back the full force of her breath so she could hear the soundscape around her. The creek was about twelve feet away. In the rosy darkness, it glittered with a bluish-green luminescence. But nothing splashed through its waters, and it was too wide to jump over in one leap. The target hadn't gone that way.

She forced herself to loosen the choking grip on her knife. Too much tension would limit her range of motion. Ears perked for any hint of a sound, Vega eased a step forward, shifting her weight by cautious degrees to keep the noise to a minimum. Her lungs burned for air. She allowed herself a slow, deep inhale and took another step.

Nothing.

Vega skirted the light, keeping herself as concealed as possible in the shadows as she slowly picked her way toward the general area where her target had disappeared.

Ten yards.

Five yards.

Except for the gentle rush of water, the forest was quiet. The disturbance of their chase had forced wildlife into momentary silence.

Vega paused by a trunk as wide as a transport and soft to the touch.

This was it. He should be here.

She traced the ground with her foot but didn't feel any indentations or soft spots to indicate a sinkhole. Impossible to see tracks in the night but if he'd changed direction, she would have heard it. The creek was too far and too exposed. She would have seen him going in that direction.

Craning her neck, she looked up into the tree canopy. The plant she was leaning on didn't look like a tree. More like a tall flower. The trunk stretched so far into the sky it would tower over anything else around, but it was smooth. No branches, no hand or footholds. Unless the guy had wings, he wouldn't have been able to climb up there without gear—which would have left marks.

As quietly as she could, Vega rounded the massive base, counting her footsteps, eyes peeled for any hint of a threat, ears sharp for betraying sounds. She traced her damaged hand along the surface all the way around to her starting point on the creek side.

And found nothing.

Her target had disappeared.

What the fuck!

Vega breathed down the tremble in her limbs. She waited for the killer to betray his presence, but he didn't show.

Minutes later, night-dwelling creatures resumed their song.

Game over.

Vega spat on the ground and thumped her head against the tree. He was gone.

How the fuck?

The creek was right in front of her, the only landmark she had, and not enough to find her way back. Vega spoke Quinn's name into her com, and her forearm lit up with a map. She followed the nav back through the trees until she saw the light of their flameless fire ahead.

Quinn had to be freaking out.

But he would have seen her looking for him and probably tracked her through the woods. He knew she was close by. Vega was proud of him for not moving to intercept her.

She scanned the ground along her path, looking for the glint of her knife. Her aim was flawless, but she hadn't picked up on the sound of impact, and her target hadn't slowed. It was possible she'd missed, and the knife had landed in soft underbrush.

After about five minutes, with no luck and the tension rising in their camp as Quinn's patience ran out, Vega gave up and stepped into the light. Quinn's hard stare made her feel like she was about to report mission failure to her CO, but much worse.

She dragged her feet all the way to the pillow he'd set down on the sleeping bag. Sheathing her knife, she sat and rubbed her face. "He got away," she confessed and, fuck, she wanted to throw up. She'd lost a civilian. In a fucking foot chase through the woods. "I'm getting us on the first shuttle out tomo—"

"Turn around," Quinn said softly, and she flinched at the violence she heard leashed in his voice.

"I'm fi—"

"Turn. Around." His tone suggested he'd make her if she didn't comply.

Vega sighed and twisted so he could see her back. She wasn't lying; the burn on her shoulder throbbed with searing pain, but plasma shots instantly cauterized the wound. There would be no blood loss or risk of infection. As long as she didn't rip it open, it would heal into another scar to add to her collection. It was nothing.

But Quinn sucked in a sharp breath when he saw it, and Vega could have sworn the temperature plummeted. His fingers brushed along her skin, far enough from the wound to be safe, but her nerve endings were frayed enough by the blast that a full half of her upper back was affected, and she tensed at the lightest touch.

She heard him gulp before he rasped out, "This was meant for me."

Yes. But she decided to lie. "We can't know that. Not anymore."

"I make a pretty damn big target, Vega. Hard to miss—unless someone *bodily throws herself into the path of the shot!*"

She elbowed him, twisting around to slap her hand over his mouth. "Keep your fucking voice down." The other camps couldn't be too far away. If the family heard him, they'd come running, and there was no way Vega could explain what just happened.

Quinn shoved her hand off him and forced her to turn back around. "And you're *not fine.*" She heard him rooting around behind her, but their packs hadn't come equipped with a first aid kit. Which, by the sound of his creative cursing, he was now discovering for himself.

"The pain patch still works," she told him. Not a lie. It would help with the pain but wasn't designed to dull so much of it in multiple locations. "You know what's funny?"

The movement behind her stopped.

"I've been through literal wars"—not to mention training exercises that had felt like wars—"and managed to get myself out of dozens of live fire skirmishes with only a handful of marks on me. I know Shadows who are covered from head to toe in scars and old injuries. Compared to them, I am basically a blank canvas." Not counting a few stab wounds and such. "But a few days with your family, and look at me. I'm a mess." As soon as she said it, the truth of her words struck her, and she laughed.

And laughed.

Until her sides hurt and tears overflowed. She listed backward to lie down, her burn forgotten until Quinn yanked her back up. He didn't seem to be sharing in her amusement.

Understandable. Someone had just tried to kill him, after all. Most likely one of his own family members. Vega made an effort to rein in her hysterics. They were unbecoming of a Shadow. And she was undeserving of such a lapse of good sense.

The gunman might not have been acting alone. She'd run headlong after him, leaving Quinn completely exposed and vulnerable to another attack.

The thought sobered her as nothing else could. "I failed you," she said. Right about now, her CO would be giving her a cold dismissal and a punishment fit for the crime of incompetence. She might get two weeks on quarter rations and double patrol duty. Or maybe he'd make her stand on the roof in a snowstorm without shelter through the night.

There was no excuse for failure among the Shadows, and nothing Vega could say would ever make up for failing to carry out a mission. But she still felt more words demanding to be spoken, and she couldn't hold them back. Quinn deserved this much, at least. "I'm…I'm sorry."

27

Day 5

After some coaxing, Vega told him what happened, how she'd tracked the gunman to a creek and then he'd disappeared into thin air. She was convinced it hadn't been a Shadow because, "A Shadow wouldn't have missed." But beyond him being male and roughly her height, that was all she'd been able to tell.

She went out there two more times, looking for her knife, both times with the com tracker turned on so he could see where she was. Both times, she came back empty-handed.

After that, they sat in the light of the flameless fire and waited while Quinn watched her flip her remaining knife back and forth and jumped at the smallest rustle in the trees. He debated bringing up the stupid treasure hunt to give them something to do with themselves, but the far-away look on Vega's face shut his mouth.

She was in pain. There was no way she wasn't. Couldn't tell by looking at her. That knife flipped from her good hand to the bad one and back again, swelling and fractured bone notwithstanding. Almost like the pain was easier to deal with than the tension of not knowing.

Quinn might have jumped at the odd rustle, but every now and again, for no reason he could discern, Vega would catch the knife in a firm grip and freeze, staring out into the woods. He could feel how she tensed, the sharpness of her gaze raising the hairs on the back of his neck. She stared unblinking for several seconds and then went back to flipping the knife as if nothing had happened.

It was the most harrowing night of his life—and he'd come through a three-year war with a bad heart.

Ela didn't have anything resembling a standardized measure of time, but devices did track sunrises and sunsets. Quinn stared at the graphic depiction of a sunburst crawling up toward the flat line representing the horizon, willing the planet to turn faster. Vega refused to move out until they had enough light to navigate the forest and see what lurked around them.

Eventually, the sky began to lighten, and Vega got up to gather everything back into the packs they'd brought. He grabbed the three heavy balls as she reached for them with her bad hand and chucked them into the trees with all his might. One of them bore a hole through a tree. Another struck something that clanged like a massive bell. The third one flew for several seconds before they heard it shatter in the distance.

Vega shrugged and kept packing.

She didn't extinguish the flame until the sun was high enough to peek through the tree canopy. Once she'd put it away, she pulled her knife again and dug into the ground where the lantern had been. The surface was stomped down hard, but underneath that it turned soft enough to dig through by hand. About four inches down, she unearthed a perfectly symmetrical cube and tossed it to him.

Quinn stared at the box in his hand, at the bright yellow WINNER etched into its polished metallic surface. "How long have you known it was there?"

"Since I put the lantern down on the only patch of smooth ground within a twenty-foot radius." She shouldered one of the packs before he could take it from her. Not a wince, not a flinch as its weight settled over her burned back. "Ready to go?"

If he never saw another tree again, it would be too soon.

Vega went in search of her knife one more time, but there was no sign of it, even in the light of day. When she came back, her mouth was pressed into a tight line and she marched past him to set course for their extraction point, as she called it.

"You can always buy more knives," he said reasonably.

She shook her head.

Quinn stopped trying to make conversation after that. Vega wasn't in the mood to participate and, frankly, neither was he.

They hiked for a good while as the forest heated up to a sauna. His clothing was plastered to every inch of him and sweat ran down his face. Meanwhile, Vega looked like she could keep going for days, barely sweating, her cheeks the slightest bit flushed.

He caught her good wrist and tugged her to a stop. "Here, you need to drink."

Vega looked at the half-full water bottle, then raised an eyebrow at him.

"The last thing you drank was that little glass of water after brunch yesterday. You're not sweating. You need to drink."

Some of the tension left her face. She accepted the bottle and took a couple of swallows before handing it over.

Quinn pushed it right back to her. "All of it."

"What about you?"

"I'll live," he retorted.

She drank some more, but left a cup's worth when she handed it back to him declaring, "I'm good. Let's go, we're almost there."

Almost there turned out to be another half-mile at least.

Quinn was so happy to emerge onto a pink-sanded beach, his heart whirred in a frenzy and all he saw was the glitter of cool, endless water. He planned to dunk himself into it immediately.

"Something's wrong."

Quinn tore his gaze away from the sealine to the miserable-looking gathering of VanWarrens a hundred and fifty yards down the beach. Nothing out of the ordinary to his civilian eyes, but something was making Vega twitchy beside him.

She dropped her backpack and put on her hoodie to hide the burn on her shoulder. "Put your arm around me and stay close."

He didn't think to question her, but he did switch sides so he wouldn't jar her injury as he settled a hand on her hip.

The sand was so loose, his feet buried into it with every step. It took them a while to half the distance and, by then, he started picking up on the subtle anomalies Vega had noticed right away. His family didn't look the way he'd expect them to look after an exciting night of treasure hunting in the wild. They were grouped together, heads bent, shoulders hunched.

Four HOVRs idled in a line nearby, all the packs tossed into a pile there, but no one had bothered to load them yet.

Quinn only saw a couple of attendants in the gathering, nodding solemnly to whatever they were being told.

One of them noticed Quinn and Vega approaching. He interrupted whoever was speaking to him and all at once, everyone in the group looked up at them.

Vega halted and tensed up so much her knees wouldn't bend to take another step.

A familiar figure split off from the group and jogged over to them.

Zach, looking haggard and ashen, his wide eyes bloodshot. The first words out of his mouth were, "Are you guys okay?"

"We're fine," Vega said with just the right amount of careless confusion and a pretty frown. "Why? What happened?"

Zach speared a hand through his hair as he looked back toward the group. By the looks of it, he'd been doing that for a while now. "There's something… I don't…" He huffed a shuddering sigh and finally blurted out, "Fuck, guys, Emmett is dead."

Quinn's stomach sank to his knees. "What?"

"What are you talking about?"

Zach shrugged, mouth working, but for a few tries no sound came out. "H-he… I guess he was teamed up with Andras. They split up to look for the treasure and… Well, Andras came back to their camp and Emmett didn't. Andras freaked out and set off the emergency beacon. They looked for him all night, and finally found him down by the creek at dawn." He turned away again, this time toward the HOVRs and the pile of packs.

Not a pile of packs.

It was a body bag laid out on the sand.

Quinn wanted to hurl.

If possible, Vega tensed even more. "D-do they know what happened?"

Zach shook his head. "I guess he slipped and fell or something. I didn't see much before they covered him up. Half his face was black and blue, and his neck was bent all weird."

Vega sagged against him.

Zach's eyes went even wider. "Shit, sorry. I shouldn't have told you that." He gulped. "I just…never saw a dead body before."

But it wasn't horror that made Vega limp. It was relief. Bruised face and bent neck meant he hadn't died of a knife wound.

"Matthew called the authorities. They're already on their way. We have to wait for them to pick up the"—another gulp—"Emmett's corpse and take our statements before we can leave."

He glanced at the family again. Most of them had turned back to their shared grief, but Andras sat on his own, head in his hands, and Geraldine was standing off to the side, hugging herself and watching them as if she couldn't wait for Zach to get back to her.

"Listen," Zach said, before facing them. "People have been whispering about what happened yesterday."

"What about what happened yesterday?" Quinn growled.

Zach reeled back.

"You think Quinn did this," Vega accused, her voice filled with horror, but he felt tension coil in her limbs.

"No!" Zach rushed to assure them. "Of course I don't. But it sounds like I may be in the minority."

They were taking too long. The others were getting visibly restless. Holden and Matthew said something to Kendry and then split off from the group, heading over.

"We were in our camp the whole night," Vega snapped, loud enough for his brothers to hear the outrage even from twenty feet away. "I was actually having fun for a while. Even with this." She held up her injured hand. "And with my father…" Quinn was mighty impressed with the emotional quiver in her voice as she turned into his side. "We were in our camp."

"And you bastards would have known that if anyone had bothered to come tell *us* that someone was missing." He hugged her to him, squeezing her shoulder before he recalled the burn there. He let up right away, but not before she shuddered, and Quinn wondered whether she'd planned it that way. It happened as Holden and Matthew joined them.

Whatever Matthew had been about to say died on the tip of his tongue as he winced and ducked his head.

"The authorities are on their way," Holden said. "They'll be questioning all of us." He glanced from Vega to Quinn, to Zach, and back to Quinn. "Did either of you see anything last night? Hear anything?"

Quinn shook his head. He didn't have Vega's gift for pulling believable bullshit out of thin air. Better for him to shut up and look shellshocked. Not exactly farfetched, under the circumstance.

"Given what happened yesterday—"

"What happened yesterday was that Emmett attacked my wife, and you refused to boot him off the estate."

Vega dug her fingers into his side in a quiet warning to shut the fuck up.

Quinn didn't heed it. "He never should have been out here in the first place."

"Yeah, make sure you tell that to the cops," Matthew retorted, shaking his head in disgust as Holden paled.

Zach swore under his breath as he retreated to Geraldine, and it dawned on Quinn too late that what he'd just said might as well have been a confession.

~

The family wasn't allowed to leave the island, but attendants who hadn't been there through the night made several trips back and forth to bring food, blankets, chairs, and umbrellas. It was a goddamn picnic on the beach while six uniformed officers led a search through the woods and two more cycled through the VanWarren interviews.

The undertakers had loaded Emmett's corpse into the back of an ambulance but, like the rest of them, it stayed there until the cops allowed it to be removed from the island.

Vega and Quinn stayed with the group, but it was clear the others had adopted a policy of non-involvement. Zach and Geraldine sat close, but even they didn't talk to either of them unless necessary. Until the cops cleared them—*if* they cleared them—Vega and Quinn were social pariahs.

Vega angled herself to keep an eye on the interview tables where VanWarren after VanWarren gave their statements. It was too far to hear, and the cops didn't give away a single clue, but every so often, one of them cast a quick glance at them and Vega knew they were saving their prime suspect for last.

Quinn hadn't been the one to punch Emmett's lights out yesterday, but he'd been in a mighty rage over the incident. And the two of them had been the last to arrive on the beach this morning. Coupled with Quinn's outburst at his brothers, it wasn't looking good. Vega ran through the scenarios in her head and concluded that they might have to buy their way out of this. It wouldn't be a long-term solution, but it would give her time to get Quinn off-world.

It was a desperate plan that Quinn definitely wouldn't like. As soon as they disappeared, the family would be exactly where Vega didn't want them: digging through the accounts and pissing off the Shadows.

But at the moment, Quinn's safety was of a much larger concern. Last night made two attempts on his life in less than a week. These people would not let him live if they had any say about it. Vega needed to get him far, far away from them—physically and in every other way.

Maybe once they regained control of their businesses, the VanWarrens would be content to let sleeping dogs lie as long as Quinn never shadowed their doorstep again. That's what they wanted, after all.

And it wasn't as if Emmett had been a beloved member of the family. Based on what she'd learned from his relatives, the man had been one rowdy night away from staining the VanWarren name in ways none of them were equipped to deal with. More than likely, once the shock wore off, they'd be relieved to not have to deal with him anymore.

By midday, the heat was almost unbearable and the attendants were running back and forth to replenish cold drinks and adjust umbrella angles. Half of the family had been interviewed, and Andras had recovered his senses enough to stare out at the sea instead of into the sand. As the last person who'd seen Emmett alive, he was as much a suspect as Quinn.

The search party returned as Geraldine walked away from her interview. One of the cops spoke softly to the captain, who nodded a casual dismissal, but Vega noted the stiff way in which he cracked his neck as the others loaded their gear back into their vehicles and set off.

He noticed her looking and held her gaze for a moment before he waved her and Quinn over.

"Any tips?" Quinn murmured in her ear on the pretext of kissing her cheek.

"Don't volunteer any details. You were pissed at Emmett, but wanted to enjoy the night with me. We didn't leave our camp until the sun came up."

They took their time walking over to the captain's table. An attendant met them there with an additional chair so they could both sit for their interrogation.

The police captain was a no-nonsense man in his mid-sixties. He had the look of someone who kept his house clean and didn't enjoy his routine being disrupted.

That didn't mean he wouldn't do his job. As evidenced by the full minute he spent staring at them to make them squirm.

"Where were you camped last night?"

Vega and Quinn shared a confused glance.

"We're new here," Quinn said. "There were maps in our packs, that's about the best I can do."

The packs had already been confiscated and searched. Each one had been matched to its original owner and the flight path of its designated HOVR.

"You stayed in that location all night?"

Quinn nodded. "Yes, sir."

"No one wandered off?"

Trick question.

"Well," Vega said, "I did for about five minutes to…you know." She made an awkward motion as she wriggled in her seat. "But other than that, we just looked at the stars and talked."

"Maybe made out a bit," Quinn added, and she shot him a hard look, tempering it enough to feign embarrassment.

"Talk to me about the incident yesterday."

Fuck.

Before Quinn could say a word, she told the story herself, the same way she'd told it to the family. Emmett had wanted to apologize for his behavior, then spiked her drink and started groping her. She'd fought him off, breaking her hand in the process.

"Were you there to witness this?" he asked Quinn.

"I heard her from the hallway and got there to see her knock his lights out."

The captain checked his notes. "Mr. Matthew VanWarren testified that you were—quote—furious and aggressive afterward."

A muscle ticked in his jaw. "Wouldn't you be?" he asked quietly.

Vega took his hand to make it unclench, and he did exactly what she knew he would. He looked at her, his gaze softening as he brushed his thumb over the back of her hand.

The captain noted the gesture, then asked, "Did you threaten Mr. Emmett VanWarren during this altercation?"

"No," Quinn said. "I did want him removed from the compound, but that's as far as it went. Obviously, he was allowed to stay."

The captain looked between them, letting the silence stretch.

It worked, too. Quinn shifted in his seat, then leaned forward a bit. "Can you tell us what happened?"

Vega wanted to kick him. She waited for the captain to pounce but, after a moment, he answered plainly. "Initial results suggest accident. He was drunk, wandered off toward the creek, slipped on some rocks, and fell at an unfortunate angle, breaking his neck."

"Damn," Vega breathed.

"So, does that mean we can leave now?"

The captain narrowed his eyes at Quinn. "How long have you known Mr. Emmett VanWarren?"

Quinn shrugged. "A few days. I never met him before we arrived on Ela."

"Are you aware of his personal history with drugs and alcohol?"

"Only what I've been told. And what I saw at the compound."

"Other than yesterday's incident, is there any reason you can think of why Mr. Emmett VanWarren would have a grudge against you?"

"Yeah, about sixty-eight billion reasons." At the captain's raised eyebrow, he clarified, "I recently inherited controlling interests in the VanWarren family estate. There are a lot of people who don't like me right now. Emmett's current business is falling apart. He is—*was*—up to his eyeballs in debt, and I had no intention of buying him out of it."

"Who would inherit the estate in the event of your death."

"My wife," he answered without hesitation.

Vega leaned forward, frowning. "What's this about, officer?"

"Captain," he corrected.

"Why are you asking about grudges against my husband?"

He took his time thinking it over. Seeming to come to a decision, he said, "My men retrieved an illegal firearm near the location where Mr. Emmett VanWarren's body was found. It appears to have been discharged. Possibly as a result of his fall."

Vega sagged back again. "What are you saying?"

Confronted with her obvious distress, he shifted in his seat as if he couldn't wait to get out of there. "I believe Mr. Emmett VanWarren might have left his camp last night with the intent to cause harm to someone else on the island. The most likely intended victim seems to be one of you."

28

Boredom was a dangerous thing. A Shadow with too much time on his hands could get himself into all sorts of unsanctioned shit without direct orders.

Like take a stroll through the family compound while half of said family was out on a camping trip.

Turned out, VanWarren security was very much hit-or-miss. Talon hadn't been able to get anywhere near the garage with so many servants running around the vehicles. But no one had stopped him, or even noticed when he'd walked right through the front door of the main house.

These people knew how to live. Their style was a little overdone for his taste, but he could forgive that. Especially when it seemed like all the rooms in the house had at least a small assortment of food and drinks set out for anyone who might wander in and find themselves needing a snack. And the liquor was smooth as shit.

Talon didn't like letting opportunities go to waste, so he'd sampled a little bit of everything as he'd toured the place from the basement up, walking right past oblivious old geezers who didn't notice a servant in their vicinity unless they ran into one, and smiling at the kids who definitely noticed someone they'd never seen before.

And his excursion had been fruitful in more ways than one.

Perched in his treetop again, watching transports fill the drive as the campers disembarked, he snorted and shook his head at the shell-shocked looks on their cosmetically enhanced faces. You'd think they'd crawled through a pit of vipers and spent the night facing down rabid beasts.

And there was his little Vega, with her bruised hand in a brace—he'd love to hear that story—and dark shadows under her eyes as if she hadn't slept again.

Curious since the field trip had taken her out of range of her leash. He'd felt it misfire when he'd tried to fuck with her long-distance shortly after sunset. He would have thought she'd sleep like a baby under the stars.

Then again, maybe her new John had kept her busy through the night.

Either way, this game was going stale. It was time to finish it.

As if the mere thought had summoned it, his wrist unit vibrated with an incoming transmission: STATUS REPORT.

Talon debated how to answer. If Commander Hughes wanted to play it terse, he could do the same. PARAMETERS UNCHANGED. Hughes wanted Vega? He'd either give Talon his wings or he could come get her himself.

RETRIEVE TARGET AND DELIVER TO DROP-OFF POINT.

Talon tapped his chin. NEGATIVE. PARAMETERS UNCHANGED.

INSUBORDINATION WILL NOT BE TOLERATED.

He almost laughed himself right out of the tree. The fuck was the prick going to do? Talon was the one holding all the cards. In fact...

Yes, why not? There was a beautiful kind of poetry to it. Talon would take a page out of Vega's playbook for this one.

TARGET ABOUT TO BECOME NON-VIABLE.

He could taste the dead air on the other end of the connection.

STAND BY.

Talon grinned. That was better. But he had no intention of waiting forever. Better give the bureaucrat a proper deadline.

20 MINUTES.

More than generous, all things considered. Enough of a cushion to allow for transmission delays but not so much that the CO got any ideas in his head about trying to circumvent the inevitable.

Never let it be said that ol' Talon wasn't a reasonable kind of guy.

29

Such a curious thing to find.

Such a small and innocuous-looking thing.

It wasn't the only one—and it wasn't M's.

M knew exactly where it had come from. Its presence wasn't a surprise, but the possible ramification struck M as reckless and wholly unnecessary. The hallmark of a Hound.

And now there was a decision to be made.

The subdermal com vibrated a pattern to communicate an incoming transmission. It was a useful thing to have when access to other devices was restricted or impossible. Even Hawks in the field needed a way to receive new orders at all times. One never knew when mission parameters might change at a moment's notice, necessitating a needlepoint pivot.

This one, however, demanded an answer.

STATUS UPDATE.

Another curious development. There had never been need of such a request in the past. It felt less like a question and more of a notification.

M studied the intrusive device on the wall for all of five seconds before walking away. A series of taps on the miniature metal disc in M's pocket relayed the expected response: NO CHANGE.

There was a strange kind of static in the air, a tingle of awareness that something big was about to happen or had already happened. M had never been the impatient type, but waiting for the new order to come down the line—because it would—was akin to torture.

Attendants in the hallway. M nodded to them and smiled, murmuring a few words to one of them. A suggestion the young woman was only too eager to run with.

And then it came.

A new assignment.

Nothing more than an alphanumerical code corresponding to one of the two pictures Command had sent two days ago and a word as clear as it could possibly be.

EXECUTE.

The static settled into a bone-deep hum. One long breath. A single smile. Then M casually walked out the side door.

The hunt was on.

30

Fifteen minutes after Talon's last transmission, he received the response and grinned. Hughes hadn't even pushed the deadline to the limit.

He sat up and straightened the stolen servant's jacket. It wasn't a Shadow uniform, but Talon wanted to look his best when he accepted his Hawk pin. Even if he wouldn't actually *get* it until he got out of this bougie shithole.

Brushing back his hair, he cleared his throat and opened the transmission.

And stared.

And stared some more as text continued to stream in, carefully indented into proper paragraphs.

Instead of the confirmation he'd expected, Commander Hughes had sent him section fifteen of the Shadow code of conduct—the one on insubordination and desertion.

Heat coiled in his chest and rose up his neck, flooding his face. He was shaking by the time the last sentence scrolled by: Failure to uphold the tenets of the Shadow code of conduct will be deemed a capital offense.

Having delivered its message, the transmission disappeared, and so did the module for secure communications on the wrist unit.

It took Talon several seconds to breathe through his rage enough to climb down the tree.

Son of a bitch wanted to play?

He'd play.

He was an expert on these kinds of games.

Back on solid ground, he crouched low and crawled to the edge of the tree line. Most all of the VanWarrens had already cleared the drive and gone into the house. No one left but a couple of servants and his targets.

Vega and her giant had stopped on the lawn to gab in the sun, but they looked like they were wrapping it up. He waited patiently for them to cross the rest of the drive to the front door.

Then waited a couple more minutes for them to get deeper into the house…

31

By the time their HOVR touched down in front of the garage on Crescent Island, Quinn was so over the whole reunion all he wanted to do was drive back to the shuttleport and wait for the next available flight—and he didn't particularly care where it took him.

But Vega had been combing the 'port schedules since last night and couldn't find a single open seat for the next three weeks. "Fucking planetary alignments," she muttered before a garage attendant came to open her door.

Apparently, it was a once-in-a-lifetime event and part of the reason why the VanWarrens had chosen this place and this time to hold the reunion. In a few days, the uber-rich denizens of this solar system would take advantage of the alignment to hop their way from planet to inhabited planet in some sort of bougie bucket list challenge.

The already limited flight schedule had been rearranged to accommodate the planet-hopping morons and, despite the astronomical price hikes, said morons had booked all the seats on all the shuttle flights. Because they could.

Quinn was exhausted, dragging his feet along the drive toward the main house. It was already nearing sunset again. After two sleepless nights, he was ready to drop. Still, the idea of going back into that house gave him chills.

Emmett was dead.

And Quinn still felt him glaring at them from every shadowed corner.

He stopped by the crescent-shaped pool. "Can we go to a hotel?"

"All booked up. I checked." Vega sounded as tired as he felt.

"Can we have one built in the next couple of hours and then go stay there?"

She huffed a weak chuckle.

He frowned. "I just realized I'm not kidding."

Vega looked up at him, squinting against the setting sun. "You really don't want to go back in there, do you?"

"Do *you*?"

She frowned. "I keep thinking about what the captain said about Emmett wanting to kill us."

"Technically, he said, *intent to cause harm.*"

Vega gave him a look like he should know better and, okay, yeah, he did. Hell, he might even understand why Emmett would be driven to such measures. But part of him still wanted to cling to denial. Aside from the Shadows, Quinn had never known a person who hated him enough to want him dead, much less multiple.

And the fact that they were all related to him shouldn't have been such a shock, given the situation. It also shouldn't have bothered him as much as it did—he'd come here expecting them to try something, after all.

But it did bother him.

And Vega knew.

She'd known it before Quinn himself had figured it out.

He still wanted to be part of this family. He wanted to belong.

Vega touched his arm. "Hey, you're not alone here."

Quinn knew what she meant. But he still heard himself saying, "Aren't I?"

Vega dropped her gaze and her hand, and it felt like she'd just ripped his brand-new heart straight out of his chest. "We talked about this."

"No, you talked. Like you always do, and I listened, because I respect your expertise on the subject. But—"

"Right," she agreed. "I am the expert. You *should* listen."

He wanted to shake her. "So I get no say in this. What I want doesn't enter into your calculations. You write me off like you do with every-thing else that isn't about the Sh—"

"What do you want, Quinn?"

"What do *you* want?" he countered. "Do you even know?"

"I need to—"

"No. Stop. I already know what you were taught to need. I want to know what you *want*." If anything. "Is there anything in there"—he pointed at her chest—"beyond knives and death?" Quinn had thought there was. He'd risked everything on the spark of goodness she'd shown him and his refugee family on Anamtaigh. The glimpses of compassion he'd seen over and over in the last few days.

But maybe it wasn't enough. Maybe, in the end, she really was just a Shadow.

Anger. True, burning anger lit up her eyes as she clenched her jaw, and Quinn half expected her to deck him. He'd welcome it. Any show of emotion from her felt like a damn milestone. "I don't get to want," she gritted out. "Wanting is for people who sleep through the night and wake up with smiles and sunshine to make breakfast for their spouse. You can't *want* when all you can think about is getting through the next day—the next hour—without seeing your or someone else's brains splattered on the ground. That's a privilege I lost a long time ago."

"I see." He nodded. "So you'll throw down for everyone else. Just not yourself."

She slumped with an exhausted sigh. "What are you talking about?"

"Do you even want to live?"

"So now I'm suicidal?"

"That would imply wanting to die. And you don't get to *want*, right? I think you just decided not to have a preference one way or the other."

Vega shook her head, turning away from him. "I don't have to listen to this."

Oh no, she didn't get to walk away yet. It was high time for Quinn to speak his piece. He caught her good arm to stop her. "How long did you look for Talon before you made a beeline for the nearest Bliss counter? How many doctors did you talk to before you gave up on that thing in your neck, too? You didn't leave Anamtaigh for a mission, you left so you wouldn't have to deal with people trying to help you. And you'll leave me for the same reason. Because it's easier to give up when you have no one fighting for you. Better to be all on your own than run the risk of the people who care for you deciding you're not worth the fight. Easier to be the one to die than the one left behind to live on."

"Been rehearsing that one a while, have you?"

"No, Vega, I'm just calling it like it is. All that bullshit bravado of yours is just armor to keep you from feeling anything that might make a difference. Well, I'm not a soldier. I can't break it down for you. All I can do is be here when you decide to do it yourself."

She stared at him, the frustration in her face draining in a rush as her lips parted to speak, but she didn't say a word. He saw it in her eyes, though, the comprehension and the immediate fear of what he'd said.

"Take as much time as you need. You'll know where to find me when you're ready."

Vega flinched when he let go and walked away. She followed slower, running through every word he'd said over and over again trying to come up with an appropriate response, but nothing came to her. Not one goddamn thing.

This mission had been a mistake.

She should have sent Quinn back to Rowe and the other ex-Shadows.

Her chest felt hollow, making everything echo strangely as she walked in the front door. The VanWarren kids were streaming out through the back, blankets and pillows in hand for what she could only assume was an impromptu sleep-out to make up for the one the adults hadn't taken them on the night before.

Attendants were carrying platters of sweets and steaming mugs out after them, while not a single VanWarren adult appeared to take an interest.

Vega followed Quinn toward the staircase. Apparently, he had energy to burn after a night spent not running around a dark forest chasing a would-be murderer. She stopped by the elevator, rolling her shoulder. The friction of her hoodie over the scorch mark on her back was a good reminder of why she needed to put some distance between them.

She'd let herself get distracted, and it had almost cost Quinn his life.

They never should have been out there in the first place.

Her mistake.

Vega couldn't afford to make another one.

Shut it down. This was not the time to get distracted. She was already compromised, and a liability in any potential altercation.

All I can do is be there…

Shut it the fuck down!

Vega raked her loose hair off her face, yanking hard enough to stretch her eyebrows up as she breathed away the words.

You'll know where to find me when you're ready.

Her jaw ached like a son of a bitch. If she tried to work it out, she'd strain something again.

Quinn didn't know what he was talking about. He'd come through a battle, gotten a new heart, a new family—a happy ending—and he thought the war was over.

But Vega was still in it. And regardless of his idealistic dreams, she would never be *out* of it.

No matter how much she wanted to.

No one ever left the Shadows—except in a body bag.

Breath returned. Her jaw loosened, and her arms relaxed down to her sides. She had to hang on for a few more days. Long enough to get Quinn out of this mess so he could live out his happily ever after. Long enough to throw a stone or ten to beat that sentimental nonsense out of his head—it would only lead to heartbreak, anyway.

By the time Vega was done, he'd be only too happy to see her walk away for good. No tears, no waiting, no mourning. Just a long, happy, carefree life.

Vega dropped her good hand on the banister. It took more effort than it should have to lift her foot onto the first stair.

The step sent a tremor through the entire house.

Vega froze as tall vases wobbled on the entry hall tables and the crystal chandelier chimed above. She felt the pressure wave roll through, heard the walls groan with it.

VanWarrens murmured all through the ground floor as attendants took off running to answer their summons. She glimpsed a face or two as they passed by in a hurry. Eyes wide, mouths set. This was not a normal occurrence on Crescent Island.

Quinn...

Vega shot up the stairs faster than she'd ever moved in her life, eyes wide, trying to see farther around the bend. "*Quinn!*"

Their suite was at the end of the hall to the right. He was five steps from the door when she reached the second-floor landing, but already heading her way. "The hell was that?"

He caught her as she ran up to him, for all the world as if she needed comfort. Vega dug her nails into his arms and yanked. "Get out," she snapped when he didn't move. "Run!"

It took him a couple of seconds to switch gears and start walking, then running back toward the staircase. But instead of heading down, he went up.

"What the hell are you doing?"

"There are people up there!"

Vega swore. Of course, that's what he'd do. *Idiot.* She caught up to him and tripped him enough to slam into the wall halfway up to the third floor. "They are not my concern. *You* are."

His mouth drew back into a snarl, ready to argue, but another shudder cut him off. This one was big enough to crack the walls and send dust raining down on them, and Quinn hunched over on instinct, yanking her into him again to shield her.

The timing…

The charges had to be small and spaced out. This place was built on a solid foundation; it would take more than a couple of little pops to shake it, but Vega had no doubt that was precisely what was happening. Someone was done playing games. They were about to bring the whole goddamn house down—with the entire family inside.

The timing…

Two minutes between blasts? Three, maybe?

She shoved her way out of Quinn's hold. "Get the fuck out of the house!"

"I'm not leaving them!" he roared back.

Vega couldn't fight him. There was no time. "Then clear the floors below. Get out as many as you can, but *do not stop moving.* You feel something start to go, you fucking run."

He stared at her.

"*Go!*"

Quinn went.

Vega raced up the rest of the stairs to the third floor. This one was smaller, at least, but fully occupied. "Everybody out!" She ordered those already in the hallway as she banged on door after closed door to rouse the ones who were too complacent to worry about the entire building shaking to the rafters.

Sixty-eight.

Sixty-nine.

Seventy.

She shoved past flabbergasted attendants, yanking on a sleeve here, an arm there, herding them all toward the staircase. "Move it! Down the stairs, get out as fast as you can—and don't take the elevator!"

Eighty-eight.

Eighty-nine…

Another blast.

People screamed and ran, panic taking over where shock had frozen them in place. They bottlenecked at the stairs, tripping into one another, barely keeping their feet under them as the rumble of destruction shook the walls. The southside wing was collapsing.

Vega stumbled down the hallway, glancing into rooms to make sure they were clear before she headed one floor below, counting seconds.

Eighty-five…

Eighty-six…

On the ground floor, Quinn's voice boomed out over the screams, giving orders as well as any commander, relentlessly steering people out through any unobstructed door or window.

Motherfucker was still inside.

Heart in her throat, Vega abandoned her sweep and headed for the staircase.

The next explosion took out half of the hallway she'd just left, sending her tumbling down the stairs. She managed to roll toward a solid corner and duck for cover as part of the ceiling came down on the staircase, boring through and leaving a ten-foot-wide hole straight down to the sublevel.

Ears ringing. She couldn't hear anything beyond the rush of her own blood. Dust filled the air, stinging her eyes, blinding her to what was around.

She had to get up.

She had to find Quinn and get him the fuck out of the house.

How long had it been since the last explosion?

Vega had lost count.

Didn't matter, anyway.

The house was half gone already. Late afternoon sunlight speared through the dust as she picked herself up, taking stock of herself. Her fractured hand was throbbing. She'd landed hard with her ribcage on the edge of a stair. Breathing hurt, and there was blood trickling down behind her left ear. Nothing else broken. Just a shit ton of bruises that would heal.

"Quinn," she called out, but her voice rasped, barely audible in the chaos.

He was still fucking there! Vega heard him somewhere in that dusty void, still yelling at people, though his words were too muffled to make out.

She coughed and tried again. "Quinn!"

The dust cleared enough to make out shapes. She put one foot in front of the other, heading for the towering shadow ahead. Was he calling for her? Vega couldn't tell. An inhale filled her lungs with dust, and she coughed. "Quinn!"

He turned and though she couldn't see his face clearly yet, she felt him spot her. She saw him take a step, heard the hum of his voice form what might have been her name.

She reached for him, vaguely noting the blood on her splinted arm, the pain in her shoulder. Her foot slipped on a piece of debris, and she went down, cracking her knees in the thick stone archway that split the entry hall into front and back.

Get up, soldier.

GET THE FUCK UP!

Vega raised her head, counting seconds out of order as her heart beat sent panicked stabs of pain through her chest. Quinn was heading her way. Not out, but deeper in.

Tiny hairs all over her body stood on end as she felt the next explosion coming.

Her eyes stung as she finally made out the look on Quinn's face, the fucking *blood* pouring down the left side of it. "*Run!*" she screamed with everything she had.

This time, the explosion was a sharp burst of sound from right below.

This time, the shock wave bowled her over and sent Quinn flying back across the entry hall.

This time, she watched the floor collapse and the ceiling come down on top of Quinn, but no one heard her scream past the din of a posh mansion breaking apart and folding in on itself around her archway.

An archway of elaborately carved solid stone. A ridiculously, uselessly expensive decorative element was all that survived the collapse—all that had just saved her life.

She was on the move before the last of the tremors had subsided, crawling through a hellscape of gaps and holes in the massive pile of debris that moments ago had been a three-story house. Quinn had been a short ten yards away. Just across the entry. Right by the front door.

He'd been so fucking close. Steps away from safety.

But he'd come back for her instead.

Vega pulled herself through an opening, careful of the hooked shard of metal poking out an inch away from her hip. A couple of feet farther, she turned to her side and slowly pulled herself across a ten-foot drop between a slat of floor paneling and a shattered bed frame. The mattress at least gave her a safe surface underneath, but above, the broken remnants of a cabinet dangled shards of glass on flimsy hinges.

One wrong move, one unexpected shift in the unstable pile, and Vega would get filleted. She didn't care.

He's alive. He's alive…

It was the only possibility she would accept. Quinn had to be alive. He had to *live*.

There!

In the faint glow of fading sunlight that wouldn't last another half hour, she spotted his hand sticking out from beneath a pile of debris. Vega crawled for it, pulling herself free of the mountain into a cavernous gap beneath three fallen ceiling beams.

She grasped his wrist. No pulse. Artificial heart—it didn't beat.

Fuck! She had to get him out of there.

That blast, the weight of the collapse, was enough to crush every bone in a person's body.

A sound, high and keening, somewhere in her vicinity.

Vega didn't have time to address it. She shoved against the debris with bloodied hands. Heaviest pieces first, to alleviate the pressure on Quinn so he could breathe.

As long as he could breathe, as long as his heart still whirred, doctors could fix the rest.

He just had to breathe.

"Breathe," she hissed, heaving a massive piece of wood off to the side. "Breathe. Breathe…"

The pile moved.

Glorious. Simply glorious.

Talon hadn't put too much thought into where he'd placed the charges, but man, they went off in a fucking symphony of destruction so beautiful he got half hard watching the walls crumble from the outside in.

People poured out from every available opening, screaming and wailing their horror to the heavens, and Talon waved his hand back and forth like the conductor he was.

But all the while, he watched for one face in particular.

Plumes of dust obscured his view; the pile of destruction hid everything and everyone who'd escaped out the back. No sign of Vega—or her overgrown boyfriend.

It couldn't be that easy, could it?

No, Vega was too smart, too *good* to get herself crushed in a building collapse. No way. She would fucking crawl out of the debris if there was a single breath left in her body. The bitch didn't have a Stop button— which used to be one of the things he'd appreciated most about her.

As the last echoes of the collapse finally settled, the crowd hushed in utter shock. Only a few columns and the decorative front façade remained of the three-story structure. There was no fire, no smoke. Just a haze of dust and piles of rubble.

And through that silence, Talon's keen hearing picked up on a muffled wail from inside the dust cloud beyond the front wall. Still alive. Of-fucking-course she was.

Her voice set the ant hill scurrying again. Naturally, not a single person approached the ruins. All of them ran headlong toward the garage, with servants herding the sheep to keep them somewhat organized.

Talon hoped Vega hadn't been counting on them to lend a hand.

What the fuck was she still doing in there? She should have been dead or out already. He had shit to do, and that list didn't include going over there to confirm his kill—

"So fucking unnecessary."

Talon sucked in a breath and almost choked on his own spittle.

It tasted suspiciously like fear.

Such wasteful destruction. Such a goddamn shame.

And all because some unhinged prick thought he could extort his way through Shadow ranks.

M watched the chaos of fleeing VanWarrens, fully aware of the pissant's every move. To his credit, what little he still had, Bigellow reacted with a healthy dose of caution now that he'd finally caught on to the fact that he had a Hawk standing at ease behind him. He'd been too busy salivating over the demolition to notice M walking up five minutes ago. Had no idea how many different ways he could already be dead.

But he'd made this personal. Having to clean up after Bigellow's mess was one thing. Having the prick interfere with M's mission was something altogether different.

"I'm genuinely curious," M said, watching the front entry for any sign of Vega Ortiz. "What in your history with the Shadows gave you the impression that we're open to negotiation?"

Bigellow turned over to sit up ever so slowly. M didn't dignify his presence with more than minimal attention. The man reeked after several days of living out in the elements. He huffed with a fury that raised his body temperature enough for M's wrist unit sensor to pick it up. "I know what Shadows will do for something they want badly enough."

"Kill," M replied. "We will kill."

But M's first shot didn't. No, the weapon was set to fifty percent power, enough to shatter Bigellow's kneecap at close range. The force of it bent the Hound's leg the wrong way and before his brain processed the sight and sensation, M shot again, shattering the other one.

Bigellow's body shook with the force of his scream, and M dropped over him, shoving the man flat and covering his mouth to keep the sound contained.

It was as good an opening as Bigellow would ever get. He might have lost any potential physical leverage but all those years of hand-to-hand combat training did not leave a Shadow without options in a situation like this. M quickly ran through all of the possibilities and smiled. Any attempt Bigellow might make to free himself would, of course, be futile. M was in a prime position to end this at any second but, for once, efficiency was not a prime concern.

There was a lesson in this clusterfuck of a situation—one that no one seemed to have bothered to teach Latham Bigellow in all his miserable years of underwhelming service. So the privilege would now fall to M, and the lesson would be the last one the Hound ever received.

Fucking with a Hawk's assignment was detrimental to one's health.

But Bigellow didn't fight.

He didn't even try to free his mouth or grab for the gun—which M fired twice more at Bigellow's hips.

Instead, he reached up and slapped a shaking hand over the side of his neck.

M frowned at the triumphant gleam in Bigellow's bloodshot eyes, even as a tortured scream echoed from the ruins of the VanWarren mansion.

Bigellow's hand slid forward like he was wiping away a stain, and the scream was cut short as Quinn VanWarren bellowed Vega's name.

34

Pain. Everywhere.

Quinn clawed his way back to consciousness, every nerve ending in his body screaming. A heavy weight pressed down on his chest, compressing his lungs until it eased off, and he was finally able to suck in a breath.

He regretted it instantly as his ribs snapped back into alignment, mending whole in a way that was most definitely *not* painless. Quinn couldn't feel his left leg past a dislocated hip, and his insides rolled and roiled like a boiling stew of shattered organs. He wanted to hurl, but the thought of moving his head in any direction made agony bloom at the base of his skull.

But he was alive.

Quinn sent up a silent prayer of thanks to whatever deity had blessed him with his higher bone density, and to Dr. Chase-Calen and her miraculous heal-all serum. Both had just saved his life. Then he shoved up against the solid piece of wood pinning him down. Newly-reconnected tendons howled but held as he shifted the weight off.

"Quinn!"

He sat up in a rush, forcing his hip joint back into alignment. His vision went black, and he ground the heels of his palms into his eye sockets, willing himself not to pass out.

Hands on his wrists, tugging. "Hey, look at me. Quinn!"

He opened his eyes, blinking back a haze of red and gray as his vision slowly cleared.

"What the…"

Quinn's legs were still pinned by a solid wooden beam, but he hauled Vega onto his lap and squeezed her as tight as he dared. Dust had turned her raven hair gray and she smelled of smoke, but she was alive and in one piece.

Holy fuck, she was alive. "Are you okay? Are you hurt?" He'd seen blood on her before the entry had exploded. "How badly are you hurt?"

"I'll live," she groaned.

Only then did he force himself to let her go and look around. His heart didn't have a beat to skip, but there was a disconcerting pitch and whirl in the frequency of its hum as he looked around.

It was all gone. The whole house.

"We have to move," Vega said, shifting toward his legs and the beam pinning them down.

She tried to move it.

Quinn would have kissed her senseless if he could. "I need room." And light. Dusk had already fallen, and everything was darkness and shadow. Quinn felt the weight, knew he could lift the beam, but not from this angle and not without displacing a lot of other shit that could potentially bury them both again.

Where the hell were the rescue teams? Surely, someone would have called for help by now.

Vega sat back on her heels, holding a hand to her side. "What do you need me to do?"

Again, that irrational impulse to stop everything and kiss her. Quinn shook himself off and tried to hold a coherent thought in his head. "Did the other buildings survive?"

"I don't know. Been a bit busy. Can't hear anyone out there, though."

Quinn dipped a grim nod. "You need to get out."

"The fuck I do."

"I'm serious, Vega. I don't know what will happen when I move this thing." He could survive another avalanche—the same way he'd survived the first one. Vega wouldn't. She was barely keeping upright as it was.

"You understand, the second I step out of here will be confirmation of life for whoever is trying to kill us, right?"

Fuck. He hadn't even thought of that. "Okay, just step back as far as you can."

Vega shifted all of five feet off to his right.

It would have to do.

The beam across his shins was about a foot wide and at least twelve feet long. The texture felt like wood, except harder and denser. He couldn't dig his fingers into it to rip it up piece by piece and breaking it at any point was out of the question. But he might have enough wiggle room to pull out his left leg. If he did that and managed to reposition himself, the new angle would provide better leverage to get his right leg free.

He gave his left foot an experimental twist and tug.

Nothing moved. Too much debris; he'd have to mangle his limbs to get them out.

Reaching forward, Quinn shoved his hands beneath the beam. *Brute force it is.*

"For the record," Vega said and he paused. "I'm glad you're alive."

It was too dark to see her face and her tone gave him no hints as to what she meant by that.

"What—"

Her scream tore through the fabric of his being as the shadow of her form contorted and collapsed.

And he froze.

He fucking froze, the same way he had in that goddamn vault on Anamtaigh, as the device in the back of her neck dropped her like a fucking stone.

For a split second, her neck *lit up* enough for him to get a glimpse of the twisting torment in her face. Then it went dark, and she fell silent.

And stopped moving all together.

"*VEGA!*"

Quinn wrenched himself sideways, reaching for her, but she was too far. His fingers missed her by inches.

She wasn't moving.

The whirr of his heart became a high-pitched zizz and he couldn't breathe fast enough to keep up. He shoved and punched at the beam, yanked on his legs to no effect. Stars danced in his dark vision. He was going to pass out.

Overheated, panting, Quinn shoved his hands underneath the beam again and put everything he had into lifting the fucking thing.

Muscles strained in his arms and twitched in his back. Something heavy groaned and debris shifted, raining down on the far side of the pile. The beam lifted all of an inch. But it was enough. Quinn mercilessly wrenched his leg sideways, dislocating his ankle to pull it out of the shoe still stuck in the debris. He barely felt the pain as he let the beam drop again and pulled his foot under him. The joint healed in seconds.

One more.

He couldn't look at Vega. Her stillness and silence short-circuited his brain. The void where she should have been sucked the air from his lungs. Quinn couldn't think his way past it.

His knee strained as he leaned farther forward to get a better hold of the beam. With his free leg bent beneath him, he had more strength to put into the lift, but it would cost him. Quinn didn't care. He grabbed the beam again, bore down, gritting his teeth against the pain of his knee bending the wrong way and bellowed, lifting up.

Something screeched and groaned as more debris dislodged, coming down all around him, on top of him, but the weight of the beam eased enough that he could shift it a few inches before he dropped it again.

Foot loose. Knee dislocated.

Quinn sat back and scooted his ass across the two feet of space he had to get his leg out from under the beam. His knee screamed, muscles and tendons twitching with involuntary movement to get the joint back into alignment, but if it did that, he'd never get his foot free.

Quinn glanced sideways.

Still too fucking far.

He took hold of his shin and twisted. His foot turned at a right angle, enough to slide free. The second it did, Quinn threw himself sideways again, dragging his momentarily useless leg behind him. "Vega..." She didn't respond. Didn't move. He pulled himself across the floor, slipping on sharp debris that tore open his forearms and stabbed into his hip. "Vega, fucking *answer me!*"

His knee snapped back into alignment as he reached her.

Limp. He pulled her closer, and it was like lifting a lifeless doll. No response. No signs of life.

Breath locked up in his throat, teeth gritted so hard they cracked,

Quinn lurched to his feet and carried her out onto the drive. There was light there, the path was lined with pretty little lamps bright enough to illuminate the borders of the gravel drive. Quinn laid Vega out on the soft grass, pressed shaking fingers to the side of her neck.

No pulse.

No breath.

"Shit…"

Quinn looked up at Zach standing a few feet away. Behind him, the sky was lit up with transports rising off the ground and speeding away into the night. His family running for their lives without a backward glance.

"I can't do CPR without crushing her," Quinn said through numb lips. "You have to do it."

Zach swore again, took a step forward, then stopped.

He stopped.

And in that second of hesitation, Quinn noted the look on Zach's face, the tense set of his shoulders, straight and pulled back. The blood on his hands.

Zach looked over his shoulder, then back at Vega. He checked the cuff on his wrist like he had all the time in the world, and there was something very familiar about it. Not just the gesture, but the device. Quinn had seen it before.

"You're—"

"A friend," Zach said in a clipped tone, tapping something on the cuff. "Today, Quinn, I'm a friend."

A dark transport emerged from behind the garage, making a beeline straight for them as Zach closed the distance and crouched down on Vega's other side.

Quinn had his hand around the son of a bitch's throat before he could touch her. He'd never felt anything like the murderous rage coursing through him. "Shadow," he growled. A Hawk. And Quinn had never seen him coming. Just like Vega had warned.

His fingers curled into the traitor's delicate flesh, and it was so easy. He would crush Zach's neck to pulp, and gift his head to Vega when she woke up—because she *would* wake up. She had to.

Zach grabbed Quinn's wrist as if he had a chance in hell of budging him. Not without a gun. And even then, it'd take a kill shot for Quinn to let up.

But Zach wasn't trying to get free. He held Quinn's gaze with the sharp focus of someone who either didn't give a shit whether he lived or died or someone who knew it would never come to that. And with his free hand, he held up a small metal square with minuscule wires hanging loose from the corners. "Trig-ger," he bit out.

Quinn blinked and let up enough for Zach to take a breath to speak as the transport came to a stop beside them, idling down low to the ground.

"Cut it out of Bigellow's neck."

"Who the fuck is Bigellow?" And why should he give a shit?

Zach's gaze dipped down, then came back up. "The guy who killed her."

Talon.

Talon was the only one with the trigger to Vega's torture device.

Quinn released Zach with a shove hard enough to send him sprawling.

He was back in two seconds, rolling his head on his shoulders to make sure it was still attached. It would take so little to rip it clear off his body.

"Where is he?"

"Dead," Zach said, checking Vega's pulse, and another stab of agony shattered through the void in Quinn's chest when he shook his head. "Consider it my pleasure. Vega deserved better." That sounded like he meant it. "This next part is me doing you a favor."

Zach twisted something clean off his cuff and yanked the neck of Vega's hoodie down to stamp it onto her chest before he picked her up and took her to the transport.

The fuck that was happening! Quinn shoved to his feet and grabbed Zach to throw him across the lawn, but the man was already stepping back from where he'd loaded Vega into the vehicle. "Get in," he said. "You don't have much time. When she wakes up, tell her she owes me."

Then he turned his back and wandered off like nothing had happened.

Quinn got in and pulled Vega into his lap as the door closed and the transport raised off the ground. It took off so fast, the force of it threw Quinn against the back rest but he felt Vega twitch in his arms. The second the transport leveled out and he regained mobility, Quinn rearranged Vega in his arms to see what the son of a bitch had done to her.

The device was blinking with a red light. And each time it blinked, she twitched. Contractions. An artificial heartbeat. Mechanical CPR, keeping her blood circulating until they reached help.

Holy shit.

He put his hand beneath her nose, but there was no breath. Quinn pinched it shut and put his mouth over hers to breathe for her.

How long had she been without a pulse? Ten minutes? More?

He clutched her tighter and kept breathing air into her lungs.

The transport came to an abrupt stop and descended straight down like it would fall out of the sky. As soon as it settled, the door opened, and there were people reaching inside, pulling Vega away from him and laying her out on a gurney.

Quinn went after them, vaguely noting emergency vehicles parked all around and an illuminated HOSPITAL sign. Three people dressed in nurse uniforms and a man in a lab coat all talked over each other as they steered Vega's gurney down the hallway. One of them had already cut away her hoodie and replaced Zach's device with a patch and a breathing mask. Another was setting up an IV, while two more rattled off her vitals and physical condition.

None of them paid a lick of attention to Quinn dogging their footsteps until they reached a door that needed an ID scan.

As they pushed her through, one of the nurses turned to see him following and stepped into his path. "You'll need to wait out here. We'll keep you up—*oof!*"

Quinn body-checked the man out of his way to follow Vega, keeping three feet of space between himself and her gurney to give the medical team room to work, but no more than that.

The doctor spared him a glance but didn't bother addressing the breech in protocol as he passed a flat scanner over her from toe to head.

They were about to turn into one of the rooms lining the hall when the scanner flashed red and the doctor snapped, "Stop!"

Everyone froze.

"How long has she been down?"

"Estimated five and a half minutes before the heart pump was applied. Oxygen levels are restored to ninety-five percent."

"Arrest CPR and put her on ice."

Nurses screamed and fled out of his way as Quinn crossed the three steps needed to grab hold of the doctor and shove him against the wall. "You're going to bring her back."

"I—"

"*Now!*"

People screamed again at his bellow, and an alarm started blaring up and down the hallway.

Quinn ignored all of it, his entire being focused on two things: the puny man who held Vega's life in his shaking hands and the soft beep of the heart monitor behind him, telling him Vega's heart was still beating and the respirator was still working to breathe for her.

"Bring—her—back."

The doctor gulped and held up his hands, one of them still clutching the scanner. "If I do that," he said with cautious precision, "the device on her spine will just kill her again."

Quinn's fingers curled into the man's shoulder hard enough to make him yelp.

"I can get it out!"

Quinn froze.

"I can"—he gasped in a pained breath—"I can get it out. Her heart stopped for over five minutes. The biofeedback loop is broken. I can remove the device safely. But only while she's dead. And that's a very short window, so if you want your girlfriend to live, we need to move now."

Quinn stared him down, swallowing past the lump in his throat to find his voice and what remained of his sanity. "She's my wife."

The doctor nodded. "I understand."

Quinn loosened his hold, allowing the doctor's feet to touch the ground again. "I'm not leaving her side."

Another nod. "Get him some scrubs."

"Doctor—"

"Just do it. And someone turn off that goddamn noise."

Two of the nurses ran for it. A few seconds later, the alarm shut off, and they were moving again, at a more measured pace.

When the nurses returned, one handed Quinn a white full-body suit that stretched too tight but didn't tear. The other held up a new IV bag filled with blue liquid.

"You will explain every step before you make it," Quinn informed them, and all movement paused.

The doctor spared him a glance before nodding to the nurse to continue. "We're going to stop her heart now and engage an artificial pump," he said, still cautious of the man who'd had him pinned to the wall moments ago. "The coolant will lower her body temperature to keep her organs and tissues from dying while we work."

Quinn curled his hands into fists, clamping down on the panic that threatened to overwhelm him at the thought.

"Remember to breathe. I can only treat one patient at a time."

Then the doctor tapped a glowing symbol on Vega's gurney, and her life support shut down.

35

Day 7

Nine hours. It took the surgeon nine hours to carefully pry eighteen microscopic, spiked tentacles out of Vega's spine and close her up again. No stitches, just an adhesive solution the doc said would heal the incision in a matter of hours without leaving a scar.

Then they put her in a neck brace, turned her over and replaced the coolant IV with a bag of warmed blood, and waited another twenty minutes until her body temperature raised enough to allow for resuscitation.

The three minutes it took to restart her heart were the most harrowing moments of Quinn's entire life. By the time they wheeled her into the recovery ward, he couldn't summon the energy to do anything more than collapse into the chair next to her bed.

She was alive. But whether or not she'd wake up, and in what condition, the doctor couldn't tell him. She'd gone a long time without oxygen. And there had been faint but visible marks on her spinal cord when they'd removed the device. There was a possibility of brain damage and mobility impairment.

Quinn didn't have it in him to entertain those risks. She was alive, and that was all that mattered. The rest was up to Vega, and how much she wanted to live; how hard she was willing to fight to get back to herself.

He closed his eyes for a second and woke up to the last rays of evening sunlight teasing open his eyelids. He'd slept through the entire day.

The nurse checking on Vega's condition smiled at him as she updated the digital chart. "Brain activity looks good. We tested neural responses earlier. There's solid feedback in all extremities. She's doing well, all things considered."

"Then why isn't she awake yet?"

The smile dimmed a little. "Her body's been through a lot. She just needs time."

Little comfort in that.

Quinn rubbed the sleep from his face. He must have gotten a few solid hours at least, despite the awkward sitting position, but exhaustion still weighed down his limbs. He ought to eat something. Maybe once his stomach unclenched enough to let him swallow food.

Vega looked so peaceful in sleep it unnerved him. She was breathing on her own, and most of the tubes and needles had been removed. Now, she only had the monitoring patch over her chest and a nutritional IV drip in her arm. They'd removed the sedative drip, too, which meant there was nothing artificial keeping her under.

Time. She needed time.

To sleep and dream the same nightmares she suffered every night—only this time she couldn't wake herself up.

"Umm…" The nurse rounded Vega's bed to his side, staring at the digital pad in her hands. "We… There was a region-wide alert sent out to all medical centers. Your last name is VanWarren, yes?"

Quinn nodded.

"And you were brought here from Crescent Island?"

Quinn figured the transport would have alerted them once they were en route.

"I just… I thought you should know. Three other centers took in patients from Crescent Island, and they're all coordinating to keep everyone up to date."

"Don't tell them we're here." Quinn had risked his life to get the rest of his family out of the house, and in their eternal gratitude, they hadn't looked back once before fleeing the island and leaving him trapped in the wreckage.

He was done.

"O-of course, Mr. VanWarren. We never share patient information without consent. But, umm… Your family did consent, and I have a summary of their conditions." She waited for him to respond and, when he didn't, read a few lines off her digital screen. "There were a lot of minor injuries. Cuts, scrapes, burns. Mostly among the adults. One had a broken arm, two suffered mild concussions, and one was treated for a sprained knee. Ingrid VanWarren suffered a heart attack upon arrival at the medical center. The team was unable to revive her. I'm so sorry for your loss. Um…. There is one person unaccounted for. They're asking if anyone has information on Geraldine VanWarren?"

Quinn's gut went stone cold.

He replayed the attack in his mind, from the first tremor to the moment the transport took off for the hospital. It was chaos, mayhem, and pain. So many faces passing by, screaming, terrified, but he couldn't distinguish between them. They were a blur of familiar features that all blended together in the end. Quinn couldn't recall seeing Geraldine. Not since Midnight Island.

"Your family's private security searched the grounds but didn't find Miss VanWarren near the site of the collapse," the nurse told him gently. "Police teams and technical crews were dispatched earlier today to search through the wreckage. If she was still in the house when it collapsed, it's…unlikely that she survived. I'm very sorry, sir."

Having delivered her news, the kindly nurse made her quiet exit.

Minutes went by as Quinn sat there in silence, watching Vega's chest rise and fall.

It didn't make sense. None of it. No matter how hard he tried, Quinn couldn't find any logic behind the last few days. Hell, the last few *years*. So much death and destruction. Grief and pain—and for what?

"You're going to wake up," he told Vega, voice hoarse, hands shaking. "You're going to wake up because Talon is dead, and there's no more leash, and… God dammit, Vega, we're married. I'm not gonna let you just fade away. You're better than that. Fight. If not for yourself then…" He swallowed the tremor in his voice and blinked back the haze. "Then for me."

A soft knock behind him.

The door was open. Quinn had insisted on it to keep the path clear for emergencies.

He didn't bother extending an invitation.

The visitor didn't appear to need one.

Measured footsteps entered the room. Color snuck in on the periphery of Quinn's vision as a vase of flowers settled on the far table. "She really did deserve better, you know."

Quinn was on his feet in a blink, facing off with Zach—if that was even his real name.

No more pretense of humanity in the face of the man who'd called himself a poor relation trying to make a good impression. This was the truth of the Hawk behind the mask. His eyes were hard, his mouth unsmiling. He'd changed clothes at some point and washed off the blood. Nothing about him betrayed how lethal he could be except the unfeeling expression on his handsome face.

The same face that hadn't quirked an eyebrow when he'd loaded Vega into his transport and told Quinn she now *owed him*.

"What do you want?"

"To see if my efforts paid off." His hands were loose at his sides. There was no tension in his spine and no hint of unease in his steady gaze. Quinn was within arm's reach of the man, close enough to crush his skull or break him in half if he wanted. And the Hawk was unafraid. Because as fast as Quinn could end him, he could end Quinn faster.

The quicksilver quirk of his eyebrow all but confirmed it.

"You saved her life." The words tasted bitter on his tongue, but they were true. "Why?"

"Which time?"

Quinn frowned. "What?"

The small patronizing smile Zach gave him was there one second and gone the next. "Emmett had twenty-nine more shots left in his weapon when he ran off from your camp. Maybe he would have left well enough alone if Vega hadn't decided to chase after him. Then again, maybe not." Zach shrugged. "I never liked him, anyway. Putrid waste of humanity. Didn't even break a sweat taking him out."

"Cops said he fell."

"Oh, he did. I just…helped him fall the *right* way."

And, by the looks of it, he'd enjoyed it.

"And then, of course, there was the case of one Latham Bigellow. I assume that he used a different name when you knew him."

"He called himself Talon."

Zach huffed a chuckle. "Arrogant fucking prick." Then he frowned. "You should know, my assignment was to monitor the VanWarrens after the old guard died and ensure our financial relationship remained intact." So the payments were going to the Shadows after all. "You were supposed to be a watch-and-wait, and Vega Ortiz wasn't a target for us at all until he showed up. She wasn't even on our radar."

Quinn didn't miss that careful choice of words. "And now?"

"Now... Things are a little different." Still no fear, even as he glanced down at Quinn's fists quivering at his sides to do irreparable damage. Still the same, relaxed pose and unconcerned expression on his face as he met Quinn's gaze again head-on.

And it still didn't make any fucking sense. What the hell kind of mind games was he playing? Why was he telling Quinn any of this? Why had he bothered helping them at all if he only ended up killing them in the end?

Or would he?

"You said you were a friend." He'd killed two people to prove it.

"Last night, I was," Zach confirmed.

"And today?"

"I'm sorry, Quinn. Today, I'm not."

Quinn was going to beat the fucker's face into mulch. "You want her? You have to go through me first."

Zach shook his head at an angle like Quinn had said something adorably ignorant. "We will. But whether or not we get her is incidental." He leaned closer to whisper, "You should be more careful about where you leave your blood."

Faster than Quinn could process, Zach raised his hand and sprayed a light mist into his face. Quinn couldn't stop the instinctual gasp. He inhaled the substance and staggered back as the world tilted and pitched under his feet. His knees gave out, and he fell against Vega's bed before dropping to the floor.

Zach's unhurried footsteps echoed in his ears. Four different versions of him crouched next to Quinn, their expressions never changing as they watched his eyes roll back in his head.

Day 10

It was dark when Vega slowly blinked open her eyes. The familiar taste of pennies on her tongue and the aching heaviness in her limbs told her Talon had yanked on her leash again. She breathed in deeply and exhaled on a pained groan. He'd hit her harder than he had in ages. The hell had crawled up his ass this time?

The smell of disinfectant registered first, then the blinking lights of a medical scanner, and finally, the large glass window. The night sky was lit up with drones forming and reforming different shapes as shuttle after shuttle took off in the distance.

Vega blinked and blinked again.

She wasn't in the vault. This wasn't Anamtaigh, and she wasn't with Talon's crew.

Everything came back then, all at once, and Vega bolted upright.

Or tried to, anyway. Her body felt like someone else was in charge of it. The smallest movement took immense effort to coordinate—and, holy fuck, it hurt. From the base of her spine to her tingling toes, Vega was one massive knot of pain. She didn't get farther than a couple of inches before it laid her out flat again. Head spinning, heart racing, she watched bright lights flash across the hospital ceiling above her.

The house had collapsed. She'd crawled through the wreckage to get to Quinn, who should have been dead. He should have been crushed to mulch beneath the debris, but he hadn't been.

He...

She'd watched a torn gash across his forehead pinch closed and the black cloud of blood clear from his eyes before the sun went down.

The scanner beeped a warning, registering a sudden spike in her heart rate, and seconds later, the light came on, and a handsome nurse with braids hanging down to his shoulders rushed in.

"You're awake!" He smiled brightly, almost with relief. "Thank the skies. You had us worried there for a while."

Vega barely managed to lift an uncoordinated hand and weakly grip the handle on her bed.

She'd watched Quinn heal before her eyes.

"It's okay," the nurse rushed to assure her as he cleared the alarm off the scanner.

Vega's hand was still in a brace. She was covered in bruises from the explosion, and her limbs buzzed with a nervy sensation she could only attribute to the fucking leash.

But Quinn hadn't had a scratch on him by the time it'd killed her.

The nurse's name tag read ASHTON, RN. Late thirties, with brown skin, unnaturally blue eyes, and bright pink lipstick.

Vega watched every move he made and couldn't spot a single Shadow tell.

Not that she would if the man was a Hawk.

And that right there was the problem.

Quinn had survived the collapse and healed from his injuries in seconds. He hadn't had that ability a few months ago, which meant it wasn't part of his particular genetic glitch.

Had she imagined it?

No, the memory was too clear and detailed to be untrue.

If anyone else saw it…

Nurse Ashton flipped a switch, and the top half of Vega's bed bent up to help her sit. "Your body took a hell of a beating. But it's a good sign that you're moving around this much."

Quinn would be a target. She had to get him out of here.

"How long have I been out?"

Nurse Ashton lifted Vega's fractured hand and turned it palm up. "A few days. Can you lift up for me?"

Days! No, that wasn't right. It couldn't be.

"There was an explosion. Push for me, *cher.*"

Vega pushed, intending to shove the man straight out the window.

She barely managed to press her forearm against his palm.

It appeared to be enough. Nurse Ashton set down her arm and took her good hand, pressing it palm to palm with his. "You were in pretty bad shape when your husband brought you in. Lucky for you, this is the best medical center in the region. Push again."

Vega couldn't catch her breath, her mouth dry and her throat aching. Days. She'd lost *days.* "W-where is he?" In the back of her mind, she registered the alarming weakness in her body, the heaviness in her limbs, but right now those concerns were secondary. She had to get Quinn off-world.

"Your husband? I'm not sure." Nurse Ashton pulled back the bottom edge of Vega's covers to reveal her feet and ran his nail along the soles. Vega's toes curled at the tickle. "He was with you the whole time you were in surgery and then wouldn't leave the room the whole next day. Bend your knee for me? Good. Now the other one. I think he went home to get some sleep," he said, ignoring the obvious effort it took Vega to bend her right knee.

No, that was too far out of character for Quinn. The man she knew wouldn't have left her bedside for longer than a couple of hours.

He'd healed himself within seconds.

The Shadows would do anything to get their hands on that kind of ability—and they might not even need Quinn alive to replicate it.

"Lean forward."

Vega leaned on the arm Nurse Ashton braced against her chest. Her neck was stiff, and so weak she wanted to let her head hang, but it didn't. Delicate fingers probed something solid connecting the back of her neck and shoulders with the base of her skull and she flinched. The movement sent another wave of zinging pain down her spine into her limbs.

"We put a stabilizer on you so you wouldn't wrench your spine when you came to. It'll stay on for the next couple of weeks and then come off on its own. Don't try to pry it. You'll rip your flesh off."

The leash had killed her.

Vega had felt its electric fire fry her synapses. She'd felt the weight of her body drop away.

Was this hell?

"All healed up. You were very lucky. The doctor said if your husband had brought you in even ten minutes later, he wouldn't have been able to remove the device."

Remove?

"*Cher*, I don't know what kind of mess you got yourself into, but if you want my advice, it's time to get out." He settled her back against the pillows and pulled something out of his pocket. "The doc said you might like to keep it as a souvenir."

Vega stared at the metal thing he placed in the middle of her palm. It was barely half an inch in length with hair-thin tethers fanning out from it. She touched the smooth brace on the back of her neck, found the opening down the middle and traced a cautious finger along her skin. There was no external wound only a deep ache in her neck that carried the memory of a surgical procedure.

"You okay?"

Okay? Vega closed her fist around the device, expecting it to bite again, but it didn't. It was out, and she was alive. She was free. "When did Qu… When did you last see my husband?"

Nurse Ashton pulled the covers back over her legs. "I told you, a few days ago."

"How many?" All of Ela might exist on a la-dee-da schedule, but hospitals had to keep proper time. Patients' lives depended on timing accuracy.

"Well, let's see. Three days, I think? Yes, I had to change out the water in your bouquet yesterday because the flowers were starting to wilt, and that was two days after your visitor stopped by to drop it off." He nodded to himself." Three days."

Vega stared at the vase sitting on a table across from her bed. "Can I see those?"

"Oh, sure!" Nurse Ashton picked up the vase, the bouquet so large he disappeared behind it as he brought it over and rested the bottom against Vega's bed. "There's a note in there somewhere. I'm pretty sure I saw one."

Oh, there was a note, all right. No envelope, just bold text hand-written on an off-white paper rectangle. Numbers and letters, vector coordinates encased in a lopsided heart shape.

It was attached to Quinn's shattered com cuff.

Vega threw back the covers and swung her legs over the side of her bed.

"Whoa! What are you doing? You can't get up yet."

Pain shot down her back and her right leg crawled with stinging ants as she pushed herself forward. Both of her knees buckled and hit the polished, disinfected floor.

Nurse Ashton set the vase away and rounded the bed, taking hold of her arm. "I told you. You're not well enough to be out of bed. Your body needs time to heal."

"I don't have time," she growled, shoving at the man, but what little strength she had in her arms wasn't anywhere near enough to deter him.

Nurse Ashton levered her up to sit on her heels, then swatted away Vega's useless hand and pinched her face to make her look at him. "You just had surgery on your cervical spine," he said, suddenly serious. "If you cause further damage, it could end up being permanent. Is that what you want?"

"I don't get to *want*," she snapped. Why did everyone have so much trouble comprehending the concept? "I am leaving, and you can either help me or stand aside, because I swear to your *skies*, if you get in my way, you'll find out exactly how much trouble *I* am."

Those horrifically blue eyes stared at her for all of five seconds before Nurse Ashton decided he'd rather not tempt fate. He pulled out his digital tablet and held it out for her. "Thumbprint to authorize a discharge against medical advice."

She gave him one.

"Stay here." He retrieved a set of clothes and a pair of plastic-wrapped shoes from one of the wall cabinets. Dropping them on the bed behind her, he left again and came back with a green case that needed a medical override to open. "I'm going to put a patch on your spine. It'll keep the pain manageable and prevent further swelling. Do not remove it."

When he reached for her, Vega moved away. "Can you remove the brace?"

"Do you want to be a paraplegic?"

Fuck. She leaned forward and let him put the patch on her. "I'll need a ride to the shuttleport." Three days. "Has the planetary alignment started?" According to the schedules she'd seen, the planetary hop was supposed to begin one week before peak alignment and keep going for another week after.

"They kicked off the celebrations last night."

The shuttles taking off in the distance.

All of them booked.

Didn't matter. Vega didn't need a ticket to get on a shuttle. On her own, she had ways of getting from place to place without anyone the wiser. She was a Shadow, after all.

A Shadow who needed Nurse Ashton to help her remove the patient gown and put on hospital-provided clothes because her limbs weren't strong enough or coordinated enough to do it for her.

One problem at a time.

At least when he lifted her to her feet, she stayed on them. Long enough for him to fetch a levchair, anyway. The tremor in her right leg was concerning. It wasn't stable enough to hold her weight and her knee seemed to have forgotten how to lock.

Relatively mobile in the chair, she maneuvered herself around the bed to the bouquet and retrieved the note and com cuff.

"*Cher*," the nurse said kindly, "whatever you think you have to do, it's not worth it."

Vega wasn't a cosmographer, but she recognized the first third of the vector coordinate set from tracking their inbound shuttle flight to Ela. They pointed to one of the three other planets in this solar system. The note might as well be an invitation: *Come get him. We'll wait.*

"You have no idea."

Vega was going to rip that world apart to get Quinn back.

37

The Shadow tranquilizers didn't last very long. Quinn had shaken off the first dose in the back of a transport, prompting a needle to the neck. He'd shaken that off long enough to recognize the smooth black walls of some kind of cargo hold before another dose knocked him out.

Quinn figured they must have set up a schedule to keep him under after that because he didn't remember anything else until he'd woken up alone in a solid white cell with no windows or doors, only a small sink and toilet that folded out of nothing, and returned back to nothing once he was done with them. And he had no idea how much time had passed.

No one came to check on him or question him. He didn't have any bruises or injuries, but then again, he wouldn't, would he? Not unless they fully amputated something, and even then, Quinn wasn't sure how far Dr. Chase-Calen's regenerative serum would go to heal the injury.

It was a pretty safe bet, though, that they would have at least taken tissue samples and performed some tests while he'd been unconscious and unable to rip limbs from bodies.

Was Vega still sleeping?

The wall to his left sprouted a rectangular hole, admitting the Shadow formerly known as Zach. He was dressed head to toe in a black uniform with midnight blue accents, and a silver pin in the abstract shape of wings on his collar. The cell's unforgiving brightness threw his utter lack of expression into stark relief. He didn't move with the clipped, heel-snapping sharpness of a soldier. He reminded Quinn of a snake gliding through water—fluid, silent, and deadly. No hint left of the easy-going man Quinn had met on Crescent Island. Only a killer with nothing but cold, merciless intelligence in his eyes.

And still Quinn dredged up enough fight to smile at the bastard. "You don't scare me."

"Good," the Hawk said, setting his food tray on the floor two feet from Quinn. "I don't want to. I don't want you for an enemy."

Quinn thumped his head back against the wall and sighed. "More mind games."

The Hawk chuckled. And then he sat down beside Quinn, mirroring his pose. Like they were buddies. They sat in silence together for a good few minutes while Quinn imagined all the ways he could paint this blank room red. But where would it get him? Even if he managed to get that door open, he'd only face more Shadows out there.

The Hawk casually lounging beside him seemed to know it, too. Whatever training he used to read him, whatever minor tells Quinn revealed, the Hawk knew the moment Quinn decided not to try his luck. Only then did he break his silence. "Your friend from the SU spent some time in a cell like this. It's built to neutralize telepathic abilities."

"Too bad I don't have any."

"No, but your friends do. The cell works both ways."

"Are you my friend today, *Zach*?"

"I'm not your enemy."

Quinn snorted. Fucking Hawks. "Food poisoned?"

"Nope."

"Drugged?"

"No."

Quinn hummed thoughtfully. "How 'bout the water?"

The Hawk grinned. "How 'bout the air?"

Shit.

"Relax. We got everything we need from you. For now."

So they had taken samples after all. "Find anything interesting?"

"Oh, yes. It appears you have foreign nucleotide segments grafted onto your DNA."

"Hmm."

"Or, I should say, *into* your DNA. It's fully integrated into the strand and present in all tissue samples. Something not mentioned in any of your medical records from even a year ago. The lab cats are saying it's impossible. You can't change a grown adult's DNA in every cell throughout an entire body." His mouth quirked the slightest bit. "It's kind of fun to watch their heads smoke whenever they come across the work of a Chase. They'd love to know how the sisters did it." Head still resting against the wall, he rolled it to the side to raise an eyebrow at Quinn. "You wouldn't know, would you?"

"Science isn't really my thing."

The Hawk grinned wider. "All brawn and no brains? That what you're trying to sell me? Come on, man. At least make it believable. I looked into the VanWarren accounts. Every single Shadow transaction for the last eight months was flagged as recently accessed. Curiously, there was no history of data exports, and no sign of AI trawl. You didn't hire an accountant, or run any algorithms. You found them all on your own. In, what, over three thousand family accounts?"

Three thousand five hundred and eighteen. Not that it mattered. Numbers and patterns were a party trick. Most days about as useful as a sewing needle in a grocery shop. "Still not science."

"Right."

Quinn decided to keep his mouth shut.

"In any case, it doesn't matter. The graft may not be transferable, but it is replicable."

Quinn's heart did a dizzying *zzzZZZZzzz*. His face heated up while his hands went cold as ice. The Hawk didn't even glance his way, but Quinn knew he picked up on his reaction. Replicable. The word kept repeating in his head. *Replicable. Replicable. Replicable…*

"Ever heard of a place called New Alaska?"

Replicable. Replicable. Replicable.

"Back in 3028, someone leaked a story to the news media networks about unsanctioned genetic experimentation being done on the inmates there. Dr. Chase—the elder—didn't know it at the time, but her blowing that whistle was the first real spark that ignited the antichem movement. People were outraged. How *dare* someone use convicted criminals in the highest security prison world in the galaxy as unwilling test subjects? And if that wasn't bad enough, now they wanted to institute human breeding programs in there? Inconceivable!"

Replicable. Unwilling test subjects. Replicable. Human breeding programs. Replicable…

"Too bad no one bothered to leak anything from Prime Gama—twenty years earlier."

Staring straight ahead, Quinn caught movement from the corner of his eye as the Hawk turned to look at him again.

"Just think, if they had, I wouldn't be here, having this conversation with you right now."

"You're going to breed my traits into new Shadows." Not only the regenerative properties Dr. Chase-Calen had given him. His natural strength, too. They would spawn an entire generation of soldiers who could shred through transports with their bare hands, break every bone in their body, and then walk away fully healed a minute or two later.

"Any opportunity for improvement gives us an advantage in the war," The Hawk said with a careless shrug. "In vitro genetic grafting still has about a thirty percent failure rate. Not too bad. And with a large enough sample size, the risk becomes more of a…standard operating cost. Surrogates can always be acquired. And a soldier *born* is far more reliable than a soldier *made*." Was that a hint of resentment?

"Over my dead fucking body."

"That won't be necessary. I told you, we have everything we need for the time being. And, once they put you in the chair, you won't be as resistant to our directive anymore."

The chair.

They would fry his brain the same way they had Finn's and Vega's, and every other Shadow's. They'd make him a compliant zombie to do their bidding. The first in a long line of indestructible soldiers to raze what was left of human society and… What then? "What's the end goal? I never quite understood. Why all this killing? What's the point?"

The Hawk shrugged again. "Who knows? More importantly, who gives a shit?"

"*I* do."

"Really? So if I told you it's all for the greater good, that the people in power seek to win this one final war to usher in a Golden Age of human evolution and development and eradicate all future conflicts from ever sprouting again, you'd go along with it? You'd accept the short-term destruction in favor of long-term peace and prosperity? Didn't think so." He pushed away from the wall and stood. "Moral and philosophical conundrums aside, there are some practical considerations to ponder—if one were inclined to do so."

"Such as?"

"Shadows maintain control by circumventing what we like to call free will. It requires EMC, of course, but also a continuous supply of clear, direct orders. Thanks to your friends at the SU, our Commander in Chief is out of commission. And with each Shadow unit possessing only enough information to do their jobs, we don't have a larger directive anymore. We're just keeping on to keep keeping on until someone else steps up to reset our course. How long do you think that can last? Especially when you factor in EMC's diminishing returns. Whether it's after twelve treatments or twelve hundred, eventually, a soldier's brain becomes resistant to further programming. They die, they break…or they reset."

Quinn frowned at him. Had he just casually revealed the Shadows' greatest weaknesses?

"No directive, fragmenting control… I don't know if the COs realize how easily we can fall into entropy. How far we have already fallen. They may have a higher clearance but, at the end of the day, they're all just grunts trained to follow orders, same as the rest of us." He tapped his temple. "Following orders and creating them don't tend to go hand in hand."

Following orders and questioning their higher purpose or long-term strategy didn't, either.

"So what does a soldier trained to destroy and kill do when he wakes up from the nightmare long enough to ask questions, and no one can tell him what he's supposed to dream next?"

The same thing John Wayland had done when he'd pulled Emma Calen out of a cell like this. The same thing Finn Rowe had done when he'd turned the executioner's ax to take off the head of a Shadow instead of his best friend. And the same thing Vega had done when she'd chosen to take a young girl's life rather than deliver her into a living hell.

"He picks a side," Quinn answered.

Holy shit. Was the Hawk saying what Quinn thought he was saying?

I don't want you for an enemy.

But he didn't call himself a friend, either.

The Hawk's chin dipped in a sage nod. "Practical considerations."

And, before Quinn could think of something to say, to somehow take advantage of the tiny, fragile lifeline, the Hawk walked out through a door that was there one moment and gone the next. Nothing left but unbroken white and an untouched food tray sitting two feet away.

Minutes—hours?—later, still reeling, Quinn began to wonder whether he'd hallucinated the whole encounter.

Every shuttleport had a blind spot. Every shuttle had security holes. They might appear once a week or on the hour, but they were obvious to anyone who knew how to look for them.

And every Shadow did.

It took Vega thirty minutes to identify the most direct flight to Mai, then two hours to get into the shuttleport and sneak into the shuttle's cargo hold. With a record number of passengers crowding through for the first stages of the planetary alignment hop, she probably could have walked right into a First-Class cabin with no one except the pass holder batting an eye. But Vega couldn't risk getting flagged and removed from the shuttle before take-off.

An hour after she awkwardly squeezed herself into a crawl space, the ground crew finished pre-flight checks, and the shuttle took off.

It wasn't a smooth launch.

To accommodate a record demand for the same route, there were so many shuttles taking off one after the other that the wind turbulence they created caused high surf advisories and tornado warnings all over Ela, and all passengers on those shuttles received a sedative to make their journey more comfortable.

Stuck in the cargo hold crawl space, Vega felt each harrowing shudder and sway rattle through her spine until pain shot down her arms and legs. Her headache turned into a pounding migraine, causing rainbow lights to flare wherever she looked in the darkness. She clenched her teeth and swallowed back against wave after wave of nausea, counting the seconds and waiting to pass the fuck out.

But she didn't.

And then the shuttle cleared the planet's atmosphere, and the ride became much smoother, allowing her to slip out of the crawl space into the cavernous cargo hold.

Thanks to the alignment, the four inhabited planets of the solar system were close enough that traveling between them didn't require dropping into subspace. But it still took twenty-six hours for a shuttle from Ela to reach Mai.

Time she needed to start wresting back control of her banged-up body. And whenever her knees buckled, whenever her arm refused to pull or push up her weight, she touched the shattered com on her wrist, thought of Quinn in a Shadow holding cell, and tried again. Pushed harder.

Twenty-six hours later, Vega had a pretty good benchmark for her current physical limits.

It wasn't pretty.

And she didn't care.

November 1, 3039 – Bilabong, Mai

Mai had sixty-seven shuttleports. Vega's flight landed her on the southernmost tip of its megacontinent, forty-seven thousand miles from where she was headed.

She was stumbling like a goddamn drunk by the time she made it out of the shuttle and got her bearings. It was nighttime, but the 'port was lit up bright as day and crawling with so many travelers they looked like schools of fish swimming here and there.

Lines twelve people long stretched out from every passenger console. Vega's back began to spasm by the time she got her turn at one of them to scope out the situation. Long-range hovers serviced cross-continental routes. The shortest one had five intermediate stops and would take almost an entire day, but at least she wouldn't have to change hovers.

Best of all, the outbound flight had plenty of seats still available.

Vega used one of her burner IDs to book the passage and added a meal plan before she dragged her feet to her gate, where boarding had just begun. Cutting the line to the front, Vega flashed her Priority Pass, shuffled through into the cabin, and collapsed into her seat, ready to pass out.

She hadn't eaten since Ela, and only a crew member's abandoned water bottle had kept her hydrated enough to last the shuttle flight. Her body wailed with aches and pains that wouldn't stop. Her grip was shot; only one of her legs could hold her weight, and she couldn't turn her head because of the stabilizer brace.

There was a good chance this trip was one-way only.

Vega tried to dredge some emotion over it, but nothing came.

She was just so goddamn tired.

But now wasn't the time to give up. Not yet.

She still had a mission to complete.

One more fight.

Get Quinn away from the Shadows, get him somewhere safe. That was all she had to do.

After that, the rest wouldn't matter, anyway.

It never had.

Shadows always had been and always would be expendable.

November 2, 3039 – Kunluni Province, Mai

A couple of solid in-flight meals and a few hours of rest in relative comfort did wonders for Vega's equilibrium. Which all got undone the moment she pulled up a map at the hover station and realized New Shangri La was on the other side of the Arakai mountain range that loomed over the province, and all vehicles were grounded due to inclement weather conditions.

Transport rental places had stopped operations.

All roadways up into the mountains were closed.

All businesses were shutting down.

Residents were being advised to stay indoors for the next day and a half.

Adorable.

It only took Vega five minutes to break into a transport in the hover station parking lot and drive off without raising any alarms.

And then the damned thing shut down on her a couple of miles outside of town.

Warning: Inclement weather forecasted for the next thirty-nine hours. Seek shelter immediately.

After forty minutes of tinkering with its wiring and a small fire that filled the cabin with noxious smoke, Vega had a vehicle that hobbled almost as badly as she did. She should have taken Rowe up on his offer to teach her how to do this right.

The warning didn't clear, blinking an angry red all across the front windshield, but the transport did rise off the ground. With the pre-programmed vertical limit now disengaged, it rose and rose, rocking wildly in a windstorm that kicked up snow vortices in the plains below.

By then, the sun had already set, and the storm had dropped the outside temperature far below freezing. Vega engaged the engine, pushing it to the max, and shot straight toward the sharp-edged mountain range.

Minutes to clear the top. Lo and behold, as soon as she began her descent into the valley, the air settled as if by magic, and the warning cleared.

New Shangri La was nestled in a flattish basin sunken into the mountain range that embraced it from all sides, creating a natural wind barrier. The valley consisted of a few scattered villages and pools that looked like aurora lights caught in liquid form. Every so often, something bright blue streaked across the sky right in front of the transport, causing Vega to flinch and veer off course. She leveled out and descended to inches above the tree line.

Laura Belden's new compound stood out on the northeast side of the basin, sprawling across a plot of land almost as big as one of the smaller villages. Its closest neighbor was a massive mansion three miles south that looked like it had been built out of ice crystals.

A half-mile-thick circle of trees bordered the property in what Vega assumed was an attempt at a fence. That didn't mean the compound wasn't protected. Hell, the VanWarrens' Crescent Island hadn't had a single wall or fence, but it still managed to deter most civilians from trespassing. Laura Belden likely had similar security measures in place.

Vega slowed to a crawl as she guided the transport right up to and then over the natural perimeter, keeping a careful eye on the console.

No warnings, no technical overrides. She crossed the non-barrier without difficulty and touched down on the other side, well within sight of the compound but veiled by shadows in the dark of night.

Vega turned off the engine and waited. Any minute now, an army of guards would swarm out to surround her. Or her brains would start leaking out of her nose. Or she'd suddenly get the urge to drive off and crash herself into a canyon.

Any minute…

She checked the time.

Fifteen minutes had passed, and still, no one appeared to have noticed that their perimeter had been breached. Did the woman have no security to speak of, human or artificial? Even if they'd recognized her at a distance and decided she wasn't a threat, Vega would have expected *someone* to come confront her.

Finnegan-fucking-Rowe was supposed to be in there. In what goddamn universe did he not notice a potential threat landing in his backyard?

The longer she sat there, waiting for something to happen, the more it pissed her off.

How comfortable, how complacent these people were.

How quickly they'd forgotten what happened to them on Anamtaigh.

Vega hadn't seen Quinn talk to anyone from his old compound the whole time she'd been with him.

Had they forgotten him, too? All for one, as long as they stayed under the same roof, and then every man for himself?

Vega shoved her way out of the transport and almost face-planted into the snow when her right knee gave out. She was shaking in the cold, her hospital-issued outfit designed for the tropical clime of Ela, not this frozen hell. In seconds, she lost feeling in her toes, but pure fury boiled in her gut, forcing one foot in front of the other as she made her way toward the front entry.

No guards were posted outside.

She tried the door—unlocked.

Vega wanted to scream. But she bit down hard on the inside of her cheek and dragged her right foot forward, limping down a brightly lit hall toward the sound of happy, carefree laughter.

Just like Crescent Island.

She thumped her right thigh, where a crawling numbness was starting to spread. Only a few more steps. Five feet.

The doorless opening framed a scene that raised her hackles. The large, open space had curved tables set up in a circle, and the seats were filled all around with adults and children alike. Happy faces, laughing voices, plates heaped with food. More of it was piled high on the self-serve tables placed along one wall. Heaters blasted the air, keeping the temperature comfortable, even with the entire back of the room open to the snowed-in garden beyond.

Blissful, wasteful ignorance.

Vega dragged her foot across the threshold, and all laughter stopped.

All eyes turned her way; every face instantly switched from carefree joy to blank terror. Adults pulled children closer to shield them from the Shadow in their midst; men rose from their seats while women covertly palmed knives off their tables.

She ignored them, focusing all of her attention on the only person who mattered.

Finnegan-fucking-Rowe, sitting at the far side of the table with his back exposed to the garden like he no longer needed anyone to watch it.

Finnegan Rowe, staring her down like he had no fucking clue she wasn't on Persephone 5 anymore. Like he hadn't expected or wanted to see her ever again.

Finnegan Rowe, who'd collected a ragtag group of ex-Shadows into Laura Belden's old, crumbling compound in Karsengale, yet somehow ended up here in this luxurious mountain retreat with his childhood sweetheart at his side, and not a single brother-in-arms to be seen.

Vega clutched Quinn's broken com tight to remind herself why she was here in the first place. She breathed down the fury, pushed her resentment aside, and focused on the face of the one person she'd wasted precious time coming to see, praying to whatever death gods dogged her footsteps that it hadn't been for nothing.

Two more limping steps brought her across the table from him. Hating to the bottom of her soul how hard she had to work to keep her hand from shaking, she unclenched her fingers and tossed Quinn's com in front of Rowe.

The cold sense of loss curled her hand back into a fist, clutching nothing.

"We need to talk."

Rowe picked up the com, turned it over in his four-fingered hand, then murmured something to Laura. Whatever he said, she didn't like, but she did sit and let him walk away from the table. "Let's go talk," he said to Vega.

She followed him out of the room, fully aware that he slowed his pace to accommodate her limp. Vega allowed him to remain upright because he didn't ask if she needed help.

He led her to a much smaller room two doors down with a card table and an open cabinet haphazardly stuffed with old-world games. Two windows facing the garden, one door in or out.

Rowe had either lost his mind or all sense of self-preservation. For a Shadow, even a former one, the two were one and the same.

He closed the door behind them for privacy and waited until she took a seat at the table. Immediately, her back curved with relief, even as the crawling numbness in her right thigh intensified.

"This is a civilian com. Or was. You wanna tell me what the fuck happened?"

She'd planned to. Vega needed a Hawk for the first phase of her plan. But the Rowe who dropped into the seat opposite her was very far from one. Despite the harsh look on his face, he'd gone civilian through and through, from his fashionably disheveled hair, to the casual clothing. Not a single weapon on him that she could see. No sign of a com, civilian or otherwise.

So, before she started talking, Vega needed something from him first. "Where are the others?" Mass, Moto-man, Owens, and Galakis. The Shadows who'd been spared in the final bloodbath on Anamtaigh. The ones who had chosen to follow Rowe rather than go off with the SU like Zigmann and Catton. She hadn't heard from them since she'd left for Persephone 5, and that was on her for not checking in.

But she was a grunt, a Hound, same as them. They all looked to Rowe, the strategic-thinking Hawk, for leadership.

And they weren't here.

"Karsengale," he said.

Her jaw went tight at that non-answer. "Why?"

"They're breaking down the compound and taking apart anything dangerous that might have been left in the vault. After that, I gave them a choice. They chose to come here. Last I spoke to Owens, they were two weeks out from take-off."

He hadn't left them behind.

Some of her tension eased enough for her to lean back. The neck brace dug into her scalp when she tried to let her head drop against the chair's backrest, and she flinched.

Rowe noticed. "Your turn."

Vega took a bracing breath, and then she talked. She laid everything out for him. From her deal with Quinn to the shitshow that was the VanWarren family and their multiple attempts on Quinn's life, to Emmett's untimely demise and how strategically the main residential building had started to topple—with everyone still inside. She hesitated only once—when it came to the aftermath and Quinn's uncanny healing abilities. But, for Quinn's sake, Rowe needed to know everything.

She briefly skimmed over the part where she'd apparently died to when she woke up at the hospital, alone, with a massive bouquet and a message.

While she talked Rowe examined the com like he expected to find a hidden clue in it. There wasn't one—she'd already checked. He only paused once to flash her a quick glance during the part about her dying. Enough of a tell to let her know she'd shocked him. When she finished, he set down the com. "What were the coordinates?"

Vega rattled them off.

He nodded. "Sounds like they gave you a direct address. You think it's Latham?"

She hadn't thought of Talon by his given name in so long it took her a second to understand whom Rowe was talking about. When it clicked, Vega realized she hadn't thought of him at all since waking up at the hospital. She'd been so focused on getting here she'd left herself completely exposed. "The leash is out," she said to remind herself as much as Rowe.

"So?"

"So, I don't give a fuck if it is him." Talon's most effective weapon against her had been neutralized, which rendered him nothing more than another Hound. Unstable as he was. "Don't care if he's alone or hiding behind a full unit. Don't care if they're Hounds or Hawks. They're still gonna die." One by one. And if she found Quinn in anything less than perfect condition, she would take her sweet time making them pay.

Rowe's steady gaze held hers for a second, then dropped in measured steps. To her neck. To her shoulder. To the brace on her wrist. To the table, and her malfunctioning leg stretched out under it. An efficient inventory of all her weaknesses and liabilities, done in three seconds flat. His face didn't reveal his final judgment when he said, "So what's the plan?"

"There's a Hawk cache about eight hundred miles south of here." At least there had been when she'd read through the full list of them during her Shadow training. One of seven on Mai. Curiously close proximity to New Shangri La. It had to be a coincidence since it predated the establishment of Laura's compound by about a decade, but Vega would bet Quinn's last credit that it lived rent-free at the back of Rowe's mind. Civilian or not, eight hundred miles had to be too close for comfort. "You're going to get me in there so I can gear up."

"I'm not a Hawk anymore."

"Your ID might still be active." And if it wasn't they could always shoot their way in. It would set off all the alarms, tip her hand to the enemy, and potentially put this place in Shadow crosshairs, but oh well. They were under SU protection and had at least one powerful telepath in residence. The risk was acceptable, considering the payoff. Without proper gear, Vega didn't stand a chance in hell of getting anywhere near Quinn.

"And then what?"

"Then I go get my husband." Even if they flagged her ID, her rank in their systems was listed as Hound. They wouldn't expect her to use her Hawk training to cut them off at the knees. Hawks had been rare among the Shadow ranks to begin with, and the war had thinned them out even more. The odds of her running into one or more of them were slim. It would give her an advantage.

Rowe's jaw twitched. "You expect me to—"

"Scan your ID at the door, then run for all I care. I don't expect anything from you beyond getting me into that cache."

His mouth compressed into a thin line, his hands clenching on top of the table. "Why the fuck not?"

The door opened with slow caution, allowing Laura Belden to slip inside. She looked exactly the way she had the last time Vega had seen her on Anamtaigh. Tall, solidly built, with a sweet face that carried the weight of her sorrows in sharp, forest-green eyes and a no-nonsense expression. Her brown hair was a little longer, and she didn't have blood leaking from her eyes and nose, but on the whole, escaping the war hadn't changed her all that much. Lucky bitch.

"You're in no condition to do this solo," Rowe snapped.

"You're not a Hawk anymore," she returned dryly. His own words, from less than two minutes ago. He didn't owe her a damn thing. If he wanted to leave his military days behind, Vega could let him. Galaxy knew he'd earned it. Not to mention, his lover would probably turn Vega's brain into mulch and go after Quinn herself before she let Rowe charge into battle yet again and risk having her erased from his mind—yet again.

Laura didn't say a word, watching the two of them, probably gauging how big of a problem Vega was about to become for her little retreat.

"Mass and Galakis can be here in four days if they leave now—"

"Quinn could be dead tomorrow."

Laura gasped.

Vega stifled a flinch. She hadn't let herself think about the possibility during the trip. Whoever had left her the coordinates wanted her to come for him, but that didn't mean they had to keep him alive. They'd left no proof of life. For all she knew, Quinn was already dead, and she was about to go meet the reaper for nothing.

Vega didn't care. Quinn's extraction was her number one priority.

If they wanted to kill her in the process, fine. But she'd take the whole fucking outpost with her.

"Catton might be closer. I'll ping him and get a unit together by tomorrow night."

"I'll move faster on my own."

He snorted. "You're a liability stepping over a threshold. You won't make it within three miles of those coordinates, much less walk away from any direct confrontation with a Shadow."

"Wanna try me, asshole?" Dysfunctional leg or not, she'd still wipe the floor with him.

"I'm not letting you go off on a suicide rescue mission, Hound. You will stand down!"

Hound. Vega drew herself up, baring her teeth in a snarl. "You don't give me orders."

"He might not," Laura said. "But I do."

Too late, Vega remembered the woman was still in the room with them. And what her particular specialty was. Intent. Manipulating people into wanting to do whatever she decided.

Vega shoved away from the table—and that was as far as she got before Laura tilted her head and said, "You're exhausted, Vega. You really want to sleep."

The floor rushed up at her as the world went dark.

Quinn's parlor trick for numbers and patterns used to make telling time a simple task. Without doing any conscious calculations, his brain recognized the stretch of time between sunrise and sunset and divided it into even intervals for hours and minutes. Back before his heart transplant, he'd also kept time by his pulse, no matter how uneven it had been.

He had no such tells here.

There were no sunrises or sunsets. The room remained bright white, the walls illuminating the space from all sides. They never dimmed, never flickered. And with his new heart humming, he had no pulse to provide an anchor there, either.

Quinn had no idea how long he'd been there. Whether it had been long enough for Vega to wake up from her coma.

Had she woken up? Was she okay? Had anyone told her what happened to him? That he hadn't just left her there, bruised and broken, all on her own on a whim…

The unbroken white messed with his mind. He started seeing spinning, dancing swirls all over the walls. Then, one of those swirls grew and deepened into an endless vortex that stretched his reality into a pinprick of infinity.

When he started to panic about it sucking him into an alternate dimension, Quinn yanked off his shirt and tied it around his eyes. The darkness helped calm him enough to regain feeling in his body.

He slept on and off when exhaustion, or whatever drug they decided to pump into the air forced him under, but woke up still tired. Sleep felt more like a conscious zone-out than true rest.

Emma Wayland had been kept in a room like this. Cut off from her senses, her telepathy crippled until it had broken her. What Quinn felt was a minor inconvenience compared to the torture a telepath would endure, but even that was enough to slowly drive him insane.

After a while, it occurred to him that he never saw anyone come in, but his food tray refreshed every so often. They were drugging him. Knocking him out long enough for someone to bring him food while he was incapacitated. He couldn't tell whether the tray was real or a tactile hallucination. Nothing on it ever tasted the way it looked. But he ate it anyway, out of sheer necessity. His body required nourishment. Like it or not, he had to take whatever they gave him.

The leftover droplets of mush on his current tray had dried to crumbs by the time the door opened, admitting his least favorite Hawk carrying a fresh meal. The door closed at his back, with Quinn still debating whether or not he was real.

The Hawk toed his empty tray aside to make room for the new one. A hunk of seared steak, two large potatoes split down the middle and a pool of thick sauce with mushrooms. He couldn't smell any of it.

The Hawk sat down again with his back to the wall, arms braced loosely on his up-drawn knees. He stared off into white nothing for a while, letting Quinn decide whether he wanted to eat or not.

He decided not and thumped his head back against the wall behind him.

"Do you think Vega still likes me?" the Hawk asked.

Quinn's immediate answer was, "No."

The Hawk frowned at him. "Why not? We hit it off pretty well on Ela."

"You're a Shadow." Which, come to think of it, she might not be aware of. She'd been dead when good ol' *Zach* had revealed himself as the snake in their midst.

The Hawk considered this for a moment, then asked, "Think she'd like me if I wasn't a Shadow?"

What the hell was he talking about? "She doesn't even know your real name." Quinn swiveled his head sideways. "What *is* your real name, anyway?"

"Never had one," the Hawk said casually as if it was no big deal. "I've always just been Operative M. M for short."

That's right, Quinn remembered. He'd mentioned something about breeding programs during his last visit. It was true, then. And M was a product of it. A soldier from birth. Not even worth a name. Less than human, his Hawk rank notwithstanding. Quinn almost felt a hint of sympathy stirring in his chest. He quelched it.

"But I think I like Zach," the Hawk mused. "Nice, normal name for a nice, normal guy. *Zzzach.* Yeah, I like that."

The look on his face said he was tasting the idea of it. The same way normal people sipped on an unfamiliar vintage to see if it would agree with them before taking a gulp. Was that how he operated, ingesting a new persona like a magical potion that instantly changed him?

The thought made Quinn want to put more space between himself and the deadly chameleon beside him.

"Maybe I'll keep it for a while. I could take a detour from my next mission. Go hang out with Geraldine for a couple of days. *She* likes me."

Her name sent a stab of pain through the hollow in Quinn's gut. "I'm sure they'll welcome you with open arms at the funeral."

M didn't move a muscle in reaction. He went so completely still Quinn half thought the hallucination had frozen in time. Not one twitch, not a blink. Not even a discernible breath.

Quinn needed the man to move, or he would lose his shit. "You didn't know? I thought you would have heard. The nurse told me right before you arrived to kidnap me away from Vega's bedside."

Daggers in his chest; acid burning through his brain at the thought of Vega, lying in that hospital bed, bandaged all over, eyes closed. So still. A different kind of still. More terrifying. Like she might never move again.

He gritted his teeth, then flexed his jaw, forcing the memory away. "Geraldine never made it out of the house. She was presumed dead in the explosion."

M didn't move for another fifteen seconds, at least. When he finally blinked, the world seemed to reset into something different. Sadder. He exhaled on a long, measured hiss. "I should have killed Bigellow a lot slower."

That almost sounded like wrath. Like true grief over the loss of someone he might have considered a friend. If such a thing was possible for someone like him.

It was dangerous to make those kinds of assumptions about a man who, by his own admission, didn't have a solid identity beyond his status among the Shadows. But that tiny hint of human emotion reminded Quinn that Geraldine had been barely out of her teenage years. A steady, supportive friend to both him and Vega from the moment they'd all sat down at the dinner table the first night.

A gifted singer and a hopeless romantic who hadn't deserved to die.

"For what it's worth," Quinn said, "I would have liked to have had her as my family, too."

M twitched a tiny nod in acknowledgment and fell silent once more.

Then, out of nowhere, as if he'd flipped a switch, M raised a wry eyebrow at Quinn. "Guess I'll have to settle for Vega."

It was a blatant attempt to provoke him. And Quinn jumped on it, grateful for the distraction. "She's married to me."

"So what? I don't mind sharing. I don't mind being shared, either. What do you say, Quinn? Want to feel what it's like to fuck a Shadow?"

Whether through genetic manipulation or plain good luck, M was one handsome son of a bitch, and he knew it, too. Probably used it the same way Vega did to lure his prey into complacency. Quinn looked him up and down. "You don't hold a candle to my wife. Not even as a Shadow."

M's sinful dark eyes danced as he heaved a dramatic sigh. "Always the bridesmaid, never the bride." He winked. "Offer stands. If you ever change your mind."

"What are you doing?"

"Propositioning you? Respecting your personal boundaries? Leaving the back door open, if you know what I mean?"

"Why are you even here, talking to me like… Like Zach?"

"I told you. I like Zach." As if that explained everything.

"But you're not him." And they were a long way from Crescent Island.

M hitched a shoulder and pushed to his feet. "Technically, I'm not anyone. But you gotta start somewhere, right?"

He would walk out again and leave Quinn alone in the white void.

Before he'd reached the door, Quinn threw out a last desperate hook to keep him there a little longer. "What's it like? Being put in the chair." They planned to do it to him eventually. He figured it wouldn't hurt to know what he was in for.

M tensed, coming to a stop. He didn't turn around as he said, "You go in one way, they flip a switch, and you come out a Shadow."

"Yeah, but, what's it *like*?"

M spared him a glance over his shoulder. Quick, but sharp as an arrow straight into his brain. "I'm told it feels like having everything you've ever known and ever wanted scorched out of your brain."

Hounds don't make decisions. They have decisions made for them.

Every time he'd asked Vega about her personal preferences, she hadn't been able to give him an answer. She hadn't had one to give. Because any time she'd shown the slightest hint of individuality in the past, those sadistic fucks would have sent her right back to that chair.

"But you'd have to confirm that with someone who had *knowns* and *wanteds* before," M said. "I never did."

I don't get to want.

They'd destroyed her.

They'd burned away who she was. Again and again. All so she would never have a reason to question an order. Never form an attachment that might split her loyalties away from the Shadows who owned her down to her soul.

No one ever leaves the Shadows—except in a body bag…

By the time Quinn collected himself back to the present moment, M was gone.

And all he had left was the memory of Vega's raw fury when he'd so stupidly thrown those hateful, ignorant accusations in her face.

Is there anything in there beyond knives and death?

Quinn had known about the basic mechanics of Shadow mind control from what little Finn had shared. But he hadn't understood. Not really.

How hard-won, how utterly miraculous and precious every little choice Vega had managed to make was.

November 4, 3039

The soft hiss-and-buzz of nearby machines had a steady rhythm totally thrown off by a squeak-thump right beside her. The discordance made Vega wince as she clawed her way back to consciousness. She blinked up at a gauzy, canopied ceiling, then followed its fabric down as far as she could track with just her eyes.

Bright, heavenly light shone through the curtains, casting her visitor in halos he damn well didn't deserve. Someone appeared to have pulled a stick out of his ass, though, because the man rocking his hospital chair on its hind legs with his head thrown all the way back was not the man she knew.

Brent Catton had locks. Teeny, tiny locks sticking out from the scalp he'd used to shave clean since she'd known him. And he was wearing shorts and a bright pink T-shirt with white silhouettes of women in suggestive poses all over it. At least he still shaved that fake scar through his right eyebrow.

Vega took a slightly deeper breath.

The hospital chair thumped down to all fours, and Catton's depthless black eyes locked on her. Eyes of a sharpshooter who missed nothing. "Repeat after me: It's okay. To ask for help. When—I—need—it."

"Oh, fuck you."

He grinned those big, bright white teeth at her, and suddenly, the sharpshooter was gone, and a laid-back stranger with crinkling crow's feet and the makings of laugh lines was winking at her. "Close enough."

Laugh lines.

On Brent Catton.

Was she dead?

Vega tried to sit up, but as soon as she tensed her neck muscles the slightest bit, the brace pulled, confirming that she was, indeed, still alive. She groaned. "What time is it?"

"About noon, I think."

Seriously, who the hell was this guy? The Catton she knew would have given her millisecond accuracy. What was this 'about noon' shit?

Wait… "That bitch kept me out for half a *day*?"

"Whoa, throttle down, killer." Catton put a scarred hand on her shoulder, keeping her prone when she tried to sit up again. "Laura *put* you out. She didn't *keep* you out. Your body just decided it was tired of your shit and took a little vacation." He coughed into his fist. "For a couple of days."

"*What!*"

He shoved harder, standing up for good measure. "Settle," he ordered, a full-on Shadow at his limits. "Or I've been authorized to tranq you until you do."

"I don't have time for this shit." Quinn didn't have time.

"Which is why we're all working nonstop to plan out this mission." Catton kicked something on the floor and her bed adjusted to sit her up. He didn't let go until he deemed her sufficiently compliant. Like she had another choice. "Zig's down south, scoping out the cache situation; Rowe found those coordinates you were given—which, by the way, are a whole-ass outpost, so's you know—and he's been mapping it inside and out; Laura's got the SU chasing down transportation for us; and her whole damn medical team is scrambling to put your Humpty Dumpty ass back together so you can actually *go*." He took a breath. "Mass and Owens are on their way to the outpost already, in case you were wondering. And while all that fun's going down, I'm stuck here on babysitter duty."

Vega blinked. "Why?"

He shrugged, making the naked silhouette at his shoulder briefly close her legs. "I drew the short straw." Then he sobered, and those black eyes pinned her with enough intensity to make her fight a cringe. "SU pulled reports from Ela. They found Talon on the island estate. Kneecaps shattered, hips shattered, neck cut open—someone went to work on him. He's dead, Vee. Positive ID and everything. And they're pinning the explosion on him as a radical act of terror."

The world went still. Talon was dead?

For a moment, she couldn't quite believe it. All of the pain and horror of his reign, the constant fear of him showing up again to pay her back for turning on him, was rooted so deep it didn't want to let go.

Talon was dead.

She sat with it, tasted the new reality on the back of her tongue, and let it seep into her chest so she could breathe.

But the wonder didn't last.

Talon was dead, but not by her hand. And certainly not by any VanWarren or their staff.

So who had killed him?

Who the fuck had taken Quinn—and why?

"Talon's *dead*," Catton repeated like he needed to say it again for his own confirmation. She heard the knowledge settle in his voice, too. It was over. After years of that psychotic prick trying like hell to break them down, they were finally free. Truly free.

Catton got himself back on track and squared his shoulders. "Talon's dead, and this ain't Anamtaigh. You got people in your corner now. Maybe let us have your back. Just this once. Won't make you any less of a rabid bitch."

Vega gritted her teeth and growled, "I will stab you."

Catton raised that shave-scared eyebrow. "Yeah? With what knives?" He bent over where she couldn't see then dropped something black and heavy in her lap and settled back into his chair, pointing an accusing finger at her. "One time, you hear? You lose these, you can ask Santa Quinn for another set. This shit's expensive, you know."

Vega tugged on the tie and unrolled the bundle. Six shining handles stuck out of their individual pockets, a honing stick neatly aligned in a seventh pocket of its own. Vega pulled out one of the knives. He'd sharpened them for her, too. "Wait, what are these zigzags?" She ran her thumb over the base of the blade where it dulled into the handle. A black, laser-etched design had been stamped into the metal. A maker's mark?

There went that grin again, all mischief and trouble. "Baby, those ain't no zigzags. That's your initials. Mrs. Vega VanWarren. Vee, Vee, Dub."

"You…monogrammed my knives?"

"Call it a belated wedding present."

"I'm not really married, you know."

He snorted. "Yeah, whatever. We're still not letting you live it down. Stone-cold killer Vega Ortiz got herself hitched. To a bleeding-heart pacifist with a literal bleeding heart. To be honest, most of us didn't even know you had a personality, let alone white picket fence fantasies. Guess you never really know a person."

The curtain at the foot of her bed pulled back, admitting a familiar, tattooed face framed by long black hair. "Knock-knock. Don't mean to interrupt, but I'd like a moment with my patient if you don't mind."

Catton threw up his hands. "The fuck took you so long? She's talking my ear off over here." He was up and heading for the curtain like he couldn't wait to get out of there.

"Catton," she said. "Mass and Owens don't make a move without me."

He rolled his eyes. "Yeah, no shit, VanWarren. Unlike you, they're not suicidal morons."

Eskel stared after him when the curtains settled back into place. "You know, he's a lot chattier than I remember him being on the shuttle flight out of Anamtaigh."

So it wasn't just her. "Guess the civilian life agrees with him. Seems to agree with you, too."

Eskel looked a hell of a lot better than the last time she'd seen him in the vault. Back then, he'd been skin and bones, dark shadows under his eyes contrasting with the solid black stripe tattooed down his chin. He'd filled out since then. And there was a lightness to him. The way he moved, and the look on his face. No longer resigned but peaceful. Purposeful.

"Wish I could say the same for you. How are you feeling?"

"We can skip the small talk. How bad is it?"

He nodded. "Fair enough." With a tap on the glass tablet in his hand, he brought up a hologram of her body scan. "Some random scrapes, cuts, bruises, and a plasma burn all healed at the hospital where they treated you. They must have had a cosmetic surgeon on call. You won't have a single scar." Naturally, a planet populated with the galaxy's richest and most famous would have a battalion of people on call to keep them looking pretty. "Your fractured hand still needs about another two weeks before the brace can come off."

"Give me a metal one." A metal gauntlet could be a great equalizer in hand-to-hand combat.

Eskel zoomed in on her neck. "And then there's this."

Yeah. That.

He zoomed in some more until her spinal cord was a foot wide, hovering over her lap.

Dread clenched her stomach muscles hard. "How badly did they fuck me up?"

"They saved your life," he said. "And considering the circumstances, they did a beautiful job removing the device with minimal damage."

"Then what's with all the red?" The borders of her spinal column were outlined in it, a warning without any descriptions. Eskel must have cleared those before he showed her.

The medic traced the nearest line with a finger that made the hologram flare brighter where he touched it. "This right here is a buildup of fluid. Pretty standard for any surgical procedure on the spine. The swelling is just your body insulating the region to protect it from damage while it heals. It might cause some temporary discomfort, but as long as you keep that brace on and don't wrench anything, the swelling should go down in another day or two. This is the bigger issue." He highlighted the six faint lines that cut diagonally across the vertical column of her spinal cord. "Scar tissue. When the device went off, it burned through your nerve endings. Basically created tiny blockages in your neural network."

Not good. "Can you fix it?"

He studied her for a moment, as if gauging whether she was stable enough to hear what he had to say.

Fuck. Very not good. "Just say it."

"Bad news: the damage is permanent. We could try neural therapy to reestablish the connections naturally, but those treatments take years, and you'd have to spend days at a time face-down on a hospital bed."

Fuck. Fuck. FUCK!

"Good news: there may be a workaround. But you're not going to like it."

Vega concentrated on her breathing as she absorbed what he was telling her. Permanent damage meant no amount of bed rest would get her leg working properly. Exercises might help her with balance and coordination, but if those neural networks didn't heal, her grip wouldn't improve any more than what she'd built up so far. And, without her grip, her aim was shot. Those pretty, monogrammed knives in her lap might as well be decorations.

"What's the work-around, and how fast can you do it?"

Eskel gave her another measuring look, then tapped on his device again. The hologram zoomed out as if to soften the blow, and then it shimmered as something new settled over it.

Vega's body reacted on instinct, jerking back deeper against the bed to get as far as it could. "No. No fucking way!"

"Hey, look at me."

Vega couldn't breathe.

"*Look at me.*" Eskel's face swam before her. His hands gripped the sides of her head, pressing hard enough to get her attention. She was shaking. The knives slid off the bed and clattered to the floor as she thrashed beneath the covers, but they were tucked in too tight, and she didn't have enough strength in them to do anything more than flail. "Breathe, Vega. *Breathe.*"

Shiny metal flatworm covering her spine, thin tentacles hugging the rope of nerves.

A zing of phantom electricity shot through the back of her neck, sending her shoulder muscles into rhythmic spasms that jarred her brace and stabbed pain through the base of her skull.

"*Vega!* Look at me and take a breath."

Eskel's thumbs moved over her cheeks. They were wet.

She blinked, forcing air into her lungs on a shaky inhale.

"Good. Again. Focus on me and breathe."

The exhale was so quick, but dragging air back in was almost impossible with her rib cage constricted by a vise of pure terror.

"I know what you're thinking. But this isn't that. This is what the Shadows bastardized to *make* that. The original device is a medical tool. It's a neural bypass. Doctors use it all the time to help people with spinal injuries walk again. It doesn't interface with anything else. It is not controllable. It's just a fancy bandage. All it does is take the impulses from your brain and skip them over the damaged region of your spine so they can go where they need to go. That's it."

Vega squeezed her eyes shut, but the image remained imprinted on the back of her eyelids.

Not that.

Not that.

She fought another breath into her lungs and held it down until the urge to scream became a physical pain. Her exhale turned into a whimper.

"It's okay," Eskel was saying. "You're okay. No one here is going to hurt you. Just breathe."

Vega sucked in more air. Blew it back out.

The next inhale was a little easier.

"That's it. You got this. In and out. I'm right here."

Little by little, Vega wrested her body back under control. It left her exhausted, head spinning and neck aching like a son of a bitch. But she opened her eyes and met Eskel's steady stare.

Last time she'd been in his care back on Anamtaigh, the medic had been Talon's POW, and she'd been the one to capture him, along with Quinn and another member of their group. She'd come to him for help—for Quinn, whose heart had started to fail. And while they'd talked, Eskel had cut open an infected stab wound in her thigh and dug out a whole mess of pus and fluids without bothering to administer a numbing agent.

Eskel had no sympathy for any of the Shadows, least of all her.

But he was looking at her now with so much remorse it bordered on pity. He knew what this meant for her. And, being the good person— the good medic—he was, Eskel wasn't presenting this to her lightly.

She swallowed the lump in her throat and rasped out, "Quinn healed his injuries in seconds on Ela."

Eskel nodded. "We know. While you were sleeping, I reached out to his SU doctor to see if she had any suggestions for your care. She said Quinn's surgery was so risky that they gave him an experimental dose of a regenerative serum to help his body accept the artificial heart."

"Could it heal me?"

Eskel shook his head. "Dr. Chase-Calen checked your medfile. You're not a good candidate."

"Who gives a shit! Do it anyway—"

"We did."

Vega paused, holding her breath. "And?"

"Do you feel your right leg?"

Her heart sank. She felt it, but just barely. Sitting as she was, the crawling numbness she'd felt before returned full force, starting at the small of her back and shooting down to below her knee. She could move her leg, bend her knee, roll her ankle, and wriggle her toes, but the larger the movement, the more effort it took. It felt like her thigh muscles had completely atrophied.

"The neural bypass is your best option to regain full mobility."

Vega clenched her jaw so tight it hurt. "Then why isn't it in me yet?" She'd been passed out for two days. Why hadn't he shot it into the back of her neck and been done with it? Talon hadn't hesitated for an instant.

"Because it needs to be your choice. You have to understand that this is a one-shot deal. Once that device goes in, it *can't* come out. *Ever*. It integrates into the spine and replaces all the neurons beneath it as they atrophy over time. Given the location of your injury, if the device gets too severely damaged, your heart will stop beating. Your lungs will stop breathing. Your body will die from the neck down. And we won't be able to fix it. Do you understand what I'm telling you?"

"Don't get stabbed in the neck. Got it."

Not that.

It wasn't a leash. It was a lifeline.

And Eskel wasn't forcing it on her. He was forcing her to decide on her own, which was so much worse.

Without the bypass, she was done.

If she tried to hobble her way into that Shadow outpost, even with Rowe and the others on her team, she would not be walking back out again. Might as well go up to the first Hound she saw and put her forehead to the barrel of his gun.

But a lifetime with that fucking thing on her spine. A constant reminder of Talon and everything he'd done. All the ways he'd broken her—and not just in body.

Quinn was waiting for her to come for him.

"Let's do it."

Another of those long, probing looks. "Are you sure this is what you want?"

She almost laughed. "I can handle it." A lifetime of nightmares and an artificial device on her spine. What else was new?

"That's not what I asked you."

God damn his bullshit medical red tape. "I, Vega Analisa Ortiz VanWarren, do hereby formally consent to the medical procedure you outlined and accept all inherent risks thereof. Happy now? Need me to sign something to make it official? Just get the fucking thing on my spine."

Eskel shut down the holograph projection. "I'll start prepping the team. The anesthesia will knock you out for—"

"No anesthesia. I can take the pain." She'd already wasted two fucking days sleeping. She needed him to get this over with so she could *go*.

Eskel set down his device and got right in her face. "Did you miss the part where this is a one-shot deal? We do this my way. You'll be under for the procedure, and you'll follow my instructions to the letter afterward. And if you give me any shit about it, your ass is staying put right here until I clear you to leave the clinic. And I'm not above keeping you sedated to do it. Understood?"

"Why bother wasting more time? You don't give a shit about me; you just need me to get Quinn back for you. So why aren't you shoving me out the door to go fetch him."

"Because Quinn is my *brother*. And *when* he comes back, I need to be able to look him in the eye and tell him I did everything I possibly could to keep his wife safe. So that his new heart doesn't break worse than the old one."

Eskel had everything prepped within the hour but forced her to sit through another hour of detailed explanations while the nutritional IV fluid dripped into her arm. To be fair, the entire medical team got the same lecture.

When he'd deemed them all sufficiently on the same page, they transferred Vega to a sterile surgery and attached dozens of tiny electrode needles all over her body to check her neural pathways and map out the problem areas. Another hour there.

Finally, with the electrodes still attached, they sat her in a backward chair with a front rest and armrests extending forward. Doctor Lucy replaced her IV bag with a new one. Nurse Kahan already had the sedative spray in his hand. He attached the soft mask that would go over her mouth and nose and nodded to Eskel.

"Make sure the seal is tight," Eskel instructed, staring at Vega.

Okay, so maybe she had briefly considered not breathing in the sedative. Every hour wasted was one less Quinn had left to breathe.

Kahan nodded. "Ready?" He had her sit up from the front rest so he could press the mask onto her face. "Take a deep breath for me."

She looked at his thumb hovering over the trigger button, then up at him. They were taking no chances. Vega rolled her eyes and took a deep breath.

Kahan pressed the button, releasing the sedative mist.

It was so fine, she barely felt…

~

Vega came to back in her original bed. This time, one side of the curtains was pulled back to show off a snowy white garden and some kind of three-pillared monument on the far side.

At the foot of her bed, an entertainment screen had unrolled from the ceiling. It was active and showed a news segment. Not for her benefit, but so Finnegan Rowe, sitting vigil on her other side, wouldn't get bored.

"Six hours," he said, never taking his eyes off a news anchor covering the planetary alignment hop. "Ninety seconds to put you under. Five minutes to apply the bypass. Two hours for it to sync to your neural frequencies and another thirty minutes to calibrate it based on the preop map. Then, three hours to let your body adjust and heal." There was the Hawk she'd come to see. All focus and no-nonsense. No weapons on him, but he had a civilian com cuff on his wrist to make up for the lack of his Shadow one.

"Eskel said he'd keep me under for less than three—total." Although she really should have known better.

"Yeah, Eskel doesn't negotiate." He took a swig from a dark blue bottle and then handed it to her.

Vega closed her eyes, taking quiet inventory of her body. She couldn't feel the device in her neck, but she still *felt* it.

Three hours to complete the procedure. Eskel had certainly taken more care applying the device than Talon.

She curled her good hand into a fist, testing her grip. It felt a lot surer than it had six hours ago. Satisfied that she wouldn't drop it, Vega accepted the bottle from Rowe and took a sip. Beer. Good beer. Probably not Eskel-approved, which made it taste even better. She handed it back with a murmur of thanks.

A careful shift of her rib cage to the left and right confirmed there was no more nervy sensation in her back. Vega pulled up her right knee. No numbness.

Breathe. The neck brace was still firmly attached, but she felt no pain beneath it.

"The three extra hours helped stabilize the application site," Rowe explained. He was still fully invested in the news but aware of her every movement. "Eskel checked on you about twenty minutes ago. Said the swelling's mostly gone down, but you still need to be careful for the next two days of PT."

"Funny, he didn't mention any PT to me."

Rowe raised an eyebrow at her. "You just had two consecutive surgeries on your spine. What did you expect?"

Breathe. "So I'm stuck here for two more days?"

"Be glad it's not two weeks. Which, by the way, is standard with something like this. Eskel's good, but he's not a miracle worker. You fuck this up, Vega, you might still end up permanently decommissioned. If I were you, I'd do what the good doctor says."

Two days. For Quinn.

"Two days." She could handle that. "And then we move."

"That's the plan. Your PT starts bright and early tomorrow morning. Eskel shot you up with some shit to make sure you don't overexert yourself before then. You can move, but you can't stand or walk. So don't."

Goddamn son of a bitch high and mighty piece of shit medic scum dragged up from the sewer end of the galaxy. "What the hell am I supposed to do until tomorrow?"

Rowe nodded toward the screen.

Vega frowned at the feed showing Matthew and Holden VanWarren addressing a group of people outdoors. Their voices were muted as the news anchor explained, *"The Port Cain community is in mourning this week over the sudden, violent attack on Crescent Island, the private residence of the VanWarren family. The VanWarrens are, of course, well known in the entertainment industry as actors, directors, and content creators."* The right side of the screen scrolled through headshots of various family members, with their names and greatest achievements, to remind viewers of who the hell they all were.

"The targeted attack was confirmed to have been orchestrated by one Latham Bigellow." And there was his pre-Shadow civilian ID photo. He looked so much younger in it. So much more sable.

But that smirk. That hint of cruelty in the twinkle of his eyes.

The Shadows hadn't broken Latham Bigellow. He'd been broken all along. They'd only sharpened his edges and taught him how to use them.

"Twenty-eight-year-old Bigellow was reported missing in 3034 and is presumed to have been a Shadow operative. He has been found dead at the scene of the crime. Authorities have not issued any warnings or security alerts to the community at large."

"A Shadow operative." Rowe snorted. "Son of a bitch finally got his wings."

"May they fly him straight to hell."

Rowe grunted his agreement and saluted her with the beer bottle.

"We are now reporting live from the VanWarren family memorial, honoring the life of Ingrid VanWarren, who tragically succumbed to her injuries, and those who went missing in the attack. Twenty-one-year-old Geraldine VanWarren was a promising singer and songwriter who performed under the stage name 'Whisper on the Wind.' Her first album, Starstruck, has been climbing up the local charts after her true identity was leaked to the media following the attack.

"Also among the victims were the recently appointed heir to the Van-Warren family estate, Quinn VanWarren, and his wife."

"Those fucking bastards." The hospital would have had records of them coming in for treatment—alive, if not all that well. Someone must have paid good money to convince them to wipe those records clean.

"The king is dead," Rowe said. "Long live the king."

"...all three VanWarrens are presumed dead at this time. Matthew and Holden VanWarren have been assigned interim control over the family estate until the victims' remains have been recovered or thirty days have passed to satisfy Ela's legal proof of life mandate."

Matthew and Holden. Not one of the aunts and uncles, or even Quinn's mother, Holly. The brothers were more devious than Vega had thought.

Curious, the news made no mention of Emmett's death the night before the attack.

"Well, that's one way to do it," Rowe mused. "Can't wait to see the looks on their faces when Quinn shows up alive and well."

On the screen, the news anchor disappeared, and the live feed stretched full-width as the audio engaged to give viewers a snippet of what was happening. Matthew stood stone-faced beside his younger brother while Holden delivered the speech.

Not a single time did Holden stutter or trip over a syllable, talking about their continued efforts to *respectfully* sort through the wreckage to recover the remains of his beloved family so they could be given the proper rites.

Remains that were not there and would never be found. But if they took long enough, they wouldn't need them.

Not once did a muscle twitch in his face as he firmly assured the public that no expense would be spared for their funerals and that they would always live on in the hearts of every VanWarren who truly knew them.

A pointed reminder of how little the VanWarrens knew her, Quinn, and even Geraldine.

The tone of the entire speech was one of warning. They knew full well that she and Quinn had made it at least as far as the hospital. Whatever the family suspected about their disappearance, this performance made it clear they had no intention of launching a search. As far as they were concerned, the long-lost heir and his wife were dead—and they'd better stay that way.

She would have expected this from any other VanWarren. But not Holden. For him to be the one drawing this public line in the sand was another subtle message. Vega read it loud and clear, and her heart ached for Quinn.

She slowly, carefully shook her head. "He won't go back."

"You think he'll leave all that money on the table for them?"

As the news crew panned the feed from left to right, Vega spied Kendry half-hidden behind Matthew. She looked almost serene. Calm and collected, and more peaceful than Vega had ever seen her. On the other end, beside Holden, stood the family patriarch, the eldest of the old guard's children: Uncle Trent. His back was ramrod straight, and he was staring off into the distance as if someone was holding a gun to his back. The distress written all over his punchable face had nothing to do with the terrifying attack or the deaths of his young family members. No, he was upset that he'd been passed over for the inheritance yet again.

The only one who showed a hint of true human emotion was his wife, Ivy, who looked haunted and almost broken. She huddled close to Trent, clearly in need of a touch, a look—some acknowledgment of what she'd been through. Some small attempt at affection.

Her husband remained coldly indifferent.

"They abandoned him," Vega told Rowe. "He stayed back to get them all out safely. He risked his life for them. And the moment they were clear, they ran for it. Not one of them looked back to see if he'd made it out." Not a single one of them had raised a shout or a hand while she'd ripped herself open crawling through the wreckage to get to him. "No one came to help. Not even the staff."

Rowe shifted in his seat. "Just shows they don't deserve him."

Very much agreed. "They never did." And wasn't that the greatest tragedy of the whole thing? Quinn might have been the best of them. Strong in ways they couldn't even imagine. And they'd buried him like a bad memory.

"News off," Rowe ordered, and the screen shut down.

Rowe did have a point, though. The VanWarren estate was massive. Even with all those failing businesses, the investments Amundsen and Beatrice had made throughout the years continued to grow. They would keep the family well-funded for generations to come.

All that money being squandered by people who deserved it so little…

"Say, Rowe… Does Laura retain lawyers on staff?"

He snorted. "Probably an army of them."

Laura's late husband might have been disinherited from the Belden family collective, but their own bylaws had provided her as William's widow with a continuous allowance for the rest of her natural life. It was a drop in the bucket for them, but for Laura, the annual sum amounted to an astronomical fortune, which she was using to fund and maintain this entire place. She would need lawyers on staff, if only to ensure the Beldens kept to the letter of those bylaws and didn't stick their anti-charity noses into her business.

"Why do you ask?"

He straightened to attention in his seat when Vega looked at him and smiled. "I'm going to need a favor."

Everything was white. From the long runner stretching down the aisle to the tufted scraps of fabric tied to chairs in lieu of flowers to the twinkling lights wrapped around cracked beams.

It was snowing outside, but the clouds had finally parted enough to let the sun shine through the gentle flurries. A bright beam of it speared down through the jagged hole in the ceiling like a portal to heaven.

Quinn blinked, and there she was. Draped in an ancient white gown with pale blue lace hand-stitched along the hemline, her shiny black hair held back by a string of white beads the children had made for her. Her bouquet was a humble bunch of daisies that had already started to wilt, and her shoes were old, scuffed leather boots two sizes too big.

But her smile…

That brilliant, joyous light in her eyes…

Quinn's chest grew tight and he couldn't take a proper breath. He could hardly keep his feet still to wait for her as she glided, step by graceful step, down the white aisle toward him.

She passed through the sunlight, catching snowflakes in her hair and on her nose. It tickled enough that she scrunched it up and laughed as the tiny flake melted. The snow followed her as she emerged from the light, a delicate train that wafted up behind her.

She was breathtaking. A vision of an angel descended from the heavens just for him. A gift he planned to treasure for the rest of his life.

Then, between one step and the next, she gasped. Her beautiful smile contorted into a mask of agony as her body turned rigid.

"Vega!" Quinn caught her as she collapsed. Spared her the impact against the jagged floor, now piled with dust and sharp debris.

But he couldn't spare her the pain.

She convulsed in his arms, and he felt the electric charge cramp his muscles where their bodies touched, but he refused to let go. Not when her dress darkened to a torn, stained hoodie or when a black brace snaked around her wrist. Not even when blood began to drip from her nose, painting a bright red line through the ash and dust covering her face.

"Don't."

Her body arched in his hold, her eyes squeezed shut, her jaw clenched so tight he heard her teeth begin to crack.

"Don't…" Quinn clutched her closer to take more of the charge. Pain shot up his arms and across his chest, but he just held on tighter. If he could take the pain for her, from her…

His bad heart gave an all too familiar stutter-beat, cramping into a halt. He couldn't take a breath. But he didn't let go.

At last, the relentless force released them both. The woman in his arms sighed, her body growing limp in his hold. So still.

So very still.

Quinn's heart whirred back to life, and his muscles unclenched enough to let him loosen his cramped hold.

He didn't.

"Vega…"

She didn't respond.

Not a single breath wafted against his skin. Not a single flutter of a heartbeat.

"Vega!"

Snow had covered the ground before him, draping over empty chairs, dimming the lights, and hiding piles and mounds of jagged debris. Its softness swallowed the echoes of his ragged shout. Pulled his voice out of his throat and rendered him as silent as the woman he held to his artificial heart. And it would not stop whirring, no matter how much he wanted it to.

Colors bleached out as his world faded.

Little by little, everything disappeared into an endless, wintry white.

Including the limp, lifeless body in his arms…

~

Quinn jerked awake on the floor of his white torture chamber, holding the mattress so tight his arms were shaking. His heart whirred so loudly it was a buzz in his ears, and he was sweating, overheated, and breathing much too hard and fast, the sensation of holding Vega, limp as a doll, still locked in his limbs.

His mind struggled to make the switch from that nightmare to this waking one.

Until his whirling gaze locked on the dark figure crouching over him, a wicked smirk on his handsome face.

M waggled his eyebrows. "What'd you dream about?"

"Squeezing the life out of you. Crushing your tiny little body like a grape."

"A happy way to die, I'm sure," he replied, dark eyes dancing.

Quinn sat up against the wall, rubbing visions of snow flurries from his eyes. They wouldn't go away. "What do you want?"

"Can't I take time out of my day to visit my favorite cousin?"

Quinn glared at him.

"Okay, fine. Although, I must say, cousin, this attitude of yours is very unflattering."

"I'm not your cousin."

"We share the same name."

"You don't have a name."

"Of course I do. Zach VanWarren." M blinked at him, an almost comical level of concern scrunching his eyebrows together. "We met on Crescent Island. Don't you remember?"

"Knock it the fuck off. Only way you're messing with my head is if you put me in the chair."

M rolled his eyes, all pretense of concern gone in a split second. "See? That's what I mean about your attitude." He sat down beside Quinn and stretched out his legs. "Also, we can't put you in the chair yet. You'll have to hang tight for a while longer."

"Why?" Quinn would have thought they'd do it immediately to ensure he wasn't a threat. Not that he'd made a single move against them since they'd locked him up.

"We don't know if your artificial heart can handle a treatment."

"I heal," Quinn reminded him.

"Yes, from physical damage. But can you heal from *death*?"

Good point. "Why would it matter? You have everything you need from me."

"We have everything we need *for now*. But those lab cats are burning through the samples like their jobs depend on it. They'll need a refill soon."

He should be happy about that. Or concerned. Some kind of emotional reaction was probably in order. But Quinn was only half paying attention. The snow was still falling. Waist-high drifts in one corner covered piles of debris, but it was the smaller one right in front of him he couldn't look away from. The one shaped like a body. His hands clenched into fists and opened again, but nothing would shake the feel of Vega's limp form from his muscle memory. The longer he stared at that drift, the harder it was to pretend it wasn't there. To stay seated when his body ached to go there and dig, to make sure it wasn't real.

He blinked, and it was gone. Along with the snow, and the debris. Nothing there but blank white walls.

And the Shadow sitting next to him.

He was still there, which had to mean he was real.

Quinn sorted through the last few minutes to reorient himself to the conversation he didn't remember taking part in. Something about genes and refills. "Science not adding up?"

"It turns out," M explained gleefully, "your unique genetic traits are recessive. Lab cats tried to use your sperm on donor eggs, and none of the embryos that survived had the genes. To make more of you, they'll need both the sperm *and* the egg to carry the traits."

"So, if I have children with Vega—"

"You won't have children with Vega."

Quinn gritted his teeth. "You won't win. I'll get out of here eventually and—"

"Shadows get sterilized as part of their intake and initial treatment. Just a small injection. One of a hundred little pricks in the grand scheme of things. But the effects are permanent and irreversible."

His muscles bulged with strain.

Another choice they'd stolen from her. Another piece she would never get back.

"Throttle down, Quinn," M warned.

"I am going to rip you all apart. Piece by piece."

M didn't move from his seat, but he watched Quinn like the Hawk he was, seemingly relaxed but ready to strike with instant and deadly force. But, despite the intensity of his focus, his tone was conversational when he said, "Maybe one day you will. Hell, who's to say the chair will even work on you? You might heal your brain right back to normal as soon as it powers down. You can probably break the restraints like they're nothing, kill the medic, and trash the shit out of the room with his lifeless corpse."

Again, that careful wording. Like he wasn't just musing about the possibilities but walking Quinn through a specific set of instructions. Some part of him, not currently screaming in mindless rage, picked up on that but immediately discarded it as useless information.

"But you need to be alive to do it. So right now, you're going to settle. Because it's not just sedatives they can pump through the air vents."

Quinn forced his fists to uncurl, but the effort made his hands shake uncontrollably to wrap around M's throat. He slammed his head back against the wall and felt it reverberate behind him. The pain was fleeting, gone in an instant. Not enough to ground him.

So he lurched to his feet. The bright white blended together, swallowing corners and seams until Quinn had no anchor to orient himself in space, except the solid surface at his back. Head spinning, he whirled around and braced his hands against it. Immediately, they curled into fists, and he drew one back to slam it into the wall.

His knuckles split. The surface of the wall rippled outward.

M didn't move from his seat, but his voice lost all pretense of friendliness. "Quinn..."

Vega's face swam before him, eyes sharp, mouth set. The face of a soldier with nothing to live for once the mission was complete.

Is there anything in there beyond knives and death?

Quinn drew back and punched the wall again—harder. Ground his bloody knuckles into the smooth surface to paint it red before his skin healed over.

"Where does the sun set, Quinn?"

Wanting is for people who sleep through the night...

Quinn punched the wall a third time.

It wasn't his skin that gave way this time. It was the wall. A small crack, but one he could feel.

"Where does the sun set?" M repeated.

That's a privilege I lost a long time ago.

The wall wasn't indestructible. The tiny crack had already expanded into a fine, dark spiderweb that set the whole chamber flickering. He could break through it. Take his chances with the Shadows on the other side.

But there was one already locked in there with him.

Quinn turned his attention to M.

"In the west," the Hawk answered his own question, still calm and unconcerned as he twisted a dial on his cuff. "Remember that."

Before Quinn could so much as reach for the bastard, the sedative gas stole away his strength, then his sight, and finally his consciousness.

He went down hard, chasing Vega's voice into shadows so dark not even all his might could claw them apart.

46

Eskel was ruthless in overseeing her PT routine. If she made the smallest move outside of his instruction, he made her regret it. It wasn't just, "Stand up. Squat down. Raise your arm. Lift your leg." Oh no. It was, "Keep your back straight, and push your heels into the floor as you stand up. Feet shoulder-width apart and parallel, then squat down this far. Now a little farther. Engage your core and raise your arm to forty-five degrees. Palm flat. Rotate palm up..."

When she raised her middle finger at him on the last move, he made her hold a shallow squat position for five minutes.

He let her walk for all of ten minutes the first day. Slowly.

And when her limp improved only enough to keep her pace somewhat even, he forbade her to run until day two.

All the exercises were so mild they could hardly be called a workout, but Eskel kept her at them all day long in measured increments of movement and rest, with occasional breaks for food and to relieve herself.

Vega's entire body was quivering and soaked with sweat by the time he called it for the day. Two of the on-call nurses had to help her into a bath. She fell asleep there.

The next day, her limp was still pronounced enough that Eskel stopped her steady jog to put her in a fancy scanner machine.

"Is the bypass not working?"

Eskel read through the long paragraphs of text the machine spat out. "It's working," he confirmed.

"Then why am I still limping?"

"Maybe because a torture device fried your neurons so much, it made proper mapping impossible," he said without an ounce of pity.

"Or it could be psychosomatic."

"You did not just tell me it's all in my head."

"The device is as calibrated as we could get it. But it's not a perfect procedure. The bypass still needs time to learn and adapt to the nuances of your body's unique neural characteristics."

"So it'll fix itself?"

"That's the hope."

"The *hope*? You told me this would cure me."

Eskel crossed his arms, glaring at her. "No, I told you it was your only option. And it is. But we're forcing the device to do in two days what it usually takes weeks to complete. There are bound to be issues."

Son of a bitch!

"The device is working. You have full range of motion, full control of all your limbs, and no pain. I don't think you realize what a miracle that is. At this point, the limp is a minor concern that will likely resolve itself in a month or two. But even if it doesn't, it shouldn't hold you back in any significant way." He raised both eyebrows in challenge. "As long as you follow the doctor's orders."

"I want to get back to work." If the device needed time to learn her body's characteristics, then she had to expedite the lesson plan and teach it everything she would require to get Quinn away from the Shadows.

Eskel glared but didn't argue.

For the next six hours, he put her through the paces of various poses and movements. Jogging was allowed, but sprinting was not. Tumbling and sparring were out of the question, but he did let her go through her knife routines and a little target practice.

For dinner, she met with Laura to go over what her lawyers had come up with.

Vega had thought she was devious for the plan she'd brewed up.

Laura's legal team had taken it ten steps further in a ruthless choreography that would bring the entire VanWarren family to their knees. Vega was impressed—and grateful to have them in her corner.

"You do realize this will mean war," Laura said.

Her hands were clenched together, but Vega noted the distinct lack of compassion in her eyes. Nervous she might be, but Laura was no push-over. And she was as protective of her people now as she had been back on Anamtaigh. Quinn belonged to her, not the VanWarrens. She would go toe to toe with them the same way she had with Talon and his crew. To her, there was no difference between the two.

Which made her one of Vega's favorite people today.

"Would you do it differently?" she asked, already knowing the answer.

Laura met her gaze, and there wasn't an ounce of hesitation in her when she said, "No."

"Then we're in accord."

They went straight from Laura's dining room into a community game room that Rowe had converted into a makeshift command central. Four different screens and three holograph projectors filled the dark space with a bunch of maps and schematics.

Catton was already there, trying to look dignified, sitting on an oversized pillow on the floor.

Rowe had already filled her in on the plan, but they still needed to get on the same page about the details and synchronize their watches.

Vega counted seconds and flipped and twirled her knives as he reviewed the mission's details and how it needed to play out.

They were waiting for the SU to line up the final leg of their transport. After that, she, Rowe, and Catton would walk out of New Shangri La to meet Zigmann down south, and only Rowe would come back.

Catton didn't like it.

Hell, Laura didn't like it. "They'll need a Hawk, Finn."

Rowe watched Vega sink a blade into the vertical gash on the far wall where the previous one had fallen out a moment ago. "They already have one."

Vega dipped her chin as much as the neck brace would allow.

"They won't like us taking their shit," the former Hawk said. "If they decide to retaliate, someone needs to be here to head them off."

"*I'll* be here," Laura argued.

"And they'll be shielded," Rowe shot back.

The Shadows had known long before the war how dangerous one telepath could be, let alone a group of them. They had developed special helmets to protect their troops from telepathic corruption. By the time they'd launched the first attack, those helmets had become standard issue.

If they came knocking, it wouldn't matter how strong Laura was or how many other telepaths she housed in this compound. Only brute force would stop a Shadow unit from killing everyone here just to prove they could.

"I know how to fight, Finn," Laura growled. A stupid thing to say, considering she'd already experienced what a Shadow raid was like. Vega had been there—she'd been the one leading it.

Thanks to the rabid disregard for life that Talon had trained into his troops, even Vega hadn't been able to prevent them from killing a number of Laura's people.

They'd captured Quinn during that raid.

Vega shut out the memory of him strung up like a slab of meat on the side of the mountain, pale-faced and hardly breathing as his bad heart struggled to keep beating.

Rowe plunged his four-fingered hand into Laura's hair and touched his forehead to hers. "I know you do, baby. But I'm here to make sure you don't have to."

Vega turned away to give them privacy as she retrieved her knives. She traced the dark monogram with her thumb, breathing down her impatience. Telling herself it was important to do this right. Quinn's life depended on it. Once they walked out of here, there would be no margin for error.

She tried and failed not to think about all the things the Shadows could do to someone who healed any injury in seconds.

Finally, word came down that everything was in place. There was a public hover waiting for them at the same station where she'd arrived. It would drop them off two blocks from the Shadow cache at an official station as part of its regular route—except they'd be the only passengers. The same hover would then take them to a nearby shuttleport, where a private shuttle, courtesy of Laura's ridiculously deep pockets, would take them up during the next batch of scheduled planetary hop launches and deposit them on Karem Shem, the fourth and farthest inhabited planet in the Karos solar system.

From there, they would be on their own.

Vega and Catton climbed into the stolen transport now covered with a foot of snow to give Rowe time to say his goodbyes.

Ten minutes later, they were airborne.

Rowe cursed when stray sparks zapped out from beneath the console. "The hell did you do to this thing?"

"It's flying, isn't it?"

"Barely."

And that's how they got it back to the hover station parking lot: barely.

But they did make it.

The hover was already waiting for them, a line of disgruntled travelers complaining about why the passenger loading doors wouldn't open to let them board.

Finn bypassed the crowd and banged on the port door, which was usually reserved for crew.

The crowd let out a cheer, swarming toward them but Catton blocked their way. "Maintenance run, folks. No passengers. You'll have to wait for the next one."

"You don't look like agency techs."

Catton stared down the old man whose skin stretched too far and thin over his face. "And you don't look like someone who should be mouthing off to me."

He hopped in after Vega and the door closed in the faces of a lot of angry rich people who were unfamiliar with the concept of not always getting their way.

"Subtle," she said.

Catton gave her a humble shrug. "I thought so."

The hover was a smaller, short-range model with a maximum speed of 500mph. The pilot pushed it as far as she could but the flight still took close to two hours.

Right before they landed, Rowe sent a quick status update to Laura.

She replied back with a message for Vega: "Everything's in place. Just say when."

"When," Vega told Rowe, who relayed the word back to Laura. Then he smashed the shit out of his com to make sure it couldn't be tracked back if they were captured. He had two others on him to use and discard as needed.

"Ready for this?"

Catton huffed a deep-voiced *woof*, the Hound equivalent of a rallying cry.

Vega nodded, stroking the knife sheathed at her thigh.

"Here we go."

The hover touched down.

The port door opened.

And three Shadows slipped out into the darkness of a snowy night.

47

While cloning was a well-established thing in the genetic industry, it tended to replicate errors and break down after a while. Not to mention, the lack of biodiversity led to additional issues later on.

The more reliable method of genetic design was to augment the chromosomes inside a broad genetic variety of haploid cells—eggs and sperms—pair them by genetic markers for viability and then use in vitro fertilization to spawn a specimen.

And that's what the lab cats have been attempting to do: graft Quinn's genetic anomalies onto a strand of DNA inside a bunch of eggs so they could then use his sperm to fertilize them. A grid of one hundred tiny petri dishes loaded with one donor egg each was now feeding into the AI machine that would graft a manufactured nucleotide segment onto their original DNA strands.

Every step was carefully monitored and recorded. Each mistake and error would be marked for future recalibration.

The boss lab cat called the time and initiated the sequence.

M watched the tray slide in; watched the AI target and map each egg on the grid. Then the robotic arm moved into place over the first petri dish and proceeded to do its thing, touching each dish in sequence, for thirteen point eight-two-six seconds apiece.

Halfway through the batch, errors started popping up all over the finished portion of the grid. One after the other, the augmented eggs started breaking down, and a long readout of data streamed across one of the screens, recording the details of what went wrong.

By the time the robotic arm had finished with the hundredth egg and settled into resting position again, all of the eggs had become nonviable.

There was a moment of silence in the lab as the medics absorbed their complete and utter failure. The lab temperature raised a tenth of a degree as their tempers rose, but none of them would risk a tantrum that might damage sensitive equipment.

M allowed himself a small, brief smile as the boss lab cat finally slumped and said, "Back to the drawing board." He looked up at M in the gallery. "We'll need more samples."

Since M had been the one to acquire the test subject, he was now in charge of anything and everything pertaining to him. Quinn might not be a telepath, but the threat level he presented was equivalent. Therefore, as far as Quinn's care, feeding, and treatment were concerned, M had the final say. The one area where his authority overrode everyone else's, short of the unit's CO, who was lightyears away, sitting pretty on his bureaucratic throne at the OSA.

And, since this outpost was half the usual size, with no CO onsite and little else going on, this round of experiments effectively put M in command. Which was why the lab cat phrased himself so carefully, making a request instead of issuing an order.

"You know where to get them," he replied.

After Quinn's spectacular loss of control, they'd had to sedate him and move him to a new cell. Because the man had destroyed the first one with a few targeted blows. The techs were still analyzing whether the cell's integrity could be restored, or whether it would be easier to demolish it and start fresh. Quinn had been either sedated or kept subdued with a mild paralytic ever since.

The lab cat winced. "It would make our work a lot easier if he was treated."

M walked out without another word. They'd been subtly pushing for Quinn to go into the chair since M had brought him in. But he hadn't lied to Quinn when he'd said there was no way to predict how his artificial heart would handle an EMC treatment. M had managed to stall the medics under the pretext of getting information from Quinn about the SU but, with multiple "interrogations" yielding nothing, he wouldn't be able to stall them much longer. For now, the CO relied on M for progress reports. But as soon as the lab cats stabilized the augmented DNA, they'd be duty-bound to report it. And then, valuable knowledge or not, the potential for more effective soldiers would make Quinn an expendable asset.

The weather had turned outside. Another massive electrical storm was poised to sweep across the region. The outpost was shielded, of course, but the soldiers were not. Electrical storms outside meant all Shadows were confined indoors until it passed. One hundred and forty-nine soldiers with nothing to do, cooped up for the next eighteen to thirty-eight hours.

Lots of eyes and ears. Watching. Listening. But neither seeing, nor hearing anything beyond the obvious.

M made his way to central command, where six separate areas monitored a variety of different things, from weather patterns, to local news, to coms channels, and more. The Hounds in each one were on twelve-hour rotations, and the eleventh hour had just passed for the one he needed. M didn't meet a single bleary-eyed gaze as he marched through the first four sections to one tucked toward the back of the open space. The Hound there had a glazed look on her face, and didn't notice, much less say a word, when M settled in front of the console at her back.

He wasn't a stranger here. The Hounds expected him to come through at least once a day to send off his reports to the CO and receive orders as pertained to his prisoner.

Today, M accessed the OSA servers as he always did and perused them at his leisure, as he always did. He tapped on a section here, let himself into a secure database there, checked the readouts and charts somewhere else—all part of a routine he'd established early on. An extensive, complex pattern of many small actions no one questioned because M had temporary command, with a direct channel of communication to their distant CO.

He heard a Hound marching toward him from a long way off and casually shut down all the different prompts before the soldier turned the corner. "Sir! We received a security alert at one of our caches on Mai."

Took them long enough. M pushed to his feet with as much purpose as would be expected of him. "Show me."

He followed the Hound to a different section. The security screens were manned by a team of eight. Either they'd recently relieved the earlier shift, or the alert had woken them up enough to pay attention. All eight were busy going through a prescribed checklist of what to do in a situation like this:

Confirm the alert. Notify the closest Shadows. Check first responder coms for signs of conflict in the region. Check all other caches in the area for activity and potential threats.

The last one would take the longest. Karos had not one but *four* inhabited planets, each one with the requisite number of supply caches, all of which would need to be checked and monitored. It would thin out their resources. Protocol demanded that additional personnel be called in to handle the workload more efficiently. They would be arriving any minute.

The Hound who'd fetched him reclaimed his seat at his console and brought up a grid of security feeds from the area. The night time scene replicated across the screen in various configurations—night vision, infrared, and AI trawl.

The first was obscured by snowfall. Thick chunked-up flakes floated down from the sky, giving them peekaboo glimpses of the nondescript building tucked away on an industrial side street with no foot traffic.

The infrared showed four figures at the cache entrance. Heat signatures indicated three males and a female. Their body language was coordinated and alert. A unit working together, the way all Shadows were trained to do.

It was the AI trawl that had sent up the alert. It had identified all four individuals and matched them to files within the Shadow database.

M leaned over the desk to get a closer look at the fine print of each file.

Brent Catton. Hound. Sharp shooter. MIA and presumed dead two and a half years ago.

Arthur Zigmann. Hound. MIA and presumed dead two and a half years ago.

Finnegan Rowe. Hawk. MIA and presumed dead over three years ago at Outpost Green 24.

And there she was. Vega Ortiz. Hound. MIA and recently identified leaving Persephone 5 en route to Ela.

"Sir, Deckler's team is closest. They've already been alerted and are standing by to intercept."

Normally, a Hawk accessing a cache would prompt action to assist.

But a Hawk accompanied by three Hounds was not a Shadow in distress. It was a raiding party. Deckler's team would be deployed not to cover them from potential threats, but to eliminate them as the threat itself.

"Sir? What are your orders?"

M watched Finnegan Rowe hold the back of his wrist to the scanner. It sent up an immediate alarm across all of their systems.

"Sir…"

This outpost wouldn't be the only one receiving the alert. But it was the closest, which meant it fell under M's jurisdiction. It was his call how to deal with it.

"Sir, should I—"

"Clear the alarm and let them in."

"Sir?"

"Are you going to make me repeat myself?"

"No, sir!" The Houd swiped his palm across the screen. The alert cleared. He tapped in an override code and, on the feed, they watched the cache door open.

Finnegan Rowe and Vega Ortiz ducked in, followed by Arthur Zigmann. A second later, an arm shoved back out the door to hand Brent Catton, the sharp shooter, a weapon, then a helmet, and finally a small, flexible riot shield.

"Should I send in Deckler, sir?"

Clever to have Catton be the lookout. With the helmet on his head giving him a detailed readout of the surrounding area, he'd see Shadows coming from half a block away. And with his sharp shooter skills, he could pick them off one by one.

A clock at the top of the screen recorded the time from the initial opening of the cache door. M watched it tick through one minute. Two. Three… "Sir, Deckler's team is requesting orders."

At the five-minute mark, M straightened from the desk and ordered, "Send them in."

Rowe was the first one through the door as soon as it opened. "Alert is out. We're on the clock." The closest Shadow outposts would be notified immediately that a cache had been accessed. Depending on where soldiers were stationed on assignment, multiple teams would likely be diverted to the cache to intercept them. They could have hours, or minutes.

As stellar as Vega's luck has been lately, she wagered minutes.

Rowe headed straight for a rack beside the door and took a couple of handguns, a riot shield, and a standard-issue surveillance helmet for Catton.

Vega and Zigmann, meanwhile, took inventory of the trove before them. Everything a soldier might need, this place had in ample supply. It was an armory, an emergency clinic, and a safe house all in one.

"Don't get greedy," Rowe warned, grabbing three backpacks already filled with standard gear. "Take only what you need." He went over to an open locker and pulled vacuum sealed bundles off the shelves. "Uniforms." He tossed three of them to Vega, then jerked his chin at Zigmann. "Leave the cuffs. You won't be able to use them."

Zig was looking over a table laid out with specialized wrist units, each neatly curled around a small protective case that held its corresponding lens.

A Hawk wrist unit was a masterpiece of warfare engineering. A covert weapon of last resort that had multiple functions for times when traditional weapons weren't an option. It could generate a plasma shield, deliver a percussion blast, and interface with the lens to give the Hawk all the readouts of a helmet visor without the bulk. Among many other, very nifty features.

Zig picked up a lens case. "Why? Are they locked to rank like the cache building?"

"No, it just takes a week to learn all the different features and commands. If you don't know what you're doing, you can easily blow yourself up with one of those."

Vega stuffed a uniform into her pack. "I forgot they can go *boom*." Wrist units were supposed to be the last part of Hawk training. Vega's CO had washed her out of the program halfway through it. She'd gotten a general overview and a couple of hands-on sessions, but not enough to master the full range of what one of those babies could do.

She paused with the second uniform halfway into Catton's pack and met eyes with Zigmann. It might be enough. "Take them all."

He grinned. "Oh, yeah." He swept half of them off the table straight into his pack but tossed a cuff and a lens to Rowe.

The backpacks already had the bare necessities, but Vega still swiped a few extra nutrition gel packs off the shelves, as well as a backup first aid kit. Weapons and more riot shields were stacked along the back wall. Standard gear for any Shadow, but not a Hawk's first choice. They would do just fine for Hounds, though. Vega strapped on a full-body set of holsters already stuffed with six handguns and four extra cartridges. There were drawers full of throwing knives, too. But the standard-issue steel didn't hold a candle to her alloy set and would only add more weight for her to carry, so she ignored them.

"Five minutes," Rowe called.

They were pushing it.

"Let's go, Zig. You don't need that shit."

Already armed with guns and knives of his own, Zigmann glared at her through the shimmery film of a riot shield. "The fuck do you mean I don't need it? I got balls to protect over here!"

"Then take an extra cup, and—"

Catton slammed backward through the half-open door and rolled across the floor. His cracked shield went flying, but he came right up to his feet, weapon raised to fire into the night. "Time's up, packrats. Scurry!"

Zigmann, riot shield still in hand, ducked under Catton's weapon to crouch in front of him, providing cover.

Rowe cursed a vicious streak as he tossed a helmet to Vega, then strapped on the cuff. A twist and a flick activated its plasma shield, and he used it to get close enough to put a helmet on Zig. Then he went flat against the wall by the door, lens in his left eye, peeking out between Catton's shots to scope out the situation.

"Three on the rooftop across the street," Catton reported. "Two more street-level—three o'clock. Two down at nine and eleven."

"Back door?" Vega asked, kicking the packs across the floor and grabbing two gun harnesses for Catton.

"They'll have it covered, too," Rowe responded, fiddling with the cuff.

"Guess we're taking 'em out head-on," Zig offered.

Catton's weapon ran out of charge. He had a backup in hand before he dropped the empty.

"I need to get out there," Rowe said.

Catton nodded. "Zig, on my mark—*go.*"

Zigmann ducked his head and put his shoulder to the shield, pushing forward against the battering force of repeated plasma blasts. Catton was right on his heels, firing back, but the Shadows out on the street had plasma shields. Unlike the cheap riot shield that was starting to warp in front of Zigmann, plasma shields absorbed and dispersed weapons fire like rainwater. Catton's skills alone wouldn't get them out of this.

Vega grabbed a couple of the lightweight riot shields and rounded the room to get to the door just as Zig and Catton pushed through it. She met eyes with Rowe and gave him a nod.

As soon as the others cleared enough room for him, he lunged out, Vega on his heels, one shield in front of her, the other over her head.

Rowe threw something too small for her to see and ducked down, shouting, "*Cover!*"

Catton immediately dropped behind Zig, and Vega threw herself toward them, raising both of her shields over all their heads, hunching down to brace against a blast.

Only there was no blast.

All Vega heard was a soft, distant whistle of a flying projectile and then a series of soft thuds as bodies dropped onto the snow-covered pavement.

A sharp screech sparked laterally across Zigmann's shield, making him flinch, and then there was silence.

Rowe slotted the throwing star back into his cuff. Not a bomb, a physical weapon engineered to seek out heat signatures outside of a set perimeter around the cuff and eliminate them. Something small and sharp enough to cut through armor, that a plasma shield was not made to counter. It would have passed right through Zigmann's shield and killed all three of them, too, if they'd been any farther away from Rowe.

Fucking brilliant.

Rowe patted the cuff with obvious affection. "Damn, I missed this thing."

Catton stared at him. "I want one."

Zigmann sniffed. "Do I smell barbecue?"

Rowe twisted to hold his arm up to the light. It was scorched in a straight line from elbow to shoulder, sleeve burned away, and skin fried to a black crisp.

Vega swore. "How the fuck did you manage that?"

"Lucky shot," Rowe said with a wince.

Catton and Zig helped him to his feet and back inside while Vega fetched a medkit.

"There will be more incoming," Rowe said. "You need to get out of here."

"Yeah, yeah, shut up." Catton tore off the sleeve, hissing at the injury.

Vega slapped a pain patch on the side of Rowe's neck. "Four hours. Then swap for a new one." She shook a canister of liquid bandage and carefully sprayed it over the wound. The plasma blast had cauterized the surface, but the tissue was fragile and could easily crack open under physical stress—such as fighting or running for one's life. The bandage would disinfect and protect it until a trained medic removed it and treated the wound properly. "I suggest you get your ass to a medic or this'll leave a hell of a nasty scar."

No names. No locations. The cache would be monitored inside and out. Someone would be watching them and listening to every word they spoke.

Rowe shook his head. The plan had been for him to stick around town for a while, drive off randomly to lead any stray Shadows on a wild goose chase to keep them off everyone's trail before he went back to the compound.

"Then kill them," Vega said. "And blow all their shit up. Not like you don't have the fire power."

Rowe groaned a chuckle. "I can handle myself."

Of that, she had no doubt.

"Not reading any more heat signatures out there," Zigmann reported from the front door.

Catton looked dubious, strapping on a weapons harness. "Think they only sent seven?"

Rowe shrugged. "Could be they only had seven close enough to send."

"Not taking the chance," Vega declared. "We're moving out. Are you good?"

Rowe cracked his neck. "I'll live."

Vega shouldered her pack, then the extra one. Gear for Mass and Owens, once they linked up with them on Karem Shem.

Catton took two more packs, and the two harnesses Vega had taken off the wall. Zig would take point. With only his own pack to carry, he had two hands free to head off another ambush.

Vega put on her helmet. The visor activated instantly, giving her a bio readout of everyone around her. Rowe's heart rate was through the roof and the temperature in his extremities was dropping. She tossed him a sealed uniform pack and a field blanket. "Watch your back," she warned.

"Fair winds and good hunting," Rowe said, saluting them out the door.

Fifteen minutes later, the three of them were back in the still-waiting hover.

Thirty-seven seconds after that, the hover raised high into the air, in time for them to watch fire engulf the Shadow cache and an EM pulse ripple across the neighborhood, causing a blackout that would disable all surveillance feeds in a ten-mile radius.

The shuttleport was two hours away at full speed ahead.

Vega counted down the seconds.

Four Shadows had gone into that cache, but only three had been seen coming out before it blew. M was still contemplating the strategy a day later as he swam against the current of an automated exercise pool.

He'd seen Vega limping on the feed. Clearly, the building collapse on Crescent Island had caused some significant damage. So why would she pick two Hounds for her team and leave her most valuable asset, a Hawk, behind?

The explosion had been a stroke of genius. But only in that it had lost them the Hawk. Finnegan Rowe had left no trail for them to follow. A minor frustration, and no less than M would have expected from someone of Rowe's caliber.

The rest of them, the Shadows on duty had tracked all the way to a shuttleport, where they'd lost them in the swarming crowds onboarding and offboarding the alignment hop. Not that M had expected to pick them up again. Plus, since the seven Hounds who had so abysmally failed in the simple assignment of apprehending four targets had been the only ones currently on the continent, there'd been no one left to catch them, anyway.

Didn't matter. M didn't need visual confirmation to know where they were headed.

The pool's current slowed to a stop. M touched his feet to the bottom and raised his head out of the water, taking his first breath in two minutes and ten seconds.

"Sir, may I have a word?"

The Hound stood at ease at the edge of the in-ground pool, looking down his nose at M with a mixture of disappointment and disgust before he raised his chin and stared straight ahead.

His name was Hui. Five-foot-eleven, two hundred pounds. High center of gravity, and not a fan of leg day. M could drop him with a quick grab for his ankles. If he put enough force behind it, the impact would slam the man's head on the floor hard enough to knock him out. It would serve him right for interrupting M's swim.

"What do you want?"

"Sir, the troops are questioning why we haven't sent additional Hounds after the perps who blew up our Mai cache."

M braced his hands on the edge of the pool and pushed himself up and out, forcing the Hound back a step or two. "Are they now?"

To his credit, Hui held his ground.

"Why would I expend more resources that I know to be inadequate to the task?"

"Sir?" So much ire in that one syllable.

"The Mai team was an embarrassment to our institution. Seven fully-armed Hounds with the element of surprise, and they couldn't take down four deserters?" He scoffed. "The best thing those soldiers did was die."

Hui drew himself up as stiff as he could. "They were stalled for a full five minutes on your order, *sir*, giving the enemy time to arm themselves with *our* weapons. The delay was not only unnecessary but disastrous. You deliberately sabotaged the mission and allowed the targets to escape."

"Is that your professional assessment?"

"Yes, sir! Our team would not have failed if you hadn't set them up to do so." A bold statement. Delivered with all the audacity of a Hound who thought he had the upper hand.

"*My* team would not have failed if I'd sent them in ten minutes later with no weapons at all."

Hui's face turned bright red.

"*My* unit has a dedicated CO onsite to ensure all soldiers maintain a training and exercise regimen, and take part in field assignments to keep their skills sharp. In the time I have been at this outpost, this gym has been empty every single day. Out of the hundred and fifty Hounds in residence, twenty-two are on duty in central command, and thirty-six are on watch around the perimeter at any given time.

Not counting medics and other non-military personnel, that means ninety-two of you sit around for hours on end with nothing better to do than incubate your balls."

Hui's nostrils flared. He was breathing hard, his jaw twitching as he clamped down on his temper. He clearly had more to say, and was just waiting for M to pause long enough to let him.

M didn't let him.

"That includes you, Hound. I've seen you in the mess hall, in the barracks, in central command, but not once have I seen you in here, or out there in the plains. I doubt you've been part of a single mission since we acquired you. And there's probably a reason for that—and for why you and the rest of this unit have been assigned to the one solar system that hasn't seen live battle since the war began. But you're going to stand there and tell *me* that *I'm* the reason the mission failed?"

"Sir, it is my duty to submit a detailed report on any action occurring in or initiated by this outpost to my commanding officer."

"Then I suggest you do so."

Hui met M's gaze with a nasty little smirk. "I already did, sir. We received a response twenty minutes ago."

"And what did Commander Hughes have to say?"

"He instructed us to relieve you of command, effective immediately. We are to take orders from no one but Commander Hughes until a dedicated CO is dispatched to take over."

Something he could and should have done immediately, instead of giving M that little speech about sabotage. Hui had a superiority complex unbefitting a Hound. He had prioritized his own reputation and authority over the efficiency and effectiveness of his outpost. And he would likely do so again.

"Excellent. Anything else?" M was starting to dry off, standing there yammering on in nothing but his swimsuit. The chill was bracing, but M was getting bored with this conversation.

"Yes, sir. Commander Hughes ordered the prisoner to be treated immediately. He expects a full report no later than twenty-one hundred hours."

Another thing Hui could have facilitated himself, instead of telling M about it. Another way to put M in his place and establish Hui's authority over the outpost.

And wasn't that a beautiful, beautiful thing?

"I'll see to it myself," M said. Accounting for transmission delays, and the time it would take to perform the procedure and compose a full report, he had four hours to get Quinn into the chair.

M picked up his towel and headed for the showers.

Hui called after him, "You're not going to dispute the charges I levered against you?"

"Nope. You did your job, Hound. And I did mine. We are all just doing what we're told."

50

The VanWarrens had somehow managed to strongarm an entire hotel into evicting their guests to make room for the family and their servants. And the moment they'd settled in, Ulysses Navarre, Captain of the Port Cain PD, had received a summons to meet with the patriarchs of the clan on some urgent matter *not* pertaining to the attack on Crescent Island.

Navarre would rather pick up a shovel and go dig through the wreckage. He'd probably be more useful there than the crews the family had hired to clean up the debris. It seemed like their contracted pace was one pebble per hour.

But that was none of his business. All Navarre wanted was to clear this mess of a family off his planet so he could go back to the way things used to be. He preferred it when his biggest concern on any given day was dispatching a bot out into the ocean where some rich yahoo's wave rider stalled too far offshore.

Instead, Navarre was currently following a shellshocked-looking woman up to the top floor, then down a corridor of doors to an antechamber that spanned the entire width of the building. He waited while she knocked on the gleaming double-doors and received the signal to enter. She opened the door and waved him inside.

Not one word.

The woman had not uttered a single word the whole time she'd been with him.

These people needed some serious professional help.

Navarre stepped through into the penthouse, keeping his gaze front and center on the two men before him. His shoes squeaked on the polished marble floor. Sunlight reflected off tapestries woven from metallic threads. He ignored the gaudy décor and the fortunes it must have cost. But he couldn't help the judgmental twist of his mouth when he picked up on a familiar scent. Out of the corner of his eye, he spotted a bright yellow log burning green in the gleaming fireplace.

The trees on Ela were so fragrant that burning a freshly cut log was equivalent to filling a room with incense. The most potent varieties, like this one, had a calming, medicinal effect. They were considered endangered and illegal to harvest. But apparently local laws didn't apply to the rich and famous VanWarrens.

The older of the brothers came forward first, extending his hand in greeting. "Mr. Navarre, thank you for coming."

"Captain," Navarre corrected, shaking VanWarren's hand and quickly letting go to shake hands with the younger brother, who only offered a nod, letting his sibling do the talking.

"Of course, I apologize."

"What is it that I can do for you, Mr. VanWarren?"

Matthew VanWarren waved him toward a com screen embedded in the wall beneath a giant hand-painted waterscape in a gilded frame. "We received this transmission from Mai a few hours ago. Take a look." He brought up the communications dashboard and selected the message in question.

An authorization request with a review receipt popped up first. It indicated that the transmission had already been opened three times—something the sender would also be able to verify. Matthew VanWarren scanned his ID chip, and then entered a verification code on the next screen. Once access was granted, the folder opened to a video recording and a series of digital documents. Each separate attachment had its own receipt count. The video had been played three times. The documents had counts ranging between three and eighteen.

VanWarren opened the video message first, and the screen expanded to show a tan-skinned, dark-haired woman with piercing eyes and a cold smile.

Navarre recognized her immediately as Vega VanWarren. It was the same woman he'd interviewed on the beach the morning of Emmett

VanWarren's death. But somehow, she looked radically different, as if another person had stepped into her skin. None of her former sweet innocence and sun-warmed blushes. This was a creature he wouldn't want to cross after dark. Cold intelligence shone out of those eyes, and a sort of heartless authority shrouded the rigid set of her shoulders as she spoke.

And her voice…

Navarre felt an unpleasant chill run down his spine and counted himself lucky that he wasn't the target of her wrath.

"Greetings. I should probably say something like, 'I hope this message finds you well,' but I think by now, we can all agree to dispense with the bullshit. This is Vega Ortiz VanWarren, wife of Quinn VanWarren, and a legally appointed chairperson of the VanWarren estate. The accompanying documents will confirm my identity, and both access and authority over the VanWarren financials. Everything has been reviewed, notarized, and verified by the legal team at Ulawatha Mannon & Tabari, hereafter referred to as UMT."

The legal team's credentials and contact information scrolled across the bottom of the screen.

"I'm sure you'll want to perform your own investigations into this, which you are, of course, welcome to do at your expense. Feel free to direct any questions or complaints to the UMT legal secretary. They are expecting your call.

"This message is intended for Misters Matthew and Holden Van-Warren, and-or the current interim head of the VanWarren family." Her smile momentarily stretched wider, more predatory. *"Hi. Be you didn't think you'd see me again. Alive, anyway."*

Navarre glanced at the brothers to gauge their reactions. Matthew VanWarren was a decent actor. He'd already had three previous views to get the surprise out of his system, but his anger still lingered in the twitch of his jaw muscles. Holden VanWarren wasn't even looking at the screen, as if he couldn't face the woman speaking to him, even though she wasn't physically there.

It appeared Vega VanWarren was correct. The brothers had, indeed, expected her to be dead. And neither looked happy to find out otherwise.

This was going to be interesting.

"I am recording this for you as a matter of courtesy. Everything I am about to say will be going into effect the moment you receive this message, so you won't have time to stop it. But most of it shouldn't come as too much of a surprise since my husband made his plans clear to both of you already. I am simply putting them into action. And taking a couple of extra steps in the direction he set." She leaned closer to the recorder. *"You might want to sit down for this next part—I guarantee you won't like it."*

Then she straightened away and became all business, reading from something on the desk before her. The recorder wasn't angled to pick it up, but the message did come annotated with reference links. *"Per the plans outlined by Quinn VanWarren in his meeting with Matthew and Holden VanWarren at the family estate on Crescent Island, Ela..."* An icon blinked in one corner of the screen, presumably a link for the recording of said meeting. *"The following businesses will be shutting down operations effective immediately."* A list of them and the names of their CEOs scrolled across the screen, with a link to one of the documents that had been attached to the message. *"All company assets will be seized, liquidated, and used to pay off any outstanding debts. The balance, if there is one, will be deposited to the primary VanWarren estate account.*

"The following businesses will remain operational." Another list scrolled through, with another document reference link. *"However, the monetary value of all investments into these businesses by Beatrice and Amundsen VanWarren and-or the primary VanWarren estate account will be reclaimed immediately and redeposited into the primary VanWarren estate account.*

"UMT has employed a team of financial experts to calculate the total sums and informed me that withdrawing these funds will force the following businesses to file for bankruptcy. Once the withdrawals are finalized, the controlling interest of each business will revert to their respective owners. Said owners can then deal with the consequences as they see fit. But they won't be getting any more family handouts." She showed no remorse whatsoever about singlehandedly sinking entire companies and throwing what had to be thousands of people into

unemployment.

Navarre swallowed back the impulse to whistle. The VanWarren family might be popular entertainers, but were they any good with money? Based on the look the brothers gave each other, no, they were not. And why would they be? With a safety net the size of a small moon, courtesy of their deceased elders, what was a little risk or two?

"Last on the business agenda, the following companies will also remain operational. Pending the owners' agreement to certain provisions, they will receive a financial investment to augment and expand. Current leadership will retain control, subject to annual review by a VanWarren estate chairperson. At present, that would be Quinn VanWarren and-or myself."

Only five businesses populated that exclusive list. Navarre made a mental note to look into them for stock options. His police captain's salary was decent, all things considered, but he did have grandbabies to think about. Would be nice if they had something to remember him by when he was gone.

"That takes care of business," Mrs. VanWarren proclaimed, sweeping her hand over the surface of her desk. *"Now let's talk about the family. Effective immediately, every VanWarren under the age of sixteen, and all future-born legitimate VanWarren children will be disinherited from the greater VanWarren estate and all its associated resources."* She looked up at the recorder. *"To be clear, no VanWarren child will be getting access to any estate-controlled accounts or accounts co-signed by the estate. Not on their own, and not through their parents."*

Navarre once again glanced at the brothers, but they showed no reaction to this news. At least not an obvious one. If memory served, neither of them had children. It appeared they therefore didn't consider this provision to be of concern to them.

The woman who seemed to have them all tightly by the balls resumed reading from her notes. *"Instead, they will have a trust fund created in their name, in the amount of two thousand credits. This money will be held in escrow and accrue an annual interest of no less than twenty percent until the child reaches eighteen years of age. At that point, the child will gain access to those funds to use as they wish.*

"If and when they become gainfully employed, productive members

of society, their access to estate resources will be restored, and they will return to the proper line of succession and inheritance. Caveats and addendums apply." Another series of links to reference documents followed. *"If not, too bad. I suppose they can just have mommy and daddy continue footing the bill for their existence."*

Boy, was Navarre glad not to be a VanWarren right about now. If the bankruptcies didn't tear the family apart, this sure as hell would. Ragmags would have a field day with this story if they ever got their hands on it. Was that why the VanWarrens had called him in? To help them keep this under wraps?

"As for the current balance of the primary VanWarren estate account. Going forward, fifty percent of all annual income will be donated to various charities and nonprofit organizations. Twenty percent will go toward stipends and grants for work-study programs to be made available to VanWarren estate employees. And the remaining thirty percent will be subdivided for trust funds and inheritances."

The screen popped up a bar chart that showed the current account balance and the annual income projected over the next twenty-five years. Beside it, said income levels were shown in pie charts to illustrate the break-down she'd described. Damn. That was a proper chunk of change right there. And it only affected money coming in, not money already there.

Vega VanWarren paused for a long beat of silence, punctuated by the crackle of burning firewood. Navarre found himself holding his breath. He could practically feel her savoring the shock she'd caused. It was written all over her face and in that small, satisfied smile she held firmly in check.

She swiped the desk clean again and focused her full attention on the recorder.

She was staring straight into Navarre's soul. He had to steel himself not to hunch his shoulders against an inexplicable feeling of guilt.

"This is the part where I, Vega Ortiz VanWarren, decide to right some wrongs on my husband's behalf. Note the distinction. I am trying to make it clear that what follows next is not Quinn's doing. He is far too forgiving. I am not."

Everything the woman had said so far would already be disastrous for the VanWarren family. Each provision would drive the wedge deeper between them. Navarre would have thought it retribution enough for whatever slight she imagined them to have delivered.

But the way she said those three little words...

Navarre swallowed nervously and shuffled back a step, sweaty palm patting along his hip for a sidearm that wasn't there.

Vega Ortiz VanWarren, whoever she was, was about to deliver a blow they would never recover from.

"I know every single VanWarren, and every credit you have to your name. And I know that all but a few of you have set yourselves up to live very comfortably at the old guard's expense. You can afford to pay for the sins of your past. Which is why, effective immediately, access to all VanWarren estate accounts will be revoked for all VanWarrens and their spouses. This includes trust funds, stipends, annuities, personal loans, and inheritances.

"The VanWarren family collectively exiled my husband as a sixteen-year-old boy to fend for himself. With nothing but the clothes on his back and a bad heart in his chest. And not one of you ever bothered to find out what became of him. Grandma Beatrice gifted Quinn two thousand credits and a warm farewell when he called her for help. So that's what you'll get from me. Two thousand credits each.

"In fact, I'll be generous. For those currently stuck on Ela, I'll throw in a one-way ticket back to your primary residence, wherever it may be. Third class. After that, you're on your own. Just like Quinn was. Let's see if you can make it as long as he did.

"Between you and me, I won't lose a single night of sleep over it if you fail. Just like you didn't when you ran from Crescent Island and left Quinn and me to dig our way out of a collapsed building on our own." She shrugged. *"Maybe if you'd stuck around to lend a hand, this conversation wouldn't be so one-sided."*

The video stopped there, on a still of Vega VanWarren staring her hatred straight at the recorder. Navarre shifted from foot to foot, feeling complicit in someone else's sins. He'd thought he was pretty well versed in the VanWarren family dynamics, with their lives hanging out there for everyone to see. But he'd had no idea how callous they could be. To toss a kid with a bad heart out on the street—after the kind of cushy life he'd had up to that point… Navarre couldn't imagine what that must have been like.

"Turn it off." The first words out of Holden VanWarren sounded rough and unsteady. He was still looking away, avoiding the sight of his judge and executioner.

Matthew VanWarren tapped the screen, and Vega VanWarren disappeared.

Navarre took a deep breath and blew it out long and slow. "I'll make some calls. Make sure this hasn't leaked to the media. If we can keep it contained, it should help minimize any public fallout—"

"I don't care about that," Matthew VanWarren said, unbending steel in his voice. "You're not here to contain this."

Navarre looked from him to Holden VanWarren and back again. "Then why am I here?"

"I want you to invalidate it."

He must have heard that wrong. "Excuse me?"

"Go through the certificates, dig into her past. Find whatever dirt you can to take her out."

"What are you asking me right now?" The certs he'd seen flash across the screen already had a police seal over them, meaning that a law enforcement AI bot had notarized and fully verified every part of it. The system had so many redundant fail-safes and security measures that it would take a hundred hackers two centuries to push one through the system. No forged document had ever passed those checks, which meant the seals were ironclad. That was why people got them. To ensure any documents they were on became unquestionable. And Vega VanWarren had at least a half dozen of them. She'd covered all her bases before she'd sent that message.

"If Quinn were alive, it would have been him talking, not that trailer trash piece of shit he hauled out of a ditch somewhere. She's not one of us. She is *nothing*. And I'll be damned if I let her drag my family into the gutter."

Holden VanWarren rubbed his face tiredly. "I think what Matthew is trying to say is that we have doubts as to the legitimacy of Vega Ortiz's marriage to our brother and the access she has to our estate finances—"

"Shut her down," Matthew VanWarren ordered.

"Listen, I get that you're upset"—understatement—"but I don't think I can help you here. The marriage license, the contracts, the account access—everything would have been verified fifty times over by every institution Quinn VanWarren and his wife touched. If *they* didn't flag any issues, I don't see how—"

"I'll pay you a fortune big enough for your children's children to live on if you make this go away."

She's not one of us.

Not one of the elite class whose bank account balances were bigger than the average person could fathom. Just one of the vermin. The masses who took up space and sullied the views. People who weren't even people to him. Easy to crush. Without the means to fight back.

Except Vega VanWarren currently had her hands on a great big club, and she wasn't shy about swinging it around.

And Navarre had to check a sudden vicious smile that would have mirrored hers. He scratched the back of his head and feigned a wince to hide it. "Gonna be tough for three generations to survive on two thousand credits, don't you think?"

If looks could kill, Navarre would drop dead where he stood.

He figured perhaps he ought to not stand there anymore.

Nodding goodbye to Holden VanWarren, who seemed to have lost himself in his misery, Navarre turned his back on the brain-melting fury Matthew VanWarren was shooting at him through his eye-lasers and walked out, softly closing the door behind him.

He had a feeling the VanWarren family would be making the news a lot in the coming months.

And wherever she was, Navarre hoped Vega VanWarren enjoyed every second of it.

51

Around the same time – Karem Shem

"Welcome to the picturesque paradise of Karem Shem. Where lightning strikes up." Owens demonstrated the direction with his middle finger as thin branches of yellow lightning sparked up from the ground toward a dark red sky all around them.

They'd been watching the storm for a while now, and though the upward lightning seemed to have calmed a bit, it hadn't stopped yet. Something about the electromagnetic properties of this particular region. And Vega imagined the majority of the planet's surface.

Just because it was habitable didn't mean Karem Shem wasn't hostile. The planet was mostly populated by scientists and rich thrill seekers who thought they'd be the first ones to tame it.

The reality of their life here seemed to be less than spectacular. The handful of communities who'd established a foothold lived in giant dome structures half hidden beneath the surface.

So why bother colonizing the planet at all?

Natural resources, of course. Karem Shem had the ideal conditions for growing some of the galaxy's most prized minerals. Extensive cave systems beneath the surface were lined with sharp crystals and thick veins of precious metal. Entire industries were salivating for a piece of that pie.

But the ICG had declared the planet illegal to harvest until further notice to preserve and observe its ecosystem. The planet was in the earliest stages of organic evolution. It had a breathable atmosphere, extensive water reservoirs, and lots and lots of energy churning all over. It was in an ideal stage for studying the origins of life. Therefore, access was strictly limited.

Of course, there were always exceptions.

Like rich people who wanted to visit four planets in one week.

Or an army for whom the word "no" didn't exist.

That was a whole-ass Shadow outpost they were looking at about five miles across the lightning field. Aboveground. Because fuck lightning, she supposed. Whoever had approved the plans for this place must have been either a sadist or an idiot.

Massimino winced next to Vega as a particularly gnarly bolt struck up right in front of their vehicle. He didn't say anything, but his unease was clear in the fine sheen of sweat over his face.

Vega closed her eyes and breathed, reminding herself that the vehicle was fully insulated and safe. They'd appropriated it from the shuttleport's emergency response center. It was specially made for this environment.

She was safe.

"Anyone else have concerns about a team of five infiltrating a fully manned Shadow outpost?" Owens asked, scratching behind his ear.

"Nope," Vega said as Catton snorted. "Ain't no Shadow outpost. See any Shadows walking around outside?"

Owens gaped at him. "There's a lightning storm!"

Vega shrugged. "I would have done it."

"You're psychotic."

"And that's exactly the point. All of us spent three years in special training under a sadistic psychopath more unhinged than any Shadow commander. They're trained to think one way. We fight feral."

"I give us one-in-fifty to get out alive," Mass said, a thoughtful, unconcerned look on his face.

"So, what? One-tenth of each of us has a chance to get out?"

"I've lived through worse," Cannot said. He wasn't kidding.

Zig shifted forward in the seat behind Vega, his weight rocking the whole vehicle on its massive, rubberized wheels. "Maybe you should think about—"

"Kicking your ass all around this oversized toy buggy?" Vega finished through clenched teeth. "Believe me, I'm thinking about it."

Zig tucked tail and hunched back into his seat, where he met with

Catton clapping him on the shoulder in comfort. "Valiant effort."

No one else said a word.

Good.

Vega didn't need them to remind her that she wasn't exactly in prime fighting form at the moment. Quinn was somewhere in that outpost. She was fine. "What's the status?"

Mass checked the dashboard screen. It was synced with the closest station for weather updates but with so much EM interference, it glitched a lot. The readings flickered and often went dark for minutes at a time. "Seems to be abating," Mass reported. "Still estimating three hours before we can safely walk out."

"Great," she said, "Just need to make sure we park close to the door." They might still use the storm for cover when they made their exit. Three hours inside a Shadow outpost. If they didn't make it out before then, they weren't making it out at all.

Mass twisted around to raise a thick eyebrow at her. "You want I should call ahead and have them save us a spot?"

"If you think it'll help."

Owens shook his head. "I ain't walking across that. Uh-uh."

Vega gave him a feral little grin. "What, you're afraid you'll get hit by a bolt of electricity that might fry your brain, loosen your bowels, and make all your muscles lock up and cramp for an hour after?"

"Well…*yeah.*"

She snorted. "Pussy."

In the back seat, Catton cackled a loud, "*Ha!*"

"Whatever," Owens muttered, turning away from her as much as the cramped cabin would allow.

"Anything on the outpost?"

Mass played with the console, then brought up a 3D hologram of the compound across the electrified plain. Like the weather report, the image glitched and flickered, but Vega saw enough to make out the basics. "Looks like we got lucky. Rowe's intel was spot on. Standard hexagonal layout. Main entrance to the south. Southwest corner is registering multiple mechanical vehicles similar to ours and some other equipment."

That side would be their escape route, then.

"Gotta figure they'll need an ecogarden for food 'n shit," Mass continued. "It's not showing up on the scan, but I'll bet it's underground."

Which meant blind spots. But those facilities were usually staffed by lower-grade non-Shadow soldiers or civilian engineers.

"What about the brig?" Zig asked. "We walk you two in, you figure they'll put you in the holding cells, or what?"

Vega frowned at him, "Your outpost had a brig?"

"Yours didn't?"

"No." Vega's outpost hadn't bothered with detaining unruly Shadows. They went straight into the chair, and if that didn't set them straight, a plasma bolt to the head usually did the trick.

"We gotta figure holding cells or medbay," Catton offered. "For all of us."

The plan was for Owens, Mass, and Zig to walk in Vega and Catton as their prisoners. Zig having turned on them, and called the other two for backup. If they played it right, the Shadows would let them straight in the front door and get them at least part of the way to Quinn.

Of course, they could decide to shoot first instead. Which was why all of them would go in wearing a Hawk wrist unit.

The shuttle flight from Mai had given them enough time to learn a few of its basic functions. Enough to give them an edge but not so much that it distracted them in the heat of battle. Tools like that had to be second nature. Taking your eyes off a Shadow, even for an instant, tended to be a fatal mistake.

"We'll need to split up," Vega said.

"We need to kick the shit out of that anthill, is what we need," Zig returned. "Get them chasing their own tails instead of ours."

Owens reached over and grabbed hold of the hologram, turning it around from every angle. He zoomed in on one spot, then shifted the view somewhere else. "Right here," he said after a moment, but the hologram went dark. He swore as it reappeared in front of Mass and reached over Vega to point again. "There. See that hotspot? Power source. There are a few smaller ones for backup, but that right there is our target."

Vega thought it over, spinning the hologram. Timing would be crucial. But if they could disable the power grid, it might buy them a small advantage. They'd need every single one to make it out of there alive. "Okay, here it is. They'll have a team waiting for us, and they'll be primed to shoot first. Catton and I are out on entry. Tranqued." No other way the rest of them could walk in two Shadow prisoners. It was either knocked out or dead. "Zig will do the talking."

He snorted. "If they let me."

"If they don't, you knock 'em out. Mass, keep the percussion pulse primed to go. If something feels wrong, give the signal and set it off. It'll buy you enough time to wake up the two of us, and then we *move*."

"What if they're not hostile?" Mass asked.

Owens gave him the look he deserved. "*Not hostile?*"

Mass winced. "Yeah, I heard it as soon as I said it."

"Best we can hope for," Vega said, "is that they give us sixty seconds to feed them the story before they search and disarm us. They find our cuffs, we're done for." She traced the outpost's corridors. "This is our path. Right here is where we split. Catton goes with Owens. You cover him until he can take out the generator, then you both haul ass to the transport bay. Shoot to kill." Only way a Shadow ever stayed down. "Mass, you're the lookout. Take position here, monitor their movements, and find us an exit path. Zig, you're with me. Everyone clear on what the mission is?"

"Quinn VanWarren," Owens answered.

Vega gave a tight nod. "Exactly. Don't get distracted. This is strictly snatch and grab. But if you happen to get a chance to hobble them some more, do it. Just try not to get shot, yeah?"

Her team *woof*ed at her in response.

"Let's go."

Mass turned on the engine and flinched when lightning zapped along the underside of the toy buggy. They set off down the hill in a straight line since there was no road to follow. The terrain was smooth enough that one wasn't necessary. At their careful, crawling pace, they would reach the south gate in approximately fifteen minutes.

Vega climbed over her seat and squeezed past Zig and Catton to the storage hold. She and Catton were the only ones still in civvies. The rest had already changed into uniforms. Vega would need to relinquish her knives to Mass for the initial entry, but the wrist unit concealed beneath her long sleeve would suffice until she got them back.

Catton climbed over the back seat after her. He had to tuck his head sideways in the cramped space. "You solid?"

"I know what I have to do."

"Ain't what I asked you."

Vega opened one of the med kits they'd pilfered from the Hawk cache. It contained two sedative patches that would knock them out immediately on contact and stop working as soon as they were removed. She handed one to Catton. "The mission is Quinn."

"And if you fall behind?"

"Then you leave me behind. Get Quinn to the SU. They'll take over from there."

Hopefully.

They didn't seem like the types to hold grudges. And, now that Vega had shuffled the shit out of the VanWarren accounts, all of the Shadow payments would naturally stop. As much a show of good faith as she could manage, circumstances being what they were. And if the Shadows decided to take it up with the VanWarrens, well, that was their problem.

Laura had helped Vega put escape plans in place for the kids. They could take refuge with her and various SU centers for what would be referred to as work-study programs. The grownups were on their own.

Catton stared her down like he expected her to break. Then he shook his head and took the patch. "You know what the most dangerous thing is in a warzone?"

"A commander with a gun and a map?"

"A soldier who doesn't care whether she lives or dies."

"Noted."

"I'm serious, Vee. You want to go down swinging, that's on you. But we're risking our lives here, too. I need to know you're not planning to make us go down with you."

"You volunteered to storm a Shadow outpost with me, and ten minutes out, you're getting cold feet?"

"I know what I signed up for."

"Then what are we talking about?"

Catton tugged on his collar to bare the side of his neck. "You go down, we leave you there. On your order. Right?"

"Right," she bit out. "The mission is Quinn."

"And if he goes rogue over you?"

Vega gritted her teeth. "You tell him whatever you have to, to get him out."

"Coming within scanner range," Owens called back. "Time to say good night."

"Roger," Vega acknowledged. "Try not to fuck things up before you wake me."

She held out her fist for Catton to bump with his own, and once he did, they both slapped the sedative patch onto their necks. Vega barely registered her hand dropping back into her lap before it took effect.

M's personal security feed alerted him to a Hound approaching his quarters. Time was up.

M straightened his uniform and met the Hound at the door so he wouldn't have to endure the indignity of being outright summoned to do his job.

At least it wasn't Hui. M nodded to the woman and passed her without pause on his way to Quinn. She followed him to where the main hallway split off toward the holding cells and waited there. Close enough to see what he was up to, but far enough not to get caught in any physical altercation. Coward. Another of Hui's incompetent pissant ilk. M didn't spare her another thought.

Quinn was laid out on his mattress, conscious but groggy and disoriented, thanks to the chemical cocktail pumping through the atmosphere. It didn't affect Shadows, so M didn't bother with a breathing filter. "Hey, cuz. How's it going?"

Quinn weakly raised his head and blinked unseeing eyes at him. "Mmmm'syou'gain."

"Yeah, I missed you, too." He brought up the environmental controls and turned off the sedative gas. It would take a few minutes to filter out of Quinn's system. Long enough for M to get him into the chair. If he even managed to get his heavy ass out of this room. "Come on, big guy. Time for your treatment. If you're good, I'll get you a lollipop after."

Quinn huffed a sigh and let his head drop, trying to roll to his back, but his back was to the wall. "Go'way."

"Love to. Can't. Now come on." M grabbed hold of Quinn's arm and gave an experimental tug. Quinn was a massive slab of solid muscle which, even at his impressive weight, would have been doable, but not when he was as floppy as a dead fish. M managed to drag him halfway across the cell before he decided there were better ways to handle this. "Hound, get in here!"

He waited for the woman to unstick her feet from the floor. It took pathetically long. When she appeared in the doorway, she had one hand on her sidearm and the other braced on the wall outside.

M rolled his eyes. "Grab his arm and help me get him up."

"We have levchairs for this sort of—"

"Grab his fucking arm, Hound!"

The barked command snapped her spine straight and got her moving. By the time she woke up and realized he had no authority to order her around, she already had Quinn's arm slung around her shoulders and she was too committed to back out.

They hauled him up between them and carried his dead weight out of the cell. His feet dragged across the floor the whole way to medbay, far enough to pass several roaming Hounds, none of whom offered to help. M's back began to burn, and he wasn't above letting the woman take more of Quinn's weight for the final stretch to the chair.

When they dropped him into it, the entire mechanism rattled and groaned. M waited for it to snap apart, but it didn't.

And now there was no going back.

The Hound was out the door before Quinn's ass had fully settled in the seat, and the medic already had all his scanners and instruments prepped to go.

Quinn started coming around during the initial workup. He blinked open eyes that were still trying to roll back in his head, and the scanners beeped with an elevated blood pressure alert as he realized he wasn't in an all-white cell anymore. He made a valiant effort to shake it off, even tried to raise his hand, but it was already strapped down tight, as were his legs.

M checked his wrist unit. None of his alarms had been tripped.

The medic completed the scan and turned his back on them to calibrate the treatment.

"I'm sorry, Quinn," M murmured, low enough that only the big guy would hear it over his incoherent mumbling. "I really thought she'd make it in time."

"System's ready," the medic announced, and M stepped away.

Quinn had grown silent, staring at the ceiling as his eyes darted wildly. A side effect of the sedative. He managed to turn his head to squint at M, opened his mouth to say something.

But he never got the chance as the medic shoved a dental guard onto his teeth and turned his head to face forward again, strapping it down for good measure.

For all the mechanical bulk of the chair, the device that turned a soldier's brain into mush was thin and delicate. A narrow white band that settled at the temples, where the skull was thinnest and easiest to penetrate.

"Scanners—check."

M allowed himself a single unhappy mouth twitch before he schooled his face into a mask of indifference.

"Calibration complete."

The room dimmed, and the medscreen switched over to the EMC controls. M read through the specs and gritted his teeth. The medic had ramped up both sides of the treatment, maxing out the charge and doubling the potency of the usual chemical blend. "Bit excessive, isn't it?"

"Given his unusual biology, we can't predict the efficacy of a standard treatment. I like to err on the side of caution."

"You're not worried about frying his brains right out of his skull?"

The medic gave him an incredulous look. "Why would I be?"

Why, indeed? It wasn't like Quinn was important or anything. Just another muscle-bound body to slot into the ranks. Expendable, and easily replaceable.

"Ready on three."

M checked his wrist unit again.

"Two."

Quinn made a sound like he wanted to speak around the mouthpiece. He was starting to come around, writhing in the seat, limbs twitching as he flexed those big muscles to break free.

The chair emitted a deep groan. Synthetic fibers began to tear in a soft, subdued crackle…

"One."

53

Shouting. Flashing lights.

The smell of charred flesh.

Vega curled up from the floor to utter chaos, and Mass standing over her, firing down the hallway. "The hell happened?"

"We're fucked up the ass, that's what happened. Get up!" Keeping his gaze trained down the barrel of his weapon, he grabbed onto her arm and yanked, forcing her to her feet. She snatched a fallen Shadow's sidearm on the way.

The hallway floor was littered with them. Eight soldiers were dead, but at least three were shooting at them from around the corner. The noise was much louder in her right ear and she realized she was hearing an echo of the same situation somewhere else in the outpost. Owens and Catton making their way to the generator.

"Guess we didn't get our sixty seconds."

"We didn't get ten. They opened fire soon as the fucking door closed behind us. Lucky Owens had his shield up. Percussion pulse took out most of them long enough for Zig to wake Catton and clear the way for them."

"Where's Zig?"

Mass shot a few more pulses, dropping one of the Shadows before he ducked back around the corner. "He's over there."

Vega bit down on the inside of her cheek. In his uniform, Zig was indistinguishable from the other Shadows laid out along the hallway. She recognized him by the shattered wrist unit hanging off his left arm. Someone had attempted to pry it off him and dislocated his elbow in the process. The arm was bent up behind his back, his fingers covering the still-smoking hole between his shoulder blades.

"He got Catton and Owens through the gauntlet and took three of the bastards with him."

Fuck! "Alarms?"

"Haven't heard any yet."

Through her com, Catton shouted something, and then she heard a crash.

"Clear!" Owens barked. They'd made it to the generator.

Vega spotted her knife sheaths wrapped around Massimino's leg. She took them from him and armed up, blinking her left eye in a familiar pattern to bring up a heat map in her lens. A squint zoomed it out to a larger schematic of the outpost, fifty yards out.

Four Shadows were pinning them down, and six more were converging on their location. Another dozen were heading the other way toward Catton and Owens. If they didn't move, they were dead. "What's that heat spike I'm picking up?" It was out of range, but the aura it threw off was large enough to bleed over. And it was nowhere near the generator.

"That's medbay," Catton responded. They would be closer to it and able to pick up more details.

She paused with the last knife brace halfway strapped to her arm.

"The chair," Mass said.

Someone was about to get their brains fried. *Quinn.*

"Owens!"

"Workin' on it!"

"Work faster." To Mass, she said, "Let's move." Handing over the pilfered weapon, she pulled up her sleeve to prep her shield, then nodded to him.

He nodded back, a gun in each hand, and stepped out from behind the corner, laying down cover fire. "Go!"

Vega ducked under his arms. Shield up, knife in hand, she ran, jumping over bodies to reach the blind corner. Soldiers on both sides of the hallway leaned out to return fire. Vega hunched lower behind her shield to give Mass a clean shot over her head.

Mass was close enough for her to hear him breathing at her back. But her shield wouldn't cover them both. He took down one Hound on the right, forcing the other to retreat.

Shifting position, Vega threw her knife at that corner. The hilt struck the wall with enough force to bounce off at an angle and impale a left-side Hound through the neck.

Vega took his last plasma blast with her shield, then ran at the left wall and launched off it. Second knife in hand, she leaped at the Shadow hiding around the right corner, bearing him to the ground, her blade in his chest. She twisted it for good measure.

Heat seared her face as a shot scorched a hole in the wall beside her head. Debris struck her cheek and neck, drawing blood. By the time she'd grabbed the dead Shadow's weapon and twisted around to take out the shooter, Mass had already done it. He discarded one of the guns to bring up his shield, covering that side of the hallway from the two Shadows coming up on them.

The ten yards they'd gained put medbay on Vega's lens map. Heat spike still growing. The sensor on her wrist unit indicated it would max out soon. "Owens…"

Swearing in her com.

Three Shadows coming at her, weapons drawn.

Vega backed up toward Mass. He had four more coming from his side. They were about to be pinned, and their shields were only designed to hold up for about five to ten minutes.

"Owens!"

"Down!" Mass barked.

Vega dropped as something sailed over her head.

She recognized the shape of an extra wrist unit. The Hounds coming at them didn't. One of them fired at it. Perfect aim—it set the device off with an explosion that blew all of them off their feet.

Vega slammed into Mass on her way down, her head whipping back and digging the edges of her neck brace into her flesh. Skin tore, her spine strained, and a zinging pain shot down her back into her right leg.

Ears ringing, it took her too many precious seconds to drag herself back up. Lights danced in her field of vision, the edges blacking out as she pushed to her feet.

If the outpost hadn't known they were under attack before, they sure as shit did now. Her lens showed fifteen more heat signatures rushing at them from both sides.

Mass groaned, getting back to his feet. He had blood coming out of his nose and ears; he spat more of it as he pulled her knife from the Shadow's neck and handed it back to her. "You ready for more?"

Vega bared her teeth in a snarl.

He gave her a bloodied grin in return. "Yo, Owens. Could use a hand here."

"Ask and ye shall receive," came the answer.

"Incoming," Vega warned, tracking the first five heat signatures about to turn the far corner as she holstered her weapon and retrieved her second knife.

She shifted her weight onto her good leg for balance, ready to launch. Medbay was in that direction. That was her path to Quinn they were blocking.

Not for long.

Her shield gave out. She didn't care. A knife in each hand, she grounded down into the ball of her foot, breathing through the crawling numbness in her leg.

Pounding footsteps approached the blind corner. The five soon-to-be-dead Hounds hurtled straight for her. No shields, no helmets, weapons still in their hip holsters.

They pulled up short when they saw her running at them full-sprint.

Then the ground shuddered beneath her feet, and the lights went out.

Quinn's mind was slow to shake the sedative. He was aware of every-thing happening around him and to him, but he was losing the battle to stay conscious. One moment, he was looking at M standing off to the side, the next his eyes rolled back in his head, and he was in the middle of a Mai jungle, wading through quicksand that dragged him deeper with every inch he gained toward the edge.

"Ready on three," a strange voice warbled.

The quicksand's grip tugged on his arms, harder and harder the more he strained to break free.

"Two."

He felt fibers start giving way, felt the quicksand groan around him as the chair they'd strapped him into began to bend to his strength.

"One."

Quinn's eyes shot wide open as the medic tapped a command on his screen to initiate his treatment.

And then everything went dark.

His eyes went blind as the world plunged into silence.

But it only lasted a few seconds before he registered sounds around him.

"*Breach!*" someone shouted far away, and then a dim red light switched on overhead, bathing the room in blood.

The medic scrambled at the controls, but his equipment was dark and unresponsive.

Quinn bore down and flexed his left arm. More fibers tore. The mechanical groan became a screech. With a snap, the entire armrest came loose, and Quinn's arm shot up.

He took the dental guard out of his mouth, then yanked the delicate white band off and ripped through the strap that held his head immobile.

By the time he tore his right arm free, the medic was screaming.

By the time he broke the restraints on his legs, the little man in a lab coat had pissed himself.

Quinn shot out of the chair and snatched the medic by the throat.

You can probably break the restraints like they're nothing, kill the medic, and trash the shit out of the room with his lifeless corpse.

What a great idea.

The medic's neck broke with the first swing. But his body stayed intact long enough to smash everything breakable on that side of the room. Glass screens shattered. Sparks flared out of electronic equipment and set the medic's lab coat on fire.

Quinn spun around and hurled the broken corpse across to the other side.

It cost him. His knees buckled and he went down, head spinning, back into quicksand. It was up to his neck now, and he was exhausted, struggling against its pull.

Burning chemicals stung his nose, glass shards dug into his hands and shins. Head lolling, he stared at the dark red floor, fighting to stay conscious.

Hands grabbed at him.

Quinn flung out his arm to shake them off. The swing was too weak to do much damage, but it worked well enough.

For a few seconds.

"Stay with me, cousin."

He knew that voice. Blinking through the red haze, Quinn recognized the blurred face attached to the hands gripping him by the arm. "Zach," he managed to say.

The man's face shifted into a grin. "I do like that name." It was gone too quickly, and Quinn couldn't focus his gaze well enough to be sure. He did pick up on the stone-cold command in the man's voice when he said, "Get up."

Quinn…tried. He pushed up and managed to get one foot planted. But when he tried to stand, his knee buckled and he slammed into the man, smashing him against the wall. He heard a grunt; felt the delicate pop of a bone breaking.

The man didn't let up. "We need to move." He tucked himself under Quinn's arm and hauled him upright, dragging him toward the door.

The world was dark red everywhere he looked. Deep shadows obscured everything but the biggest shapes around, and even those were too blurry, moving too quickly for Quinn to identify them beyond a vague sense that they *shouldn't* be moving at all.

"Where'r we goin'?"

"Where does the sun set, Quinn?"

His free shoulder slammed into a doorframe as they barreled through it. Quinn shook his head and squinted. The world had finally stopped spinning, but he still couldn't get his eyes to work all the way right.

"West," Zach answered himself, ducking behind an open door as a group of soldiers ran past them. Dark blobs with shiny helmets reflecting red light straight into Quinn's brain.

Noises filtered through the ringing in his ears. Shouting and explosions. He couldn't tell whether the ground shook or if that was still part of the sedative's side effects, but Quinn leaned harder against the wall to keep his feet under him.

"West," Zach repeated, and bright lights came on overhead.

They shut off almost instantly, and now the reds flared and dimmed like an erratic heartbeat.

Zach looked out from behind their door, then yanked Quinn away from the wall. "You gotta help me out here, buddy. I can't carry you the whole way."

Quinn rubbed some feeling back into his face, bit the inside of his cheek to ground himself. It helped enough that, by the time they rounded the corner into a long hallway, he could walk on his own, just not in a straight line.

Zach kept him moving forward through the din of blaring alarms and smoke pouring in from somewhere else. It tasted corrosive.

"Almost there. Come on."

They were coming up on an intersection and from the way Zach shoved his whole weight against Quinn, he figured they were supposed to turn left.

But then the lights flared again, and when they dimmed, a figure emerged from the smoke on the right in a limping march. Covered in dust and gore. Long hair braided in a rope. Blood on her face and murder in her eyes.

Quinn almost went to his knees again at the sight of her. "Vega."

But she didn't spare him a single glance, wholly intent on his guide. "Target acquired," she said in the scariest tone he'd ever heard from her.

Zach pushed away from Quinn—or rather pushed Quinn into the wall to free himself as he said, "Hey, Vega."

Quinn caught a glint of metal right before it buried in Zach's gut, cutting off his greeting with a grunt.

"Vega!"

She didn't acknowledge him for a second, staring straight into Zach's face as he grinned at her. "Are you trying to turn me on?"

The knife twisted.

"Vega, stop!"

Only when Zach's legs started to give out from under him did she step back, leaving her knife behind.

Zach collapsed on the floor, his back against the wall. He clutched at the wound in his gut, but didn't pull out the knife. A wet chuckle rattled from his chest. "I knew you liked me."

Vega turned her back on him and took his place against Quinn's side, pulling him away from the wall.

"Sunset," Zach called after them.

Vega didn't take them the way she'd come. Without a word, she took the left hallway where Zach had been steering them earlier. "Are you hurt?" she asked.

"Dizzy. He was getting me out."

"That's why he's still breathing."

"We need to go back—"

"Keep walking." She picked up her pace, forcing him to keep up or drag her down with him.

"Blood," he said, looking down at what little he could see of her in the red gloom.

"Yep."

Another explosion rocked the ground beneath his feet. Definitely not a hallucination this time. Vega veered off course and they stumbled into a small, dark utility closet. She braced him against a rack of shelves. One bloodied hand flat against his chest to keep him steady, she looked out into the hallway. "Sound off."

Quinn figured she was talking to someone else.

"Head to the transport bay. We'll meet you there."

When she turned back to him, it was with heel-snapping momentum that sent her shifting a few unsteady inches to the side. She didn't seem to notice, cupping his face to make him look at her. "You good?"

Balance restored, vision back to normal. But a deep lethargy still made his spine want to curl. He let it, leaning over to touch his forehead to Vega's. "Love you, wife." He sounded drunk. Quinn didn't care. He needed to say it. Needed her to know, in case they didn't make it out. "Don't leave me."

"Only in a body bag," she said, pressing a too-brief kiss to his mouth.

Then they were on the move again.

Still too many fucking Shadows. Owens' little pranks had sent them into a tailspin, but they were far from neutralized. Vega kept Quinn moving toward the transport bay, splitting her focus between the path before them and the hallway behind them. Every time she twisted to check their six, she felt the neck brace bite. The tingling in her right leg was back, her limp more pronounced than it had been after surgery.

It had nearly cost her everything several times already.

"One more!" Owens barked in her com.

"Abort," Mass snapped back. *"You did enough. Haul your asses out."*

Owens had more than done it. He hadn't just taken out the primary generator. Whatever clever trick he'd come up with, it had caused a chain reaction within the whole system. Two of the auxiliary backups had already exploded, keeping the Shadows literally in the dark.

"Southside clear," Mass reported. He'd fallen behind to head off the stragglers. *"Twenty yards behind you, Vee."*

Good. She couldn't support Quinn on her own for much longer.

"Registering eight heat signatures in the transport bay," Catton informed her. *"Those boys haven't moved the whole time. You're gonna need a distraction."*

"Negative. Keep moving. Owens, abort—*now*."

They'd made up enough ground for their wrist units to show in the 3D schematic hovering in her left field of vision. Mass was closest.

Owens and Catton swept in from an eastern corridor, then detoured way the fuck off course. *"Just one more,"* Owens was saying. His voice sounded strained.

"Catton, you got four Hounds on your six. Abort!"

There was a crash in her right ear, then three of the heat signatures following her men faded out. Catton shouted something unintelligible, his heat signature clashing with the remaining Shadow.

Owens kept going. Right off her virtual map and out of range again. *"We need to disable them. Only way we're getting out of this."*

She couldn't see where he was headed; couldn't predict what he might be walking into. Darkness wouldn't keep the Shadows distracted for very long, and the only advantage Owens had was that he was wearing the same uniform as the rest of them.

But Catton was not. Soon as the Shadows saw them together, they attacked. After all that huffing and puffing about her state of mind, Catton was doing exactly what he'd warned her against: going off-script.

To cover Owens. So he could get all of them out of there.

"Owens—"

"Get us a ride," he said. *"Then you can pick us up on the way."*

Catton groaned out a curse. *"Five minutes. If we go silent, leave."*

"The fuck that's happening!" Mass snapped, echoing her thoughts so loudly she heard him from several yards behind her, and catching up fast.

Vega was so focused on the northern part of the facility, the entire schematic map in her vision skewed away from her immediate surroundings, glitching as it attempted to create an image her sensor was too far to read. All it managed was to zoom in on the northern boundary, which kept shifting in the wrong direction the farther she and Quinn hobbled away from it.

But she had to see. She had to know what the fuck was happening over there. Owens and Catton had gone silent. No more sounds coming through from them, which meant they weren't hearing her, either.

"Five minutes," she gritted out, grateful Quinn wasn't asking any questions. She wouldn't know what to tell him.

Mass rounded the corner behind them, shouting at her.

His warning came too late.

A few feet ahead, one of the doors opened right into her path. A Shadow came charging at Vega through the virtual map, bowling her over and away from Quinn. Her back slammed into the floor, a snarling face right above hers, and it was all she could do to keep him at arm's length.

There was shouting nearby; sounds of fighting somewhere off to her right where she couldn't twist to look. The Hound roared in her face, showering her with spittle as he forced the tip of his knife toward her throat. It was half an inch from her skin.

And then it was gone. And so was the Shadow.

Quinn had snatched him by the leg and swung him in an arc over his head, slamming him with all of his might into the floor. The soldier's body shattered on impact.

"Holy shit," Mass whispered. Now that her focus had shifted by necessity, the virtual map in her left eye snapped back to her part of the building, showing his heat signature where he'd come to a stop ten feet behind her. And there he stayed, likely doing the same thing Vega was: trying to count the bodies by the bits of them scattered on the ground and, in a few cases, embedded in the walls.

Vega levered herself up to sit, swallowing back the bile rising in her throat.

Covered in gore, Quinn gripped her under the arms and lifted her off the ground and off her feet until they were nose to nose. "Fuck your body bag."

He set her back on her feet but gripped her fractured hand—her whole hand, up to the wrist—to tug her back into motion.

Mass caught up to them on Quinn's other side and met her gaze behind his back. "Did you know he could do that?"

"I do now."

But right now, they had much bigger problems.

By her admittedly unreliable count, five minutes had come and gone.

And her com was still silent.

Smart call to take out the generator.

But whose dumbass idea had it been to split up?

M watched the faint blue dots of Vega's infiltration team glide across his field of vision. Half one way, half the other. What was the play here? They'd already hobbled the outpost. Security feeds were down. Environmental controls were shot to shit. Shadows caught off guard were literally running into the fucking walls, scrambling to get their shit together. What more was there to do?

Ah.

Central command. Someone was going rogue to take out the last auxiliary generator and shut down emergency coms. Someone clearly more suicidal than the rest of them.

Too bad it wouldn't matter. The distress call had already been sent. The transmission delay would give their team a few extra minutes to get out, but a backup force was probably already en route, which meant the detour was a pointless waste of time they didn't have.

M doubted Vega had authorized it. She didn't seem like the type to leave a man behind.

He winced, shifting against the wall. Every breath he took scraped the edges of his broken rib together. That's what happened when a two-ton mammoth accidentally flattened someone against a wall—bones popped like toothpicks.

Still better than the searing agony of stomach acid leaking into his gut around Vega's blade.

Dear, sweet Vega. More class in her little pinky than her entire clan of in-laws had in their combined, overbred DNA. He'd miss her.

"Oh my, how the mighty have fallen."

Funny that should have been his opening line. M blinked through the virtual dots to look at Hui crouching before him with a shit-eating grin on his face. "Didn't anyone warn you not to grimace or your face will freeze that way?"

"What, this?" Hui smiled wider. "I'm just enjoying watching you bleed out, *Hawk*." His face was starting to blur in the darkness. Probably not a good sign. "You knew they would be coming here, didn't you?"

M attempted a shrug and instantly regretted it. "Seemed like a logical conclusion, considering where and how I acquired my target."

Hui hummed his agreement. "Nice touch, getting us all to focus on our PT in the gym and away from our most effective weapons."

"Never told you to leave your sidearm under your pillow."

"I should drag you before Hughes myself so I can watch him finish what your traitorous little friend started. Oh, I really want to see that."

Despite the pain, M felt like smiling back. "So what'll be your excuse this time?"

"Say what?"

"One hundred and fifty Shadows inside this fully-operational outpost, Hound. With you in charge. How in the ever-loving fuck did you manage to let a handful of defected soldiers bring it crashing down around you *and* steal a valuable asset in the process?"

A painfully deep breath brought a bit more oxygen to M's brain. It cleared his vision for a moment so he could see Hui's grin become a snarl. His chubby-cheeked face couldn't handle that level of ferocity. He looked like a child throwing a tantrum.

Accurate.

"I'll just tell him the truth. You've been sabotaging us from the moment you stepped through the door. You sent our men to their deaths, let the enemy arm themselves with Hawk equipment, and then led the prisoner out of our medbay, straight into their arms. Funny, how they didn't seem to appreciate your efforts. Left you behind to take the fall for them."

"The hell are you talking about? I went down trying to save your pathetic life." He sighed. More air. He needed more air. "Just a shame I wasn't fast enough."

Hui frowned. "What?"

M clenched his teeth and surged up from his slouch, yanking Vega's blade out of his gut. Unlike her, he aimed it much higher. Directly into Hui's chest. Four quick jabs perforated his heart before the incompetent blowhard registered what was happening.

He wasn't smiling anymore. All big, round eyes and gaping mouth. Maybe he'd forgotten how to.

Well, M had warned him, after all.

Grabbing the Hound by the throat to hold him steady, M slashed the knife through those chubby cheeks, etching a permanent grin onto his face. Shame the pissant died before he finished.

M let the Hound's body drop as his own sagged back against the wall.

Losing too much blood. And stomach acid. Should probably do something about that. So he reinserted the knife back into his wound and promptly passed out.

56

"Catton. Owens. Come in."

Silence answered her.

Vega met eyes with Mass. He didn't have an easy answer for her either. Her mission. Her call. And her orders had been clear. Quinn was the priority.

Her wrist unit sensor range now reached into the transport bay. Six of the eight heat signatures had split off to head north, leaving two to guard the vehicles. Vega shoved Quinn flat against a shadowed part of the wall as those six crossed the corridor intersection some fifteen yards ahead. They were in too much of a hurry to notice three intruders in the red gloom, shouting into their coms and not getting any more of a response than Vega had over hers.

Owens must have done it. He'd taken down their coms. Which meant the only way anyone would find them now was if they physically came looking for them. That put Vega and her team two steps ahead.

But it still left them separated, with their only way out being guarded by two Shadows with access to an entire transport bay of fully armed assault vehicles.

Vega checked her wrist unit tools. The shield was depleted. The percussion pulse would need another half-hour to recharge, and the heat-seeking throwing star was gone. That left her with her knives and the meager advantage of sensors. In other words, fuckall.

She made sure the Shadows were well clear of them before she tugged Quinn back into motion toward the intersection, Mass covering their rear. "Transport bay to the south of us," she said for Quinn's benefit, setting their course as she tapped her ear and snapped, "Owens!"

At the corner, Quinn stopped in his tracks, arresting her momentum right along with him. He was staring straight down the hallway they were in. "West," he said.

"Yeah, that's west," Mass confirmed, then pointed down the branch-off. "Transport bay is that way."

He went around them to keep going, but Quinn grabbed the back of his collar to stop him, too. "No." Hauling the Hound back, he pushed him ahead and pulled Vega after him, keeping their course straight—away from the transport bay.

Vega tugged against his hold. "Quinn! We need to go that way."

"Where does the sun set?" he countered.

Mass cursed up a long, creative streak but didn't make a move against the man who'd obliterated at least two trained Shadows with his bare hands less than five minutes ago.

"West," Quinn insisted. "We go west."

Vega clenched her molars until her jaw muscles twitched. "Because the Hawk said so?"

Quinn shrugged a big shoulder. "He's my cousin, why would he lead me wrong?"

"That was a joke, right?"

He grinned at her and winked.

"Vee, are you seeing what I'm seeing?"

"Pretend I'm not." She wasn't picking up any heat signatures, other than the six heading away from them, and the two holding steady in the transport bay. But the hallway curved slightly up ahead and about twenty-five yards beyond that, the map went apeshit. A thick wall of sparking, flashing static.

"Storm hasn't cleared," Mass said. "It's interfering with the sensors. But look up."

Up? Vega nudged the virtual map a few degrees higher. In the sea of static, a solid shell carved out a flat, egg-shaped object hovering above the level of the compound roof.

"Son of a bitch."

"What is it?" Quinn asked as they rounded the curve.

"Hover," Mass told him and picked up speed, forcing Quinn to release him. "Unguarded. Probably concealed."

Quinn raised an I-told-you-so eyebrow at her.

Vega rolled her eyes. "Hundred different ways this could be a trap."

Mass had his weapon at the ready as he approached the exterior door. The small window flashed with the lightning still raging outside.

Vega wiped her face and tapped her com again. "Catton, Owens, sound off."

Mass watched her for an update. He had the same com; he heard the same silence.

"Repeat: sound off."

Nothing.

"Could be somewhere shielded," Mass offered weakly. "We would have heard something if they went down."

"Catton. Owens. Come on, guys, someone answer me."

The silence stretched on.

"Vee, we gotta go," Mass said.

Fuck.

She didn't meet Quinn's gaze; couldn't stomach it. This was her fault. Her mission. Her failure.

But it wasn't finished.

"Can you access the hover controls from here?" She could. Her wrist unit was already attempting to link up with the hover, which meant Mass' was, too. Only one of them could sync up, and it had to be Mass.

He held up a finger, his eyes darting as he navigated the virtual view in his lens. Then he nodded to confirm the sync.

Vega's lens flashed a FAIL, then removed the hover options from her view. She nodded back. "Get it low enough to open the hatch."

"Roger."

Quinn came up behind her, not touching, but close enough for her to feel his warmth. How easy it would be to melt into him and let the rest of the world fade.

It killed her to know he'd see this next part as a betrayal.

But she couldn't leave her men—her *friends*—behind.

Outside, the hover descended as close to the building as it could get. Its cloaking technology rendered it invisible to the naked eye under normal circumstances. With the electrical storm still active, the hover became a lightning rod. A flurry of bolts crackled and buzzed as they connected with the hull's underside, revealing its outline.

The cloak fractured as the hatch opened, a gangway hinging and extending out at a low angle. It didn't touch down all the way, but it held steady enough, the insulated surface clear and safe to walk on.

"Go!" Vega snapped, shoving into the door to open it.

Mass ran out, scoping the perimeter along the way to ensure it was clear. Small branches of lightning snapped at his feet and calves, but he kept going until he reached the edge of the gangway, hovering at chest level. With a running start, he hauled himself up easily.

His voice came through to her right ear. *"Hover is clear. Fully charged and ready to fly. Let's go!"* He held out his hand, beckoning.

Okay, fine. So maybe the Hawk hadn't fucked them over.

That didn't mean she trusted him. Whatever long game he was playing was his business. But he'd dragged Quinn into it. Vega would not forget that. Or forgive.

"Go," she repeated, shoving Quinn out the door.

He didn't hesitate, running headlong for Mass. Seconds to get himself up. Mass immediately shoved him along inside, and he went, trusting that Vega would be right on his heels.

Mass knew better. *"Hover's sensors have a longer range. Sending you a full map of the outpost and the boys' last known location. There are utility passageways all over the place. If they're anywhere, they'll be in there."*

"Copy."

Mass ran up the gangway, disappearing into the dark cargo hold.

Vega waited for the hatch to close and the hover to rise up out of range.

Instead, Mass returned to throw something at her.

She only reached far enough out the door to catch the pack that came flying at her, but it was enough for a bolt of lightning to snap at her metal wrist brace. Vega fumbled the pack as her arm muscles seized up to her shoulder.

Whose fucking idea had it been to exchange her mesh brace for a metal one?

Oh, yeah. Hers.

Luckily, her wrist unit was on the other arm.

Retrieving the pack, she saluted Mass and ducked inside. Through the window, she watched the gangway start to close as Quinn came back. He saw the closed outpost door, made to dive out of the hover, but the hatch slid shut before he could.

Then, the hover rose into the air again and disappeared from her line of sight.

"You better haul ass," Mass warned through the com to a chorus of bangs, crashes, and curses in the background. *"Your pet juggernaut is gonna tear this thing apart before we can take off."*

"Keep him busy," she said, working out the cramps in her arm.

The pack Mass had tossed her was a standard emergency escape kit for when a hover went down on mission. She left behind everything except the brace of side arms and three pulse grenades that would definitely come in handy.

"I'm patching you into the hover coms—Don't touch that!" More crashing noises, and then her audio feed became louder and more echoed. *"Got your twenty on-screen—Say hello to your wifey, big guy."*

"Vega! What the fuck?"

Yeah, he was pissed. "I need to get my team."

"You need to get out of there."

"Yep." With the hover's systems at her disposal, Vega was able to zoom out on the whole compound, aboveground and below. There was an entire complex of tunnels and chambers beneath the surface, with a whole lot of heat signatures moving around. Impossible to tell whether they were Shadows or not, but they weren't her problem. Just an easy target to take out once she and her team were safely onboard the hover.

Vega took off toward the spot where Catton and Owens had disappeared. Not far from there, her map showed a chamber about half the size of the transport bay, and too many heat signatures to count. Those would definitely be Shadows. Either on duty, or summoned to stand guard.

No sign of her team. No record of com failure.

They had to be somewhere shielded.

She tuned out Mass and Quinn's shouting match and traced several paths through the outpost, marking convenient exits, hiding places, and potential death traps. Not a lot of the former. Too many of the latter.

Up ahead, a door-sized panel built into the wall marked a utility station. The outpost was too big to transport supplies and equipment by hand. Instead, right beneath the floor, sandwiched between the two levels, was a web of maglev tracks that conveyed carts full of materials throughout the place at speeds that would splatter any human who happened to step into one's path. At each station, the carts pushed the corresponding cargo up or down to its location for delivery.

With the power grid disrupted, the maglev track was disabled, and the passages would be safe and clear as long as she didn't run into a stalled cart. Better, it was shielded, which meant she would be invisible to anyone scanning for her location.

Vega looked back to make sure she hadn't tracked any blood, then sprinted for the station. She shoved the panel inward the two inches it would go, then attempted to slide it sideways into the wall to get it open. It budged all of half an inch, her hands slipping over the surface without any traction. She needed to open a big enough crack to get her fingers in there, but the damn door was at least two hundred pounds of solid metal, and not intended to be moved manually.

She wiped her hands on her thighs and tried again, putting all of her remaining strength into it. One inch. She just needed one inch—

The door moved, sliding open so quickly Vega jumped back on pure instinct, pulling her weapon on whoever was on the other side, her finger already squeezing the trigger.

The plasma blast flared through the pitch-black space, briefly illuminating a familiar pink shirt before it melted a ten-inch circle of the inner wall into a red-hot target over Catton's hunched shoulders.

Catton froze, peeking up at her, then straightened with a glare. He was waist deep in the recessed space, the only reason why his head was still intact. Not that he seemed to appreciate it. "Your watch broke or something, Ortiz?"

She raised her gun again. "You want a fresh one, asshole?"

In her right ear, Mass snapped, *"Is that Catton?"*

The Hound in question shook his head at her as he pulled himself out of the hole. As soon as his upper body cleared the doorway, Vega's lens picked up his location and com. "Alive," he said, but he wasn't putting his full weight on his left leg. Reaching back in, he helped haul Owens out after him. "Limping, but alive."

Vega's stomach dropped. Owens' right side was burned from the top of his head all the way down his arm. Not bad enough to cost him an eye or an ear, but enough that he would need treatment STAT. "What the fuck happened?" she demanded, holstering her weapon to help him up.

"Minor miscalculation," Owens said. "We gotta move. They're deaf and blind for now, but they'll be coming to rout us any minute. And I think they called for reinforcements before I took out their coms."

"Sure did," Mass confirmed. *"Just picked up the response. We've got incoming in thirty."*

Vega braced Owens on one side and took the lead back the way she'd come, Catton following behind. "On our way," she told Mass. "Prep the weapons. Target the com center and transport bay. No loose ends." With any luck, those two strategic hits would be enough to cripple them. At the very least, it would keep them busy long enough for her team to make a clean escape.

"Movement in the transport bay," Catton warned.

"I see it. Take Owens. I'll cover."

She could hear the hover lowering outside, drawing the storm in a flurry.

"This is gonna hurt," Owens said as the door opened, but they didn't pause for a beat, hobbling out toward the hatch already opening for them. With Mass at the controls, it was Quinn who reached down to haul both men up onto the platform.

And Vega still hadn't crossed the threshold.

There was too much lightning. If she stepped outside the insulated building, she'd be a walking lightning rod. She could take the pain, but if the spinal bypass couldn't handle the charge, she'd end up worse than dead.

The map in her lens flashed with movement. Two heat signatures were approaching fast from the transport bay. Vega pivoted to fire at them before they'd cleared the corner. One went down, but the other managed to duck out of the line of fire.

She pulled out one of the pulse grenades, twisting it active, and hurled it down the corridor. The explosion caught the Hound as he peeked out and knocked him back on his ass.

It wouldn't have killed him. She had to make sure he stayed down.

Vega took all of one step in his direction when a big, bulky arm clamped around her waist, lifting her off her feet. "I really don't like to repeat myself, wife," Quinn growled. Tucking her into his chest, he hunched over her and backed out into the storm.

Vega flinched, her whole body tensing in anticipation of a world of pain but it never came. Not the way she expected. Lightning bit at her dangling feet, but the bulk of its fury was redirected at larger targets—Quinn and the hover.

He tossed her up onto the gangway, where Catton dragged her ass across the rough surface to make room for Quinn to climb onboard.

Then the hatch closed, and the hover raised into the air. The sudden motion knocked Catton off his feet and both of them took a brutal hit as they collided with the airlock.

"*We cleared the blast radius,*" Mass said through the hover's com system. "*Targeting transport bay. Locked on.*"

Vega allowed Quinn to pull her upright. "Fire at will."

Catton was already hobbling toward the cockpit, leaving them behind.

The hover didn't even rock as Mass discharged its weapons. By her estimate, he wouldn't need more than a couple of blasts to level that part of the facility. The explosives inside the vehicles stored there would do the bulk of the work for him.

"*Target destroyed,*" Mass said, then the hover tilted as he turned it toward the next one.

"Zach's still in there," Quinn reminded her. Clearly, he'd built some kind of unhealthy bond with the Hawk.

"*Targeting com center. Locked on. Movement in the compound. They're spreading out.*"

Quinn's eyes pleaded with her.

"*Shadow hover twenty minutes out,*" Owens piped in. "*They're calling out on all frequencies.*"

They were out of time. "Tell them to leave a message," she ordered. "Mass, target the com center *only.*"

"Copy. Locked on."

"He should be well out of range," she assured Quinn. Although, she wouldn't lose sleep over it if the Hawk did get caught in the blast. "And the reinforcements will be coming for him soon." Likely to apprehend him as an accomplice, but Quinn didn't need to know that.

He nodded but didn't look convinced.

Taking the gesture as permission, Vega pulled him into motion again. "Fire at will."

The hover delivered another volley of shots that went unseen, unheard, and unfelt as Vega and Quinn made their way to the cockpit. By the time they got there, the view out the front window was filled with fire and smoke.

"Target destroyed," Mass reported.

Owens was shaking like a leaf beside him, but he didn't pause whatever he was doing at the controls.

"You might wanna strap in," Catton told them, already in his seat, a medkit at his feet. "It's about to get bumpy."

"Got it!" Owens leaned back with an exhausted sigh and muttered, "Frequencies scrambled. Keep her low to the ground and the storm will cloak us. 'long as we can get on a shuttle right away, we should be clear."

"Thank you," Quinn said soberly. "All of you."

No one responded.

They'd done their job. They'd saved a life.

And lost one in the process.

Mass steered the hover to circle the outpost once, a final salute to their fallen friend. "Bye, Zig," Vega whispered.

"Sleep tight, buddy," Mass added.

As one, the Hounds in the shuttle raised a hand to their brow.

Then Mass turned the hover south. "Setting course for the shuttleport. Full speed ahead."

The force of their acceleration slammed Vega back into her seat.

She couldn't turn her head to look at Quinn sitting beside her.

Instead, he took her hand and squeezed, letting her know he was there.

So she'd know she wasn't alone.

57

November 15, 3039 – Glassor City, Planet Daedalus

Quinn got the whole story on the shuttle flight out of Karem Shem—on a private shuttle the SU had apparently provided. It was mostly Catton doing the narrating. He told Quinn all about how Vega had shown up on Laura's doorstep and "scared the shit out of some kids," Eskel's medical treatments, their mission planning, and the "epic clap-back" Vega had delivered to the VanWarren clan on her way to "get her man."

Blow after blow, after emotional blow. Quinn didn't know how he managed to sit through it all without his artificial heart blowing up.

And the whole time, Vega barely spoke.

On recommendation from the medbot, she spent most of the three-day flight on a bed specially made to keep her spine steady. Her body had sustained the bulk of the damage. The new device that now kept her mobile was safe and unaffected. But her injuries were still significant enough that Quinn saw her wince through certain movements when she thought he wasn't looking.

It was pack instinct for all of them to stay in the clinic with her. A bunch of wounded animals sleeping huddled together for safety. Metaphorically speaking. Quinn didn't mind the company. But with every hour they flew, he felt Vega withdrawing more into herself.

Losing Zigmann had hit them all hard, but Quinn felt the weight of it smothering Vega. Zig had come out of hiding for her—they all had—and Quinn could practically see the chorus looping through her thoughts whenever she got that faraway look in her eyes. *No one ever leaves the Shadows—except in a body bag.*

Quinn couldn't make it better, nor was it his place to try. But the reserved and quiet Massimino summed it up pretty well on the last day when their stumbling flow of conversation stalled for a bit too long. "They made us fight wars we never believed in. Zig got to die fighting one that finally mattered. It was a good death. Don't diminish it with guilt. It's not yours to take."

A few hours later, they landed outside of Glassor City and an SU contingent picked them up and took them to their local HQ. They spent the next week there recounting everything in as much detail as they could provide. Medics checked on all of them and got the guys back on their feet. They came to say goodbye before they each went their separate ways.

At last, the branch supervisor called in Quinn and Vega for a discharge interview. She confirmed a few lingering details, gave Vega a comprehensive physical therapy plan, and sent them on their way with a smile and a wave.

They made it as far as the sidewalk outside before Vega stopped in her tracks, looking around as if she didn't know where to go next.

It was summer in this part of the world. The trees were in bloom, sprinkling delicate white petals on the breeze. The day was warm but pleasant, without the oppressive humidity of Ela's tropical clime. The perfect weather for stringing up a hammock and taking a nap in the garden.

Specifically, his garden.

Glassor City was his home now. The first thing he'd bought with his inherited fortune had been a little house that bordered an orchard across a meandering stream in his backyard. It was in the residential district about four miles away. A quick drive or a nice, long walk.

"Are you hungry?" he asked, keeping his tone as casual as he could manage. "There's a good fusion place a couple blocks away I think you might like. We can get take-out on the way home."

This was it. The final crossroads.

Talon was dead, Quinn was safe, his family was taken care of. And Vega had delivered a blow to the Shadows that would take them a while to recover from—if what Zach had told him was true.

Her mission was finished. She could walk away now and never look back if she wanted to, and Quinn would probably never find her again.

By the looks of it, she was thinking the same thing.

The SU had provided them both with new clothes. Vega got stretchy black pants and a tank top with her signature black leather boots. But she'd taken one of his white shirts to put on in place of a light jacket. It was massive on her. The sleeves were rolled several times up to her elbows, and the shoulder seams drooped halfway down her upper arms. She'd tied the hem at her waist to make the outfit a bit more casual, but nothing could ever dull the hard edge of danger she exuded.

Except for the lost, haunted look in her eyes when she blinked up at him and cracked something vital in his soul.

Stay, he wanted to plead, but he'd already done that. The state she was in, if he pushed too much, he'd push her right out the door. Vega was a masterful strategist, an unmatched warrior, but deeper emotions were a foreign concept to her, and after everything they'd been through the last few weeks, she had to be drowning in far too many of them.

If he wanted her to stay, Quinn needed to give her the space to decide on her own.

So he waited. He made himself breathe in the sweet summer breeze and tried to tell himself he could let her walk away if that was what she wanted. Even if it killed him.

Vega's throat worked on a swallow, and then she slowly dipped her chin in a half-nod. "I could eat." It was tentative and hesitant, and the most beautiful thing Quinn had ever heard.

He took her hand in his and set a slow pace down the sidewalk of his favorite city with his favorite person by his side. "I wonder if Ela exports those centipede things."

Vega huffed a chuckle, leaning into his side, and the world somehow got even brighter.

58

The concert hall was completely sold out, and thousands more people filled the plaza outside, breathlessly watching the show on massive holoprojections cast into the air. Millions more would be streaming the event from their homes all across the galaxy.

Ensconced in their private box, well away from the suffocating crowds, Vega and Quinn watched as the orchestra filed onto the stage, each musician taking their designated place.

At the front, Amanda VanWarren and her daughter bowed to uproarious applause before taking up their instruments.

This was their show. A special concert composed by the VanWarren musicians to honor the memory of the talented Geraldine, whose sweet music had spread like wildfire after her death. Just as she'd always wanted.

Vega only wished the girl was still alive to see it.

The last few weeks had been a whirlwind of madness, with the VanWarrens trying and failing to win the battle for their money, the media trying and failing to drag Quinn into the spotlight, and Vega trying and failing to resist the deep sense of comfort that settled over her a little more the longer she spent with him.

Quinn's home was exactly what she would expect it to be. Cozy, with small touches of old-world nostalgia to compensate for a lifetime of hardship. He had a room full of bookshelves and fluffy couches for reading. An attic hideaway with skylights for stargazing. And a porch with a swinging couch overlooking a garden overgrown with wildflowers.

It was home.

And every day and night, Quinn went out of his way to make sure she knew it was *hers*.

Vega kept expecting him to wake up one day and decide her nightmares were too much or that he deserved better than her taciturn moods. Every day, the thought crossed her mind that their marriage was a sham, and Quinn was only letting her stay with him until she recovered enough to be on her own again.

She didn't dare ask him about it. Didn't want to have to leave the cozy nest he'd made for her. Vega had grown accustomed to feeling his solid arm around her throughout the night and the sound of his deep voice singing in the shower in the morning. His smiles lit up her days, and his touch made her forget life didn't used to be worth living.

She liked living with him. She liked the books he read. She liked it when they cooked together, and she even liked the mindless task of cleaning up the dishes afterward. Quinn's home felt like the safest place in all the worlds for her to just *be*. Whoever it was she wanted to be. No judgment—ever. In fact, Quinn seemed to enjoy encouraging her to try anything and everything, no matter how weird, messy, or questionable in nature.

He wanted her to be happy.

The least she could do was make sure he didn't get hurt again.

Quinn didn't know it, but she'd made a few improvements to his home. With a little help from Rowe and his new connections, she'd set up a security system and alerts to monitor neighborhood activity. If anyone who wasn't supposed to be there came within a mile of their home, Vega knew about it. And she always had a wrist unit and lens either on her person, or within easy reach, just to be safe.

The only thing she couldn't protect him from was the poison of his family. Even with most of their direct communications being filtered by the UMT legal team, they seemed to be going out of their way to make their thoughts public. And the media ate it up. Which meant a day rarely went by when they didn't see or hear mention of one of the Van Warren brothers on the news.

She knew it hurt Quinn to see them publicly slandering him at every opportunity.

She'd offered to engineer an "accident" for one or both of them. Quinn had politely declined. He said he had everything he needed and more than he'd ever dreamed he could have. That nothing good ever came without a price and that his could have been much, much worse.

There were still a handful of VanWarrens who seemed to genuinely care. Aunt Ivy had sent Quinn a box of paper books, the first batch her publishing company had printed, accompanied by a long, hand-written letter. The books alone would have been a clear bid for connection—a thoughtful one, too, considering Quinn's love of the written word. The letter all but brought him to tears. Aunt Ivy had poured her heart into it, sharing her grief over what happened and her hope that they could still keep in touch, even if it was just an annual "happy birthday."

And then Aunt Amanda had sent a recording, personally inviting them to this concert. She'd secured the private box for them and assured Quinn that his brothers had not been invited and would not be welcome.

So here they were, listening to some of the most beautiful music Vega had ever heard, and she thought maybe it could be safe to relax and enjoy this strange new life. Just a little. For a few hours.

The string instruments drew out the last note of a song, and the concert hall boomed with echoing applause. As everyone switched out their music sheets, the conductor went over to Aunt Amanda, and a short, quiet conversation took place. Amanda touched her heart, smiling as she nodded her thanks.

Then, the conductor returned to his station and faced the audience. He waited until everyone quieted before he spoke. "Honored guests, our next song will be a special addition to tonight's performance. You will not find it listed in your programs. You will not find recordings of it available afterward. We have been granted permission to cover it only this once, as it was the last song Miss Geraldine VanWarren wrote for her family mere days before her passing."

An appreciative hum swept the crowds.

Vega glanced at Quinn to find him already watching her.

"We play it for you here tonight to honor not only Miss VanWarren's life and work but also her love and devotion to those she held dear."

With a courteous bow, he once again faced the orchestra.

The familiar melody, delivered with such sweet gravity, made Vega's throat thicken and her eyes sting. She blinked back the tears, not wanting to miss a single detail. Every note plucked at her heart. Every movement on stage engraved itself into her memory. In those few minutes, she could almost see Geraldine sitting next to her, her nose scrunching up with self-consciousness despite her smile.

Oh, she would have loved this.

"I have something for you," Quinn murmured at her ear, placing a small box into her lap.

Now? With *this* song—*their* song—playing?

Vega dragged herself away from the melody to meet his gaze. She couldn't read his expression, but the way he looked at her made the world feel too small to contain it. She opened the box and found herself staring at two intricate rings nestled inside. With the house lights dimmed, it was hard to make out details until the stage spotlights swept over the audience and flashed across the box. Three metallic colors glittered beneath a smooth, glassy surface, and she noticed…

"Is that…?"

"I know, I know, it's sappy and sentimental and not your style. But I figured it was the closest thing we have to a meaningful memento of our wedding day."

The earrings they'd used for wedding rings on the shuttle flight to Ela.

She could see the clasps encased in a crystalline structure along the top curve of each ring.

"Wh—How…?"

"Remember our walk in Port Cain? We passed by a jeweler's shop. When we got back, I sent them the earrings to make something special. They messaged me a while ago that the rings were finished and asked where to ship them." He hitched up a shoulder. "Wanted to wait for the right moment to give them to you."

Now. With their song being played on stage by a full orchestra.

Vega took out the smaller of the two rings. The jeweler had kept the original earring at its core and weaved two strands of gold and platinum over and under it in such a way that the circumference was covered by an even pattern of infinity symbols. And at the top, where a gemstone would be, the jeweler had grown a diamond shell over the clasp and stretched it out to cover the whole ring in a fine, crystalline sheen.

"It's forever," Quinn said. "You and me. No matter what, no matter where, no matter how. If you want it."

"Do you?"

"Forever," he said.

Vega swallowed past the lump in her throat. "Been rehearsing that a while?"

He chuckled. "Forever." He took her hand and slid the ring onto her finger. It fit perfectly.

Vega was terrified she'd drop the bigger ring before it ever got on his finger, her hands shook so much. But then it was on, and it fit perfectly, just like hers. Just like him.

Quinn wove their fingers together and pulled her into him, his kiss stealing the happy laugh from her lips as the song onstage reached its sweet, romantic end.

For them, it was only the beginning.

59

Date unknown – Somewhere far away…

The world burned inside his head. His body cramped from head to toe, tearing muscles, straining tendons, and creaking joints. His brain felt too big for the confines of his skull but empty somehow as if there were pieces carved out of it.

Harsh light stabbed into his eyes. When he squinted, he felt his face for the first time. Slack, drooping. Tired. His jaw was loose, tongue dry, even as he felt drool sliding down his chin.

The light disappeared, leaving floating globs of white in his vision.

Who are you?

Who are you?

A hard sting across his face. "Who are you?"

He struggled to form thoughts into meaning. A response came at the ready, but giving it a voice was harder than it should have been. His mouth didn't want to move.

Another hard slap.

He forced air out through his vocal cords to mumble, "No one."

"Where do you reside?"

He squeezed his eyes shut. Opened them wide, working the muscles in his jaw to touch his teeth together. "Nowhere," he said, a little more comprehensible.

It wasn't enough.

"What do you do?"

Another instinctual answer came to him at once. "What needs to be done."

Hard fingers gripped his jaw, forcing his face up. He couldn't make out the man standing before him. Didn't particularly care to.

The man released him, and then the straps around his arms came loose. "Get some rest, soldier. You will be briefed for your next mission at twenty-seven hundred."

"What's my name?"

The man walking away from him stopped and turned back. "You are Operative M."

M. Yes, that was correct.

Wasn't it?

"But what's my name?"

Heel-snapping steps brought the stranger back to his chair. He didn't see the blow coming. But it exploded across his cheekbone and snapped his head to the side.

"*Who are you, soldier,*" the stranger boomed.

"No one," he answered at once.

"Where do you reside?"

"Nowhere." More conviction this time. That's what the stranger wanted.

"What do you do?"

"What needs to be done—*sir!*"

A long, scrutinous silence.

Then, "Dismissed."

Operative M unstrapped his legs from the chair and pushed up to stand. His legs were unsteady, but he locked his knees and straightened to his full height despite the world twisting and diving all around him. He saluted the commanding officer and marched out of medbay, following instincts he didn't recognize, down one hallway, then another, to one unmarked door among many. It was locked but opened at his touch to allow him inside.

Operative M unlaced and removed his boots, stripped out of his uniform, and stepped into the shower. The water was cold. He preferred it that way.

He thought.

The soap dispensed automatically, and he scrubbed himself from head to toe, wincing at an unfamiliar pain in his gut. Finished with his wash, he stepped out and yanked a towel off its rack. He scrubbed himself dry, then twisted and bent into the light to examine his torso.

There was no scar or any external sign of injury, but deeper in his abdomen, a dull ache lingered. Vague flashes of memory told him it had to have been a stab wound.

He'd been stabbed?

The mirror held no answers for him, only a stranger staring back at him, equally clueless.

But there was something…

There was supposed to be something…

Operative M dressed quickly and set about searching what he assumed were his quarters. All of the clothes fit. Everything was arranged in a way he liked. Whatever he might need was precisely where he would want it to be.

In the closet, he found uniforms, shoes, and standard gear.

On the desk, he had a brace of weapons and a wrist unit with the paired lens.

The bed was made, with the pillow shifted a few inches off-center.

He moved it and discovered a small, transparent disc underneath.

The moment he touched it, a voice spoke up at his back. "Who are you?"

Operative M swiveled to face the desk at attention and answered, "No one!" before he registered it was a holoprojection of his own face looking at him and his voice demanding, "Where do you reside?"

"Nowhere," he responded, more hesitantly this time.

"What do you do?"

He gulped. "What needs to be done."

His holoself nodded, as if it heard him. "Two of those are a lie. Now pay attention."

Next to the holoface, text began streaming up at a rapid pace. Too fast for almost anyone to read. But not M. M caught every detail, because it was his. Somehow, he had done this. Recorded this. Compiled all this information for himself, knowing what would happen. He'd anticipated his own memory wipe and preserved everything he'd need to remember once it was done.

His mind didn't pick out individual details of the information his eyes were seeing. It simply absorbed everything in a steady flow. And with each word, his eyes went a little rounder. With each sentence, his body tensed a little tighter. With every bit of new-old information, another puzzle piece fell neatly into place.

"Who are you?" his holoself asked.

With the text still streaming, he answered, "Zachary VanWarren." He liked the sound of that. The shape of it on his tongue. But not the feeling it brought up deep in his chest. Too complex to examine now. But later, the hurt would come again. It wasn't his, but he'd claimed it, and so he would carry it—always.

Worse than the stab wound.

Missed opportunities always were.

"Where do you reside?"

"One-eight-eight-six Enmity Row. Chairo. Valhale 602." Not his true home—he didn't have one of those. It was the address he needed to find at any cost. A place he might never leave again. But it was the only safe haven he had now. His only chance of surviving what was to come. Small as it was.

The final paragraph streamed through, gifting him with a database of access codes and account details that could get him killed a hundred different ways.

"What do you do?"

Zach rubbed feeling back into his face, straightened his spine, and put his head on straight. "What needs to be done."

His holoself stared at him as if gauging his commitment.

It was absolute, and both of them knew it.

Both of them knew what he had to do next.

"Run."

ALIANNE DONNELLY is an avid lover of stories of all kinds. Raised on a healthy diet of fairy tales in a place where they almost seemed real, she grew into a writer who seeks magic in the modern age and enjoys sharing a little bit of it with the world through every story she writes. Her books span the spectrum from fantasy to science fiction with varying degrees of romance sprinkled throughout. Alianne now lives in California, where she spends her free time reading, writing, and daydreaming.

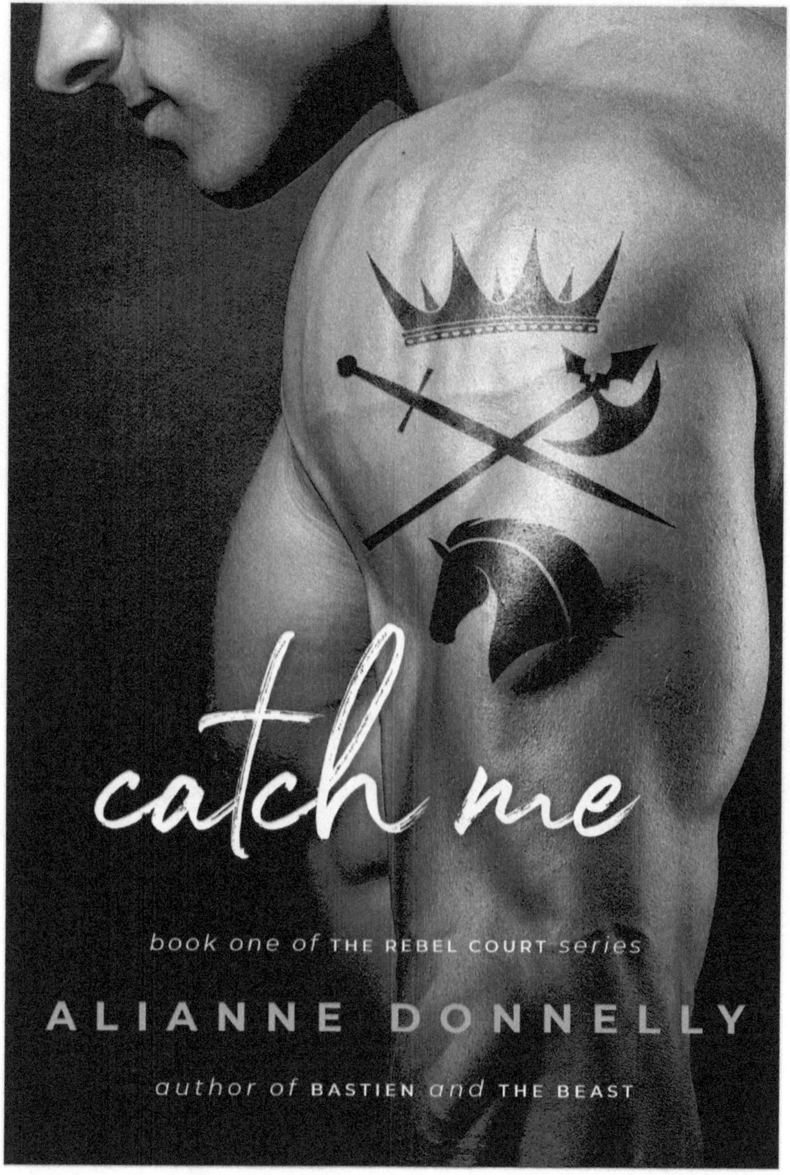
catch me
book one of THE REBEL COURT series
ALIANNE DONNELLY
author of BASTIEN and THE BEAST

As the most loyal of Snow White's dedicated Rebel Court, Haig Cavanaugh has never failed to complete a mission. Now that the war is over, he might be spending his time on far more pleasurable pursuits, but a soldier never truly stops being a soldier. When Snow White once again calls on her trusted allies, Haig is ready and willing to answer.

There's only one problem. His partner for this task is the Huntsman's beautiful daughter, Aislin and to her, mixing business with pleasure is a totally foreign concept. Happily, their mission leads into the depths of the mysterious Elderwood, where all sorts of things have been known to happen.

The nights are warm, the ground is soft, and Haig happens to be a very practical kind of guy. Who cares if he's the hunter or the prey? All that matters is that he gets Aislin naked and willing in his arms in the end. And that she doesn't find out what their mission really entails…

CHAPTER 1

"Bloody fucking hell, I thought we were done with this shite when she took the throne."

"As eloquent as ever, Graeme," Haig drawled, his gaze following the sway of a truly exemplary female ass down the opulent corridor. As if she felt his gaze, the woman's shoulders stiffened, and she paused to look over her shoulder. Haig gave her his most winning grin and a bold once-over, delighted when she blushed and rushed off around the corner. He craned his neck to prolong the sight, but damn, she was quick!

There was a distinct note of an eye roll in Graeme's voice when he muttered, "And you're still a whore."

Beau sighed. "Haig, leave Miss Juliana alone."

Haig raised an eyebrow at his comrade. Of all of them, Beau was the only one who'd weathered the war without apparent injury. To be expected, given he'd never actually seen any of the battles he'd strategized. Foot soldiers met the enemy in the field. Men like Beau conducted them like a well-trained orchestra from behind the scene. "Miss Juliana, is it? You saving her for yourself? You dirty dog, you."

The glare Beau spared him would have been truly frightening, if not for the blush coloring his pale cheeks. "You know full well the royal staff is off limits."

"Or are you saving yourself for her?" Haig winked. "That it?" When the rest of the rebels joined Beau in the glaring contest, Haig decided to be merciful. "You're all just jealous that I get more pussy in a day than you did in all of last year."

"Sebastian's got you beat," Beau returned. "*Handily.*"

Haig scowled at that. It wasn't a competition! "Where is he, anyway?"

"In treatment," Declan said in a tone that signaled the discussion was over. Haig had long ago stopped being intimidated by the Ravenskin's piercing silver gaze, but when Declan glowered like that, even the strongest resolve to win the staring contest failed miserably. At an imposing six feet five inches, and with his skin as black as a raven's feather—hence the name—he was intimidating as hell at the best of times.

Haig held up his hands in mock surrender.

Graeme growled, tugging on the collar of his dress shirt. "How much bloody longer will she make us wait?" He shoved to his feet to pace the hallway, checking his watch every five seconds. "This is bullshite. The summons said noon sharp."

"Yeah, and that's still five minutes away." Haig couldn't help staring at the man in horrified wonder. Graeme took issue with fancy clothes. Even their tasteful uniforms, made to size and specially for them, seemed to make his shaggy hair stand on end. Haig had been told Graeme used to be something to look at back in the day. He couldn't see it. To him, Graeme was and forever would be a rude, werewolf-looking guy who was allergic to razor blades, chewed his nails off when they got too long, and bit people who tried to cut his hair.

Animal...

Darius, having observed the exchange quietly until now, frowned in thought. "What do you think this is about? Beau, did she say anything to you?"

Beau raised an eyebrow. "Did the queen of Valefort tell me why she was summoning the leaders of her uprising all at once on short notice? No. It never came up."

Haig snorted. "What did?"

Darius ignored him. "You're her right hand. Surely you know something."

Beau shrugged uncomfortably. "Nothing concrete. Just whispers. The Network's been buzzing and the castle's been upside down ever since Snow White took the crown. Could be anything."

"Gentlemen, gentlemen," Haig quickly interjected. Darius was like a tick. Once he latched on to a mystery, he didn't let go until he was fully satisfied. "Why waste the energy wondering? In two minutes, we'll be called in and find out exactly what's what. Take a page out of Saxon's book. He couldn't care less."

Judging from his slouch and the tilt of his head, Saxon not only didn't care, he was fast asleep. Again. *How the hell does he do that?*

The grandfather clock at the end of the corridor struck noon and the grand door opened. As if on cue, at precisely the same moment, Sebastian rounded the corner and jogged up to the rest of them, still buttoning his shirt. Haig shook his head, reminding himself, *It's not a contest.*

Snow White's herald, a proud, but ancient, withered little man did his best to fill the doorway while they all stood up. Saxon had to be shoved awake, but to his credit, he recovered quickly. The herald looked down his beaked nose at them for a moment, then inclined his head a fraction of an inch as if he'd judged them acceptable—barely. "Her Majesty thanks you for your audience." All of them started forward to enter, but the herald stayed them. "One at a time, if you please. Her Majesty will see Master Haig first."

They shared a look amongst them. This was new.

Haig grinned wide at his comrades. "I'll try not to wear her out too much."

They rolled their eyes at him, so he flipped them off and followed the herald.

Since Snow White's ascension, Valefort wasn't so much a kingdom as it was a thriving corporation with Snow as the CEO, and her receiving room reflected that. Queen Zorana's garishly appointed, cavernous throne room had been stripped of all gild and trimmings. The golden tapestries had been replaced with TV monitors showing the latest economic trends and forecasts, the dais had been demolished, and a massive circle of high-gloss ebony tables took up the middle, surrounded by cushy power chairs.

Snow White—Queen Snow now—stood at the far side of the table, dressed in a stylish business suit, her raven hair woven into a single braid over one shoulder. She smiled in welcome. "Haig. It's been too long."

Haig grinned and shocked a gasp out of the herald when he rounded the tables in ground-eating strides and hugged the queen off her feet.

Snow was still laughing when he set her back on them. "Marlow, that'll be all for now. Thank you."

The herald bowed away and closed the door behind him.

"It's good to see you again, brat," Haig said, tugging on her braid. "Where's that no good husband of yours?"

"Marcus won't be joining us today," she replied easily enough, but something in her tone put Haig on guard. Reading his expression with her signature know-it-all-ness, Snow gasped. "Oh, no! There's nothing wrong between us. We're blissfully happy. Really. It's just that… I don't want to involve him in this. It's something of a delicate matter."

A delicate matter she couldn't share with the rest of her allies—men who'd saved her life, sheltered her, protected her, and led her to victory against the murderous Queen Zorana. Men she'd lovingly dubbed her Rebel Court, once upon a time. Haig's ever-present good humor faded. "Then we'd better get down to business."

She allowed him to seat her, then motioned for him to take the adjacent chair. "What I'm about to tell you cannot leave this room. You can't tell anyone, not even the other six, and Marcus must never find out. If he did, he'd turn it into a witch hunt, and that's the last thing I need right now."

"You want someone disappeared." It was a logical conclusion.

"Yes. I'm afraid I do."

Good humor definitely gone. This had to be serious. Snow only had to speak a word and any enemy, political or otherwise, could be dispatched by an expert marksman or a spell. She wouldn't have called him in for something as easy as an assassination. His presence here meant that whoever had drawn Snow's wrath needed to be erased quietly and completely. "Who's the mark?"

She took a deep breath. "Zorana's son."

Haig frowned. "Zorana had a son?"

"Believe me, I was as surprised as you are," she retorted. "Although, I really shouldn't have been, given what we know about her."

His mind refused to wrap all the way around that. "You may need to back up a little here. What exactly do we know and how did we find out?"

Snow gave him a half-hearted smile. "Funny things you come across when you go through your traitor stepmother's things. Among the *many* ledgers of illegal magic dealings, I found bundles of personal diaries."

"So now you know all of Zorana's sordid secrets?"

"Emphasis on sordid." Her expression turned pained, hands twisting in her lap. Given that Zorana had hated Snow enough to want her dead in a way most foul, whatever she may have written into her diaries couldn't have been pleasant for Snow to read.

Haig caught her hand in his, squeezed lightly. "Take your time."

Snow shook off her gloom and smiled. "Anyway, yes. Apparently, Zorana had a son several months after she married my father. It's all just obscure enough that there's no way to tell whether the issue was legitimate."

"You know he's not."

"Do I?"

"Will it make a difference, anyway?"

Snow shook her head in the negative. "By the word of our Charter, any child born after the wedding takes place is considered true and legitimate, and the crown legally belongs to the first-born *son*, only to pass to a daughter if no male heir exists at the time of the monarch's death."

"Which means this boy could challenge your rule, and by the word of our Charter, you'd have to abdicate to him or risk another civil war."

"And there would definitely be a war. We may have won against Zorana's armies, but she still has too many sympathizers among the noble court. People who have lost a lot in terms of wealth and standing when she was executed. It wouldn't take much to incite them against me."

"So we take care of the problem," Haig offered with a shrug. "Easy enough. Where is he?"

Snow winced. "That's kind of the problem."

Haig glowered. "I'm not going to like this, am I?"

"From what I could decipher, Zorana hid the boy somewhere in the Elderwood."

"Aw, fuck." While the castle city of Kesteran and most towns of a certain size were modernized with electricity, indoor plumbing, heat, and refined magic, a large portion of the land was still mired in the Dark Ages of brow sweat and raw magic only. People in the Elderwood lived in hovels and hauled water from the creek—if one happened to be nearby. And the worst part was, because of the effects raw magic had on the environment, no modern technology worked there. No phones, tracking devices, combustion engines, even weapons. "How am I supposed to find him?"

"You'll be working with—"

"Absolutely not!"

"—a partner for this assignment," she finished, ignoring his outburst. "I know you don't want anyone knowing about your…skills. I swore to you I would never tell anyone, and I haven't—I won't. But you can't find a needle of a teenage boy in a haystack the size of the Elderwood on your own."

"Oh, and I can just imagine the natural wonder you chose to help me track him."

"Aislin Crane," she answered regally.

Haig gaped at her. "The Huntsman's daughter?"

"She's the best tracker in Valefort." And considering Zorana had her father quartered for allowing Snow to escape, Haig could see how Aislin might be motivated to strike back at the bitch. "But I don't want her to know who the mark is."

"What? Why?"

She gave him a look. "Because she might balk if she finds out the boy you're about to take out is only fifteen years old."

"Well how the hell is she going to track him if she doesn't know who he is?"

Snow shrugged. "You have your gifts, she has hers."

"Fan-*fucking*-tastic."

Snow's face shuttered, and she drew herself up. "Will you do this or not?"

He scoffed. "Do I get a choice?"

She gave him a sweet smile and pressed a button on her desk to open an automatic door.

Grumbling under his breath, Haig pushed to his feet and squared his shoulders in preparation to meet his new partner.

CHAPTER 2

Y our Majesty," the woman said right by Haig's shoulder.

"*Gah!* Don't you make noise?" The last word drew out of him as he turned to face her.

Aislin was tall, just a couple of inches shorter than him, dressed in soft, clinging leathers that hugged her curves in all the right places. They were sewn together from odd-colored pieces, in a pattern that invited the eye to follow a meandering path from her exposed collarbones, down the valley of her pillowy cleavage, across her flat stomach to just past her loins.

That's where Haig stuck, hissing a breath. *Mercy...* She had nicely rounded hips, ripe for gripping, and long, supple legs that would easily lock around him as he thrust into her. Gods, he loved long-legged women. He loved all women, but there was something special about the leggy ones. An elegance and a sensuality usually reserved for swans and does.

"That would be counterproductive for a hunter," she retorted, drawing his attention—slowly—back up to her face. She'd braided her thick, black hair tightly against her scalp, throwing her features into stark relief. Haughtily arched eyebrows, cold, piercing green eyes, a narrow, aristocratic nose, high cheekbones...she had all the makings of an ice queen. But her soft skin was the color of warm, creamy caramel and her mouth was plump and generous, the lower lip thicker than the upper, hinting at rich reserves of passion he'd love to mine. The things he could do to that mouth alone...

Suddenly the boardroom was gone, and Haig's magic hijacked his mind, thrusting him into another place, another time, into another version of him in some alternate reality where...

The Huntsman's daughter stood naked at the edge of a lake, her face turned up to the light of a bright, full moon. She smiled at him with a challenge in her eyes as she backed into the water until the surface waves lapped at the juncture of her thighs.

She shivered, her dark nipples beading instantly, and Haig almost went to his knees. The sight of her like this—wild, unabashed, utterly beautiful—caused an ache in his chest. He wanted to stare at her for hours, and at the same time, he wanted desperately to be in that lake with her—inside her. Somehow, he came forward, joined her in the water, fully dressed, his pants straining across a raging cockstand. For her and no one else.

The random thought should have scared the shit out of him, but when Aislin lay back, floating weightless on the water, with moonlight burnishing her soft skin in cool, silver hues like a magical gift laid out just for him, Haig no longer cared…

Snow cleared her throat, dragging him out of the vision and back to the present. "Haig Cavanaugh, I'd like to introduce Aislin Crane." Under her breath she added, "You're staring."

Of course he was staring! She'd just introduced him to sex on a stick, whom he was apparently sexing up right now in at least one other reality. How was he supposed to get anything done, knowing that—*seeing* it? "Hi," he said, buying himself time to recover his power of speech. *Down!* he commanded his dick. It had no effect whatsoever.

Aislin scoffed delicately, and the room temperature plunged into arctic levels when she gave him a careless once-over. "You're supposed to be the expert?"

Despite her arch tone, Haig fought down a hot shiver. She had a soft, just-been-thoroughly-fucked kind of voice that shot straight to his groin. "Jack of all trades," he heard himself saying, "and master of quite a few. Care to give me a try?" Instinctively, he knew she'd be just as quiet in bed and, gods, he itched to break her of that. He knew how to do things to her that would drive her out of her head with pleasure. He could make her scream his name and weep with gratitude. And beg him for more—

Dismissing him off hand, Aislin turned to Snow, giving him a full-body view of her profile: a proud, straight line from the top of her head to the heel of her soft-soled boot, disrupted only by the curve of her breasts and ass. Her arms were bare, visibly toned, but not mannish. She'd smeared them with soot, presumably for camouflage. He noticed the crossbow she clutched in her left hand. A bolt quiver was strapped to her right thigh.

Oh, man. Haig's mouth watered just thinking about all the ways he could disarm her and strip her naked. He swayed on his feet, plunging right back into his vision. Only this time…

He stood between Aislin's thighs, and her head was tilted back, her mouth open on a passionate sigh. He saw his own hands on her; felt the heated silk of her skin, the curl of her legs around him, and he thought, It's even better than in a bed.

The folds of her sex rubbed up and down over his cock, each stroke bringing him to the very edge of her pussy, teasing with the promise of entrance.

She was magnificent, stunning, an otherworldly nymph, and he felt so…grateful. Aislin arched, crying out as an orgasm shivered through her exquisite body—but how could she deny him the sight of her face? With her legs squeezing him to her, Haig lowered to his haunches in the water, bringing her upright into his arms. Eyes unfocused, Aislin sighed his name, just as Haig thrust up, plunging straight into heaven…

"…choose your horse from the stables," Snow was saying, "and have the kitchen prepare supplies for—"

With his attention still halfway in visionland, Haig licked his suddenly dry lips, staring hard at the true Huntress standing before him. Only, in his mind, she was still naked, and very, very wet. And he still felt her sheath squeezing his cock. "What are you, a size six? Eight?" he asked, hoarse-voiced.

Snow gaped at him.

Aislin speared him with a hateful glare. "I make my own clothes."

"Yeah, I bet you do."

"From the skins of my enemies," she added with a savage smile. "I save the foreskins for polishing rags."

Haig's balls pulled up so tight he almost went soprano for a second. "And I'll bet you can't wait to get your hands on mine." This cruel streak was so unlike the sensual version of her from his vision, it jarred him fully back to the present, but his interest didn't abate at all. In fact, he almost liked this Aislin better. Haig had always loved a good challenge, and hers promised to be epic.

Then she raised an eyebrow and he realized what he'd just said. "Wait, that didn't come out right."

"What is wrong with you?" Snow hissed, blushing furiously. "No, you know what? Don't answer that. Just get out of my sight. Both of you."

Aislin bowed and strode to the corridor leading directly to the stables.

Haig watched the sway of her hips, savoring the athleticism and power encased in her sexy leathers. That one would be a ride he'd remember for the rest of his life. He knew it for a fact because, in an alternate reality somewhere, another version of him already did.

He had just enough brain power left not to adjust himself in the queen's presence. But he couldn't help grinning at her. "I'm going to enjoy this."

Snow crossed her arms. "If you do anything to make her regret taking you along, I will personally cut off your genitals and gift them to her for polishing rags."

"What is it with you two and polishing things with my junk? You can't come up with a better use for it? Seriously, I thought *you* at least would have more imagination than that."

She rubbed her brow and sighed in exasperation. "Just do the job, okay? That's all I ask."

"Oh, I'll do the job. If anyone can do the job, it's me." Haig winked. "I'll do that job *real* nice."

Fuming, she pointed to the corridor after Aislin.

With a heel-clicking salute, he loped off in pursuit of his lovely Huntress.

"Hey, wait up!"

Aislin picked up her step. The corridor split into two up ahead. With any luck, he'd take the wrong turn and end up in the dungeons.

Useless, annoying waste of a man! Never would Aislin have imagined the pragmatic queen pairing her with that…that whore! There wasn't a female in Kesteran who didn't know Haig Cavanaugh. If not personally, then by reputation. He was a wastrel, a libertine. How he'd managed to earn such high honors during the war she'd never know. His only true skill seemed to be fucking.

The only thing that kept Aislin from refusing this mission was her faith that Queen Snow *was* a pragmatic regent. Which meant she had to have a reason for pairing them together. *Just ignore the stupidity,* she told herself. *Focus on the mission. Find the target. The sooner you do that, the sooner you can put this whole embarrassment behind you.*

Footsteps pounded behind her with all the subtlety of a stampeding moose. "Hey, partner," Haig called, delivering a sound smack on her ass as he passed by. "Race you there!"

She had a bolt drawn and aimed at the back of his head in two seconds. But her hands shook too much with the force of her fury to make the shot. Her ass tingling where he'd pawed her, she removed the bolt, but clutched it like a dagger as she stalked him into the stables.

"Goran," she greeted the hostler with a respectful nod.

He tipped his hat in return. Having been appraised of the situation already, he'd brought forth two horses already saddled and burdened with gear, and she was gratified to see her favorite, a lovely brown mare by the name of Emer, was one of them. Aislin fastened her crossbow in place on the saddle hook, then checked over the mare and the saddlebags to make sure her necessities had been included.

"So," the whore murmured by her ear, and for just a second, she froze, barely stifling a shiver. How had he managed to sneak up on her? "Shall we get this sexual tension between us taken care of now or after?"

Aislin whirled around and grasped him by the throat, a bolt in her free hand, but to her utter shock, he was faster. With a laugh, he caught her bolt hand as his foot slipped around hers. With a deft twist, he knocked her off balance and her back met a stall door. Her other hand, still at his neck, went limp as he leaned into her. "Straight to the point. I like that in a woman."

"How did you do that?" She could have thrown him a dozen different ways, yet her body remained pliant. Because, somehow, he felt…familiar.

Haig's sinful blue eyes danced with mirth behind a stray lock of blond hair. Almost nose to nose with her, he leaned in closer still, his body pinning her in place from chest to hip. Just enough to feel his weight, the lean muscles of his torso, and the hard ridge of his erection. "I'll never tell," he whispered, his mouth a hair's breadth from hers.

Aislin pressed her lips together into a firm line. *Get ahold of yourself! This is Haig bloody Cavanaugh!* Bracing a foot against the wall, she tensed to shove him off her.

But before the thought could translate into action, his nose brushed hers, and then his mouth was at her ear. "I can feel the fight in you." His tongue darted out to touch her lobe. "You're all aquiver to break free." He put his nose to the sensitive skin of her neck and sucked in a deep breath. "But it's not me you're fighting." His teeth caught the small golden hoop of her earring, tugged a little, eliciting a surprised gasp. "The sooner you admit it, the better off both of us will be."

"Get—off—me," she grated, struggling to keep her breathing even.

"If looks could kill," he murmured with a satisfied smirk, "yours would scorch me to the bone." He released her, his knuckles brushing down her side, seemingly by accident.

Aislin doubted anything this man did was accidental. It was all a deliberate ploy—a look here, a touch there, all with one final goal in mind: seduction. She knew that, dammit! So why was her body still humming?

"I'll meet you at the castle gate at sunset," he called over his shoulder, heading out on foot.

Her mind was slow to catch up. "What? What do you mean? We're leaving now!" She chased him around the horses just in time to watch him stroll out into the courtyard with his hands in his pockets.

"Got stuff to do," he tossed back. "Things to pick up. Goodbyes to say. Long, languorous love to make." Turning mid-stride, he grinned while walking backwards away from her. "See? If you'd just admitted your lust for me, we could have saved *hours*."

Look for **CATCH ME** at your favorite online bookstore!